The Ocean Waifs
A Story Of Adventure
On Land And Sea

by

Mayne Reid

Double 9
BOOKS

The ocean waifs
A story of adventure on land and sea
by Mayne Reid

ISBN: 978-93-64289-79-5

Published by

DOUBLE 9 BOOKS
2/13-B, Ansari Road
Daryaganj, New Delhi – 110002
info@double9books.com
www.double9books.com
Tel. 011-40042856

ABOUT THE AUTHOR

Thomas Mayne Reid, known as Mayne Reid, was an Irish-American novelist celebrated for his adventure novels that captured the imaginations of readers in the 19th century. Mayne Reid was born in Ballyroney County Down, Ireland, the son of a Presbyterian minister. He grew up in an environment that valued education and was well-read from a young age. This literary foundation would later influence his writing career. His experiences in the war provided rich material for his future writings, as he participated in several significant battles and witnessed the harsh realities of military life. After the war, Reid settled in Philadelphia and began his career as a writer. His first successful novel, "The Rifle Rangers" (1850), drew heavily from his war experiences and set the stage for his prolific output of adventure novels. Adventure and Exploration: Reid's novels often feature exotic locations and daring exploits, reflecting his own adventurous spirit. Vivid Descriptions: He had a talent for painting vivid scenes, bringing to life the landscapes and settings of his stories. Action-Packed Narratives: His stories are known for their fast pace and exciting plotlines. Heroism and Resilience: Themes of bravery and survival against the odds are central to his works. "The Scalp Hunters" (1851),"The Desert Home" (1852),"The White Chief" (1855),"The Headless Horseman" (1865),"The Ocean Waifs" (1863). These novels were well-received and made Reid a popular author in both the United States and Europe. Mayne Reid's works have had a lasting impact on the genre of adventure fiction. His ability to weave thrilling stories with authentic details from his own experiences captivated a wide audience. His novels were not just entertaining but also provided readers with a window into the diverse and often perilous world of the 19th century.

CONTENTS

Chapter One
The Albatross

The "vulture of the sea," borne upon broad wing, and wandering over the wide Atlantic, suddenly suspends his flight to look down upon an object that has attracted his attention.

It is a raft, with a disc not much larger than a dining-table, constructed out of two small spars of a ship,—the dolphin-striker and spritsail yard,—with two broad planks and some narrower ones lashed crosswise, and over all two or three pieces of sail-cloth carelessly spread.

Slight as is the structure, it is occupied by two individuals,—a man and a boy. The latter is lying along the folds of the sail-cloth, apparently asleep. The man stands erect, with his hand to his forehead, shading the sun from his eyes, and scanning the surface of the sea with inquiring glances.

At his feet, lying among the creases of the canvas, are a handspike, a pair of boat oars, and an axe. Nothing more is perceptible of the raft, even to the keen eye of the albatross.

The bird continues its flight towards the west. Ten miles farther on it once more poises itself on soaring wing, and directs its glance downward.

Another raft is seen motionless upon the calm surface of the sea, but differing from the former in almost everything but the name. It is nearly ten times as large; constructed out of the masts, yards, hatches, portions of the bulwarks, and other timbers of a ship; and rendered buoyant by a number of empty water-casks lashed along its edges. A square of canvas spread between two extemporised masts, a couple of casks, an empty biscuit-box, some oars, handspikes, and other maritime implements, lie upon the raft; and around these are more than thirty men, seated, standing, lying,—in short, in almost every attitude.

Some are motionless, as if asleep; but there is that in their prostrate postures, and in the wild expression of their features, that betokens rather the sleep of intoxication. Others, by their gestures and loud, riotous talk, exhibit still surer signs of drunkenness; and the tin cup, reeking with rum, is constantly passing from hand to hand. A few, apparently sober, but haggard and hungry-like, sit or stand erect upon the raft, casting occasional glances over the wide expanse, with but slight show of hope, fast changing to despair.

Well may the sea-vulture linger over this group, and contemplate their movements with expectant eye. The instincts of the bird tell him, that ere long he may look forward to a bountiful banquet!

Ten miles farther to the west, though unseen to those upon the raft, the far-piercing gaze of the albatross detects another unusual object upon the surface of the sea. At this distance it appears only a speck not larger than the bird itself, though in reality it is a small boat,—a ship's gig,—in which six men are seated. There has been no attempt to hoist a sail; there is none in the gig. There are oars, but no one is using them. They have been dropped in despair; and the boat lies becalmed just as the two rafts. Like them, it appears to be adrift upon the ocean.

Could the albatross exert a reasoning faculty it would know that these various objects indicated a wreck. Some vessel has either foundered and gone to the bottom, or has caught fire and perished in the flames.

Ten miles to the eastward of the lesser raft might be discovered truer traces of the lost ship. There might be seen the *débris* of charred timbers, telling that she has succumbed, not to the storm, but to fire; and the fragments, scattered over the circumference of a mile, disclose further that the fire ended abruptly in some terrible explosion.

Upon the stern of the gig still afloat may be read the name *Pandora*. The same word may be seen painted on the water-casks buoying up the big raft; and on the two planks forming the transverse pieces of the lesser one appears *Pandora* in still larger letters: for these were the boards that exhibited the name of the ship on each side of her bowsprit, and which had been torn off to construct the little raft by those who now occupy it.

Beyond doubt the lost ship was the *Pandora*.

Chapter Two
Ship on Fire

The story of the *Pandora* has been told in all its terrible details. A slave-ship, fitted out in England, and sailing from an English port,—alas! not the only one by scores,—manned by a crew of ruffians, scarce two of them owning to the same nationality. Such was the bark *Pandora*.

Her latest and last voyage was to the slave coast, in the Gulf of Guinea. There, having shipped five hundred wretched beings with black skins,— "bales" as they are facetiously termed by the trader in human flesh,—she had started to carry her cargo to that infamous market,—ever open in those days to such a commodity,—the barracoons of Brazil.

In mid-ocean she had caught fire,—a fire that could not be extinguished. In the hurry and confusion of launching the boats the pinnace proved to be useless; and the longboat, stove in by the falling of a cask, sank to the bottom of the sea. Only the gig was found available; and this, seized upon by the captain, the mate, and four others, was rowed off clandestinely in the darkness.

The rest of the crew, over thirty in number, succeeded in constructing a raft; and but a few seconds after they had pushed off from the sides of the ship, a barrel of gunpowder ignited by the flames, completed the catastrophe.

But what became of the *cargo*? Ah! that is indeed a tale of horror.

Up to the last moment those unfortunate beings had been kept under hatches, under a grating that had been fastened down with battens. They would have been left in that situation to be stifled in their confinement by the suffocating smoke, or burnt alive amid the blazing timbers, but for one merciful heart among those who were leaving the ship. An axe uplifted by the arm of a brave youth—a mere boy—struck off the confining cleats, and gave the sable sufferers access to the open air.

Alas! it was scarce a respite to these wretched creatures,—only a choice between two modes of death. They escaped from the red flames but to sink into the dismal depths of the ocean,—hundreds meeting with a fate still more horrible: for there were not less than that number, and all became the prey of those hideous sea-monsters, the sharks.

Of all that band of involuntary emigrants, in ten minutes after the blowing up of the bark, there was not one above the surface of the sea! Those of them that could not swim had sunk to the bottom, while a worse fate had befallen those that could,—to fill the maws of the ravenous monsters that crowded the sea around them! At the period when our tale commences, several days had succeeded this tragical event; and the groups we have described, aligned upon a parallel of latitude, and separated one from another by a distance of some ten or a dozen miles, will be easily recognised.

The little boat lying farthest west was the gig of the *Pandora*, containing her brutal captain, his equally brutal mate, the carpenter, and three others of the crew, that had been admitted as partners in the surreptitious abstraction. Under cover of the darkness they had made their departure; but long before rowing out of gun-shot they had heard the wild denunciations and threats hurled after them by their betrayed associates.

The ruffian crew occupied the greater raft; but who were the two individuals who had intrusted themselves to that frail embarkation,— seemingly so slight that a single breath of wind would scatter it into fragments, and send its occupants to the bottom of the sea? Such in reality would have been their fate, had a storm sprung up at that moment; but fortunately for them the sea was smooth and calm,—as it had been ever since the destruction of the ship.

But why were they thus separated from the others of the crew: for both man and boy had belonged to the forecastle of the *Pandora*?

The circumstance requires explanation, and it shall be briefly given. The man was Ben Brace,—the bravest and best sailor on board the slave-bark, and one who would not have shipped in such a craft but for wrongs he had suffered while in the service of his country, and that had inducted him into a sort of reckless disposition, of which, however, he had long since repented.

The boy had also been the victim of a similar disposition. Longing to see foreign lands, he had *run away to sea*; and by an unlucky accident, through sheer ignorance of her character, had chosen the *Pandora* in which to make his initiatory voyage. From the cruel treatment he had been subjected to on board the bark, he had reason to see his folly. Irksome had been his existence from the moment he set foot on the deck of the *Pandora*; and indeed it would have been scarce endurable but for the friendship of the brave sailor Brace, who, after a time, had taken him under his especial protection. Neither of them had any feelings in common with the crew with whom they had become associated; and it was their intention to escape from such vile companionship as soon as an opportunity should offer.

The destruction of the bark would not have given that opportunity. On the contrary, it rendered it all the more necessary to remain with the others, and share the chances of safety offered by the great raft. Slight as these might be, they were still better than those that might await them, exposed on such a frail fabric as that they now occupied. It is true, that upon this they had left the burning vessel separate from the others; but immediately after they had rowed up alongside the larger structure, and made fast to it.

In this companionship they had continued for several days and nights, borne backward and forward by the varying breezes; resting by day on the calm surface of the ocean; and sharing the fate of the rest of the castaway crew.

What had led to their relinquishing the companionship? Why was Ben Brace and his *protégé* separated from the others and once more alone upon their little raft?

The cause of that separation must be declared, though one almost shudders to think of it. It was to save the boy *from being eaten* that Ben Brace had carried him away from his former associates; and it was only by a cunning stratagem, and at the risk of his own life, that the brave sailor had succeeded in preventing this horrid banquet from being made!

The castaway crew had exhausted the slender stock of provisions received from the wreck. They were reduced to that state of hunger which no longer revolts at the filthiest of food; and without even resorting to the customary method adopted in such terrible crises, they unanimously resolved upon the death of the boy,—Ben Brace alone raising a voice of dissent!

But this voice was not heeded. It was decided that the lad should die: and all that his protector was able to obtain from the fiendish crew, was the promise of a respite for him till the following morning.

Brace had his object in procuring this delay. During the night, the united rafts made way under a fresh breeze; and while all was wrapped in darkness, he cut the ropes which fastened the lesser one to the greater, allowing the former to fall astern. As it was occupied only by him and his *protégé*, they were thus separated from their dangerous associates; and when far enough off to run no risk of being heard, they used their oars to increase the distance.

All night long did they continue to row against the wind; and as morning broke upon them, they came to a rest upon the calm sea, unseen by their late comrades, and with ten miles separating the two rafts from each other.

It was the fatigue of that long spell of pulling—with many a watchful and weary hour preceding it—that had caused the boy to sink down upon the folded canvas, and almost on the instant fall asleep; and it was the apprehension of being followed that was causing Ben Brace to stand shading his eyes from the sun, and scan with uneasy glance the glittering surface of the sea.

Chapter Three
The Lord's Prayer

After carefully scrutinising the smooth water towards every point of the compass,—but more especially towards the west,—the sailor ceased from his reconnoissance, and turned his eyes upon his youthful companion, still soundly slumbering.

"Poor lad!" muttered he to himself; "he be quite knocked up. No wonder, after such a week as we've had o't. And to think he war so near bein' killed and ate by them crew o' ruffians. I'm blowed if that wasn't enough to scare the strength out o' him! Well, I dare say he's escaped from that fate; but as soon as he has got a little more rest, we must take a fresh spell at the oars. It 'ud never do to drift back to *them*. If we do, it an't only him they'll want to eat, but me too, after what's happened. Blowed if they wouldn't."

The sailor paused a moment, as if reflecting upon the probabilities of their being pursued.

"Sartin!" he continued, "they could never fetch that catamaran against the wind; but now that it's turned dead calm, they might clap on wi' their oars, in the hope of overtakin' us. There's so many of them to pull, and they've got oars in plenty, they might overhaul us yet."

"O Ben! dear Ben! save me,—save me from the wicked men!"

This came from the lips of the lad, evidently muttered in his sleep.

"Dash my buttons, if he an't dreaming!" said the sailor, turning his eyes upon the boy, and watching the movements of his lips. "He be talkin' in his sleep. He thinks they're comin' at him just as they did last night on the raft! Maybe I ought to rouse him up. If he be a dreamin' that way he'll be better awake. It's a pity, too, for he an't had enough sleep."

"Oh! they will kill me and eat me. Oh, oh!"

"No, they won't do neyther,—blow'd if they do. Will'm, little Will'm! rouse yourself, my lad."

And as he said this he bent down and gave the sleeper a shake.

"O Ben! is it you? Where are they,—those monsters?"

"Miles away, my boy. You be only a dreamin' about 'em. That's why I've shook you up."

"I'm glad you have waked me. Oh! it was a frightful dream! I thought they had done it, Ben."

"Done what, Will'm?"

"What they were going to do."

"Dash it, no, lad! they an't ate you yet; nor won't, till they've first put an end o' me,—that I promise ye."

"Dear Ben," cried the boy, "you are so good,—you've risked your life to save mine. Oh! how can I ever show you how much I am sensible of your goodness?"

"Don't talk o' that, little Will'm. Ah! lad, I fear it an't much use to eyther o' us. But if we must die, anything before a death like that. I'd rather far that the sharks should get us than to be eat up by one's own sort.—Ugh! it be horrid to think o't. But come, lad, don't let us despair. For all so black as things look, let us put our trust in Providence. We don't know but that His eye may be on us at this minute. I wish I knew how to pray, but I never was taught that ere. Can you pray, little Will'm?"

"I can repeat the Lord's Prayer. Would that do, Ben?"

"Sartain it would. It be the best kind o' prayer, I've heerd say. Get on your knees, lad, and do it. I'll kneel myself, and join with ye in the spirit o' the thing, tho' I'm shamed to say I disremember most o' the words."

The boy, thus solicited, at once raised himself into a kneeling position, and commenced repeating the sublime prayer of the Christian. The rough sailor knelt alongside of him, and with hands crossed over his breast in a supplicating attitude, listened attentively, now and then joining in the words of the prayer, whenever some phrase recurred to his remembrance.

When it was over, and the "Amen" had been solemnly pronounced by the voices of both, the sailor seemed to have become inspired with a fresh hope; and, once more grasping an oar, he desired his companion to do the same.

"We must get a little farther to east'ard," said he, "so as to make sure o' bein' out o' their way. If we only pull a couple of hours afore the sun gets hot, I think we'll be in no danger o' meetin' *them* any more. So let's set to, little Will'm! Another spell, and then you can rest as long's you have a mind to."

The sailor seated himself close to the edge of the raft, and dropped his oar-blade in the water, using it after the fashion of a canoe-paddle. "Little Will'm," taking his place on the opposite side, imitated the action; and the craft commenced moving onward over the calm surface of the sea.

The boy, though only sixteen, was skilled in the use of an oar, and could handle it in whatever fashion. He had learnt the art long before he had thought of going to sea; and it now stood him in good stead. Moreover, he was strong for his age, and therefore his stroke was sufficient to match that of the sailor, given more gently for the purpose.

Propelled by the two oars, the raft made way with considerable rapidity, —not as a boat would have done, but still at the rate of two or three knots to the hour.

They had not been rowing long, however, when a gentle breeze sprung up from the west, which aided their progress in the direction in which they wished to go. One would have thought that this was just what they should have desired. On the contrary, the sailor appeared uneasy on perceiving that the breeze blew from the west. Had it been from any other point he would have cared little about it.

"I don't like it a bit," said he, speaking across the raft to his companion. "It helps us to get east'ard, that's true; *but* it'll help them as well—and with that broad spread o' canvas they've rigged up, they might come down on us faster than we can row."

"Could we not rig a sail too?" inquired the boy. "Don't you think we might, Ben?"

"Just the thing I war thinkin' o', lad; I dare say we can. Let me see; we've got that old tarpaulin and the lying jib-sail under us. The tarpaulin itself will be big enough. How about ropes? Ah! there's the sheets of the jib still stickin' to the sail; and then there's the handspike and our two oars. The oars 'll do without the handspike. Let's set 'em up then, and rig the tarpaulin between 'em."

As the sailor spoke, he had risen to his feet; and after partially drawing the canvas off from the planks and spars, he soon accomplished the task of setting the two oars upright upon the raft. This done, the tarpaulin was spread between them, and when lashed so as to lie taut from one to the other, presented a surface of several square yards to the breeze,—quite as much sail as the craft was capable of carrying.

It only remained for them to look to the steering of the raft, so as to keep it head on before the wind; and this could be managed by means of the handspike, used as a rudder or steering-oar.

Laying hold of this, and placing himself abaft of the spread tarpaulin, Ben had the satisfaction of seeing that the sail acted admirably; and as soon as its influence was fairly felt, the raft surged on through the water at a rate of not less than five knots to the hour.

It was not likely that the large raft that carried the dreaded crew of would-be cannibals was going any faster; and therefore, whatever distance they might be off, there would be no great danger of their getting any nearer.

This confidence being firmly established, the sailor no longer gave a thought to the peril from which he and his youthful comrade had escaped. For all that, the prospect that lay before them was too terrible to permit their exchanging a word,—either of comfort or congratulation,—and for a long time they sat in a sort of desponding silence, which was broken only by the rippling surge of the waters as they swept in pearly froth along the sides of the raft.

Chapter Four
Hunger.—Despair

The breeze proved only what sailors call a catspaw, rising no higher than just to cause a ripple on the water, and lasting only about an hour. When it was over, the sea again fell into a dead calm; its surface assuming the smoothness of a mirror.

In the midst of this the raft lay motionless, and the extemporised sail was of no use for propelling it. It served a purpose, however, in screening off the rays of the sun, which, though not many degrees above the horizon, was beginning to make itself felt in all its tropical fervour.

Ben no longer required his companion to take a hand at the oar. Not but that their danger of being overtaken was as great as ever; for although they had made easterly some five or six knots, it was but natural to conclude that the great raft had been doing the same; and therefore the distance between the two would be about as before.

But whether it was that his energy had become prostrated by fatigue and the hopelessness of their situation, or whether upon further reflection he felt less fear of their being pursued, certain it is he no longer showed uneasiness about making way over the water; and after once more rising to his feet and making a fresh examination of the horizon, he stretched himself along the raft in the shade of the tarpaulin.

The boy, at his request, had already placed himself in a similar position, and was again buried in slumber.

"I'm glad to see he can sleep," said Brace to himself, as he lay down alongside. "He must be sufferin' from hunger as bad as I am myself, and as long as he's asleep he won't feel it. May be, if one could keep asleep they'd hold out longer, though I don't know 'bout that bein' so. I've often ate a hearty supper, and woke up in the mornin' as hungry as if I'm gone to my bunk without a bite. Well, it an't no use o' me tryin' to sleep as I feel now, blow'd if it is! My belly calls out loud enough to keep old Morphis himself from nappin', and there an't a morsel o' anything. More than forty hours have passed since I ate that last quarter biscuit. I can think o' nothing but our shoes, and they be so soaked wi' the sea-water, I suppose they'll do more harm than good. They'll be sure to make the thirst a deal worse than it is, though the Lord knows it be bad enough a'ready. Merciful Father!—nothin' to eat!—nothin' to drink! O God, hear the prayer little Will'm ha' just spoken and I ha' repeated, though I've been too wicked to expect bein' heard, 'Give us this day our daily bread'! Ah! another day or two without it, an' we shall both be asleep forever!"

The soliloquy of the despairing sailor ended in a groan, that awoke his young comrade from a slumber that was at best only transient and troubled.

"What is it, Ben?" he asked, raising himself on his elbow, and looking inquiringly in the face of his protector.

"Nothing partikler, my lad," answered the sailor, who did not wish to terrify his companion with the dark thoughts which were troubling himself.

"I heard you groaning,—did I not? I was afraid you had seen them coming after us."

"No fear o' that,—not a bit. They're a long way off, and in this calm sea they won't be inclined to stir,—not as long as the rum-cask holds out, I warrant; and when that's empty, they'll not feel much like movin' anywhere. 'Tan't for them we need have any fear now."

"O Ben! I'm so hungry; I could eat anything."

"I know it, my poor lad; so could I."

"True! indeed you must be even hungrier than I, for you gave me more than my share of the two biscuits. It was wrong of me to take it, for I'm sure you must be suffering dreadfully."

"That's true enough, Will'm; but a bit o' biscuit wouldn't a made no difference. It must come to the same thing in the end."

"To what, Ben?" inquired the lad, observing the shadow that had overspread the countenance of his companion, which was gloomier than he had ever seen it.

The sailor remained silent. He could not think of a way to evade giving the correct answer to the question; and keeping his eyes averted, he made no reply.

"I know what you mean," continued the interrogator. "Yes, yes,—you mean that we must die!"

"No, no, Will'm,—not that; there's hope yet,—who knows what may turn up? It may be that the prayer will be answered. I'd like, lad, if you'd go over it again. I think I could help you better this time; for I once knew it myself,—long, long ago, when I was about as big as you, and hearin' you repeatin' it, it has come most o' it back into my memory. Go over it again, little Will'm."

The youth once more knelt upon the raft, and in the shadow of the spread tarpaulin repeated the Lord's Prayer,—the sailor, in his rougher voice, pronouncing the words after him.

When they had finished, the latter once more rose to his feet, and for some minutes stood scanning the circle of sea around the raft.

The faint hope which that trusting reliance in his Maker had inspired within the breast of the rude mariner exhibited itself for a moment upon his countenance, but only for a moment. No object greeted his vision, save the blue, boundless sea, and the equally boundless sky.

A despairing look replaced that transient gleam of hope, and, staggering back behind the tarpaulin, he once more flung his body prostrate upon the raft.

Again they lay, side by side, in perfect silence,—neither of them asleep, but both in a sort of stupor, produced by their unspoken despair.

Chapter Five
Faith.—Hope

How long they lay in this half-unconscious condition, neither took note. It could not have been many minutes, for the mind under such circumstances does not long surrender itself to a state of tranquillity.

They were at length suddenly roused from it,—not, however, by any thought from within,—but by an object striking on their external senses, or, rather, upon the sense of sight. Both were lying upon their backs, with eyes open and upturned to the sky, upon which there was not a speck of cloud to vary the monotony of its endless azure.

Its monotony, however, was at that moment varied by a number of objects that passed swiftly across their field of vision, shining and scintillating as if a flight of silver arrows had been shot over the raft. The hues of blue and white were conspicuous in the bright sunbeams, and those gay-coloured creatures, that appeared to belong to the air, but which in reality were denizens of the great deep, were at once recognised by the sailor.

"A shoal o' flyin'-fish," he simply remarked, and without removing from his recumbent position.

Then at once, as if some hope had sprung up within him at seeing them continue to fly over the raft, and so near as almost to touch the tarpaulin, he added, starting to his feet as he spoke—

"What if I might knock one o' 'em down! Where's the handspike?"

The last interrogatory was mechanical, and put merely to fill up the time; for as he gave utterance to it he reached towards the implement that lay within reach of his hands, and eagerly grasping raised it aloft.

With such a weapon it was probable that he might have succeeded in striking down one of the winged swimmers that, pursued by the bonitos and albacores, were still leaping over the raft. But there was a surer weapon behind him,—in the piece of canvas spread between the upright oars; and just as the sailor had got ready to wield his huge club, a shining object flashed close to his eyes, whilst his ears were greeted by a glad sound, signifying that one of the vaulting fish had struck against the tarpaulin.

Of course it had dropped down upon the raft: for there it was, flopping and bounding about among the folds of the flying-jib, far more taken by surprise than Ben Brace, who had witnessed its mishap, or even little William, upon whose face it had fallen, with all the weight of its watery carcass. If a bird in the hand be worth two in the bush, by the same rule a fish in the hand should be worth two in the water, and more than that number flying in the air.

Some such calculation as this might have passed through the brain of Ben Brace; for, instead of continuing to hold his handspike high flourished over his head, in the hope of striking another fish, he suffered the implement to drop down upon the raft; and stooping down, he reached forward to secure the one that had voluntarily, or, rather, should we say, involuntarily, offered itself as a victim.

As it kept leaping about over the raft, there was just the danger that it might reach the edge of that limited area, and once more escape to its natural element.

This, however naturally desired by the fish, was the object which the occupants of the raft most desired to prevent; and to that end both had got upon their knees, and were scrambling over the sail-cloth with as much eager earnestness as a couple of terriers engaged in a scuffle with a harvest rat.

Once or twice little William had succeeded in getting the fish in his fingers; but the slippery creature, armed also with its spinous fin-wings, had managed each time to glide out of his grasp; and it was still uncertain whether a capture might be made, or whether after all they were only to be tantalised by the touch and sight of a morsel of food that was never to pass over their palates.

The thought of such a disappointment stimulated Ben Brace to put forth all his energies, coupled with his greatest activity. He had even resolved upon following the fish into the sea if it should prove necessary,—knowing that for the first few moments after regaining its natural element it would be more easy of capture. But just then an opportunity was offered that promised the securing of the prey without the necessity of wetting a stitch of his clothes.

The fish had been all the while bounding about upon the spread sail-cloth, near the edge of which it had now arrived. But it was fated to go no farther, at least of its own accord; for Ben seeing his advantage, seized hold of the loose selvage of the sail, and raising it a little from the raft, doubled it over the struggling captive. A stiff squeeze brought its struggles to a termination; and when the canvas was lifted aloft, it was seen lying underneath, slightly flattened out beyond its natural dimensions, and it is scarcely necessary to say, as dead as a herring.

Whether right or no, the simple-minded seaman recognised in this seasonable supply of provision the hand of an overruling Providence; and without further question, attributed it to the potency of that prayer twice repeated.

"Yes, Will'm, you see it, my lad, 'tis the answer to that wonderful prayer. Let's go over it once more, by way o' givin' thanks. He who has sent meat can also gie us drink, even here, in the middle o' the briny ocean. Come, boy! as the parson used to say in church,—let us pray!"

And with this serio-comic admonition—meant, however, in all due solemnity—the sailor dropped upon his knees, and, as before, echoed the prayer once more pronounced by his youthful companion.

Chapter Six
Flying-Fish

The flying-fish takes rank as one of the most conspicuous "wonders of the sea," and in a tale essentially devoted to the great deep, it is a subject deserving of more than a passing notice.

From the earliest periods of ocean travel, men have looked with astonishment upon a phenomenon not only singular at first sight, but which still remains unexplained, namely, a fish and a creature believed to be formed only for dwelling under water, springing suddenly above the surface, to the height of a two-storey house, and passing through the air to the distance of a furlong, before falling back into its own proper element!

It is no wonder that the sight should cause surprise to the most indifferent observer, nor that it should have been long a theme of speculation with the curious, and an interesting subject of investigation to the naturalist.

As flying-fish but rarely make their appearance except in warm latitudes, few people who have not voyaged to the tropics have had an opportunity of seeing them in their flight. Very naturally, therefore, it will be asked what kind of fish, that is, to what *species* and what *genus* the flying-fish belong. Were there only one kind of these curious creatures the answer would be easier. But not only are there different species, but also different "genera" of fish endowed with the faculty of flying, and which from the earliest times and in different parts of the world have equally received this characteristic appellation. A word or two about each sort must suffice.

First, then, there are two species belonging to the genus *Trigla*, or the Gurnards, to which Monsieur La Cepède has given the name of *Dactylopterus*.

One species is found in the Mediterranean, and individuals, from a foot to fifteen inches in length, are often taken by the fishermen, and brought to the markets of Malta, Sicily, and even to the city of Rome. The other species of flying gurnard occur in the Indian Ocean and the seas around China and Japan.

The true *flying-fish*, however, that is to say, those that are met with in the great ocean, and most spoken of in books, and in the "yarns" of the sailor, are altogether of a different kind from the gurnards. They are not only different in genus, but in the family and even the order of fishes. They are of the genus *Exocetus*, and in form and other respects have a considerable resemblance to the common pike. There are several species of them inhabiting different parts of the tropical seas; and sometimes individuals, in the summer, have been seen as far north as the coast of Cornwall in Europe, and on the banks of Newfoundland in America. Their natural habitat, however, is in the warm latitudes of the ocean; and only there are they met with in large "schools," and seen with any frequency taking their aerial flight.

For a long time there was supposed to be only one, or at most two, species of the *Exocetus*; but it is now certain there are several—perhaps as many as half a dozen—distinct from each other. They are all much alike in their habits,—differing only in size, colour, and such like circumstances.

Naturalists disagree as to the character of their flight. Some assert that it is only a leap, and this is the prevailing opinion. Their reason for regarding it thus is, that while the fish is in the air there cannot be observed any movement of the wings (pectoral fins); and, moreover, after reaching the height to which it attains on its first spring, it cannot afterwards rise higher, but gradually sinks lower till it drops suddenly back into the water.

This reasoning is neither clear nor conclusive. A similar power of suspending themselves in the air, without motion of the wings is well-known to belong to many birds,—as the vulture, the albatross, the petrels, and others. Besides, it is difficult to conceive of a leap twenty feet high and two hundred yards long; for the flight of the *Exocetus* has been observed to be carried to this extent, and even farther. It is probable that the movement partakes both of the nature of leaping and flying: that it is first begun by a spring up out of the water,—a power possessed by most other kinds of fish,—and that the impulse thus obtained is continued by the spread fins acting on the air after the fashion of parachutes. It is known that the fish can greatly lighten the specific gravity of its body by the inflation of its "swim-bladder," which, when perfectly extended, occupies nearly the entire cavity of its abdomen. In addition to this, there is a membrane in the mouth which can be inflated through the gills. These two reservoirs are capable of containing a considerable volume of air; and as the fish has the power of filling or emptying them at will, they no doubt play an important part in the mechanism of its aerial movement.

One thing is certain, that the flying-fish can turn while in the air,—that is, diverge slightly from the direction first taken; and this would seem to argue a capacity something more than that of a mere spring or leap. Besides, the wings make a perceptible noise,—a sort of rustling,—often distinctly heard; and they have been seen to open and close while the creature is in the air.

A shoal of flying-fish might easily be mistaken for a flock of white birds, though their rapid movements, and the glistening sheen of their scales—especially when the sun is shining—usually disclose their true character. They are at all times a favourite spectacle, and with all observers,—the old "salt" who has seen them a thousand times, and the young sailor on his maiden voyage, who beholds them for the first time in his life. Many an hour of *ennui* occurring to the ship-traveller, as he sits upon the poop, restlessly scanning the monotonous surface of the sea, has been brought to a cheerful termination by the appearance of a shoal of flying-fish suddenly sparkling up out of the bosom of the deep.

The flying-fish appear to be the most persecuted of all creatures. It is to avoid their enemies under water that they take *fin* and mount into the air; but the old proverb, "out of the frying-pan into the fire," is but too applicable in their case, for in their endeavours to escape from the jaws of dolphins, albicores, bonitos, and other petty tyrants of the sea, they rush into the beaks of gannets, boobies, albatrosses, and other petty tyrants of the sky.

Much sympathy has been felt—or at all events expressed—for these pretty and apparently innocent little victims. But, alas! our sympathy receives a sad shock, when it becomes known that the flying-fish is himself one of the petty tyrants of the ocean,—being, like his near congener, the pike, a most ruthless little destroyer and devourer of any fish small enough to go down his gullet.

Besides the two *genera* of flying-fish above described, there are certain other marine animals which are gifted with a similar power of sustaining themselves for some seconds in the air. They are often seen in the Pacific and Indian oceans, rising out of the water in shoals, just like the *Exoceti*: and, like them, endeavouring to escape from the albicores and bonitos that incessantly pursue them. These creatures are not fish in the true sense of the word, but "molluscs," of the genus *Loligo*; and the name given to them by the whalers of the Pacific is that of "Flying Squid."

Chapter Seven
A Cheering Cloud

The particular species of flying-fish that had fallen into the clutches of the two starving castaways upon the raft was the *Exocetus evolans*, or "Spanish flying-fish" of mariners,—a well-known inhabitant of the warmer latitudes of the Atlantic. Its body was of a steel-blue, olive and silvery white underneath, with its large pectoral fins (its wings) of a powdered grey colour. It was one of the largest of its kind, being rather over twelve inches in length, and nearly a pound in weight.

Of course, it afforded but a very slight meal for two hungry stomachs,— such as were those of Ben Brace and his boy companion. Still it helped to strengthen them a little; and its opportune arrival upon the raft—which they could not help regarding as providential—had the further effect of rendering them for a time more cheerful and hopeful.

It is not necessary to say that they ate the creature without cooking it; and although under ordinary circumstances this might be regarded as a hardship, neither was at that moment in the mood to be squeamish. They thought the dish dainty enough. It was its quantity—not the quality—that failed to give satisfaction.

Indeed the flying-fish is (when cooked, of course) one of the most delicious of morsels,—a good deal resembling the common herring when caught freshly, and dressed in a proper manner.

It seemed, however, as if the partial relief from hunger only aggravated the kindred appetite from which the occupants of the raft had already begun to suffer. Perhaps the salt-water, mingled with the saline juices of the fish, aided in producing this effect. In any case, it was not long after they had eaten the *Exocetus* before both felt thirst in its very keenest agony.

Extreme thirst, under any circumstances, is painful to endure; but under no conditions is it so excruciating as in the midst of the ocean. The sight of water which you may not drink,—the very proximity of that element,—so near that you may touch it, and yet as useless to the assuaging of thirst as if it was the parched dust of the desert,—increases rather than alleviates the appetite. It is to no purpose, that you dip your fingers into the briny flood, and endeavour to cool your lips and tongue by taking it into the mouth. To swallow it is still worse. You might as well think to allay thirst by drinking liquid fire. The momentary moistening of the mouth and tongue is succeeded by an almost instantaneous parching of the salivary glands, which only glow with redoubled ardour.

Ben Brace knew this well enough; and once or twice that little William lifted the sea-water on his palm and applied it to his lips, the sailor cautioned him to desist, saying that it would do him more harm than good.

In one of his pockets Ben chanced to have a leaden bullet, which he gave the boy, telling him to keep it in his mouth and occasionally to chew it. By this means the secretion of the saliva was promoted; and although it was but slight, the sufferer obtained a little relief.

Ben himself held the axe to his lips, and partly by pressing his tongue against the iron, and partly by gnawing the angle of the blade, endeavoured to produce the same effect.

It was but a poor means of assuaging that fearful thirst that was now the sole object of their thoughts,—it might be said their only sensation,— for all other feelings, both of pleasure or pain, had become overpowered by this one. On food they no longer reflected, though still hungry; but the appetite of hunger, even when keenest, is far less painful than that of thirst. The former weakens the frame, so that the nervous system becomes dulled, and less sensible of the affliction it is enduring; whereas the latter may exist to its extremest degree, while the body is in full strength and vigour, and therefore more capable of feeling pain.

They suffered for several hours, almost all the time in silence. The words of cheer which the sailor had addressed to his youthful comrade were now only heard occasionally, and at long intervals, and when heard were spoken in a tone that proclaimed their utterance to be merely mechanical, and that he who gave tongue to them had but slight hope. Little as remained, however, he would rise from time to time to his feet, and stand for a while scanning the horizon around him. Then as his scrutiny once more terminated in disappointment, he would sink back upon the canvas, and half-kneeling, half-lying, give way for an interval to a half stupor of despair.

From one of these moods he was suddenly aroused by circumstances which had made no impression on his youthful companion, though the latter had also observed it. It was simply the darkening of the sun by a cloud passing over its disc.

Little William wondered that an incident of so common character should produce so marked an effect as it had done upon his protector: for the latter on perceiving that the sun had become shadowed instantly started to his feet, and stood gazing up towards the sky. A change had come over his countenance. His eyes, instead of the sombre look of despair observable but the moment before, seemed now to sparkle with hope. In fact, the cloud which had darkened the face of the sun appeared to have produced the very opposite effect upon the face of the sailor!

Chapter Eight
A Canvas Tank

"What is it, Ben?" asked William, in a voice husky and hoarse, from the parched throat through which it had to pass. "You look pleased like; do you see anything?"

"I see that, boy," replied the sailor, pointing up into the sky.

"What? I see nothing there except that great cloud that has just passed over the sun. What is there in that?"

"Ay, what is there in't? That's just what I'm tryin' to make out, Will'm; an' if I'm not mistaken, boy, there's it 't the very thing as we both wants."

"Water!" gasped William, his eyes lighting up with gleam of hope. "A rain-cloud you think, Ben?"

"I'm a'most sure o't, Will'm. I never seed a bank o' clouds like them there wasn't some wet in; and if the wind 'll only drift 'em this way, we may get a shower 'll be the savin' o' our lives. O Lord! in thy mercy look down on us, and send 'em over us!"

The boy echoed the prayer.

"See!" cried the sailor. "The wind is a fetchin' them this way. Yonder's more o' the same sort risin' up in the west, an' that's the direction from which it's a-blowin'. Ho! As I live, Will'm, there's rain. I can see by the mist it's a-fallin' on the water yonder. It's still far away,—twenty mile or so,—but that's nothing; an' if the wind holds good in the same quarter, it *must* come this way."

"But if it did, Ben," said William, doubtingly, "what good would it do us? We could not drink much of the rain as it falls, and you know we have nothing in which to catch a drop of it."

"But we have, boy,—we have our clothes and our shirts. If the rain comes, it will fall like it always does in these parts, as if it were spillin' out o' a strainer. We'll be soakin' wet in five minutes' time; and then we can wring all out,—trousers, shirts, and every rag we've got."

"But we have no vessel, Ben,—what could we wring the water into?"

"Into our months first: after that—ah! it be a pity. I never thought o't. We won't be able to save a drop for another time. Any rate, if we could only get one good quenchin', we might stand it several days longer. I fancy we might catch some fish, if we were only sure about the water. Yes, the rain's a-comin' on. Look at yon black clouds; and see, there's lightning forkin' among 'em. That 's a sure sign it's raining. Let's strip, and spread out our shirts so as to have them ready."

As Ben uttered this admonition he was about proceeding to pull off his pea-jacket, when an object came before his eyes causing him to desist. At the same instant an exclamatory phrase escaping from his lips explained to his companion why he had thus suddenly changed his intention. The phrase consisted of two simple words, which written as pronounced by Ben were, "Thee tarpolin."

Little William knew it was "the tarpauling" that was meant. He could not be mistaken about that; for, even had he been ignorant of the sailor's pronunciation of the words, the latter at that moment stood pointing to the piece of tarred canvas spread upright between the oars; and which had formerly served as a covering for the after-hatch of the *Pandora*. William did not equally understand why his companion was pointing to it.

He was not left long in ignorance.

"Nothing to catch the water in? That's what you sayed, little Will'm? What do ye call that, my boy?"

"Oh!" replied the lad, catching at the idea of the sailor. "You mean—"

"I mean, boy, that there's a vessel big enough to hold gallons,—a dozen o' 'em."

"You think it would hold water?"

"I'm sure o't, lad. For what else be it made waterproof? I helped tar it myself not a week ago. It'll hold like a rum-cask, I warrant,—ay, an' it'll be the very thing to catch it too. We can keep it spread out a bit wi' a hollow place in the middle, an' if it do rain, there then,—my boy, we'll ha' a pool big enough to swim ye in. Hurrah! it's sure to rain. See yonder. It be comin' nearer every minute. Let's be ready for it. Down wi' the mainsail. Let go the sheets,—an' instead o' spreadin' our canvas to the wind, as the song says, we'll stretch it out to the rain. Come, Will'm, let's look alive!"

William had by this time also risen to his feet; and both now busied themselves in unlashing the cords that had kept the hatch-covering spread between the two oars.

This occupied only a few seconds of time; and the tarpauling soon lay detached between the extemporised masts, that were still permitted to remain as they had been "stepped."

At first the sailor had thought of holding the piece of tarred canvas in their hands; but having plenty of time to reflect, a better plan suggested itself. So long as it should be thus held, they would have no chance of using their hands for any other purpose; and would be in a dilemma as to how they should dispose of the water after having "captured it."

It did not require much ingenuity to alter their programme for the better. By means of the flying-jib that lay along the raft, they were enabled to construct a ridge of an irregular circular shape; and then placing the tarpauling upon the top, and spreading it out so that its edges lapped over this ridge, they formed a deep concavity or "tank" in the middle, which was capable of holding many gallons of water.

It only remained to examine the canvas, and make sure there were no rents or holes by which the water might escape. This was done with all the minuteness and care that the circumstances called for; and when the sailor at length became satisfied that the tarpauling was waterproof, he took the hand of his youthful *protégé* in his own, and both kneeling upon the raft, with their faces turned towards the west watched the approach of those dark, lowering clouds, as if they had been bright-winged angels sent from the far sky to deliver them from destruction.

Chapter Nine
A Pleasant Shower-Bath

They had not much longer to wait. The storm came striding across the ocean; and, to the intense gratification of both man and boy, the rain was soon falling upon them, as if a water-spout had burst over their heads.

A single minute sufficed to collect over a quart within the hollow of the spread tarpauling; and before that minute had transpired, both might have been seen lying prostrate upon their faces with their heads together, near the centre of the concavity, and their lips close to the canvas, sucking up the delicious drops, almost as fast as they fell.

For a long time they continued in this position, indulging in that cool beverage sent them from the sky,—which to both appeared the sweetest they had ever tasted in their lives. So engrossed were they in its enjoyment, that neither spoke a word until several minutes had elapsed, and both had drunk to a surfeit.

They were by this time wet to the skin; for the tropic rain, falling in a deluge of thick heavy drops, soon saturated their garments through and through. But this, instead of being an inconvenience, was rather agreeable than otherwise, cooling their skins so long parched by the torrid rays of the sun.

"Little Will'm," said Ben, after swallowing about a gallon of the rain-water, "didn't I say that He 'as sent us meat, in such good time too, could also gi' us som'at to drink? Look there! water enow to last us for days, lad!"

"'Tis wonderful!" exclaimed the boy. "I am sure, Ben, that Providence has done this. Indeed, it must be true what I was often told in the Sunday school,—that God is everywhere. Here He is present with us in the midst of this great ocean. O, dear Ben, let's hope He will not forsake us now. I almost feel sure, after what has happened to us, that the hand of God will yet deliver us from our danger."

"I almost feel so myself," rejoined the sailor, his countenance resuming its wonted expression of cheerfulness. "After what's happened, one could not think otherwise; but let us remember, lad, that He is up aloft, an' has done so much for us, expecting us to do what we can for ourselves. He puts the work within our reach, an' then leaves us to do it. Now here's this fine supply o' water. If we was to let that go to loss, it would be our own fault, not his, an' we'd deserve to die o' thirst for it."

"What is to be done, Ben? How are we to keep it?"

"That's just what I'm thinkin' about. In a very short while the rain will be over. I know the sort o' it. It be only one o' these heavy showers as falls near the line, and won't last more than half an hour,—if that. Then the sun 'll be out as hot as ever, an' will lick up the water most as fast as it fell,—that is, if we let it lie there. Yes, in another half o' an hour that tarpolin would be as dry as the down upon a booby's back."

"O dear! what shall we do to prevent evaporating?"

"Jest give me a minute to consider," rejoined the sailor, scratching his head, and putting on an air of profound reflection; "maybe afore the rain quits comin' down, I'll think o' some way to keep it from evaporating; that's what you call the dryin' o' it up."

Ben remained for some minutes silent, in the thoughtful attitude he had assumed,—while William, who was equally interested in the result of his cogitations, watched his countenance with an eager anxiety.

Soon a joyful expression revealed itself to the glance of the boy, telling him that his companion had hit upon some promising scheme.

"I think I ha' got it, Will'm," said he; "I think I've found a way to stow the water even without a cask."

"You have!" joyfully exclaimed William. "How, Ben?"

"Well, you see, boy, the tarpolin holds water as tight as if 'twere a glass bottle. I tarred it myself,—that did I, an' as I never did my work lubber-like, I done that job well. Lucky I did, warn't it, William?"

"It was."

"That be a lesson for you, lad. Schemin' work bean't the thing, you see. It comes back to cuss one; while work as be well did be often like a blessin' arterward,—just as this tarpolin be now. But see! as I told you, the rain would soon be over. There be the sun again, hot an' fiery as ever. There ain't no time to waste. Take a big drink, afore I put the stopper into the bottle."

William, without exactly comprehending what his companion meant by the last words, obeyed the injunction; and stretching forward over the rim of the improvised tank, once more placed his lips to the water, and drank copiously. Ben did the same for himself, passing several pints of the fluid into his capacious stomach.

Then rising to his feet with a satisfied air, and directing his *protégé* to do the same, he set about the stowage of the water.

William was first instructed as to the intended plan, so that he might be able to render prompt and efficient aid; for it would require both of them, and with all their hands, to carry it out.

The sailor's scheme was sufficiently ingenious. It consisted in taking up first the corners of the tarpauling, then the edges all around, and bringing them together in the centre. This had to be done with great care, so as not to jumble the volatile fluid contained within the canvas, and spill it over the selvage. Some did escape, but only a very little; and they at length succeeded in getting the tarpauling formed into a sort of bag, puckered around the mouth.

While Ben with both arms held the gathers firm and fast, William passed a loop of strong cord, that had already been made into a noose for the purpose, around the neck of the bag, close under Ben's wrists, and then drawing the other end round one of the upright oars, he pulled upon the cord with all his might.

It soon tightened sufficiently to give Ben the free use of his hands; when with a fresh loop taken around the crumpled canvas, and after a turn or two to render it more secure, the cord was made fast.

The tarpauling now rested upon the raft, a distended mass, like the stomach of some huge animal coated with tar. It was necessary, however, lest the water should leak out through the creases, to keep the top where it was tied, uppermost; and this was effected by taking a turn or two of the rope round the uppermost end of one of the oars, that had served for masts, and there making a knot. By this means the great water-sack was held in such a position that, although the contents might "bilge" about at their pleasure, not a drop could escape out either at the neck or elsewhere.

Altogether they had secured a quantity of water, not less than a dozen gallons, which Ben had succeeded in stowing to his satisfaction.

Chapter Ten
The Pilot-Fish

This opportune deliverance from the most fearful of deaths had inspired the sailor with a hope that they might still, by some further interference of Providence, escape from their perilous position. Relying on this hope, he resolved to leave no means untried that might promise to lead to its realisation. They were now furnished with a stock of water which, if carefully hoarded, would last them for weeks. If they could only obtain a proportionate supply of food, there would still be a chance of their sustaining life until some ship might make its appearance,—for, of course, they thought not of any other means of deliverance.

To think of food was to think of fishing for it. In the vast reservoir of the ocean under and around them there was no lack of nourishing food, if they could only grasp it; but the sailor well knew that the shy, slippery denizens of the deep are not to be captured at will, and that, with all the poor schemes they might be enabled to contrive, their efforts to capture even a single fish might be exerted in vain.

Still they could try; and with that feeling of hopeful confidence which usually precedes such trials, they set about making preparations.

The first thing was to make hooks and lines. There chanced to be some pins in their clothing; and with these Ben soon constructed a tolerable set of hooks. A line was obtained by untwisting a piece of rope, and respinning it to the proper thickness; and then a float was found by cutting a piece of wood to the proper dimensions. And for a sinker there was the leaden bullet with which little William had of late so vainly endeavoured to allay the pangs of thirst. The bones and fins of the flying-fish—the only part of it not eaten—would serve for bait. They did not promise to make a very attractive one; for there was not a morsel of flesh left upon them; but Ben knew that there are many kinds of fish inhabiting the great ocean that will seize at any sort of bait,—even a piece of rag,—without considering whether it be good for them or not.

They had seen fish several times near the raft, during that very day; but suffering as they were from thirst more than hunger, and despairing of relief to the more painful appetite, they had made no attempt to capture them. Now, however, they were determined to set about it in earnest.

The rain had ceased falling; the breeze no longer disturbed the surface of the sea. The clouds had passed over the canopy of the heavens,—the sky was clear, and the sun bright and hot as before.

Ben standing erect upon the raft, with the baited hook in his hand, looked down into the deep blue water.

Even the smallest fish could have been seen many fathoms below the surface, and far over the ocean.

William on the other side of the raft was armed with hook and line, and equally on the alert.

For a long time their vigil was unrewarded. No living thing came within view. Nothing was under their eyes save the boundless field of ultramarine,—beautiful, but to them, at that moment, marked only by a miserable monotony.

They had stood thus for a full hour, when an exclamation escaping from the lad, caused his companion to turn and look to the other side of the raft.

A fish was in sight. It was that which had drawn the exclamation from the boy, who was now swinging his line in the act of casting it out.

The ejaculation had been one of joy. It was checked on his perceiving that the sailor did not share it. On the contrary, a cloud came over the countenance of the latter on perceiving the fish,—whose species he at once recognised.

And why? for it was one of the most beautiful of the finny tribe. A little creature of perfect form,—of a bright azure blue, with transverse bands of deeper tint, forming rings around its body. Why did Ben Brace show disappointment at its appearance?

"You needn't trouble to throw out your line, little Will'm," said he, "that ere takes no bait,—not it."

"Why?" asked the boy.

"Because it's something else to do than forage for itself. I dare say its master an't far off."

"What is it?"

"That be the *pilot-fish*. See! turns away from us. It gone back to him as has sent it."

"Sent it! Who, Ben?"

"A shark, for sarten. Didn't I tell ye? Look yonder. Two o' them, as I live; and the biggest kind they be. Slash my timbers if I iver see such a pair! They have fins like lug-sails. Look! the pilot's gone to guide 'em. Hang me if they bean't a-comin' this way!"

William had looked in the direction pointed out by his companion. He saw the two great dorsal fins standing several feet above the water. He knew them to be those of the *white shark*: for he had already seen these dreaded monsters of the deep on more than one occasion.

It was true, as Ben had hurriedly declared. The little pilot-fish, after coming within twenty fathoms of the raft, had turned suddenly in the water, and gone back to the sharks; and now it was seen swimming a few feet in advance of them, as if in the act of leading them on!

The boy was struck with something in the tone of his companion's voice, that led him to believe there was danger in the proximity of these ugly creatures; and to say the truth, Ben did not behold them without a certain feeling of alarm. On the deck of a ship they might have been regarded without any fear; but upon a frail structure like that which supported the castaways—their feet almost on a level with the surface of the water—it was not so very improbable that the sharks might attack them!

In his experience the sailor had known cases of a similar kind. It was no matter of surprise, that he should feel uneasiness at their approach, if not actual fear.

But there was no time left either for him to speculate as to the probabilities of such an attack, or for his companion to question him about them.

Scarcely had the last words parted from his lips, when the foremost of the two sharks was seen to lash the water with its broad forked tail,—and then coming on with a rush, it struck the raft with such a force as almost to capsize it.

The other shark shot forward in a similar manner; but glancing a little to one side, caught in its huge mouth the end of the dolphin-striker, grinding off a large piece of the spar as if it had been cork-wood!

This it swallowed almost instantaneously; and then turning once more in the water appeared intent upon renewing the attack.

Ben and the boy had dropped their hooks and lines,—the former instinctively arming himself with the axe, while the latter seized upon the spare handspike. Both stood ready to receive the second charge of the enemy.

It was made almost on the instant. The shark that had just attacked was the first to return; and coming on with the velocity of an arrow, it sprang clear above the surface, projecting its hideous jaws over the edge of the raft.

For a moment the frail structure was in danger of being either capsized or swamped altogether, and then the fate of its occupants would undoubtedly have been to become "food for sharks."

But it was not the intention of Ben Brace or his youthful comrade to yield up their lives without striking a blow in self-defence, and that given by the sailor at once disembarrassed him of his antagonist.

Throwing one arm around a mast, in order to steady himself, and raising the light axe in the other, he struck outward and downward with all his might. The blade of the axe, guided with an unswerving arm, fell right upon the snout of the shark, just midway between its nostrils, cleaving the cartilaginous flesh to the depth of several inches, and laying it open to the bones.

There could not have been chosen a more vital part upon which to inflict a wound; for, huge as is the white shark, and strong and vigorous as are all animals of this ferocious family, a single blow upon the nose with a handspike or even a billet of wood, if laid on with a heavy hand, will suffice to put an end to their predatory courses.

And so was it with the shark struck by the axe of Ben Brace. As soon as the blow had been administered, the creature rolled over on its back; and after a fluke or two with its great forked tail, and a tremulous shivering through its body, it lay floating upon the water motionless as a log of wood.

William was not so fortunate with his antagonist, though he had succeeded in keeping it off. Striking wildly out with the handspike in a horizontal direction, he had poked the butt end of the implement right between the jaws of the monster, just as it raised its head over the raft with the mouth wide open.

The shark, seizing the handspike in its treble row of teeth, with one shake of its head whipped it out of the boy's hands: and then rushing on through the water, was seen grinding the timber into small fragments, and swallowing it as if it had been so many crumbs of bread or pieces of meat.

In a few seconds not a bit of the handspike could be seen,—save some trifling fragments of the fibrous wood that floated on the surface of the water; but what gave greater gratification to those who saw them, was the fact that the shark which had thus made "mince-meat" of the piece of timber was itself no longer to be seen.

Whether because it had satisfied the cravings of its appetite by that wooden banquet, or whether it had taken the alarm at witnessing the fate of its companion,—by much the larger of the two,—was a question of slight importance either to Ben Brace or to William. For whatever reason, and under any circumstances, they were but too well pleased to be disembarrassed of its hideous presence; and as they came to the conclusion that it had gone off for good, and saw the other one lying with its white belly turned upwards upon the surface of the water—evidently dead as a herring—they could no longer restrain their voices, but simultaneously raised them in a shout of victory.

Chapter Eleven
A Lenten Dinner

The shark struck upon the snout, though killed by the blow, continued to float near the surface of the water its fins still in motion as if in the act of swimming.

One unacquainted with the habits of these sea-monsters might have supposed that it still lived, and might yet contrive to escape. Not so the sailor, Ben Brace. Many score of its kind had Ben coaxed to take a bait, and afterwards helped to haul over the gangway of a ship and cut to pieces upon the deck; and Ben knew as much about the habits of these voracious creatures as any sailor that ever crossed the wide ocean, and much more than any naturalist that never did. He had seen a shark drawn aboard with a great steel hook in its stomach,—he had seen its belly ripped up with a jack-knife, the whole of the intestines taken out, then once more thrown into the sea; and after all this rough handling he had seen the animal not only move its fins, but actually swim off some distance from the ship! He knew, moreover, that a shark may be cut in twain,—have the head separated from the body,—and still exhibit signs of vitality in both parts for many hours after the dismemberment! Talk of the killing of a cat or an eel!—a shark will stand as much killing as twenty cats or a bushel of eels, and still exhibit symptoms of life.

The shark's most vulnerable part appears to be the snout,—just where the sailor had chosen to make his hit; and a blow delivered there with an axe, or even a handspike, usually puts a termination to the career of this rapacious tyrant of the great deep.

"I've knocked him into the middle o' next week," cried Ben, exultingly, as he saw the shark heel over on its side. "It ain't goin' to trouble us any more. Where's the other un?"

"Gone out that way," answered the boy, pointing in the direction taken by the second and smaller of the two sharks. "He whipped the handspike out of my hands, and he's craunched it to fragments. See! there are some of the pieces floating on the water!"

"Lucky you let go, lad; else he might ha' pulled you from the raft. I don't think he'll come back again after the reception we've gi'ed 'em. As for the other, it's gone out o' its senses. Dash my buttons, if't ain't goin' to sink! Ha! I must hinder that. Quick, Will'm, shy me that piece o' sennit: we must secure him 'fore he gives clean up and goes to the bottom. Talk o' catching fish wi' hook an' line! Aha! This beats all your small fry. If we can secure it, we'll have fish enough to last us through the longest Lent. There now! keep on the other edge of the craft so as to balance me. So-so!"

While the sailor was giving these directions, he was busy with both hands in forming a running-noose on one end of the sennit-cord, which William on the instant had handed over to him. It was but the work of a moment to make the noose; another to let it down into the water; a third to pass it over the upper jaw of the shark; a fourth to draw it taut, and tighten the cord around the creature's teeth. The next thing done was to secure the other end of the sennit to the upright oar; and the carcass of the shark was thus kept afloat near the surface of the water.

To guard against a possible chance of the creature's recovery, Ben once more laid hold of the axe; and, leaning over the edge of the raft, administered a series of smart blows upon its snout. He continued hacking away, until the upper jaw of the fish exhibited the appearance of a butcher's chopping-block; and there was no longer any doubt of the creature being as "dead as a herring."

"Now, Will'm," said the shark-killer, "this time we've got a fish that'll gi'e us a fill, lad. Have a little patience, and I'll cut ye a steak from the tenderest part o' his body; and that's just forrard o' the tail. You take hold o' the sinnet, an' pull him up a bit,—so as I can get at him."

The boy did as directed; and Ben, once more bending over the edge of the raft, caught hold of one of the caudal fins, and with his knife detached a large flake from the flank of the fish,—enough to make an ample meal for both of them.

It is superfluous to say that, like the little flying-fish, the shark-meat had to be eaten raw; but to men upon the verge of starvation there is no inconvenience in this. Indeed, there are many tribes of South-Sea Islanders— not such savage either—who habitually eat the flesh of the shark—both the blue and white species—without thinking it necessary even to warm it over a fire! Neither did the castaway English sailor nor his young comrade think it necessary. Even had a fire been possible, they were too hungry to have stayed for the process of cooking; and both, without more ado, dined upon raw shark-meat.

When they had succeeded in satisfying the cravings of hunger, and once more refreshed themselves with a draught from their extemporised water-bag, the castaways not only felt a relief from actual suffering, but a sort of cheerful confidence in the future. This arose from a conviction on their part, or at all events a strong impression, that the hand of Providence had been stretched out to their assistance. The flying-fish, the shower, the shark may have been accidents, it is true; but, occurring at such a time, just in the very crisis of their affliction, they were accidents that had the appearance of design,—design on the part of Him to whom in that solemn hour they had uplifted their voices in prayer.

It was under this impression that their spirits became naturally restored; and once more they began to take counsel together about the ways and means of prolonging their existence.

It is true that their situation was still desperate. Should a storm spring up,—even an ordinary gale,—not only would their canvas water-cask be bilged, and its contents spilled out to mingle with the briny billow, but their frail embarkation would be in danger of going to pieces, or of being whelmed fathoms deep under the frothing waves. In a high latitude, either north or south, their chance of keeping afloat would have been slight indeed. A week, or rather only a single day, would have been as long as they could have expected that calm to continue; and the experienced sailor knew well enough that anything in the shape of a storm would expose them to certain destruction. To console him for this unpleasant knowledge, however, he also knew that in the ocean, where they were then afloat, storms are exceedingly rare, and that ships are often in greater danger from the very opposite state of the atmosphere,—from *calms*. They were in that part of the Atlantic Ocean known among the early Spanish navigators as the *Horse Latitudes*,—so-called because the horses at that time being carried across to the New World, for want of water in the becalmed ships, died in great numbers, and being thrown overboard were often seen floating upon the surface of the sea.

A prettier and more poetical name have these same Spaniards given to a portion of the same Atlantic Ocean,—which, from the gentleness of its breezes, they have styled "*La Mar de las Damas*" (the Ladies' Sea).

Ben Brace knew that in the Horse Latitudes storms were of rare occurrence; and hence the hopefulness with which he was now looking forward to the future.

He was no longer inactive. If he believed in the special Interference of Providence, he also believed that Providence would expect him to make some exertion of himself, — such as circumstances might permit and require.

Chapter Twelve
Flensing a Shark

The flesh of the shark, and the stock of water so singularly obtained and so deftly stored away, might, if properly kept and carefully used, last them for many days; and to the preservation of these stores the thoughts of the sailor and his young companion were now specially directed.

For the former they could do nothing more than had been already done,—further than to cover the tarpauling that contained it with several folds of the spare sail-cloth, in order that no ray of the sun should get near it. This precaution was at once adopted.

The flesh of the shark—now dead as mutton—if left to itself, would soon spoil, and be unfit for food, even for starving men. It was this reflection that caused the sailor and his *protégé* to take counsel together as to what might be done towards preserving it.

They were not long in coming to a decision. Shark-flesh, like that of any other fish—like haddock, for instance, or red herrings—can be dried in the sun; and the more readily in that sun of the torrid zone that shone down so hotly upon their heads. The flesh only needed to be cut into thin slices and suspended from the upright oars. The atmosphere would soon do the rest. Thus cured, it would keep for weeks or months; and thus did the castaways determine to cure it.

No sooner was the plan conceived, than they entered upon its execution. Little William again seized the cord of sennit, and drew the huge carcass close up to the raft; while Ben once more opened the blade of his sailor's knife, and commenced cutting off the flesh in broad flakes,—so thin as to be almost transparent.

He had succeeded in stripping off most of the titbits around the tail, and was proceeding up the body of the shark to *flense* it in a similar fashion, when an ejaculation escaped him, expressing surprise or pleasant curiosity.

Little William was but too glad to perceive the pleased expression on the countenance of his companion,—of late so rarely seen.

"What is it, Ben?" he inquired, smilingly.

"Look 'ee theer, lad," rejoined the sailor, placing his hand upon the back of the boy's head, and pressing it close to the edge of the raft, so that he could see well down into the water,—"look theer, and tell me what you see."

"Where?" asked William, still ignorant of the object to which his attention was thus forcibly directed.

"Don't you see somethin' queery stickin' to the belly of the shark,—eh, lad?"

"As I live," rejoined William, now perceiving "somethin'", "there's a small fish pushing his head against the shark,—not so small either,—only in comparison with the great shark himself. It's about a foot long, I should think. But what is it doing in that odd position?"

"Sticking to the shark,—didn't I tell 'ee, lad!"

"Sticking to the shark? You don't mean that, Ben?"

"But I do—mean that very thing, boy. It's as fast theer as a barnacle to a ship's copper; an' 'll stay, I hope, till I get my claws upon it,—which won't take very long from now. Pass a piece o' cord this way. Quick."

The boy stretched out his hand, and, getting hold of a piece of loose string, reached it to his companion. Just as the snare had been made for the shark with the piece of sennit, and with like rapidity, a noose was constructed on the string; and, having been lowered into the water, was passed around the body of the little fish which appeared adhering to the belly of the shark. Not only did it so appear, but it actually was, as was proved by the pull necessary to detach it, and which required all the strength that lay in the strong arms of the sailor.

He succeeded, however, in effecting his purpose; and with a pluck the parasite fish was separated from the skin to which it had been clinging, and, jerked upwards, was landed alive and kicking upon the raft.

Its kicking was not allowed to continue for long. Lest it might leap back into the water, and, sluggish swimmer as it was, escape out of reach, Ben, with the knife which he still held unclasped in his hand, pinned it to one of the planks, and in an instant terminated its existence.

"What sort of a fish is it?" asked William, as he looked upon the odd creature thus oddly obtained.

"Suckin'-fish," was Ben's laconic answer.

"A sucking-fish! I never heard of one before. Why is it so-called?"

"Because it sucks," replied the sailor.

"Sucks what?"

"Sharks. Didn't you see it suckin' at this 'un afore I pulled it from the teat? Ha! ha! ha!"

"Surely it wasn't that, Ben?" said the lad, mystified by Ben's remark.

"Well, boy, I an't, going to bamboozle ye. All I know is that it fastens onto sharks, and only this sort, which are called *white sharks*; for I never seed it sticking to any o' the others,—of which there be several kinds. As to its suckin' anythin' out o' them an' livin' by that, I don't believe a word o' it; though they say it do so, and that's what's given it its name. Why I don't believe it is, because I've seed the creature stickin' just the same way to the coppered bottom o' a ship, and likewise to the sides o' rocks under the water. Now, it couldn't get anything out o' the copper to live upon, nor yet out o' a rock,—could it?"

"Certainly not."

"Then it couldn't be a suckin' them. Besides, I've seed the stomachs o' several cut open, and they were full of little water-creepers,—such as there's thousands o' kinds in the sea. I warrant if we rip this 'un up the belly, we'll find the same sort o' food in it."

"And why does it fasten itself to sharks and ships,—can you tell that, Ben?"

"I've heerd the reason, and it be sensible enough,—more so than to say that it sucks. There was a doctor as belonged in the man-o'-war where I sarved for two years, as was larned in all such curious things. He said that the suckin'-fish be a bad swimmer; and that I know myself to be true. You can tell by the smallness o' its fins. Well, the doctor, he say, it fastens on to the sharks and ships so as to get carried from place to place, and to the rocks to rest itself. Whenever it takes a notion, it can slip off, and go a huntin' for its prey; and then come back again and take a fresh grip on whatever it has chosen to lodge itself."

"It's that curious thing along the back of its head that enables it to hold on, isn't it?"

"That's its sticking-machine; and, what be curious, Will'm, if you were to try to pull it off upwards or backwards you couldn't do it wi' all your strength, nor I neither: you must shove it forrard, as you seed me do just now, or else pull it to pieces before it would come off."

"I can see," said William, holding the fish up to his eyes, "that there are rows of little teeth in that queer top-knot it's got, all turned towards the tail. It is they, I suppose, that prevent its slipping backwards?"

"No doubt, lad,—no doubt it be that. But never mind what it be just now. Let us finish flensin' o' the shark; and then if we feel hungry we can make a meal o' the sucker,—for I can tell you it's the best kind o' eatin'. I've ate 'em often in the South-Sea Islands, where the natives catch 'em with hooks and lines; but I've seen them there much bigger than this 'un,—three feet long, and more."

And so saying, the sailor returned to the operation, thus temporarily suspended,—the *flensing* of the shark.

Chapter Thirteen
The Sucking-Fish

The fish that had thus singularly fallen into their hands was, as Ben had stated, the sucking-fish, *Echeneis remora*,—one of the most curious creatures that inhabit the sea. Not so much from any peculiarity in appearance as from the singularity of its habits.

Its appearance, however, is sufficiently singular; and looking upon it, one might consider the creature as being well adapted for keeping company with the ferocious tyrant of the deep, on whom it constantly attends.

Its body is black and smooth, its head of a hideous form, and its fins short and broadly spread. The mouth is very large, with the lower jaw protruding far beyond the upper, and it is this that gives to it the cast of feature, if we may be permitted to speak of "features" in a fish.

Both lips and jaws are amply provided with teeth; and the throat, palate, and tongue are set profusely with short spines. The eyes are dark, and set high up. The "sucker" or buckler upon the top of its head consists of a number of bony plates, set side by side, so as to form an oval disc, and armed along the edges with little tentacles, or teeth, as the boy William had observed.

His companion's account of the creature was perfectly correct, so far as it went; but there are many other points in its "history" quite as curious as those which the sailor had communicated.

The fish has neither swim-bladder nor sound; and as, moreover, its fins are of the feeblest kind, it is probably on this account that it has been gifted with the power of adhering to other floating bodies, by way of compensation for the above-named deficiencies. The slow and prowling movements of the white shark, render it particularly eligible for the purposes of the sucking-fish, either as a resting-place or a means of conveyance from place to place; and it is well-known that the shark is usually attended by several of these singular satellites. Other floating objects, however, are used by the sucking-fish,—such as pieces of timber, the keel of a ship; and it even rests itself against the sides of submerged rocks, as the sailor had stated. It also adheres to whales, turtles, and the larger kinds of albacore.

Its food consists of shrimps, marine insects, fragments of molluscous animals, and the like; but it obtains no nutriment through the sucking-apparatus, nor does it in any way injure the animal to which it adheres. It only makes use of the sucker at intervals; at other times, swimming around the object it attends, and looking out for prey of its own choice, and on its own account. While swimming it propels itself by rapid lateral movements of the tail, executed awkwardly and with a tortuous motion.

It is itself preyed upon by other fish,—diodons and albacores; but the shark is merciful to it, as to the pilot-fish, and never interferes with it.

Sucking-fish are occasionally seen of a pure white colour associating with the black ones, and also attending upon the shark. They are supposed to be merely varieties or *albinos*.

When sharks are hooked and drawn on board a ship, the sucking-fishes that have been swimming around them will remain for days, and even weeks, following the vessel throughout all her courses. They can then be taken by a hook and line, baited with a piece of flesh; and they will seize the bait when let down in the stillest water. In order to secure them, however, it is necessary, after they have been hooked, to jerk them quickly out of the water; else they will swim rapidly to the side of the ship, and fix their sucker so firmly against the wood, as to defy every attempt to dislodge them.

There are two well-known species of sucking-fish,—the common one described, and another of larger size, found in the Pacific, the *Echeneis australis*. The latter is a better shaped fish than its congener, can swim more rapidly, and is altogether of a more active habit.

Perhaps the most interesting fact in the history of the *Echeneis* is its being the same fish as that known to the Spanish navigators as the *remora*, and which was found by Columbus in possession of the natives of Cuba and Jamaica, *tamed, and trained to the catching of turtles!*

Their mode of using it was by attaching a cord of palm sennit to a ring already fastened round the tail, at the smallest part between the ventral and caudal fins. It was then allowed to swim out into the sea; while the other end of the cord was tied to a tree, or made fast to a rock upon the beach. The *remora* being thus set—just as one would set a baited hook—was left free to follow its own inclinations,—which usually were to fasten its sucking-plates against the shell of one of the great sea-turtles,—so famed at aldermanic feasts and prized by modern *gourmets,* and equally relished by the ancient Cuban *caciques.*

At intervals, the turtle-catcher would look to his line; and when the extra strain upon it proved that the *remora* was *en rapport* with a turtle, he would haul in, until the huge *chelonian* was brought within striking distance of his heavy club; and thus would the capture be effected.

Turtles of many hundreds' weight could be taken in this way; for the pull upon the *remora* being towards the tail,—and therefore in a backward direction,—the sucking-fish could not be detached, unless by the most violent straining.

It is a fact of extreme singularity, that a similar method of capturing turtles is practised on the coast of Mozambique at the present day, and by a people who never could have had any communication with the aborigines of the West Indian Islands, much less have learnt from them this curious craft of angling with a fish!

A smaller species of the sucking-fish is found in the Mediterranean,— the *Echeneis remora.* It was well-known to the ancient writers; though, like most creatures gifted with any peculiarity, it was oftener the subject of fabulous romance than real history. It was supposed to have the power of arresting the progress of a ship, by attaching itself to the keel and pulling in a contrary direction! A still more ridiculous virtue was attributed to it: in the belief that, if any criminal in dread of justice could only succeed in inducing the judge to partake of a portion of its flesh, he would be able to obtain a long delay before the judge could pronounce the verdict of his condemnation!

Chapter Fourteen
A Sail of Shark-Flesh

It wanted but a little while of sunset, when the sailor and his young comrade had finished flensing the shark. The raft now exhibited quite an altered appearance. Between the two upright oars several pieces of rope had been stretched transversely, and from these hung suspended the broad thin flitches of the shark's flesh, that at a distance might have been mistaken for some sort of a sail. Indeed, they acted as such; for their united discs presented a considerable breadth of surface to the breeze, which had sprung up as the evening approached, and the raft by this means moved through the water with considerable rapidity.

There was no effort made to steer it. The idea of reaching land was entirely out of the question. Their only hope of salvation lay in their being seen from a ship; and as a ship was as likely to come from one direction as another, it mattered not to which of the thirty-two points of the compass their raft might be drifting. Yes, it *did* matter. So thought Ben Brace, on reflection.

It might be of serious consequence, should the raft make way to the westward. Somewhere in that direction—how far neither could guess—that greater raft, with its crew of desperate ruffians,—those drunken would-be cannibals,—must be drifting about, like themselves, at the mercy of winds and waves: perhaps more than themselves suffering the dire extreme of thirst and hunger. Perhaps, ere then, one of their own number may have been forced to submit to the horrid fate which they had designed for little William; and which, but for the interference of his generous protector, would most certainly have befallen him.

Should he again fall into their clutches, there would be but slight chance of a second escape. His protector knew that. Ben knew, moreover, that his own life would be equally sure of being sacrificed to the resentment of the ribald crew, with whom he had formerly associated.

No wonder, as he felt the breeze blowing on his cheek, that he looked towards the setting sun, to ascertain in what direction the raft was being borne. No wonder that his anxious glance became changed to a look of satisfaction when he perceived that they were moving eastward.

"To the east'ard it are, sure enough," said he, "and that be curious too. 'T an't often I've see'd the wind blow from the westward in these latitudes. Only another catspaw in the middle o' the calm. 'T won't last long; though it won't matter, so long's it don't turn and blow us t'other way."

The expressed wish not to be blown "t'other way" needed no explanation. William understood what that meant. The fearful scene of the preceding day was fresh in his memory. That scene, where half a score of fiend-like monsters, threatening his life, were kept at bay by one heroic man,—that was a tableau too terrible to be soon forgotten.

Nor had he forgotten it, even for a moment. Perhaps, during that brief conflict with the sharks, the nearer danger may have driven it for an interval out of his mind; but that over, the dread remembrance returned again; and every now and then,—even while engaged in the varied labours that had occupied them throughout the day,—in a sort of waking dream he had recalled that fearful vision. Often—every few minutes in fact—had his eyes been turned involuntarily towards the west,—where, instead of looking hopefully for a ship, his anxious glance betrayed a fear that any dark object might be seen in that direction.

On finishing their task, both were sufficiently fatigued,—the strong sailor as well as his feebler companion. The former still kept his feet, anxiously scanning the horizon; while the latter laid himself along the bare boards of the raft.

"Little Will'm," said the sailor, looking down at the boy, and speaking in gentle tones, "you'd better spread the sail under ye, and get some sleep. There be no use in both o' us keeping awake. I'll watch till it gets dark, an' then I'll join you. Go to sleep, lad! go to sleep!"

William was too wearied to make objection. Drawing the skirt of the sail over the raft, he lay down upon it, and found sleep almost as soon is he had composed himself into the attitude to enjoy it.

The sailor remained standing erect; now sweeping the horizon with his glance, now bending his eye restlessly upon the water as it rippled along the edge of the raft, and again returning to that distant scrutiny,—so oft repeated, so oft unrewarded.

Thus occupied, he passed the interval of twilight,—short in these latitudes; nor did he terminate his vigil until darkness had descended upon the deep.

It promised to be a dark, moonless night. Only a few feebly gleaming stars, thinly scattered over the firmament, enabled him to distinguish the canopy of the sky from the waste of waters that surrounded him. Even a ship under full spread of canvas could not have been seen, though passing at a cable's length from the raft.

It was idle to continue the dreary vigil; and having arrived at this conviction, the sailor stretched himself alongside his slumbering companion, and, like the latter, was soon relieved from his long-protracted anxiety by the sweet oblivion of sleep.

Chapter Fifteen
The Mysterious Voice

For several hours both remained wrapped in slumber, oblivious of the perils through which they had passed,—equally unconscious of the dangers that surrounded and still lay before them.

What a picture was there,—with no human eye to behold it! Two human forms, a sailor and a sailor-boy, lying side by side upon a raft scarce twice the length of their own bodies, in the midst of a vast ocean, landless and limitless as infinity itself both softly and soundly asleep,—as if reposing upon the pillow of some secure couch, with the firm earth beneath and a friendly roof extended over them! Ah, it was a striking tableau, that frail craft with its sleeping crew,—such a spectacle as is seldom seen by human eye!

It was fortunate that for many hours they continued to enjoy the sweet unconsciousness of sleep,—if such may be termed enjoyment. It was long after midnight before either awoke: for there was nothing to awake them. The breeze had kept gentle, and constant in the same quarter; and the slight noise made by the water, as it went "swishing" along the edge of the raft, instead of rousing them acted rather as a lullaby to their rest. The boy awoke first. He had been longer asleep; and his nervous system, refreshed and restored to its normal condition, had become more keenly sensitive to outward impressions. Some big, cold rain-drops falling upon his face had recalled him to wakefulness.

Was it spray tossed up by the spars ploughing through the water?

No. It was rain from the clouds. The canopy overhead was black as ink; but while the lad was scrutinising it, a gleam of lightning suddenly illumined both sea and sky, and then all was dark as before.

Little William would have restored his cheek to its sail-cloth pillow and gone to sleep again. He was not dismayed by the silent lightning,—for it was that sort that had flickered over the sky. No more did he mind the threatening rainclouds. His shirt had been soaked too often, by showers from the sky and spray from the sea, for him to have any dread of a ducking.

It was not that,—neither the presence of the lightning nor the prospect of the rain,—that kept him awake; but something he had heard,—or fancied he had heard,—something that not only restrained him from returning to repose, but inspired him with a fear that robbed him of an inclination to go to sleep again.

What was it he had heard or fancied? A noise,—a *voice*!

Was it the scream of the sea-mew, the shriek of the frigate-bird, or the hoarse note of the nelly?

None of these. The boy-sailor was acquainted with the cries of all three, and of many other sea-birds besides. It was not the call of a bird that had fallen so unexpectedly on his ear, but a note of far different intonation. It more resembled a voice,—a human voice,—the voice of a child! Not of a very young child,—an infant,—but more like that of a girl of eight or ten years of age!

Nor was it a cry of distress, though uttered in a melancholy tone. It seemed to the ear of the lad—freshly awakened from his sleep—like words spoken in conversation.

But it could not be what he had taken it for! Improbable,—impossible! He had been deluded by a fancy; or it might be the mutterings of some ocean bird with whose note he was unacquainted.

Should he awake his companion and tell him of it? A pity, if it should prove to be nothing, or only the chattering of a sea-gull. His brave protector had need of rest. Ben would not be angry to be awaked; but the sailor would be sure to laugh at him if he were to say he had heard a little girl talking at that time of night in the middle of the Atlantic Ocean. Perhaps Ben might say it was a mermaid, and mock him in that sort of style?

No: he would not run the risk of being ridiculed, even by his best of friends. Better let the thing pass, and say nothing about it.

Little William had arrived at this resolution, and had more than half determined to treat the sound he had heard as an *aurical* delusion. He had even replaced his cheek upon the sail-cloth pillow, when the very same sound again fill upon his ear,—this time more distinctly heard, as if either the utterance had been clearer or the being that made it was nearer!

If it was not the voice of a girl,—a very young girl,—then the boy-sailor had never listened to the prattling of his younger sister, or the conversation of his little female playmates. If it was a young mermaid, then most assuredly could mermaids talk: for the sound was exactly like a string or series of words uttered in conversation!

Ben must be aroused from his slumber. It could not be an illusion. Either a talking mermaid, or a little girl, was within earshot of the raft.

There was no help for it: Ben must be aroused.

"Ben! Ben!"

"Ho—hah—ow—aw—what's the row?—seven bells, I bean't on the dog-watch. Hi, hi, oh! it's you, little Will'm. What is't, lad?"

"Ben, I hear something."

"Hear somethin'! Well, what o' that, boy? Theer 's allers somethin' to be heerd: even here, in the middle o' the Atlantic. Ah! boy, I was dreamin' a nice dream when ye woke me. I thought I war back on the ole frigate. 'T wa'nt so nice, eyther, for I thought the bos'n war roustin' me up for my watch on deck. Anyhow, would a been better than this watch here. Heerd something ye say? What d'ye mean, little Will'm?"

"I heard a voice, Ben. I think it was a voice."

"Voice—o' a human, do ye mean?"

"It sounded like that of a little girl."

"Voice o' a little girl! Shiver my timbers, lad, you're goin' demented! Put yer face close to mine. Let me see ye, boy! Are ye in yer senses, Will'm?"

"I am, Ben. I'm sure I heard what I've said. Twice I heard it. The first time I wasn't sure; but just now I heard it again, and if—"

"If there hadn't been gulls, an' boobies, an' Mother Carey's chickens, as squeals and chitters just like little childer, I'd a been puzzled at what ye be a tellin' me; but as I knows there be all o' these creators in the middle o' the broad ocean,—and mermaids too, I dare say,—then, ye see, little Will'm, I must disbelieve that ye heard anything more than the voice of—a man, by—!"

As the sailor terminated his speech with this terrible emphasis, he started into an upright attitude, and listened with all his ears for another utterance of that harsh monotone that, borne upon the breeze and rising above the "sough" of the disturbed water, could easily be distinguished as the *voice of a man.*

"We're lost, Will'm!" cried he, without waiting for a repetition of the sound; "we're lost. It's the voice of Le Gros. The big raft is a bearin' down upon us wi' them bloodthirsty cannibals we thought we'd got clear o'. It's no use tryin' to escape. Make up your mind to it, lad; we've got to die! we've got to die!"

Chapter Sixteen
Other Waifs

Had it been daylight, instead of a very dark night, Ben Brace and his youthful comrade would have been less alarmed by the voices that came up the wind. Daylight would have discovered to them an object, or rather collection of objects, which, instead of repelling, would have attracted them nearer.

It was not the great raft that was drifting to leeward, nor was it the voice of Le Gros or any of his wicked companions, that had been heard; though, in the excitement of their fears, that was the first thought of the two castaways.

Could their eyes have penetrated the deep obscurity that shrouded the sea, they would have beheld a number of objects, like themselves, adrift upon the water, and like them, at the mercy of the winds and waves. They would have seen pieces of timber, black and charred with fire; fragments of broken spars, with sails and cordage attached and trailing after them; here and there a cask or barrel, sunk to the level of the surface by the weight of its contents; pieces of packing-cases, torn asunder as if by some terrible explosion; cabin-chairs, coops, oars, handspikes, and other implements of the mariner's calling,—all bobbing about on the bosom of the blue deep, and carried hither and thither by the arbitrary oscillations of the breeze.

These various objects were not all huddled up together, but scattered unequally over a space of more than a square mile in extent. Had it been daylight, so that the sailor could have seen them, as they appeared mottling the bright surface of the sea, he would have experienced no difficulty in determining their character. At a glance he would have recognised the *débris* of the burnt ship, from which he and his companion had so narrowly escaped,—the slave-bark *Pandora*.

He would have looked upon these objects with no very great surprise, but in all likelihood with a feeling of considerable satisfaction: as offering the means for recruiting the strength of his own slight embarkation, which was barely sufficient to sustain the weight of himself and his companion, and certainly not strong enough to withstand the assault of the most moderate of storms.

In the midst of the "waifs" above enumerated, however, there was one not yet named, — one that differed greatly from all the rest, — and which, had it been seen by them, would have caused extreme surprise both to Ben Brace and little William.

It was a raft, not a great deal larger than their own, but altogether of different construction. A number of planks most of them charred by fire, with a sofa, a bamboo chair, and some other articles of furniture, had been rudely bound together by ropes. These things, of themselves, would have made but a very clumsy craft, no better for navigating the great ocean than that upon which Ben and the boy were themselves embarked. But the buoyancy of the former was secured by a contrivance of which the sailor had not had the opportunity of availing himself. Around its edge were ranged hogsheads or water-casks, evidently empty. They were lashed to the plank; and being bunged up against the influx of the water, kept the whole structure afloat, so that it would have carried a ton or two without sinking below the surface.

There was a smaller cask floating alongside, attached to the timbers by a piece of rope that was tightly looped around the swell. But this could not have been designed to increase the buoyancy of the raft: since it was itself almost submerged, evidently by the weight of something it contained.

Such a congeries of objects might have drifted side by side by chance, or the caprice of the currents; but they could not have tied themselves together in such fashion. There was design in the arrangement; and in the midst of the circle of empty hogsheads might have been seen the contriver of this curious craft. He was, of course, a human being, and a man; but such an one as, under any circumstances, would arrest the attention of the beholder; much more in the singular situation in which he was then met with. He was a black man, in the fullest sense of the word; a true negro, with a skin shining like ebony; a skull of large size, and slightly square in shape, covered with a thick crop of curling wool, so close and short as to appear *felted* into the skin. A brace of broad ears stood prominently out from the sides of his head; and extending almost from one to the other, was a wide-gaping mouth, formed by a pair of lips of huge thickness, protruding far forward, so as to give to the countenance those facial outlines characteristic of the chimpanzee or gorilla.

Notwithstanding his somewhat abnormal features, the expression of the negro's face was far from being hideous. It was not even disagreeable. A double row of white teeth, gleaming between the purplish lips, could be exhibited upon ordinary occasions in a pleasant smile; and the impression derived from looking upon the countenance was, that the owner of it was rather good-natured than otherwise. Just then, as he sat upon the raft, gazing over the bulwark of hogsheads, its expression was one of profound and sombre melancholy. No wonder!

The negro was not alone. Another individual shared with him the occupancy of the raft;—one differing from him in appearance as Hyperion from the Satyr. A few feet from him, and directly before his face, was a little girl, apparently about ten or twelve years of age. She was seated, or rather cowering, among the timbers of the raft, upon a piece of tarpauling that had been spread over them, her eyes bent upon her black companion, though occasionally straying, with listless glance, over the sombre surface of the sea. Although so young, her countenance appeared sad and despondent, as if under the belief that there was little hope of escape from the fearful situation in which she was placed, and as if her little spirit had long ago surrendered to despair.

Though not a negro like her companion, the girl could scarce be called *white*. Her complexion was of that hue known as olive; but her hair, although curling, hung in long locks down over her shoulders; and the crimson hue deeply tinting her cheeks told that in her blood there was more Caucasian than negro.

Any one who had visited the western coast of Africa, on seeing this little girl, would easily have recognised in her features the type of that mixed race which has resulted from long intercourse between the Portuguese "colonists" and the sable indigenes of the soil.

Chapter Seventeen
How Snowball escaped from the Slaver

On this curious embarkation, drifting about amid the remains of the wrecked ship, there were only the two human figures,—the negro and the little girl. It is superfluous to say that they were also a portion of the wreck itself,—other castaways who had, so far, succeeded in saving themselves from the fearful doom that had overtaken, no doubt, every one of the wretched beings composing the *cargo* of the slaver.

The negro upon the raft, though black as the blackest of his unfortunate countrymen, was not among the number of those who had been carried as *freight*. On the contrary, he was one of the crew,—the lord of the caboose, and known upon the slave-bark by the satirical *soubriquet* of "Snowball."

Although originally a slave from Africa, and by race a Coromantee, Snowball had long been in the enjoyment of his liberty; and, as cook or steward, had seen service in scores of ships, and circumnavigated the globe in almost every latitude where circumnavigation was possible.

Though not naturally of a wicked disposition, he was by no means particular as to the company he kept, or the sort of ship he sailed in,—so long as the wages were good and the store-room well supplied; and as these conditions are usually found on board of a slaver, it was not Snowball's first voyage in a vessel of the kind. It is true that he had never sailed in company with a more ribald crew than that of the *Pandora*; but it is only justice to say, that, long before the fatal interruption of that voyage, even he had become tired of their companionship, and had been almost as eager to get away from the ship as Ben Brace or little William.

He, too, had been deterred from attempting to escape while upon the African coast, by the knowledge that such an attempt would have been worse than idle. In all likelihood it would have ended in his being captured by his own countrymen,—or, at all events, by people of his own colour,—and sold once more into that very slavery from which he had formerly succeeded in emancipating himself.

Though Snowball's morality was far from being immaculate, there was one virtue which he was not wanting,—gratitude. But for the possession of this, he might have been alone upon the raft, and, perhaps, less caring in what direction the winds and waves might carry him. As it was, his sole thought and anxiety was about his little companion, whose safety was as dear to him as his own.

It will be asked why Snowball felt this unselfish solicitude. The child could not be his own? Complexion, features, everything forbade the supposition that there could be anything of kinship between her and her sable protector.

Nor was there the slightest. On the contrary, the little girl was the daughter of one who had once been Snowball's greatest enemy,—the man who had sold him into slavery; but who had afterwards won the negro's gratitude by restoring to him his freedom. This person had formerly owned a trading fort on the coast of Africa, but of late years had been a resident of Rio in Brazil. His daughter, born in the former country, previous to his leaving it, was crossing the great ocean to rejoin him in his new home in the western world. Hence her presence on board the *Pandora*, where she had been a passenger under the protection of Snowball.

And well had the negro performed his duty as protector. When all the others had forsaken the ship, and the flames were fast spreading over her decks, the faithful negro had gone below, and, rousing the girl from her sleep,—for she had been slumbering unconscious of the danger,—had borne her amidst flames and smoke, at the imminent risk of his own life, and passing through the cabin windows with his burden in his arms, he had dropped down into the sea under the stern of the burning bark.

Being an excellent swimmer, he had kept afloat for some minutes, sustaining both himself and his burden by his own strength; but after a while he succeeded in clutching on to the davit-tackle by which the gig had been let down into the water, and having passed his foot through a loop in the end of it, he remained half suspended, half afloat on the water. Soon after came the explosion, caused by the ignition of the gunpowder; and as the vessel was blown to pieces, the sea around became strewed with fragments of shattered timber, cabin furniture, sea-chests, and the like. Laying hold on those pieces that were nearest, he succeeded in forming a rude sort of raft, upon which he and his *protégé* were enabled to pass the remainder of the night.

When morning dawned, Snowball and the little Lalee—such was the name of the child—were the only beings who appeared to have survived the catastrophe,—the wretched creatures who at the last moment had escaped from the "'tween-decks" were no longer in existence.

Having been brought from the interior of the African continent,—and from a district where there are no great lakes or rivers,—but few of them could swim; and those few had become the prey of the sharks, that in scores were swimming around the frail craft. As the sun rose over the ocean, and lit up the scene of that terrible tragedy, Snowball saw not a living creature save his own *protégé*, the sharks, and their satellites.

The negro knew, however, that the *Pandora's* own people had escaped. He had witnessed the clandestine departure of the gig, containing the skipper and his confederates.

This he had seen, while gazing through the windows of the cabin, previous to launching himself upon that last desperate leap. He had also been a witness to the departure of the great raft carrying the crew.

It may appear strange that he did not swim towards it, and share the fortunes of his former associates. Why he did not do so is easily explained. By an accident, arising from his own negligence, the ship had been set on fire. He was aware of this; and he knew also that both captain and crew were equally cognisant of the fact. The former, just after the discovery, assisted by the brutal mate, had administered to him (Snowball) such a chastisement as he would not soon forget; while the crew, on becoming acquainted with the circumstance, were upon the point of tossing him into the sea; and would no doubt have carried their design into execution, but for the presence of the appalling danger impelling them to look to their own safety. The negro knew, therefore, that, were he to seek safety on the great raft, it would only be to throw himself into merciless hands, certain to spurn him back with vengeful indignation, or fling him into the jaws of the hideous monsters already swimming around the ship, and quartering the sea in every direction.

For this reason had Snowball chosen to trust to his own strength,—to chance,—to anything rather than the mercy of his old associates, with whom, for a long period past, he had been far from a favourite.

Perhaps it had turned out for the best. Had he succeeded in reaching the great raft, and been permitted to share with its occupants their chances of safety, it is more than probable that the little Lalee might have become the victim of that horrid attempt from which the little William had so narrowly escaped!

Chapter Eighteen
Snowball amid the Drift

The adventures of Snowball and his *protégé*, from the blowing up of the *Pandora* until six suns had risen and gone down over the ocean, if not so varied as those of Ben Brace and his *protégé*, were nevertheless of sufficient interest to deserve a brief narration.

Supported by the few sticks which he had been able to draw together, he had remained during the rest of the night in the midst of the floating fragments.

He had listened to the wild shouts of vengeful rage, proceeding from the throats of the slaves as they clutched at the great raft, and were beaten back by those who occupied it. He had seen the broad sail suddenly hoisted, and the dark mass gradually gliding away over the ocean. He had heard many an agonising yell as, one by one, the few strong swimmers who survived the rest either sank by exhaustion or were dragged down in the jaws of the numerous sharks; until, the last shriek having sounded in his ears, all became silent as the tomb, while the sombre surface of the sea once more lay motionless around him. Even the ravening monsters, for a moment, seemed to have forsaken the spot, — as if each, having secured a sufficient prey, had gone down to devour it undisturbed in the dark unfathomed caverns of the deep.

When morning dawned upon the scene, although many objects met the eye of the negro and his companion, there was no human being within sight; and Snowball knew that, with the exception of the six men who had rowed off in the gig, and the crew upon the great raft, there were no other survivors of the slaver.

The crew having spread a sail to get out of reach of the drowning wretches who were clutching at their raft, the latter was soon carried out of sight; while the six in the gig had rowed off as fast as they were able, in order to get out of reach of their own companions! For these reasons, when day broke over the ocean, neither boat nor raft were visible from the spot where the catastrophe had occurred.

It may appear strange that none of the living cargo of the slaver had succeeded in saving themselves, by clinging to some fragment of the wreck; and Snowball thought so at the time.

The truth was, that those who could swim had struck out after the raft, and had followed it so far that they were not able to swim back to the burning vessel; while the others, in the wild terror produced by the proximity of the flames, had leaped despairingly into the sea, and sunk upon the instant.

The early sunbeams, as they fell slantingly over the surface of the sea, told the negro that he was alone,—alone with the little Lalee,—alone in the middle of the Atlantic Ocean,—afloat upon a few sticks,—without a morsel of food to eat, without a drop of water to drink!

It was a terrible situation,—sufficient to produce despair even in the stoutest heart.

But Snowball was not one of the despairing sort. He had been too often in peril of life—both by sea and land—to be unnerved even in that dread hour; and instead of permitting his spirits to become prostrated, he bethought him of how he might make the best of the circumstances by which he was surrounded.

An object that came under his eye, just as the day began to break, kindled within him a faint gleam of hope, and urged to making an effort for the salvation of himself and his helpless companion. This object was a small keg, or beaker, which chanced to be floating near him, and which, from some mark upon it, Snowball recognised. He knew that it had been standing in a corner of the caboose, previous to the blowing up of the bark; and, moreover, that it contained several gallons of fresh water, which he had himself surreptitiously abstracted from the common stock, previous to the time that the slaver's crew had agreed to being put upon rations.

It was but the work of a minute to secure this keg, and attach it by a strong cord to the piece of timber on which the ex-cook was seated astride.

But for this unexpected supply of water Snowball might probably have yielded to despair. Without water to drink he could not have reckoned on a long lease of life,—either for himself or his *protégé*. So opportunely had the keg come before his eyes as to seem a Providential interference; and the belief or fancy that it was so stimulated him to a further search among the fragments of the shattered ship.

There were many queer things around him,—like himself bobbing about upon the tiny waves. One, however, soon monopolised his attention;

and that was a barrel of somewhat flimsy structure, and about the size of those usually employed for carrying flour. Snowball recognised it also as an old acquaintance in the store-room, and knew that it was filled with the best kind of biscuit,—a private stock belonging to the captain.

Its contents could not fail to be saturated with salt-water, for the barrel was not water-tight; but the ex-cook could dry them in the sun, and render them, if not palatable, at least eatable.

The biscuit-barrel was soon fished up out of the water, and placed high and dry upon the little raft.

Snowball was next struck with the necessity of improving the quality of his craft, by giving it increase both in size and strength. With this intention— after having possessed himself of an oar, out of several that were adrift—he commenced paddling about among the floating fragments, here and there picking up such pieces as appeared best suited to his purpose.

In a short while he succeeded in collecting a sufficient number of spars and other pieces of timber,—among which figured a portion of his own old tenement, the caboose,—to form a raft as large as he might require; and to his great satisfaction he saw around him the very things that would render it *seaworthy*. Bobbing about on the waves, and at no great distance, were half a dozen empty water-casks. There had been too many of them aboard the slaver: since their emptiness was the original cause of the catastrophe that had ensued. But there were not too many for Snowball's present purpose; and, after paddling first to one and then another, he secured each in turn, and lashed them to his raft, in such fashion, that the great hogsheads, sitting higher in the water than the timbers of the raft, formed a sort of parapet around it.

This task accomplished, he proceeded to collect from the wreck such other articles as he fancied might be of service to him; and, thus occupied, he spent several days on the spot where the *Pandora* had gone to pieces.

The slight breezes that arose from time to time, and again subsided, had not separated his raft from the other objects still left floating near. In whatever direction they went, so went he: since all were drifting together.

The idea had never occurred to the negro to set up a sail and endeavour to get away from the companionship of the inanimate objects around him,—souvenirs as they were of a fearful disaster. Or rather it had occurred to him, and was rejected as unworthy of being entertained. Snowball, without knowing much of the theory of navigation, had sufficient practical acquaintance with the great Atlantic Ocean,—especially that part of it where lies the track of the dreaded "middle passage,"—long remembered by the transported slave,—Snowball, I say, was sufficiently acquainted with his present whereabouts, to know that a sail set upon his raft, and carrying him hither and thither, would not add much to the chances of his being rescued from a watery grave. His only hope lay in being picked up by some passing vessel; and, feeling convinced of this, he made no effort to go one way or the other, but suffered himself to be drifted about, along with the other waifs of the wreck, whithersoever it pleased the winds or the currents of the ocean to carry him.

Chapter Nineteen
Snowball at Sea on a Hencoop

For six days had Snowball been leading this sort of life, along with the little Lalee,—subsisting partly on the sea-steeped biscuit found in the barrel, and partly upon other provisions which had turned up among the drift; while the precious water contained in the keg had hitherto kept them from suffering the pangs of thirst.

During these six days he had never wholly surrendered himself up to despair. It was not the first, by several times, for the old sea-cook to have suffered shipwreck; nor was it his first time to be cast away in mid-ocean. Once had he been blown overboard in a storm, and left behind,—the ship, from the violence of the wind, having been unable to tack round and return to his rescue. Being an excellent swimmer, he had kept afloat, buffeting with the huge billows for nearly an hour. Of course, in the end, he must have gone to the bottom, as the place where the incident occurred was hundreds of miles from any land. But just as he was on the point of giving in, a hencoop came drifting past, to which he at once attached himself, and this being fortunately of sufficient size to sustain his weight, hindered him from sinking.

Though he knew that the hencoop had been thrown out of the ship by some of his comrades, after he had gone overboard, the ship herself was no longer in sight; and the unlucky swimmer, notwithstanding the help given him by the hencoop, must eventually have perished among the waves; but the storm having subsided, and the wind suddenly changing into the opposite quarter, the vessel was wafted back on her old track, and passing within hail of Snowball, his comrades succeeded in rescuing him from his perilous situation.

With the retrospect of such an experience,—and Snowball could look back upon many such,—he was not the man to yield easily to despair. On the contrary, he now acted as if he believed that there was still not only some hope, but a considerable chance of being delivered from the dilemma in which the late disaster of the *Pandora* had placed him.

Scarce an hour during the six days had he permitted to pass in idleness. As already stated, he had collected ample materials from the wreck floating around him. Out of these he had formed a good-sized raft, having spent much time and labour in giving it strength and security. This accomplished, and all the provisions he could find safely stored upon it, he had devoted the rest of his time to fishing.

There were many fish in the neighbourhood of the wreck. Fearful fish they were too: for they were sharks: the same that had made such havoc among the unfortunate creatures who had constituted the cargo of the slaver. These voracious monsters,—though satiated for a time with their human prey,—had not forsaken the spot where the *Pandora* had gone to pieces; but on the square mile of surface strewed by the floating fragments of the wreck they could still be seen in pairs, and sometimes in larger numbers, with their huge sail-like fins projecting high above the water, veering about as if once more hungry, and quartering the sea in search of fresh victims.

Snowball had not succeeded in capturing any of the sharks, though he had spared no pains in endeavouring to do so. There were other large fish, however, that had made their appearance in the proximity of his raft, attracted thither by the common prospect of food promised by the wreck of the slaver. There were albacores, and bonitos, and dolphins, and many other kinds of ocean fish, rarely seen, or only upon such melancholy occasions. With a long-handled harpoon, which Snowball had succeeded in securing, he was enabled to strike several of these creatures; so that by the evening of the sixth day, his larder was considerably increased,—comprising, in the way of fish, an albacore, a brace of bonitos, with three satellites of the sharks,—a pilot-fish and two sucking-fish.

All these had been ripped open and disembowelled, after which their flesh, cut into thin slices, and spread out on the tops of the empty water-casks that surrounded the raft, was in process of being cured by drying in the sun.

Befriended by the fine weather, Snowball had succeeded, one way and another, in accumulating no mean store of provisions; and, so far as food went, he felt confident, both for himself and his companion, of being able to hold out not only for days, but for weeks or even months.

He felt equal confidence in regard to their stock of water. Having gauged the keg in his own rude way, and satisfied himself as to the quantity of its contents, he had made a calculation of how long it might last, and found that by a careful economy it could be depended upon for a period of several weeks.

Reposing upon these pleasant data, on the night of the sixth day he had gone to rest with a feeling of confidence that soon enticed his spirit into the profoundest slumbers.

Not that Snowball had gone without sleep during the other five nights spent upon his raft. He had slept a little on each of them. Only a little, however; for, as most of them had been moonlight nights, he had kept awake during the greater portion of each, on the lookout over the surface of the ocean, lest some ship, sailing near, might glide past silently and unseen, and so deprive him of a chance of being picked up.

The little Lalee had also borne part in these nocturnal vigils,—taking her turn when Snowball became too weary to keep awake; and so, in alternate watches, had the two been in the habit of tiring out the long hours of the night. To this practice the sixth night had proved an exception. There was no moon in the sky; there were no stars; not a glimmer of light, either in the firmament of the heavens or on the face of the deep. The sky above and the sea below were both of one colour,—the hue of pitch. On such a night it was idle to keep watch. A ship might have passed within a cable's length of the raft, and still remained unseen; and, filled with this conviction, both Snowball and his companion, after the night had fairly closed over them, stretched their bodies along the pieces of sail-cloth that formed their respective couches, and surrendered their spirits to the sweet enchantment of sleep.

Chapter Twenty
The Flash of Lightning

Snowball began to snore almost as soon as he had closed his eyelids, and as if the shutting of his eyes had either occasioned or strengthened the current of breath through his nostrils.

And such a sound as the snore of the Coromantee was rarely heard upon the ocean,—except in the "spouting" of a whale or the "blowing" of a porpoise.

It did not wake the little Lalee. She had become accustomed to the snoring of Snowball,—which, instead of being a disturber, acted rather as a lullaby to her rest.

It was only after both had been asleep for many hours after midnight,—in fact when Lalee was herself sleeping less soundly, and when a snore, more prolonged and prodigious than any that had preceded it, came swelling through the nostrils of the sea-cook,—it was only then that the young girl was awakened.

Becoming aware of what had awakened her, she would have gone to sleep again; but just as she was about re-composing herself upon her sail-cloth couch, a sight came before her eyes that caused her not only to remain awake, but filled her with a feeling of indescribable awe.

On the instant of opening her eyes, the sky, hitherto dark, had become suddenly illumined by lightning,—not in streaks or flashes, but as if a sheet of fire had been spread for an instant over the whole canopy of the heavens.

At the same time the surface of the sea had been equally lighted up with the vivid gleam; and among the many objects drifting around the raft,—the remnants of the wreck, with which the eyes of the little Lalee had now become familiarised,—she saw, or fancied she saw, one altogether new to her.

It was a human face and figure, in the likeness of a beautiful boy, who appeared to be kneeling on the water, or on some slight structure on a level with the surface of the sea!

The lightning had revealed other objects beside him and over him. A pair of slender sticks, standing some feet apart, and in a perpendicular position, with some white strips suspended between them, in the gleam of the lightning shone clear and conspicuous.

It is not to be wondered at that the little Lalee should feel surprise at an apparition,—so unexpected, in such a place, and under such circumstances. It is not to be wondered at that her first impulse should be to rouse her companion out of his snoring slumbers.

She did so upon the instant, and without waiting for another flash of lightning either to confirm her belief in what she had seen, or convince her that it was only an apparition,—which her fancy, disturbed by the dreams in which she had been indulging, had conjured up on the instant of her awaking.

"Wha's dat you say?" inquired Snowball, abruptly awakened in the middle of a superb snore; "see something! you say dat, ma pickaninny? How you see anyting such night as dis be? Law, ma lilly Lally, you no see de nose before you own face. De 'ky 'bove am dark as de complexyun ob dis ole nigga; you muss be mistake, lilly gal!—dat you muss!"

"No, indeed, Snowball!" replied Lalee, speaking in gumbo Portuguese, "I am not mistaken. It wasn't dark when I saw it. There was lightning; and it was as clear as in daylight for a little while. I'm sure I saw some one!"

"What was de some one like?" interrogated Snowball, in an accent that proclaimed incredulity. "Was 'um a man or a woman?"

"Neither."

"Neider! Den it muss ha' been,—ha! maybe it war a mermaid!"

"What I saw looked like a boy, Snowball. O, now I think of it, like that boy."

"What boy you 'peak 'bout?"

"He who was aboard the ship,—the English boy who was one of the sailors."

"Ah! you mean de little Will'm, I 'pose. I reck'n dat 'ere lad hab gone to de bott'm ob de sea long afore dis, or else he get off on de big raff. I know he no go 'long wi' de cappen, 'case I see de little chap close by de caboose after de gig row 'way. If he hab go by de raff dem ruffins sure eat him up,—dat be if dey get hungry. Dey sure do dat! Hark! what's dat I heer? Sure's my name be Snowball, I hear some 'un 'peak out dere to win'ard. D'you hear anything, lilly Lally?"

"Yes, Snowball: I think I did."

"What you tink you?"

"A voice."

"What sort o' voice?"

"Like a boy's voice,—just like *his*."

"Who you mean?"

"The boy-sailor aboard the ship. O, listen! There it is again; and surely I hear another?"

"Gorramity! little gal, you 'peak de troof. Sure 'nuff dere am a voice,—two ob dat same. One am like de boy we 'peak 'bout,—odder more like a man o' full groaf. I wonder who dey can be. Hope 't an't de ghoses of some o' de *Pandoras* dat ha' been drowned or eat up by de sharks. Lissen 'gain, Lally, an' try make dem out."

Having imparted this injunction, the negro raised himself into a half-erect attitude; and facing to windward with his arms resting upon one of the empty casks,—which, as already stated, formed a sort of circular parapet around his raft,—he remained silent and listening.

The little Lalee had also assumed a half-erect attitude; and, by the side of her sable companion, kept peering out into the darkness,—in the hope that another flash of lightning might again reveal to her eyes the features of that beautiful boy, who, alone of all upon that fated ship, had made upon her mind an impression worthy of being remembered.

Chapter Twenty One
To the Oars

"We've got to die!"

As the sailor gave utterance to these words of fearful import, he started from his recumbent position, and, half-erect upon the raft, remained listening,—at the same time endeavouring with his glance to pierce the darkness that shrouded the surface of the deep.

Little William, terrified by the speech of his protector, made no rejoinder, but with like silence continued to look and listen.

There was nothing visible save sea and sky; and these, in the dim obscurity, were not to be distinguished from each other. A raft or boat,— even a large ship,—could not have been seen at two cables' distance from that on which they were drifting along; and the only sounds now heard were the sighing of the night breeze, and the "swish" of the water as it swept along the sides of their slight embarkation.

For five minutes or more there was nothing to interrupt this duetto of winds and waves, and Ben was beginning to believe he had been mistaken. It might not have been the voice of a man, nor a voice at all. He was but half awake when he fancied hearing it. Was it only a fancy,—an illusion? It was at the best very indistinct,—as of some one speaking in a muttered tone. It might be the "blowing" of a porpoise, or the utterance of some unknown monster of the sea: for the sailor's experience had taught him that there are many kinds of creatures inhabiting the ocean that are only seen at rare intervals even by one who is constantly traversing it, and many others one may never see at all. Could the sounds have proceeded from the throat of some of these human-like denizens of the deep, known as *dugongs, lamantins, manatees,* and the like?

It was strangest of all that William had heard the voice of a girl: for the lad still adhered to the belief that he had done so. That might have been the cry of a bird, or a mermaid; and Ben would have been ready enough to accept the latter explanation. But the voice of a young girl, coupled with that of a man, rendered the circumstance more mysterious and altogether inexplicable.

"Didn't you hear a man's voice, lad?" he asked at length, with a view either of dissipating his doubts or confirming them.

"I did," replied the boy. "Yes, Ben; I'm sure I did, not loud, but muttered like. But I don't know whether if was Le Gros. O, if it was!"

"Thee have good reason to know his ugly croak, the parleyvooin' scoundrel! That thee have, Will'm! Let's hope we are both mistaken: for if we're to come across them ruffins on the big raft, we needn't expect mercy at their hands. By this time they'll be all as hungry as the sharks and as ravenin' too."

"Oh!" exclaimed William, in accents of renewed fear, "I hope it's not them!"

"Speak low, lad!" said the sailor, interrupting him, "only in whispers. If they be near, the best thing for us are to keep quiet. They can't see us no more than we can them; anyhow, till it come mornin'. If we could hear the sound again so as to make out the direction. I didn't notice that."

"I did," interrupted William. "Both the voices I heard were out this way."

The boy pointed to leeward.

"To leuart, you think they wur?"

"I'm sure they came from that quarter."

"That be curious, hows'ever," said the sailor. "If't be them on the big raft they must a passed us, or else the wind must a veered round, for we've been to leuart o' them ever since partin' wi' 'em. Could the wind a gone round I wonder? Like enough. It be queer, — and it's blowing from the west in this part o' the Atlantic! 'Tan't possible to say what point it be in, hows'ever, — not without a compass. There bean't even the glimmer o' a star in the sky; and if there wur we couldn't make much o' it; since the north star bean't seen down in these latitudes. Thee be sure the sound come from leuart?"

"O, I am quite sure of it, Ben; the voices came up the wind."

"Then we'd best go the same way and gie 'em as wide a berth as possible. Look alive, lad! Let's down wi' them flitches o' the shark-meat: for it's them that's driftin' us along. We'll take a spell at the oars, and afore daylight we may get out o' hearin' o' the voices, and out of sight o' them as has been utterin' o' them."

Both rose simultaneously to their feet, and commenced taking down the slices of half-dried shark-flesh, and placing them upon the sail-cloth,—with the intention, as the sailor had counselled it, to unship the oars that had been doing duty as masts, and make use of them in their proper manner.

While engaged in this operation both remained silent,—at intervals stopping in their work to listen.

They had got so far as to clear away the suspended flitches, and were about unfastening the cords where they were looped around the upright oars, when another cord, attached to one of the latter, caught their attention. It was the piece of rope which closed the mouth of their tarpauling water-bag, and held the latter in such a position as to keep the "cask" from leaking.

Fortunately they were doing things in a deliberate manner. If they had been acting otherwise, and had rashly "unstepped" the mast to which that piece of rope was attached, their stock of fresh water would have been rapidly diminished,—perhaps altogether spilled into the salt sea, before they should have become aware of the disaster. As it was, they perceived the danger in good time; and, instead of taking down the oar, at once desisted from their intention.

It now became a question as to whether they should proceed any further in the design of rowing the raft to windward. With a single oar they could make but little way; and the other was already occupied in doing a duty from which it could not possibly be spared.

It is true there were still left the fragments of the hand spike that had been ground between the teeth of the surviving shark, and afterwards picked up as they drifted past it. This might serve instead of the oar to support the mouth of the water-bag; and as soon as this idea occurred to them they set about carrying it into execution.

It took but a few minutes of time to substitute one stick for the other; and then, both oars being free, they seated themselves on opposite sides of the raft, and commenced propelling it against the wind,—in a direction contrary to that in which the mysterious voices had been heard.

Chapter Twenty Two
Ship Ahoy!

They had not made over a dozen strokes of their oars,—which they handled cautiously and in silence, all the while listening intently,—when their ears were again saluted by sounds similar to those first heard by little William, and which he had conjectured to be the voice of a young girl. As before, the utterance was very low,—murmured, as if repeating a series of words,—in fact, as if the speaker was engaged in a quiet conversation.

"Shiver my timbers!" exclaimed the sailor, as soon as the voice again ceased to be heard. "If that bean't the palaver o' a little girl, my name wur never Ben Brace on a ship's book. A smalley wee thing she seem to be; not bigger than a marlinspike. It sound like as if she wur talkin' to some un. What the Ole Scratch can it mean, Will'm?"

"I don't know. Could it be a mermaid?"

"Could it? In course it could."

"But are there mermaids, Ben?"

"Maremaids! Be theer maremaids? That what you say? Who denies there ain't? Nobody but disbelevin land-lubbers as never seed nothin' curious, 'ceptin' two-headed calves and four-legged chickens. In coorse there be maremaids. I've seed some myself; but I've sailed with a shipmate as has been to a part o' the Indyan Ocean, where there be whole schools o' 'em, wi' long hair hangin' about their ears an' over their shoulders, just like reg'lar schools o' young girls goin' out for a walk in the outskirts o' Portsmouth or Gravesend. Hush! theer be her voice again!"

As the sailor ceased speaking, a tiny treble, such as might proceed from the tongue of a child,—a girl of some eight or ten years old,—came trembling over the waves, in tones that betokened a conversation.

A moment or two elapsed; and then, as if in reply to the words spoken by the child, was heard another voice,—evidently that of a man!

"If the one be a maremaid," whispered Ben to his companion, "the other must be a mareman. Shiver my timbers, if it ain't a curious confab! Moonrakers and skyscrapers! what can it mean?"

"I don't know," mechanically answered the boy.

"Anyhow," continued the sailor, apparently relieved by the reflection, *"It ain't the big raft.* There's no voice like that little 'un among its crew o' ruffins; and that man, whosomever he be, don't speak like Le Gros. I only thought so at first, bein' half asleep.

"If it be a school o' maremaids," pursued he, "theer an't no danger, even wi' theer men along wi' 'em. Leastwise, I never heerd say there wur from maremaids more'n any other weemen; an' not so much, I dare ay. Sartin it bean't the Frenchman, nor any o' that scoundrel crew. Lord o' mercy! It might be a ship as is passing near us!"

As this thought occurred to the speaker, he raised himself into an erect attitude, as if to get a better view.

"I'll hail, Will'm," he muttered; "I'll hail 'em. Keep your ears open, lad; and listen for the answer. *Ship ahoy!"*

The hail was sent in the direction whence the mysterious sounds appeared to have proceeded. There came no response; and the sailor, after listening attentively for a second or two, repeated the "Ship ahoy!" this time in a louder key.

Quick as an echo the words came back, though it could not be an echo. There are no echoes upon the ocean; besides, the voice that repeated the well-known phrase was quite different from that of him who had first pronounced it. Though different both in tone and accent, it was evidently a human voice; and, as evidently, that of a man. A rude, rough voice it was; but it is superfluous to say that, to the ears of Ben Brace and his youthful companion, it sounded sweeter than any music to which they had ever listened. The words "Ship ahoy!" were soon succeeded by others, proceeding from the same lips.

"Gorramity!" spoke the strange voice, "who de debbil call dar? Dat some'dy in de boat? Dat you, Capten? Am it you, Massa Grow?"

"A negro," muttered Ben to his companion. "It's Snowball, the cook. It can't be anybody but him. In the name o' Neptune how has the darkey got there? What's he aboard o'? He warn't on the great raft wi' the rest. I thought he'd gone off in the captain's gig. If that wur so, then it's the boat that is near us."

"No," replied William, "I'm sure I saw Snowball by the caboose after the gig had rowed away. As he wasn't with them on the big raft, I supposed he'd been drowned, or burned up in the ship. Surely, it's his voice? There it is again!"

"Ship ahoy-hoy-hoy!" once more came the words pealing over the water in a loud prolonged drawl. "Ship ahoy, some'dy call out dar? What ship am dat? Am it a ship at all? Or am it some o' de wreck Pandoray?"

"Castaways," responded Ben. "Castaways of the bark *Pandora*, Who calls? Snowball! Be it you?"

"Dat same chile,—who am you? Am it you, massa Capten,—in de gig?"

"No."

"Massa Grow, den, on de big raff?"

"Neither," responded the sailor. "It's Ben,—Ben Brace."

"Golly! you say so, Massa Brace! How you be dar, unless you on de big raff?"

"I'm on a raft of my own. Have you one, Snowball?"

"Ya, massa Ben, ya! I make um out o' de wreck an de water-cask."

"Are ye all alone?"

"Not 'zackly dat. The pickaninny be long wi' me,—de cabing gal. You know de lilly Lalee?"

"Oh! she it be!" muttered Ben, now remembering the little cabin passenger of the Pandora. "You bean't movin', be you?"

"No," responded Snowball, "lying on de water like a log o' 'hogany wood. Han't move a mile ebba since de bustin' ob de powder ball."

"Keep your place then. We've got oars. We'll row down to you."

"We—you say we? You got some'dy sides yaself on dat raff?"

"Little Will'm."

"Lilly Willum,—ah? dat ere brave lilly lad. See 'im jess as I go down in de cabin fo' get de pickaninny. See 'im forrard with axe,—he knock off de gratin' ob de fore-hatch,—he set all dem 'ere niggas free. It warn't no use,—

not bit good o' dem. Dey all got eat up by de shark, or dey go down straight to de bottom. Gorramity! how dey s'riek an' 'cream, an' jump overboard into de water!"

Neither the sailor nor Little William paid any heed to the negro's half-soliloquised narrative, further than to make use of his voice to guide them through the darkness towards the spot whence it proceeded. On discovering that it was Snowball who was near, both had turned upon their own craft, and were now rowing it in the opposite direction to that in which, but the moment before, they had been so eagerly propelling it.

As they now pulled to leeward, they had the wind in their favour; and by the time the negro arrived at the end of his disjointed narrative, they were within half a cable's length of him, and, through the darkness, were beginning to distinguish the outlines of the odd embarkation that carried Snowball and his *protégé*.

Just then the lightning blazed across the canopy of heaven, discovering the two rafts,—each to the other. In ten seconds more they were *en rapport*, and their respective crews congratulating each other, with as much joyfulness as if the unexpected encounter had completely delivered them from death and its dangers!

Chapter Twenty Three
The Rafts en Rapport

Two travellers meeting in the midst of a lone wilderness, even though strangers to each other, would not be likely to pass without speaking. If old acquaintances, then would they be certain to make the longest pause possible, and procrastinate their parting till the last moment allowed by the circumstances. If these circumstances would permit of their reaching their respective destinations by the same route, how sorry would each be to separate, and how happy to enter into a mutual alliance of co-operation and companionship!

Just like two such travellers, or two parties of travellers, meeting in the midst of the desert,—a wilderness of land,—so met, in the midst of the ocean,—the wilderness of water,—the two rafts whose history we have hitherto chronicled. Their crews were not strangers to each other, but old acquaintances. If not all friends in the past, the circumstances that now surrounded them were of a kind to make them friends for the future. Under the awe inspired by a common danger, the lion will lie down with the lamb, and the fierce jaguar consorts with the timid capivara no longer trembling at the perilous proximity.

But there was no particular antipathy between the crews of the two rafts thus singularly becoming united. It is true that formerly there had been some hostility displayed by the negro towards Little William, and but little friendship between the former and Ben Brace. These, however, were things of the past; and during the last days of their companionship on board the *Pandora* the sentiments of all three had undergone a change. An identity of interests had produced a certain three-cornered sympathy,—obliterating all past spite, and establishing, if not positive friendship, at least a sort of triangular forgiveness. Of course this affection was of the isosceles kind,— Ben and Little William being the *sides*, and Snowball the *base*. It is scarce necessary to say, that, meeting again under the circumstances described, all past spite, had there been any, would have been forgiven and forgotten.

Fortunately this had been already done. Between Ben and Snowball, and Snowball and Little William, the hatchet had been long ago buried; and they now met, not as enemies, but as old acquaintances,—almost as friends: nay, we might say, *altogether* as friends. If not so before, the common danger had made them so now, and amicably did they greet one another.

After such an encounter, it is superfluous to say that no thought of again separating entered into the minds of any of the party. The crews of both rafts knew that their destinations were identical.

Each was an *ocean waif*, seeking to escape from the wilderness of waters,—longing for deliverance from a common danger. In company they might have a better chance of obtaining it. Why should they separate to search for it?

The question did not occur to either,—in thought or in word. From the moment of their meeting, instinct told them that their destinies were the same,—that their action in future should be united.

After the two rafts had collided together, and those involuntary but joyful salutations were exchanged between their crews, the respective skippers became occupied with the more serious business of uniting the frail embarkations into one, and rendering them for the future inseparable.

"Snowball!" inquired the sailor, "have you got any spare rope?"

"Plenty o' dat 'ere," responded the ex-cook of the *Pandora*.

"Yar am a coil o' strong sinnet. Dat do?"

"That's the stuff," responded Ben. "Heave it this way, ye son of a sea-cook! Heave!"

"Now," continued he, laying hold of the coil of sennit, and tossing back one end over an empty water-cask. "Make fast there, Snowey! I dare say we can lay alongside safe enough till daylight! After that we'll splice together in a better sort o' way."

The ex-cook, obedient to the injunctions of the seaman, seized hold of the end of rope thrown to him, and made it fast to one of the spars which comprised his singular craft; while at the same time Ben busied himself in tying the other end to the piece of handspike erected upon his own.

Soon each completed his task; and after some time spent in a mutual detail of the adventures that had befallen them since the hour of separation on the deck of the ill-fated Pandora, it was agreed that all should go to rest for the remainder of the night, and with the earliest light of day take measures to perpetuate the union of the two wandering waifs thus unexpectedly brought into companionship.

Chapter Twenty Four
Reconstructing the Raft

The crews of both rafts were astir by early dawn, the sailor arousing one and all from their slumbers. The rising sun, as it shone over the ocean, fell upon four faces, all wearing a very different expression from that which they had exhibited at his setting on the day before. If not positively cheerful, there was at least hopefulness in their looks: for their renewed companionship had mutually inspired one and all with renewed hopes of deliverance. Indeed, it was evident even to the youngest of the party, that this unexpected union of strength would materially increase the chances of escape from the common danger; since the two strong men working together could do many things that would have been impossible to either of them alone, — to say nothing of the encouragement and confidence always springing from concerted action.

The very fact of their having come together in the way they had done seemed something more than accidental. It looked less like mere accident than that they had been favoured by the hand of Providence; and even the rude seaman, and the still ruder sea-cook, were only too glad to give way to the fancy that Providence was interfering on their behalf.

Certainly, the succession of fortunate events with which both had been favoured, — and which had not only hitherto sustained them, but promised to preserve their lives for a still longer period, — certainly, these circumstances were sufficient to beget the belief that they were specially under the protection of some power less capricious than mere chance.

The fact of their having encountered each other — even when one of them had been in the act of taking measures to avoid the encounter — was of itself something to strengthen this conviction, and increase their hopefulness for the future.

This very effect it produced; and it was for that reason that Ben Brace was so early astir, and so early in arousing the others.

The sailor had had too much experience in the capriciousness of the wind to believe that such calm weather as they had been enjoying for days would last much longer; and he had got up betimes with a view of uniting the two rafts, and strengthening the structure that might spring out of their union, so that it might resist whatever storm should threaten.

To attempt constructing a craft of such capability did not seem so hopeless to the skilful seaman. Before it had appeared so; but now, with the materials composing the two rafts, and others which the morning sun disclosed drifting about upon the surface of the sea, the thing looked less of an impossibility. In fact, it did not appear at all impossible; and for this reason Ben and the black at once came to the determination to attempt it.

After a short time spent in deliberation, it was resolved to break up the lesser raft,—that which had hitherto carried the sailor and little William. The planks composing it could be transferred to the larger and better structure which Snowball had got together; and this was furthermore to be reconstructed and considerably enlarged.

It was not designed to make any great alteration in the shape or fashion which Snowball had chosen for his craft, which displayed great ingenuity on the part of its designer. As it was deemed proper enough, his design was to be retained,—only the construction was to be on a larger scale.

Before setting to work, it was essential that something in the shape of a breakfast should be swallowed. This was drawn from the stores which Snowball had been engaged for days in accumulating, and consisted simply of biscuit and dried "bonito."

In the absence of any fire, the ex-cook had no opportunity to exercise his peculiar vocation, else the meal might have been more palatable. The biscuits from having had a salt bath were a little briny to the taste; but that signified little to such sharp appetites as they were called upon to satisfy; and it was not such a bad breakfast, when washed down, as it was, with a little *wine* and water.

You may be asking whence came the wine; and this was the very question which the sailor addressed to Snowball, on discovering such a commodity upon his craft.

The answer was easy enough. A small cask of "Canary" had been one of the items among the cabin stores. At the explosion it had been pitched into the sea; and not being quite full had freely floated on the surface. Snowball had taken possession of it by attaching it to his timbers.

Breakfast over, the work of reconstruction commenced. As a preliminary, the flitches of shark-meat were removed from the little raft, now doomed to destruction; while that ingenious contrivance of the sailor,—the canvas water-cask,—now no longer required, was emptied of its contents; which, with the greatest care, were decanted into the safe depository of one of the empty hogsheads that had been hitherto acting as supports to the embarkation of Snowball.

The oars, sail-cloth, piece of handspike, axe, and tarpauling were also transferred to the latter; and then the planks, and fragments of yards and spars, were loosed from their lashings, and one by one distributed into their proper places in the new structure.

All day long did the work continue,—only an interval of an hour being appropriated to the midday meal. Excursions, too, were made from point to point,—the oars serving to propel the half-constructed craft: the object of these excursions being to pick up such pieces of timber, ropes, or other articles as Snowball had not already secured. The aid of the others now rendered many items available which Snowball had formerly rejected as useless,—because unmanageable by himself while acting alone.

The sun set upon their task still unfinished; but they retired hopefully to rest: for the sky promised a continuance of the calm weather, and they knew that if the promise was kept, a few hours in the morning of the following day would suffice to complete the construction of a raft,—one that would not only give them ample accommodation for the stowage both of themselves and their stores, but would in all probability ride out any gale likely to be encountered in that truly *pacific* part of the Atlantic Ocean.

Chapter Twenty Five
The Catamaran

Next morning, as soon as there was light enough for them to see what they were about, the work was resumed; and the timbers having been put together in a fashion to satisfy all hands, were lashed to one another as tightly as the united strength of the sailor, Snowball, and Little William could draw the ropes around them.

The structure when completed was of an oblong shape, —somewhat resembling a punt or flat-bottomed ferry-boat, —nearly twenty feet in length by about half as much in breadth of beam. The empty hogsheads were placed around the edge in a regular manner. One lay crosswise at the head, while another was similarly situated as regarded the stern. The other four—there were six in all—were lashed lengthwise along the sides, —two of them opposite each other on the larboard and starboard bows, while the other two respectively represented the "quarters." By this arrangement a certain symmetry was obtained; and when the structure was complete, it really looked like a craft intended for navigation, and by Ben Brace, —its chief architect, —it was facetiously christened *The Catamaran*.

By noon of the second day the *Catamaran* was completed, —so far as the *hull* was concerned. Had Snowball been by himself he would have left it in that state: for the black did not yet believe that there was the slightest probability of reaching land by means of such an embarkation.

But the sailor, —more skilled in such matters, —was of a different way of thinking. He believed it not only possible, but probable enough, that this feat might be accomplished. He knew that they were in the very centre of the southern trade-wind; and that the raft, even if left to itself, would in time drift onward to some point on the coast of South America. With a sail its speed would be accelerated; and although, thus furnished, such a clumsy structure could not sail very swiftly, there was still a chance of its carrying them safely, —if slowly, —to land. Ben knew it was simply a question of time, —dependent upon how long their provisions might last them, —but more especially their supply of water.

Having formed in his own mind a sort of rough calculation as to the chances, and finding them rather in favour of the scheme, he determined on making trial of it, by erecting a mast upon the raft, and to this bending a sail. At the worst, their chances of being picked up would be quite as good while sailing with the wind, as if they allowed themselves to lie adrift upon the ocean.

Fortunately the materials for both mast and sail were on hand, and in abundance. They had found the "spanker" of the *Pandora* floating about, with its boom and all the cordage attached. By using the boom as a mast, and another smaller spar as a boom, they could rig up such a sail as would carry the *Catamaran* through the water with considerable velocity.

As soon as he had fully considered it in his own mind, the sailor, aided by Snowball and Little William, proceeded to rig the *Catamaran*, and by the close of the third day from the commencement of their labours a tall mast stood up out of the centre of that curious craft, midships between stem and stern, with boom and guy, and a broad sail hanging loosely along its yard,— ready to be spread to the first breath of wind that might blow westward over the ocean.

The breeze which had brought Ben and little William back among the wreck-drift of the slave-bark, leading to a renewal of intercourse with their old shipmate, Snowball, had been blowing in the contrary direction to that in which the sailor intended to steer. This breeze, however, was not such as was to be looked for in that latitude. It was only a mere puff,—a cat's-paw,—in the midst of the calm that had continued for many days after the destruction of the slaver. It had lulled again on the same night in which the rafts had become united; and ever since,—during the three days they had been at work in the construction of the *Catamaran*,—the calm had continued without intermission.

On the fourth day things remained the same,—not a breath stirring from any quarter to ruffle the glassy surface of the sea; which, like a mirror, reflected the odd image of the *Catamaran*, with her six hogsheads set like bulwarks around her sides, and her stout mast tapering tall and solitary out of her midst.

Neither her captain,—Ben Brace of course,—nor those of her crew who were capable of reflecting on the future, and providing for its probable contingencies, regretted this inaction,—forced upon them by the continuance of the calm. Indeed, although becalmed, the "Catamarans" were not inactive.

There was work worthy of their activity, and which occupied them during the whole of the day. By the aid of oars,—several of which were fortunately in their possession,—they kept the new craft in constant motion; quartering the square mile of sea-surface, upon which floated the fragments of the ill-fated *Pandora*.

Many a waif did they pick up, and stow away on their new craft against the contingency of some future need.

Among other "floating fragments" Ben chanced upon his own sea-chest; which secured him a change of linen,—to say nothing of a full suit of "Sunday go-ashores" and variety of knick-knacks likely to prove of service on the problematical voyage he proposed making.

The chest itself was retained to serve as a useful "locker."

The fourth day being spent in such fashion, the Catamarans retired to rest,—little William, at the request of the sailor, repeating the Lord's Prayer, and ending it, by the dictation of the latter, with a short petition for a wind that would waft them to the westward!

It seemed as if that simple petition had been heard and granted. As the sun once more rose over the ocean, its glossy surface became broken into tiny corrugations by a breeze blowing as if from the sun himself. The sail was run up the slippery mast; it was tightly sheeted home; and the *Catamaran*, rushing rapidly through the water, soon cleared herself from that fatal spot where the slaver had perished.

"Westward ho!" cried Ben Brace, as he saw the sail swell out, and the craft, the product of his own skill, walking proudly away through the water like a "thing of life."

"Westward ho!" simultaneously echoed Snowball and Little William; while the eyes of Lilly Lalee sparkled with joy, as she beheld the enthusiastic bearing of her companions.

Chapter Twenty Six
Little William and Lilly Lalee

The wind was favourable in more senses than one. Besides blowing in the desired direction, it kept steady and continuous,—never rising above a gentle breeze, nor again returning to that calm from which they had just escaped, and the recurrence of which, to the captain of the *Catamaran*, would have been almost as unwelcome as a gale.

It was just the sort of wind for the trial of a new craft—barely ruffling the surface of the sea, and yet filling the sail till its sheet was as taut as a bow-string. As it blew direct from the east, that part of the *Catamaran* which Ben had christened her *head* was pointed due westward; and to hinder the craft from veering round, or luffing back into the eye of the wind, her builders had constructed a steering apparatus at the stern. It was simply a very large oar,—one that had appertained to the longboat of the *Pandora*,—placed fore and aft across the swell of the stern water-cask. It was held in that position by ropes attaching it to the cask, at the same time that they permitted it to play through the water, and perform the office of a rudder. By means of this simple contrivance,—which had been rigged before starting on her cruise,—the *Catamaran* could be steered to any point of the compass, and kept either before the wind, or luffed up as close to it as she was capable of sailing.

Of course it required one or other of them to be always at the "wheel," as Ben facetiously styled the steering apparatus, and the first spell of this duty the captain had taken upon himself, considering it too important,—so long as it was only on trial,—to be intrusted either to Snowball or little William. After they should get fairly under way, and there could be no longer any doubt as to the sailing qualities of the *Catamaran*, both the above-mentioned individuals would be expected to take their turn "at the wheel."

For more than an hour the *Catamaran* continued her course, without anything occurring to interrupt the "even tenor of her way." Her captain, seated in the stern, and still in charge of the steering-oar, was the only one occupied in the conduct of the craft. Snowball was busy among his stores,— most of which lay in a mass amidships,—arranging them into some sort of order, and placing each article in the most suitable position to withstand any sudden assault of the winds and waves.

Little William and Lilly Lalee were far forward against the cask which represented the head of the craft, and which, being quite empty, stood high above the surface of the water.

Neither was engaged in any particular employment,—except in talking kindly to each other, and at intervals exchanging expressions of joy at the fortune that had so singularly reunited them under two such courageous protectors.

It is true that, on board the slaver,—during that brief voyage, brought to such an abrupt and disastrous termination,—the two had seen but little of one another, and knew less. The pretty little Portuguese had been kept within the cabin, never going beyond the confines of the "quarter"; while the English lad, in continual fear of receiving rough treatment from either the captain or mates, rarely ventured within that sacred precinct unless in obedience to some command from his dreaded superiors.

Then stayed he only long enough to execute the order as speedily as possible,—knowing that to linger by the cabin would be to expose himself to rude insult,—perhaps to be pitched into the scuppers or kicked back to the forecastle.

Under such disadvantageous circumstances, it is not to be wondered at that the sailor-boy found but few opportunities of holding communication with the half-caste girl, who, by the singular chances already stated, had been his fellow-voyager on board the ill-fated bark.

Though he had held but slight converse with his youthful *compagnon du voyage*, and knew but little either of her moral or intellectual character, he was nevertheless most intimately acquainted with her personal appearance. There was not a feature in her pretty, sweet face, not a ringlet in her jetty curling hair, with which his eyes were not perfectly familiar.

Ofttimes had he stood,—half-screened behind the sails,—gazing upon her as she loitered by the cabin hatch, surrounded by rude ruffian forms, like a little white lamb in the midst of so many wolves.

Ofttimes had the sight caused his pulse to beat and his heart to throb with throes in which pain and pleasure were equally commingled, but the cause of which he could not comprehend.

Now, seated side by side with this young creature on board the *Catamaran*,—even on that frail embarkation, which at any moment might be scattered to the winds, or whelmed under the black billows of the sea,—the sailor-boy no longer felt pain while gazing in her face, but only that sweet incomprehensible pleasure.

Chapter Twenty Seven
Too Late!

Nearly two hours had transpired since the starting of the *Catamaran*,— during which time but little change took place in the relative positions of those on board. Then, however, Snowball having finished the stowage of his stores, proposed taking his turn at steering. The offer was willingly accepted by the sailor, who, relinquishing his hold upon the oar, went forward amidships. There he had placed his old sea-chest; and, kneeling in front of it, he commenced rummaging among its contents, with the design of making himself more familiar with them, and seeing whether he might not discover some article inside that would be serviceable under the circumstances.

William and Lilly Lalee still remained by the head,—the boy habitually keeping a lookout over the ocean, but at frequent intervals turning his glances towards her who sat by his side, and endeavouring to interest her with his conversation.

The girl could not speak English,—only a few phrases which she had picked up from English or American seamen, who had visited her father's fort upon the African coast. These, though by her repeated in all innocence, were neither of the most refined character, nor yet sufficiently comprehensive to enable her to hold any lengthened dialogue. It was in her own tongue that the conversation between her and William was carried on: for the lad had picked up a somewhat extensive vocabulary of Portuguese among the sailors of the *Pandora*—many of whom were of that nation. It was a sort of "lingoa geral" spoken along the seaboard of Africa,—not unlike a similar Portuguese patois, current on the coasts and large rivers of tropical South America.

In this language, little William, by the aid of signs and gestures, was able to keep up an occasional conversation with Lilly Lalee.

During the two hours which the sailor had remained at the steering-oar,—and for some time after,—no incident occurred to interrupt the tranquillity of the *Catamaran's* crew.

A very odd sort of fish, swimming about a cable's length ahead of the craft, had attracted the attention of William and the girl,—exciting their curiosity so much as to cause them to rise to their feet and stand watching it.

The interest which this creature had inspired was not, however, of a pleasant kind. On the contrary, both looked upon it with feelings of repugnance, almost amounting to awe; for it was in reality one of the ugliest monsters to be met with in the great deep.

In size it it as about equal to the body of a man; but much more elongated, and lessening gradually towards the tail. It seemed to possess a double quantity of fins,—lunated along their outer margins, and set thickly over its body, so as to give it a bristling aspect. Unlike other fishes, its neck was more slender than its head and shoulders,—imparting to it a sort of human shape. But it was in its head that the hideousness of the creature was more especially conspicuous; the skull being prolonged on each side outwards to the distance of several inches, and set upon its neck after the fashion of a mallet upon its shaft! At the end of these lateral protuberances appeared the eyes, with gleaming golden irides, glancing horridly to the right and left.

The mouth was not less abnormal in shape and position. Instead of being in the hideous head already described, it was in the breast,—where at intervals it could be seen yawning wide open, and displaying a quadruple row of sharp serrated teeth, that threatened instant destruction to any substance, however hard, that might chance to come between them.

Little William knew not what sort of fish it was; for though common enough in some parts of the ocean, he had not had the good or ill fortune to see one before. As his companion had put the question, however,—and also to satisfy his own curiosity,—he appealed to Ben.

The latter, raising his eyes above the top of his chest, and looking in the direction pointed out by the lad, at once recognised the animal which appeared to have attached itself as an escort to the *Catamaran*.

"Hammer-head!" said Ben; "a shark he be; an' the ugliest o' his ugly tribe."

Saying this, the sailor once more ducked his head under the lid of the chest, and continued his exploration,—altogether heedless of the "hammer-head," from whose proximity they had nothing to fear.

So believed Ben Brace at the moment.

It proved a feeling of false security. In less than ten minutes from that time the sailor was within six feet of the "hammer-head's" open mouth,— in imminent danger of being craunched between those quadruple tiers of terrible teeth, and taken into the monster's capacious maw.

By the phrase "hammer-head," so laconically pronounced by the captain of the *Catamaran*, little William recognised in the fish a creature which, although never seen by him before, he had read of in books, both of travel and natural history. It was the "hammer-head" shark, or *balance-fish*, so-called from the peculiar formation of its head,—the *zygaena* of the naturalists, and one of the most voracious of that devouring tribe to which genetically it belongs.

The individual in question was, as is already stated, about a cable's length from the raft, right ahead; and through the translucent water its form could be distinctly traced in all its hideous outlines. Swimming in the same direction, and at a like rate of speed, it preserved a regular distance from the raft; and appeared like some guide or *avant courier* conducting the *Catamaran* across the Atlantic!

William and Lalee watched the fish for a considerable time; but as no change took place either in its movements or the position it held in relation to the raft, their curiosity at length became satisfied, and their eyes were turned in a different direction.

But the gaze of the boy-sailor soon became fixed; and upon an object which caused him to give utterance to two distinct exclamations,—distinct in point of time, as different in signification. The first was an ejaculation, or rather a series of phrases expressing a jocular surprise,—the second a cry of serious alarm.

"Ho!" cried he, on turning round and glancing towards the stern of the *Catamaran*, "Snowball asleep! Ha! ha! ha! See the old sea-cook! Verily, that steering-oar has escaped from his hand!"

Almost instantly succeeded the shout that betokened alarm, followed by a series of hurried phrases, indicating the danger itself.

"The boom,—the boom! 'Tis coming round! Look out, Lalee! look out!"

As he gave utterance to these words of warnings the boy sprang towards his companion, with arms outstretched, to protect her.

The action came too late. The steering-oar, held in the hands of the sleeper, hung suspended high above the water. The *Catamaran*, left without control, luffed suddenly round beam-end to the wind; the boom obeyed the impulse of the breeze; and Lilly Lalee, uplifted upon its end, was brushed off from the craft, and jerked far out upon the blue bosom of the ocean!

Chapter Twenty Eight
"Overboard!"

The cry came from little William, as the Portuguese girl, lifted on the end of the boom, was pitched far out into the sea.

The utterance was merely mechanical; and as it escaped from his lips, the sailor-lad rushed towards the edge of the raft, and placed himself in an attitude to plunge into the water,—with the design of swimming to the rescue of Lalee.

Just then the boom, suddenly recoiling, came back with a rapid sweep; and, striking him across the shins, sent him sprawling over the shoulders of Ben Brace, and right into the sea-chest, in front of which the sailor was still kneeling.

Ben had heard that significant cry of alarm, and almost simultaneously the "plash" made by the little Portuguese as her body dropped down upon the water. He had slewed himself round, and was making a hurried effort to get to his feet, when the boy, flung with violence upon his stooping back, once more brought him to his knees.

As William was chucked right over him into the chest the sailor soon recovered from the shock, and rising erect, cried out in a half-confused manner,—"Overboard! Who? Where? *Not* you, Will'm! What is't, boy?"

"O Ben! Ben!" answered William, as he lay kicking among the contents of the kit, "Lilly Lalee, she's knocked overboard by the boom! Save her! save her!"

The sailor needed neither the information nor the appeal thus addressed to him. His interrogations had been altogether mechanical, for the plunge he had heard, and the absence of the girl from the raft,—ascertained by a single glance,—told him which of the *Catamaran's* crew it was who had fallen overboard.

The circling eddies in the water showed him the spot where the girl had gone down; but, just as he got to his feet again, she had turned to the surface; and, uttering half-stifled screams, commenced buffeting the water with her tiny hands, in an instinctive endeavour to keep herself afloat.

In a crisis of this character, the brave English sailor was obstructed by no ambiguity as to how he should act. A single bound carried him across the Catamaran,—another landed him upon the top of one of the casks, and a third launched him six feet outward into the sea. Had he been apprised of the accident only a score of seconds sooner, less than that number of strokes would have sufficed him to reach the spot where the child had first fallen into the water. Unfortunately in the collision with little William, that had brought him back to his knees, some time had been expended. During this interval—short as it was—the craft, though under an uncontrolled sail, was still making considerable way; and when the rescuer at length succeeded in leaping from the cask, the struggling form had fallen into the wake of the Catamaran to the distance of nearly a cable's length.

If the girl could only keep afloat for a few minutes, there need be no great danger. The sailor knew that he could swim, sustaining a heavier weight than was the little Lalee. But it was evident the child could not swim a stroke, and was every moment in danger of sinking for the second time.

Her rescuer perceived this danger as he started to her aid; and therefore pressed rapidly towards her, cleaving the water with all the strength that lay in his muscular arm and limbs.

Meanwhile little William had also regained his feet; and, having extricated himself from the chest in which he had been temporarily encoffined, ran towards the after part of the raft. Quickly mounting upon the water-cask at the stern, he stood astride the steering-oar,—an anxious and trembling spectator,—his eyes alternately fixed on the strong swimmer and the struggling child.

Snowball was still dormant, buried in a slumber profound and unconscious,—such as only a "darkey" can enjoy. The cry "Overboard!" uttered by little William had made no impression upon the tympanum of his wide-spread ears,—nor the exclamations that succeeded in the harsher voice of the sailor. Equally unheard by him had been the scream coming across the water, though along with it he might have heard the utterance of his own name!

As none of these sounds had been sufficient to arouse him from his torpor, he was likely to remain for some time longer unconscious of what was occurring. The sailor swam in silence, — the cries of the child, now more distant, were growing feebler and feebler; while little William — Snowball's only companion upon the raft — was too much absorbed in the scene and its issue to allow even a breath to escape him.

In this moment of agony, — intense to all the others of the *Catamaran's* crew, — Snowball was sleeping as soundly and sweetly as if he had been stretched along the bench of his caboose, and rocked to rest by the undulations of a good ship going at easy sail.

Up to this time, William had not thought of awakening him; for, to say the truth, the boy had not yet quite recovered his presence of mind. The shock of consternation caused by the accident was still vibrating through his brain; and his actions, in running aft, and springing up on the cask, were half mechanical. There, enchained by the spectacle, and waiting with intense anxiety for its *dénouement*, he had not a thought to give either to Snowball or his slumberings.

The silence continued only for a short period of time, though it may have seemed long enough both to actors and spectator in that thrilling drama. It was terminated by a cry of joyous import from the lips of little William, — in short, a loud *hurrah*, evoked by his seeing the swimmer come *en rapport* with the child, raise her sinking form above the surface, and holding it in one hand, strike out with the other in the direction of the rail.

Chapter Twenty Nine
Saved!

"Brave Ben!—brave fellow! he has saved her! Hurrah!"

Whether it was the violent gestures that accompanied this ebullition of feeling that caused the water-cask to lurch from under his feet,—or whether it arose from his nervous system suddenly becoming relaxed after such a spell of intense anxiety,—certain it is that the sailor-lad, as he repeated the final "Hurrah!" lost his balance upon the task, and, staggering over, he fell with all his weight upon the prostrate body of the slumbering sea-cook.

The latter, in his sleep more sensible to touch than hearing, was at length aroused.

"Gorramity!" cried he, suddenly starting to his knees, and endeavouring to disembarrass himself of the weight of little William, still scrambling upon his back. "Gorramity! What all dis *fracas* 'bout? Someb'dy shout 'Hurrah?'—Ha! you, lilly Willy? you shout dat jess now? I tink I hear ye in ma 'leep. What for you hurrah? Golly! am dar a ship in sight? I hope dar am—Wha's Mass' Brace?—wha's de lilly gal? Augh?"

This string of interrogations was put in such rapid succession as to give the lad no opportunity of replying to them. But, indeed, a reply was not needed, as may be deduced from the final ejaculation of the questioner.

Snowball, having swept the surface of the *Catamaran* with a quick, searching glance, and missing from it not only its captain, but—what was of greater moment—his own *protégé*, became equally the victim of surprise and consternation.

His eye was at once turned towards the water; and, like all men accustomed to the sea, was intuitively directed sternward. The missing individuals could not be elsewhere than in the wake of the craft going under sail.

He was soon satisfied of the correctness of his conjecture. On the instant of his turning he beheld Ben Brace,—or rather, only the head of that individual,—just visible above the rippling surface of the sea. Close by was another head, of smaller size, with dark ringlets floating on both sides of it, and a tiny arm stretched out and apparently clinging to the shoulder of the seaman.

Snowball needed no one—not even little William—to interpret what he saw. At a glance he comprehended what had occurred during his sleep,—all except the cause. Little did he suspect that the disaster had its origin in his own negligence. But it did not need that thought to beget within him a feeling of anxiety,—or, rather, of intense alarm.

This feeling did not arise on the instant. Seeing the girl sustained by such a strong swimmer as he knew his old shipmate to be, he had but little fear for the result,—so little that he checked his first impulse, which was to leap overboard and swim to the assistance of both.

A moment's reflection, however, satisfied him that there was still danger both for Lalee and her brave rescuer,—a danger which little William while giving utterance to that joyful "Hurrah!" had not taken into account. The lad had seen the girl picked up by the strong seaman; and, having an unlimited faith in the prowess of his own protector, he had no other thought than that the latter would soon swim back to the *Catamaran*, bearing his light burden along with him.

In his joy little William had overlooked the circumstance that the *Catamaran* was *under sail*, and moving through the water at a rate of speed that the swiftest swimmer, unembarrassed with the slightest weight, might in vain attempt to overtake her!

This sinister circumstance, in the excitement of the hour overlooked by the youthful sailor, was even, for a moment, unthought of by the more experienced mariner,—for Snowball, in addition to being a sea-cook, was also a competent seaman. Not for long, however, did the latter continue unconscious of the danger. Almost on the instant did he perceive it; and quickly squatting himself in front of the cask, he took hold of the steering-oar,—which he had so culpably neglected,—and, although still ignorant of the fact that his own negligence had caused the disaster, he bent all his energies towards remedying it.

Under the strong arm of the Coromantee, the *Catamaran* was fast coming round towards the wind,—and so shortening the distance between the swimmer and the craft,—when an object came under the eye of her steersman that caused him to drop the oar as if either his arm had become suddenly paralysed, or the piece of rounded ash grasped between his hands had become transformed into a bar of red-hot iron!

The former it could not be; since paralysed arms could not act, as did those of Snowball on that instant. On dropping the oar, his right hand was suddenly carried towards his left thigh, where a long knife hung suspended in its sheath. Upon the hilt of this his fingers rested for a moment, evidently not with the intention of drawing it, but apparently to assure himself that the knife was in its place.

In an instant the hand was withdrawn; but during the action the negro had hastily risen to his feet; and, having already abandoned the oar, he rushed towards the edge of the raft and leaped overboard into the water!

Chapter Thirty
The Zygaena

The conduct of the Coromantee in thus relinquishing the rudder and springing overboard into the sea was inexplicable,—at least, to little William it seemed so for the time. What could be Snowball's object in taking to the water? The sailor's strength was sufficient to sustain both himself and the little girl. He appeared to have no difficulty in holding her above the surface; and as to getting back to the raft, Snowball was surely doing more service in steering the raft towards them? Had he continued at the rudder a few minutes longer, the *Catamaran* must have come very near where the swimmer was struggling; where as, on his dropping the oar, she once more luffed round, and began to make way in the opposite direction.

Little William, however, did not observe this sinister circumstance; or if he did, it was for the moment driven out of his mind by one still more sinister, that just then came under his observation.

Only for a few seconds had he remained watching the negro, and wondering, with unpleasant thoughts, why the latter before leaping overboard had half drawn the knife from his belt and then resheathed it. Something like a suspicion passed through the mind of the youth. What could the negro want with a knife, if his object was to give help to the swimmer? Could a fiendish conception have occurred to the Coromantee, to lessen the number of those who might require food and water?

It is true the suspicion had barely shaped itself in the brain of the boy. Still, it had shaped itself, to be succeeded by a feeling of remorse for the wrong which he had done to Snowball in entertaining it. Almost on the instant did he become conscious of this wrong, by an object coming under his eyes and which at once accounted for the conduct of the Coromantee, that had seemed strange. Snowball was swimming towards Ben Brace,—not to destroy,—but with the intention of saving him.

From what? Was the sailor really in danger of sinking, so as to stand in need of support both for himself and his burden?

Little William did not put such an interrogatory. All his conjectures were ended. The peril threatening his patron,—and little Lalee as well,—was plainly outlined before his eyes, in all its frightful reality. That flattish, dark disc, with lunetted edge, rising erect above the surface, and cutting keenly through the rippling water, was an object not to be mistaken for any moving thing met with amid the ocean, save the dorsal fin of a shark, and William knew at a glance that such in reality it was.

He saw, moreover, it was the same he and little Lalee had so late been contemplating in security,—the dreaded zygaena: for through the translucent water he could distinguish its hammer-shaped head, and lurid eyes gleaming out from their protuberant sockets,—hideous to behold!

The boy now became spectator,—sole spectator,—of a scene of thrilling, even terrible interest. The characters in the drama were Snowball, the zygaena, and Ben Brace with his burden.

Just as William had arrived at the comprehension of the Coromantee's behaviour, the *dramatis persona* were placed relatively to each other in a triangular position,—an isosceles triangle, in which Snowball and the shark represented the angles at the base, while Ben with his charge occupied the apex. The latter point was almost stationary, while both the former were moving towards it in converging lines, fast as shark and man could swim.

The situation was easily explained. The zygaena, hitherto holding its course ahead of the *Catamaran*, had become apprised of the catastrophe occurring among the crew. The plash occasioned by little Lalee as she was flung upon the water, and the heavier concussion of Ben's body as he plunged overboard, had reached the monster's ears; and, with that fell instinct peculiar to its tribe, it had suddenly turned in the water, and commenced swimming toward the wake of the craft; where it knew that anything, whether human or otherwise, falling overboard, must inevitably drift.

While passing the *Catamaran* towards the wake, Snowball had caught sight of its fan-like fin,—which apprised him of the direction it was taking, at the same time revealing to him its design.

The plunge which Snowball had made as he sprang out into the water had caused the zygaena to swerve from its course; and for some moments it swam towards *him*, as if determined upon changing the object of its attack; but whether not liking the looks of the Coromantee or frayed by his bold attitude in making directly towards it, it shied back into its former course, and kept on towards the others.

Of course, the sailor, encumbered as he was by the half-lifeless form of the girl, would stand but little chance of making a successful defence against a shark, — more especially such a monster as the zygaena; and it was the knowledge of this that had summoned Snowball to the rescue.

Against such an adversary a more capable combatant than the Coromantee could scarce have been found on the waters of the ocean, or even *in* them. He could swim like a swan, and dive like a sea-duck; nor was it the first time for him to have fought the shark in its own element; neither would it be the first time should he prove conqueror in the combat.

On launching into the lists, his chief dread had not been for himself, but for those he was proceeding to rescue.

In point of time the shark had had the start of him; and, although on parting from the raft the distances each would have to traverse were not very unequal, Snowball knew that his scaly competitor far excelled him in the quality of speed.

It was this thought that was causing him anxiety, — amounting almost to anguish, — that caused him to plunge wildly through the water, — to utter loud cries, and make other noisy demonstrations, — with a view of distracting the attention of the zygaena from the victims it had fore-chosen, and drawing its attack upon himself.

His shouts and gesticulations proved equally unavailing. The cunning zygaena took no heed of either; but with its dark dorsal fin, set like a well-bent sail, it kept straight on towards the easier victims.

The sides of the isosceles triangle were gradually growing unequal, — gradually and slowly, but, alas! surely. Already was it an irregular *scalene*. Snowball perceived the change, — each moment becoming more perceptible, each moment augmenting his fears.

"Poor lilly Lally!" cried he, in a voice that betrayed his anxiety. "O Mass' Ben! fo' de lub o' Gorramity, swum to de right, — round dat away, an' let me git 'tween you an de ravenin' beast. To de right! — da's de way. Do yer bess, Mass' Brace, an' gi' me time get up. I take care o' de lubber ef I once get im widin reach o' dis chile's arm."

The injunction thus uttered had the desired effect. Up to that time the sailor, sunk low in the water by reason of the extra weight, had not become fully cognisant of the peril of his position. Hitherto his mind had been more occupied with the idea of overtaking the raft, than any danger to be dreaded from sharks. He was not even aware of the zygaena's approach; for the fin, which had betrayed the monster's presence to those on the *Catamaran*, — from being seen *en profile*, — could not so easily be distinguished when viewed in "front-face." No wonder, therefore, that the victims which the zygaena had selected for its attack remained unconscious of its approach; and it was only on seeing Snowball spring out from the *Catamaran*, and swim towards him, that the sailor suspected the proximity of a shark. At the same instant, also, he remembered the interrogatory that had been addressed to him by little William, and his own laconic reply designating the individual as a *hammerhead*. From these various circumstances he could tell that there was a shark bearing down upon him; but in what direction he could not conjecture, until the hurried words of Snowball admonished him to "make way to de right."

The sailor had too much respect for the experience of the ex-cook to disregard the injunctions thus given; and of hearing them, he at once swerved in the direction indicated, and "made way to de right" as fast as a man could swim with only one hand free for the stroke.

Fortunately for all parties, the one arm proved sufficient. The new direction entered upon by the swimmer soon changed the relative position of all parties. The triangle became resolved into a right line, — the shark at one extremity, — the sailor with his charge at the other, — Snowball midway between!

Chapter Thirty One
Face to Face

By this change in the position of the parties, the zygaena had lost its advantage. Instead of having for the object of its attack an exhausted swimmer encumbered with a weight, without a weapon, or even an arm free to wield one, it would now have for its antagonist a strong man,— fresh and vigorous,—armed with a long-bladed knife; one, moreover, who from earliest youth had lived a half-amphibious life, and who was almost as much at home in the water as the shark itself. At all events, the Coromantee could calculate on keeping himself *above* water for several hours without rest, and *under* it as long as any other animal whose natural element was the earth or the air.

Snowball, however, had no intention to go *wider,*—not an inch deeper than he could possibly help: for therein would lie his danger, and he knew it. As we have already said, it was not the first time for him to encounter a shark in its own element; and though, perhaps, not so familial with the *hammer-head* as with the white shark, he was not altogether unacquainted with the habits and peculiarities of the former species.

He knew that the zygaena, like others of its congeners, in seizing an object, requires to have that object *under* it; otherwise, it is compelled to turn upon its back or side, just in proportion as the prey it would seize lies high or low in the water. If altogether on the surface, the shark is forced to make a complete roll, belly upward; and this necessity,—arising from the peculiar position of the animal's mouth, and the conformation of its jaws,—is well-known among mariners, and better among true shark-fighters, who use it to their advantage. Among the pearl-divers of the Vermilion Sea (Gulf of California), the attack of the common shark is but little dreaded. The only weapon used by them is a piece of stick (the *estaca*), sharpened at both ends, and hardened by fire. Provided with this simple weapon, which they carry, stuck through a loop in their leathern belt, they dive without fear among the sharks that frequent the waters of the pearl-oyster fishery. When attacked by one of these voracious creatures, they wait for the moment when the shark makes its semi-somersault, and opens its cavernous mouth. Then, with an adroitness drawn from practice, and a fearlessness which only great confidence can give, they thrust the *estaca*, gag-fashion, between the creature's jaws, leaving it no alternative but to retreat with its jaws wide open, or to close them to its own certain destruction. Among these pearl-fisheries, however, a species of shark occasionally shows itself that cannot be destroyed in such a simple fashion. It is known as the *tintorera*, and is as much dreaded by the pearl-divers as the common shark is by the ordinary mariner.

Fierce as is the zygaena and dreaded above all others of its tribe,—half the dread no doubt is attributable to its hideous configuration. Snowball knew that before it could injure him, it must make the half-turn, and, therefore, approached it with the determination to keep well upon the surface of the water, and not let it get above him.

The conflict was now inevitable: for the shark, although apparently a little put about by the transposition that had taken place, had determined upon having a meal of human flesh. Its white victims had escaped it for the time, but it was not particular as to the colour of the skin, and Snowball might be as sweet to its palate as Ben Brace or Lilly Lalee.

We are not going to assert that it reasoned after this fashion, or that any thoughts whatever passed through its huge mallet-shaped skull. Indeed, there was not much time for reflection: for as Snowball interposed his body between the zygaena and its intended victims, the woolly head of the Coromantee and the hammer-head of the shark were scarcely three lengths of a handspike from each other.

It was a fearful situation for a human being to be in; and any other than an old shark-fighter would, at such a moment, have succumbed from sheer terror.

Not so Snowball, who appeared to enter the lists with as little dread and as much confidence as if his *fetisch* had given him full assurance of victory.

Little William, standing upon the stern of the *Catamaran* with suspended breath, noting every turn of the spectacle, could see Snowball drawing the knife from his belt. Not for long, however, did he hold it clutched in his hand. For greater convenience, and to give his hands free play, while evading the attacks of his finny antagonist, he transferred the knife to his mouth, where it was seen set transversely across his cheeks, the blade tightly held between his teeth. In this strange fashion did Snowball meet his enemy,—the truculent tyrant of the deep.

Chapter Thirty Two
A Ring Performance

It might be supposed that the shark would have rushed instantaneously upon its antagonist, regardless of aught save making a meal of him. But no, the zygaena, notwithstanding its great voracity, like the rest of its tribe, is endowed with certain instincts of caution. The sea-tiger, as well as that of the land, can tell instinctively whether the object of its attack is likely to become an easy prey, or turn out a dangerous adversary.

Some such—shall we call it an idea?—seemed to enter the unshapely skull of the hammer-head,—suggested no doubt by the bold attitude which Snowball had assumed. In all likelihood, had the negro been making away, instead of swimming towards it, and showing signs of a desire to escape, its onset would have been made on the instant.

As it was, the shark saw itself *vis-à-vis* to an adversary nearly as large as itself and quite as courageous; and it is possible also that its pilot-fish,—a brace of which had advanced close to Snowball's snout, and after submitting his dusky carcass to a brief examination returned to their master,—it is just possible that these emissaries had reported to their patron, that the game he was in pursuit of must be approached with caution.

At all events something had been communicated that produced a sudden change in the tactics of the zygaena. Instead of rushing recklessly on to the attack,—or even keeping up the swimming pace by which it had hitherto been making its approach,—on arriving within some half-score fathoms of Snowball's face, it gradually slackened speed, until its brown, fan-like fins, gently oscillating along its sides seemed no longer to propel its body through the water.

Moreover, on drawing nearer, it swerved slightly from its course,—as if with the design either of attacking its adversary in the rear, or passing him altogether!

Strange enough, the two parasites appeared to direct this movement: for both kept swimming alongside the zygaena, one of them opposite each of its huge eyeballs.

The negro seemed slightly perplexed by this unexpected manoeuvre. He had anticipated an instantaneous attack, and had made every preparation to receive and repel it. He had even taken the knife from his teeth, and was holding it tightly clutched in his right hand, ready to deal his deadly blow.

The shyness of the shark produced a disappointment.

Something besides: for it now occurred to Snowball that the cunning zygaena was trying to pass him, with the design of making a *razzia* towards the helpless party in his rear.

The moment this suspicion arose to him he turned short in the water, and struck out in a direction that would enable him to head the shark, and, if possible, intercept it.

Whether the creature intended to pursue his original plan of attacking the sailor and his charge, or whether he was manoeuvring to *turn* the Coromantee, it mattered not. In either case Snowball was pursuing the correct strategy. He knew that if his supple antagonist could once get round to his rear, his chances of safety for himself or the others would be sadly diminished. Should the zygaena once get past him and continue on towards the sailor, swift swimmer as Snowball was, he could have no chance of overtaking a fish.

At this crisis a thought occurred to him which promised to avert the calamity he most dreaded,—that is, the shark getting past him, and continuing on to the others. The thought found expression in speech.

"Ho! Massa Brace!" he cried, once more taking the steel from between his teeth. "Swim roun' to de right. Keep a-gwine in de circle. For de Lord sake, keep ahind me, or you loss fo' sartin!"

The sailor scarcely needed the counsel. He saw the danger before Snowball had spoken, and had already commenced the movement which the Coromantee was requesting him to make.

Once more the tableau changed. The *dramatis persona* in their relative positions first formed an isosceles triangle, then a scalene, afterwards a right line. Now all were moving in a circle, or rather in three circles concentric to one another; the sailor, with his charge, revolving round the centre, Snowball in mid radius, while the shark, flanked by his satellites, went gliding along the outer circumference, his lurid eyes glaring continually inward, as if watching for an opportunity to break the line so carefully guarded by the Coromantee!

For full five minutes was this "ring" performance kept up, without any great alteration occurring in the relative positions of the parties. But it was a game in which the outside player had all the advantage; for, although the zygaena had by far the greater distance to traverse, what was but sport to it was fatigue and the danger of drowning to its adversaries.

Had its skull been of a different formation, and filled with a better set of brains, it would have endeavoured to keep up that game, without in the least degree changing the mode of playing it. In due time, its chief antagonist, Snowball, must have cried quarter or gone to the bottom; and far sooner must have sunk the weighted swimmer in his wake.

But sharks, like other creatures both aquatic and terrestrial, have their moments of impatience and anger; and the zygaena, yielding to these passions, common to both piscine and human nature, at length determined to break through the rules of the game, and bring the play to an abrupt termination.

In obedience to this impulse, it suddenly swerved from its circular course, and, heading towards the spot where Ben Brace, with Lilly Lalee clinging to his shoulder, was performing his shorter revolutions, it made a reckless and determined rush for the centre,—equally regardless of the admonition of its brace of monitors and the cold steel of the Coromantee, gleaming clear under the water through which it would have to make its way. So near had it to pass to the negro's flat nose that its glutinous skin would be almost in contact with his prominent lips, and with his outstretched hand he need have no difficulty in striking his slippery antagonist.

Had Snowball been anticipating this change of tactics, he could not have acted more adroitly, or with greater promptness. As the zygaena was gliding onward, and just as its rough *pectoral* passed within an inch of his nose, he suddenly returned the knife between his teeth, and, simultaneously using both hands and limbs, he sprang upward in the waiter, and, with a vigorous effort, launched himself on its back!

In the next instant he was seen,—or might have been seen,—with one hand, the left, firmly grasping the bony protuberance of the zygaena's left eye, his muscular fingers deeply imbedded in the socket, while his right, clutching the long knife, was inflicting a series of stabs against the side of his adversary, now flashing high in the air, now gleaming under water, going up and down with all the measured regularity of a trip-hammer.

When it pleased the Coromantee to dismount from his slippery saddle, the zygaena floated by his side,—a carcass stained with its own blood, that for fathoms around encrimsoned the azure waters of the ocean!

Chapter Thirty Three
The Chase of the Catamaran

As we have said, little William, standing near the stern of the *Catamaran*, had watched the spectacle with suspended breath. It was only after seeing the zygaena float lifeless on the water, and becoming satisfied that Snowball had come out of the struggle safe as well as victorious, that the boy gave utterance to a shout. Then, unable longer to restrain himself, he raised a cry of joyful exultation.

It was neither prolonged nor repeated. It had scarce passed his lips, ere it was succeeded by another of very different import. This was the very opposite to a shout of joy: rather was it a cry of consternation. That little drama of the ocean, of which he had been the sole spectator, was not yet over. There was another act to come of equally thrilling interest with that just ended,—an act in which he himself would be called upon to play an important part along with the others.

It had already commenced; and the wild cry which escaped from the lips of the sailor-lad announced his first perception of the new phase into which the drama had entered.

Absorbed in the contemplation of the combat between Snowball and the shark, he had hitherto remained unobservant of a circumstance of the most alarming character,—one that threatened not only the destruction of the Coromantee, but Ben Brace as well, and Lilly Lalee, and in time little William himself,—in short, of the whole party.

The lives of all were at that moment in the hands of the sailor-lad, or if not in his hands, then were all of them doomed to certain destruction.

You may be wondering what strange circumstance this was, fraught with such a terrible contingency. There was nothing mysterious in or about it. It was simply that the *Catamaran*, carrying its large spread sail, was drifting to leeward, and rapidly increasing the distance between itself and the swimmers.

Relieved from the anxiety with which he had regarded the conflict, little William at once became aware of this new danger,—hence his cry of consternation. Ben Brace either perceived it at the same instant, or else the shout of his *protégé* had drawn his attention to it; for, quick succeeding the latter, the voice of the sailor went rolling across the water in words of direction intended for the ears of little William.

"Will'm! Will'm!" shouted he, raising his lips above the surface so as to enunciate more distinctly. "For marcy's sake, lad, lay hold on the steerin' oar. Try to tack round, or we're lost one an' all o' us!"

At the same instant Snowball sputtered out some very similar orders; but being sadly out of breath from his exertions in the long-continued struggle with the zygaena, what proceeded from his mouth less resembled words than the snorting of a porpoise; and was, in truth, altogether unintelligible.

Little William needed no instructions,—neither to hear nor understand them. He had perceived the danger, and, with intuitive promptness, had commenced taking measures to avoid it. Partly guided by his own thoughts and partly by the directions of Ben Brace, he sprang suddenly towards the steering-oar; and, grasping it in both hands, he worked with all his might to bring the *Catamaran* about. After a time he succeeded in getting her head as close to the wind as such a craft was capable of sailing, but it soon became evident to him that the manoeuvre would be of little or no avail. Although the raft did not make leeway quite as much as before, still with its great sail, rudely bent as it was, she made sufficient to preserve the distance from the swimmers; and, as William anxiously observed, still slightly increasing. Even Snowball, who, after giving the *coup de grâce* to the zygaena, had struck direct towards the *Catamaran,*—even he, unencumbered by aught save his wet shirt and trousers, although easily passing the others in his course, did not appear to gain an inch upon the runaway raft.

It was an anxious time for all parties; and the anxiety reached its height when they perceived, as one and all soon did, that the unmanageable craft was keeping its distance, if not gaining a greater.

That state of things could not continue long. Both the swimmers had already begun to show signs of flagging. Snowball, sea-duck that he was, might have held out a good while; but the sailor, weighted with Lalee, must soon "go under." Even Snowball could not swim forever; and, unless some incident should arise to change the character of this aquatic chase, and arrest the *Catamaran* in her leeward course, sooner or later must the Coromantee become also the prey of the all-swallowing ocean.

For several minutes—they seemed hours to all—did the struggle continue between man and *Catamaran*, without any very great advantage in favour of either. It is true some change had taken place in the relative positions of the parties. The Coromantee, at starting in pursuit of the raft, had been some fathoms in the wake of Ben Brace and his *protégé*. They were now in his wake, falling, alas! still farther behind him. Unfortunately for all, Snowball, while increasing his distance from them, was not lessening it from the *Catamaran*; and therefore the advantage he was gaining over the sailor could be of no use, so long as the raft proved swifter as a sailer than he was as a swimmer.

Snowball's original idea in striking out in pursuit of the *Catamaran* was to get aboard; and, by making a better use of the steering-oar than he had hitherto done, to bring the craft back within *saving* distance of the exhausted swimmer. Confident in his natatory powers, he had at first believed this feat to be not only possible, but probable and easy. It was only after several minutes spent in the pursuit, and the distance between him and the *Catamaran* seemed to grow greater instead of less, that the negro really began to feel anxiety about the result.

This anxiety kept increasing as the minutes passed, and the broad stretch of blue water between him and the *Catamaran* appeared to grow no narrower, strike out as he would with all the strength of his sinewy arms, and kick as he might with all the muscular energy that lay in his stout legs.

His anxiety became anguish, when, after one of his most vigorous efforts, he believed, or fancied, that all had been in vain, and that the *Catamaran* had actually gained upon him. Whether fancy or not, it produced conviction in his mind that to overtake the craft was impossible; and all at once he discontinued the attempt. He did not, however, remain stationary in the water. Far from that. On abandoning the pursuit of the *Catamaran*, he turned like an otter, and looked back in the direction from which he had come. In this direction, nearly two hundred fathoms distant, two dark objects, so close together as to seem one, were visible over the "curl" of the water.

They were just visible to an eye elevated several inches above the surface; and Snowball was obliged to buoy himself into an erect attitude,—like a seal taking a survey of the circle around it, or a dog pitched unexpectedly into a deep pond,—before he could see them.

He saw them, however; he knew what they were; and, without a moment's pause or hesitation, he recommenced cleaving the water in a line leading directly towards them.

The mind of the Coromantee, hitherto distracted by conflicting emotions, had now but one thought. It was less purpose than a despairing instinct. It was to support the child who had been intrusted to him—the Lilly Lalee—above water as long as he should have strength; and then to go down along with her into that vast, fathomless tomb, that leaves no trace and carries no epitaph!

Chapter Thirty Four
The Sail out of Sight

The sea-cook and the sailor were now swimming towards each other. It is true that Ben was not making very rapid way, nor did Snowball return on his course with any great alacrity. Despair had rendered the latter somewhat irresolute; and he scarcely knew why he was swimming back, unless it was to be drowned in company with the others; for drowning now appeared their inevitable fate.

Slowly as both swam, they soon came together,—the countenances of both, as they met, exhibiting that fixed, despairing look which bespeaks the utter extinction of hope.

The *Catamaran* was now at such a distance, that even could she have been suddenly arrested in her course, and brought to an anchor, it was doubtful whether either Snowball or the sailor could have reached her by swimming. The raft itself and the water-casks lashed around it were no longer to be seen. Only the white sail, that like a bit of fleecy cloud, equally fleeting, was fast lessening to a speck upon the distant horizon. No wonder that hope had forsaken them!

The sailor wondered that the sail was still set. During the first moments, while endeavouring to come up with the craft, he had shouted to William to let go the halliards. He had kept repeating this order, until his voice, already hoarse and faltering, grew almost inarticulate from sheet exhaustion of breath, and the rail, moreover, had drifted to such a distance that it was not likely the lad could hear him. Under this impression he had at length discontinued his feeble cries, and swam on in slow and gloomy silence, wondering why William had not obeyed his injunctions, feeling chagrin at his not doing so, and with good reason, since the lowering of the sail might have still given them some chance of overtaking the craft.

It was just as the sailor had given over calling out, and relapsed into sullen silence, that Snowball was seen returning towards him. It was an additional argument for despair this abandonment of the chase on the part of the Coromantee. When such a swimmer had given it up, Ben knew it was hopeless.

In a moment after they met face to face. The glance exchanged between them was mutually understood without a word spoken by either. Each tacitly read in the eyes of the other the dread destiny that awaited them,— near, and soon to be fulfilled,—drowning!

Snowball was the first to break the terrible silence.

"You nigh done up, Massa Ben,—you muss be! Gib me de lilly gal. You Lally! you lay hold on ma shoulder, and let Massa Brace ress a bit."

"No,—no!" protested the sailor, in a despairing tone. "It bean't no use. I can carry her a bit longer. 'Tain't much longer as any o' us 'll be—"

"Sh! Massa Brace," interrupted the negro, speaking in a suppressed whisper, and looking significantly towards the child. "Hope dar 's no danger yet," he added, in a voice intended for the ear of Lalee. "We oberhaul de *Catamaran* by 'm by. De wind change, and bring dat craff down on us. 'Peak in de French, Massa Ben," he continued, at the same time adroitly adopting a *patois* of that language. "De *pauvre jeune fille* don't understan' de French lingo. I know it am all ober wi' boaf you an' me, and de gal, too but doan let her know it to de lass minute. It be no use to do dat,—only make her feel wuss."

"*Eh bien!* all right!" muttered Ben, indiscriminately mingling his French and English phrases. "*Pauvre enfant!* She shan't know nothin' from me o' what be afore her. Lord a marcy on all o' us! I don't see the raft any more! Whar be it? Can you see it, Snowball?"

"Gorramity, no!" replied the black, raising himself up in the water to get a better view. "Gone out o' de sight altogedder! We nebba see dat *Catamaran* any more,—no, nebba!"

The additional accent of despair with which these words were uttered was scarce perceptible. Had there been a hope, it would have been shattered by the disappearance of the raft,—whose white sail was now no longer visible against the blue background of the horizon. But all hope had previously been abandoned; and this new phase of the drama produced but slight change in the minds of its chief actors. Death was already staring them in the face with that determination which promised no prospect of avoiding it, and none was cherished. The only change that occurred was in the action. The swimmers no longer directed themselves in a particular course. There was none for them to follow. With the disappearance of the sail they no longer knew in what direction to look for the raft. For all they now knew of it, it might have gone to the bottom, leaving them alone upon the bosom of the limitless ocean.

"No use swimmin' on'ards!" said Ben, despairingly. "It'll only waste the bit of strength that be left us."

"No use," assented the negro. "Less lay to, and float on de water. Dat be easier, and we can keep up de longer. Do, Massa Ben,—gib me de gal. You mo' tired dan I. Come, lilly Lally, you grasp hold on ma shoulder! Dat's de bess way. Come, now,—come, dear lilly gal."

And as Snowball spoke, he swam close alongside the girl and, gently detaching her hand from the shoulder of the sailor, transferred its feeble grasp to his own.

Ben no longer offered resistance to this generous action on the part of his old comrade: for, in truth, he stood in dire necessity of the relief; and, the transfer having been effected, both continued to float upon the water, sustaining themselves with no more effort than was absolutely necessary to keep their heads above the surface.

Chapter Thirty Five
Waiting for Death

For several minutes the wretched castaways of the *Catamaran* remained in their perilous position,—almost motionless in the midst of the deep blue water,—precariously suspended upon its surface,—suspended between life and death!

Under any circumstances the situation would have been trying to the stoutest nerves,—even under circumstances where a hope of deliverance might have been indulged in. Without this it was awful.

Neither black man nor white one any longer contemplated the *danger* of death: both believed in its *certainty*.

How could they doubt it?

Had either been standing upon the scaffold, with the condemned cap drawn over his eyes and the rope adjusted around his neck, he could not have felt surer of the nearness of his end.

Both believed it to be simply a question of time; an hour or two,— perhaps not so much, since the fatigues and struggles through which they had just passed had already made sad inroads upon their strength,—but an hour or two at most, and all would be over. Both must succumb to the laws of Nature,—the laws of gravitation,—or rather of specific gravity,—and sink below the surface,—down, down into the fathomless and unknown abysm of the ocean. Along with them, sharing their sad fate, Lilly Lalee,—that pretty, uncomplaining child, the innocent victim of an ill-starred destiny, must disappear forever from a world of which she had as yet seen so little, and that little of the least favourable kind.

Throughout the whole affair the girl had shown but slight signs of the terrible affright that, under the circumstances, might have been expected. Born in a land and brought up among a people where human life was lightly and precariously held, she had been often accustomed to the spectacle of death,—which to some extent robs it of its terrors. At all events, they who are thus used appear to meet it with a more stoical indifference.

It would be a mistake to suppose that the girl appeared indifferent. Nothing of the sort. She exhibited apprehension,—fear sufficient; but whether her mind was overwhelmed by the extreme peril of the situation, or that she was still ignorant of its being extreme, certain it is that her behaviour, from beginning to end, was characterised by a calmness that seemed supernatural, or at all events superhuman. Perhaps she was sustained by the confidence she had in the brace of brave protectors swimming alongside of her,—both of whom, even in that extreme hour, carefully refrained from communicating to her the belief which they themselves in all fulness entertained,—that their lives were fast approaching to a termination.

The minds of both were fully imbued with this conviction, though not in the same degree of fulness. If possible, the white man felt more certain of the proximity of his end than did the negro. It is not easy to tell why it was so. The reason may, perhaps, be found in the fact, that the latter had been so often on the edge of the other world, had so often escaped entering it, that, despite the impossibility of escaping from his present peril,—to all appearance absolute,—there still lingered in his breast some remnant of hopefulness.

Not so with the sailor. From the bosom of Ben Brace every vestige of hope had vanished. He looked upon life as no longer possible. Once or twice the thought had actually entered his mind to put an end to the struggle, and, along with it, the agony of that terrible hour, by suspending the action of his arms, and suffering himself to sink to the bottom of the sea. He was only restrained from the suicidal act, by the influence of that instinct of our nature, which abhors self-destruction, and admonishes, or rather compels us, to abide the final moment when death comes to claim us as its own.

Thus, by different circumstances, and under different influences, were the three castaways of the *Catamaran* sustained upon the surface of the water,—Lilly Lalee by Snowball,—Snowball, by the slightest ray of hope still lingering in a corner of his black bosom,—the sailor by an instinct causing him to refrain from the committal of that act which, in civilised society, under all circumstances, is considered as a crime.

Chapter Thirty Six
A Chest at Sea

All conversation had come to an end. Even the few phrases at intervals exchanged between Snowball and the sailor,—the solemn import of which had been zealously kept from the child by their being spoken in *French*— were no longer heard.

The swimmers, now wellnigh exhausted, had for a long interval preserved this profound silence, partly for the reason of their being exhausted, and partly that no change had occurred in the circumstances surrounding them,—nothing that required a renewal of the conversation. The awe of approaching death,—now so near, that twenty minutes or a quarter of an hour might be regarded as the ultimate moment,—held, as if spellbound, the speech both of Snowball and the sailor.

There were no other sounds to interrupt the silence of that solemn moment,—at least none worthy of being mentioned. The slightest ripple of the water, stirred by a zephyr breeze, as it played against the bodies of the languid swimmers, might have been heard, but was not heeded. No more did the scream of the sea-mew arrest the attention of any of them, or if it did, it was only to add to the awe which reigned above and around them.

In this moment of deep silence and deepest misery, a voice fell upon the ears of the two swimmers that startled both of them, as if it had been a summons from the other world. It sounded sweet as if from the world of eternal joy. There was no mystery in the voice; it was that of the Lilly Lalee.

The child, sustained upon the shoulder of the buoyant black, was in such a position that her eyes were elevated over the surface of the water several inches above those either of him who supported her, or the sailor who swam by her side. In this situation she had a better view than either; and, as a consequence of this advantage, she saw what was visible to neither,—a dark object floating upon the surface of the sea at no great distance from the spot where the exhausted swimmers were feebly struggling to sustain themselves.

It was the announcement of this fact that had fallen with such startling effect upon the ears of the two men, simultaneously rousing both from that torpor of despair which for some time had held possession of them.

"Who you see, Lilly Lally? Who you see?" exclaimed Snowball, who was the first to interrogate the girl. "Look at 'im 'gain,—look, good lilly gal!" continued he, at the same time making an effort to elevate the shoulder which gave support to his *protégé*.

"Wha be it? I ain't de raff,—de *Catamaran*? Eh?"

"No, no," replied the child. "It isn't that. It's a small thing of a square shape. It looks like a box."

"A box? how come dat? A box! what de debbel!"

"Shiver my timbers if 'tain't my old sea-kit," interrupted the sailor, rearing himself aloft in the water like a spaniel in search of wounded waterfowl.

"Sure as my name's Ben Brace it be that, an' nothing else!"

"Your sea-chess?" interrogated Snowball, elevating his woolly cranium above the water, so as also to command a view. "Golly! I b'lieve it am. How he come dar? You leff 'im on de raff?"

"I did," replied the sailor. "The very last thing I had my hands upon, afore I jumped overboard. Sure I bean't mistaken,—ne'er a bit o' it. It be the old kit to a sartainty."

This conversation was carried on in a quick, hurried tone, and long before it ended,—in fact at the moment of its beginning,—the swimmers had once more put themselves in motion, and were striking out in the direction of the object thus unexpectedly presented to their view.

Chapter Thirty Seven
An improvised Life-Preserver

Whether it should turn out to be the sea-chest of Ben Brace or no, it appeared to be a chest of some sort; and, being of wood, buoyantly floating on the water, it promised to help in supporting the swimmers,—now so utterly exhausted as to be on the point of giving up, and going to the bottom.

If the sailor had entertained any doubts as to the character of the object upon which they were advancing, they were soon brought to an end. It *was* a sea-chest,—his own,—to him easy of identification. Well knew he that close-fitting canvas cover, which he had himself made for it, rendered waterproof by a coat of blue paint,—well knew he those hanging handles of strong sennit, he had himself plaited and attached to it; and, as if to provide against any possible dispute about the ownership of the chest, were the letters "B.B.,"—the unmistakable initials of Ben Brace,—painted conspicuously upon its side, just under the keyhole, with a "fouled anchor" beneath, with stars and other fantastic emblems scattered around,—all testifying to the artistic skill of the owner of the kit.

The first thought of the sailor, on recognising his chest, was that some misfortune had happened to the raft, and that it had gone to pieces.

"Poor little Will'm!" said he. "If that be so, then it be all over wi' him."

This belief was but of short duration, and was followed by a reflection of a more pleasant kind.

"No!" he exclaimed, contradicting his first hypothesis, "It can't be that. What could 'a broke up the raft? There 's been no wind, nor rough weather, as could 'a done it. Ha! I have it, Snowy. It's Will'm 's did this. He's throwed over the chest in the behopes it might help float us. That's how it's got here. Huzza for that brave boy! Let's cling on to the kit. There may be hope for us yet."

This suggestion was superfluous: for the idea of clinging to the kit was intuitive, and had entered the minds of both swimmers on their first perceiving it. It was with that view they had simultaneously set themselves in motion, and commenced swimming towards it.

The chest certainly offered an attractive object to men circumstanced as they were at that moment,—something more than a straw to be clutched at. It was floating bottom downwards, and lid upwards,—just as it might have been placed opposite Ben's own bunk in the forecastle of a frigate,—and it appeared to be kept steadily balanced in this position by the weight of some iron cleeting along the bottom, which acted as ballast. Otherwise the chest sat so high upon the water, as to show that it must either be quite empty or nearly so; for the sennit handles at each end, which were several inches below the level of the lid, hung quite clear above the surface.

These handles offered the most salient points to seize upon; so tempting, too, that it was not necessary for the sailor to suggest that Snowball should lay hold of one, while he himself sought the support of the other.

This arrangement appeared to offer itself tacitly to the Instinct of each; and, on arriving near the chest, they swam to opposite ends,—and each laid hold of a handle, as soon as he came within the proper distance to grasp it.

This kept the chest properly balanced; and although the weight they added to it caused it to sink several inches in the water, to their great joy its top still stood well above the surface. Even when the light form of Lilly Lalee lay resting along the lid, there were still several inches between the water line and its upper edge,—the only place where sea-water could possibly find admission into the kit of the English sailor.

Chapter Thirty Eight
Conjectures about the Catamaran

In less than three minutes after coming in contact with the kit, the three castaways formed a group, curious and peculiar. On the right of the chest was the sailor, his body stretched transversely along its end, with his left arm buried to the elbow in the sennit loop forming its handle. Half of his weight being thus supported by the buoyant box, it was only necessary for him to keep his right arm in regular motion to sustain himself above the surface. This, even wearied as he was, he was enabled to accomplish without difficulty: for the new position was one rather of rest than of labour.

At the opposite end of the chest, in a *pose* precisely similar, the sea-cook had placed himself, — the only difference being in the uses respectively made of their arms. Snowball's right arm was the one thrust through the handle, his left being left free for swimming.

As already hinted, Lilly Lalee had been transferred from Snowball's shoulder to a more elevated position, — upon the top of the chest where, lying upon her breast, and grasping the projecting edge of the lid, she was enabled to keep her place without any exertion.

It is not necessary to say that this change in the situation and circumstances of the party had also produced a change in their prospects. It is true that death might have appeared as inevitable as ever. They were still at its door, — though not quite so near entering as they had been but a few minutes before. With the help of the capacious chest — forming, as it did, a famous life-preserver — they might now sustain themselves for many hours above the surface, — in fact, as long as hunger and thirst would allow them. Their holding out would be simply a question of strength; and had they been only assured of a supply of food and drink, they might have looked forward to a long voyage performed in this singular fashion: that is, provided the sea around them should keep clear of storms and sharks.

Alas! the approach of one or the other of these perils was a contingency to be looked for at any moment, and to be dreaded accordingly.

Just at that moment they were not thinking of either, nor even of the probability of perishing by hunger or its kindred appetite, — thirst. The singular coincidence that the chest should come floating that way, just when they were on the point of perishing, had produced a remarkable effect on the minds both of the sailor and the sea-cook, begetting not positive conviction, but a pleasant presentiment that there might be other and more permanent succour in store for them; and that, after all, they were not destined to die by drowning,—at least not just then Hope,—sweet, soothing hope!—had again sprung up in the bosom of both; and, along with it the determination to make a further effort for the saving of their lives. They could now exchange both speech and counsel with perfect freedom; and they proceeded to discuss the situation.

The presence of the chest required explanation. The theory, which at first sight of it had suggested itself to its owner (that the raft had gone to pieces and that the kit was one of the scattered fragments) was not tenable, nor was it entertained for a moment. There had been no convulsion, either of winds or waves, to destroy the *Catamaran*; and this curiously-fashioned fabric, in all its fantastic outlines, must still be intact and afloat somewhere upon the surface of the sea.

It is true they could see nothing of it anywhere; neither could Lilly Lalee, who, from her more elevated position, was instructed to survey the circle of the horizon,—a duty which the child performed with the greatest care.

If the craft had been anywhere within the distance of a league or two, the large lateen sail should have been sufficiently conspicuous to have caught the eye of the girl. But she saw it not. She saw nothing,—so ran her report,—but the sea and sky.

From this it might have been inferred (even supposing the *Catamaran* to be still afloat) that it must have drifted to such a distance as to have destroyed all chance of their ever overtaking it. But the sage seaman did not give way to this form of reasoning. His conjectures were of a more consolatory character,—founded upon certain data which had presented themselves to his mind. On reflection, he came to the conclusion that the presence of the sea-chest upon the bosom of the blue water was no accidental circumstance, but a design,—the design of little William.

"I be sure o't, Snowy," said he; "the lad ha' chucked the kit overboard, knowin' as how we mout overhaul it, when we could not come up wi' the *Catamaran*. The chest war amidships, when I parted from it. It couldn't a' got into the water o' itself no-howsomever; besides, it war full o' heavy things, and now I'm sartin it be empty,—else how do it float so? Sure he must a' whammelled it upside down, and spilled out the things afore he pitched it overboard. It was thoughtful o' him; but he be just the one for that. I've seed him do some'at similar afore. Only think o' the dear boy!"

And Ben, after this burst of enthusiasm, for a moment indulged his admiration in silence.

"Dat's all berry likely,—berry likely," was the rejoinder of the Coromantee.

"I know what he did next," said Ben, continuing the thread of his conjectures.

"Wha' you tink, Massa Brace?"

"He tuk in sail. I don't know why he didn't do it sooner; for I called to him to do that, an' he must ha' heerd me. I've jest got a idea that the fault was not his'n. When I hauled up that bit o' canvas, I've a sort o' recollection o' puttin' a ugly knot on the haulyards. Maybe he warn't able, wi' his little bits o' digits, to get the snarl clear, as fast as mout a' been wished; an' that'll explain the whole thing. Sartin he got down the sail at last,—eyther by loosin' the belay, or cuttin' the piece o' rope, and that's why there be no canvas in sight. For all that, the *Catamaran* can't be so fur off. She hadn't had time to a' drifted to such a great distance,—'specially if the sail were got down the time as we missed it."

"Dat am true. I miss de sail all ob a sudden,—jess as if it had come down, yard an' all, straight slap bang."

"Well, then, Snowy," continued the sailor, in a tone of increased cheerfulness, "if't be as we conjecture, the craft ain't far ahead o' us yet. Maybe only a knot or two; for one can't see far over the water who happens to be neck-deep under it as we be. In any case she be sure to be lying to leuart o' us; and, without the sail, she won't drift faster than we can swim, nor yet so fast. Let us do the best we can to make a mile or two's leeway; an' then we'll know whether the old Cat's still crawling about, or whether she's gin us the slip altogether. That's the best thing we can do,—ain't it?"

"De berry bess, Massa Brace. We can't do nuffin' better dan swim down de wind."

Without further parley, the two set themselves to the task thus proposed; and one striking with his right hand, the other with his left,—both buffeting the waves with equal vigour and resolution,—they were soon sweeping onward with a velocity that caused the sea to surge along the sides of the chest, until the froth rose to the fingers of Lilly Lalee as she lay grasping its lid!

Chapter Thirty Nine
Down the Wind

They had not proceeded very far, when a cry from the girl caused them to suspend their exertions. While the others were occupied in propelling the chest, Lalee, kneeling upon the lid, had been keeping a lookout ahead. Something she saw had elicited that cry, which was uttered in a tone that betokened, if not joy, at least some sort of gratification.

"Wha is it, Lilly Lally?" interrogated the black, with an air of eagerness; "you see someting. Golly! am it de *Cat'maran*?"

"No,—it is not that. It's only a barrel floating on the water."

"Only a ba'l,—what sort o' a ba'l you tink 'im?"

"I think it's one of the empty water-casks we had tied to the raft. I'm sure it is: for I see ropes upon it."

"It is," echoed Ben, who, having poised himself aloft, had also caught sight of the cask. "Shiver my timbers! it do look like as if the Cat had come to pieces. But no! Tain't that has set the cask adrift. I set it all now. Little Will'm be at the bottom o' this too. He has cut away the lashin's o' the barrel, so as to gie us one more chance, in the case o' our not comin' across the chest. How thoughtful o' the lad! Just like 'im, as I said it war!"

"We bess swim for de cask an' take 'im in tow," suggested the sea-cook; "no harm hab 'im 'longside too. If de wind 'pring up, de ole chess be no use much. De cask de berry ting den."

"You're right, Snowy! we musn't leave the cask behind us. If the kit have served us a good turn, the other 'ud be safer in a rough sea. It be dead ahead, so we may keep straight on."

In five minutes after, they were alongside the cask,—easily recognised by its rope lashings, as one of those they had left attached to the raft. The sailor at the first glance saw that some of the chords encircling it had been cut with a knife, or other sharp instrument,—not severed with any degree of exactitude, but "haggled," as if the act had been hurriedly performed.

"Little Will'm again! He's cut the ropes wi' the old axe, an' it were blunt enough to make a job for him! Huzza for the noble lad!"

"Tay!" cried Snowball, not heeding the enthusiastic outburst of the sailor. "You hold on to de chess, Massa Brace, while I climb up on de cask, and see what I can see. May be I may see de *Catamaran* herseff now."

"All right, nigger. You had better do that. Mount the barrel, an' I'll keep a tight hold o' the kit."

Snowball, releasing his arm from the sennit loop, swam up to the floating cask; and, after some dodging about, succeeded in getting astride of it.

It required a good deal of dexterous manoeuvring to keep the cask from rolling, and pitching him back into the water. But Snowball was just the man to excel in this sort of aquatic gymnastics; and after a time he became balanced in his seat with sufficient steadiness to admit of his taking a fair survey of the ocean around him.

The sailor had watched his movements with a sage yet hopeful eye: for these repeated indications of both the presence and providence of his own *protégé* had almost convinced him that the latter would not be very distant from the spot. It was nothing more than he had prepared himself to expect, when the Coromantee, almost as soon as he had steadied himself astride of the water-cask, shouted, in a loud voice—

"The *Cat'maran*!—the *Cat'maran*!"

"Where?" cried the sailor. "To leuart?"

"Dead in dat same direcshun."

"How fur, cookey? how fur?"

"Not so fur as you might hear de bos'n's whissel; not more dan tree, four length ob a man-o'-war cable."

"Enough, Snowy! What do you think best to be done?"

"De bess ting we can do now," replied the negro, "am for me to obertake dat ere craff. As you said, de sail am down; an' de ole Cat no go fasser dan a log o' 'hogany wood in a calm o' de tropic. If dis child swim affer, he soon come up; and den wif de oar an' de help ob lilly Willy, he meet you more dan half-way,—dat fo' sartin."

"You think you can overtake her, Snowball?"

"I be sartin ob dat ere. You tay here wif Lilly Lally. Keep by de chess and de cask boaf,—for de latter am better dan de former. No fear, I soon bring de *Cat'maran* long dis way, once I get 'board o' her."

So saying, the negro gave the cask a "cant" to one side, slipped off into the water; and, with a final caution to his comrade to keep close to the spot where they were parting, he stretched out his muscular arms to their full extent, and commenced surging through the water,—snorting as he went like some huge cetacean of the tribe of the *Mysticeti*.

Chapter Forty
Launching the Life-Preserver

It is scarce necessary to say that, during all this time. Little William, on board the *Catamaran*, was half wild with anxious thoughts. He had obeyed the first instructions shouted to him by Ben Brace, and taken to the steering-oar; but, after struggling for some time to get the craft round, and seeing that his efforts were of no avail, he dropped it to comply with the still later orders given by the sailor: to let loose the halliards and lower the sail. Ben had wondered, and with a slight feeling of chagrin, why this last order had not been executed,—at least more promptly,—for at a later period he knew the sail had been lowered; but Ben was of course ignorant of the cause of the delay.

His conjecture, however, afterwards expressed, when he half-remembered having put "a ugly knot on the haulyards"; which he, little William, "maybe warn't able to get clear as fast as mout a been wished," was perfectly correct; as was also the additional hypothesis that the sail had been got down at last, "either by loosin' the belay or cuttin' the piece o' rope."

The latter was in reality the mode by which the sailor-lad had succeeded in lowering the sail.

As Ben had conjectured, the belaying loop had proved too much for the strength of William's fingers; and, after several fruitless efforts to untie the knot, he had at length given it up, and, seizing the axe, had severed the halliard by cutting it through and through.

Of course the sail came down upon the instant; but it was then too late; and when William again looked out over the ocean, he saw only the ocean itself, with neither spot nor speck to break the uniformity of its boundless bosom of blue.

In that glance he perceived that he was alone,—he felt for the first time that he was alone upon the ocean!

The thought was sufficient to beget despair, — to paralyse him against all further action; and, had he been a boy of the ordinary stamp, such might have been the result. But he was not one of this kind. The spirit which had first impelled him to seek adventure by sea, proved a mind moulded for enterprise and action. It was not the sort of spirit to yield easily to despair; nor did it then.

Instead of resigning himself up to fate or chance, he continued to exert the powers both of his mind and body, in the hope that something might still be done to retrieve the misfortune which had befallen the crew of the *Catamaran*. He again returned to the steering-oar; and, hastily detaching it from the hook upon which it had been mounted as a rudder, he commenced using it as a paddle, and endeavoured to propel the raft against the wind.

It is scarce necessary to say that he employed all his strength in the effort; but, notwithstanding this, he soon became convinced that he was employing it in vain. The huge *Catamaran* lay just as Snowball had characteristically described her, — "like a log o' 'hogany wood in a calm ob de tropic."

Even worse than this; for, paddle as he would, the sailor-lad soon perceived that the raft, instead of making way against the wind, or even holding its ground, still continued to drift rapidly to leeward.

At this crisis another idea occurred to him. It might have occurred sooner, had his mind not been monopolised with the hope of being able to row the raft to windward. Failing in this, however, his next idea was to throw something overboard, — something that might afford a support to the swimmers struggling in the water.

The first object that came under his eyes promising such rapport was the sea-kit of the sailor. As already stated, it was amidships, — where its owner had been exploring it. The lid was open, and little William perceived that it was wellnigh empty; since its contents could be seen scattered on all sides, just as the sailor had rummaged them out, forming a *paraphernalia* of sufficient variety and extent to have furnished the forecastle of a frigate.

The sight of the chest, with its painted canvas covering, which Little William knew to be water-tight, was suggestive. With the lid locked down, it might act as a buoy, and serve for a life-preserver. At all events, no better appeared to offer itself; and, without further hesitation, the lad slammed down the lid, which fortunately had the trick of locking itself with a spring, and, seizing the chest by one of the sennit handles, he dragged it to the edge of the raft, gave it a final push, and launched it overboard into the blue water of the ocean.

Little William was pleased to see that the kit, even while in the water, maintained its proper position,—that is, it swam bottom downwards. It floated buoyantly, moreover, as if it had been made of cork. He was prepared for this; for he remembered having listened to a conversation in the forecastle of the *Pandora*, relating to this very chest, in which Ben Brace had taken the principal part, and in which the sea-going qualities of his kit had been freely and proudly commented upon. William remembered how the *ci-devant* man-o'-war's-man had boasted of his *craft*, as he called the kit, proclaiming it "a reg'lar life-buoy in case o' bein' cast away at sea," and declaring that, "if 't war emp'y,—as he hoped it never should be,—it would float the whole crew o' a pinnace or longboat."

It was partly through this reminiscence that the idea of launching the chest had occurred to little William; and, as he saw it receding from the stern of the *Catamaran*, he had some happiness in the hope, that the confidence of his companion and protector might not be misplaced; but that the vaunted kit might prove the preserver, not only of *his* life, but of the life of one who to little William was now *even* dearer than Ben Brace. That one was Lilly Lalee.

Chapter Forty One
A Lookout from Aloft

After launching the kit, little William did not think of surrendering himself to inaction. He bethought him that something more should be done,—that some other *waifs* should be turned adrift from the *Catamaran*, which, by getting into the way of the swimmers, might offer them an additional chance of support.

What next? A plank? No; a cask,—one of the empty water-casks? That would be the thing,—the thing itself.

No sooner thought of than one was detached. The lashings were cut with the axe, in default of his finding a knife; and the cask, like the kit, soon fell into the wake. Not very rapidly it was true; for the *Catamaran* now, deprived of her sail, did not drift so fast to leeward as formerly. Still she went faster than either the kit or the cask, however; on account of the breeze acting upon her stout mast and some other objects that stood high upon her deck; and William very reasonably supposed that to swimmers so much exhausted,—as by that time must be both Ben and Snowball,—even the difference of a cable's length might be of vital importance.

It occurred to him also, that the greater the number of waifs sent in their way, the better would be their chance of seeing and getting hold of one of them. Instead of desisting therefore, as soon as he had detached the first cask, he commenced cutting loose a second, and committing it to the sea in like manner.

Having freed a second, he continued on to a third, and then a fourth, and was actually about to sever the lashings of a fifth one, with the intention to leave only the sixth one—that which contained the stock of precious water—attached to the *Catamaran*. He knew that the raft would still float, without any of the casks to buoy it up; and it was not any fear on that score that caused him to desist, when about to give the cut to the cords that confined cask Number 5. It was an observation which he had made of an entirely different nature; and this was, that the third cask when set loose, and more especially the fourth, instead of falling into the wake of the *Catamaran*, kept close by her side, as if loath to part company with a craft to which they had been so intimately attached.

William wondered at this, but only for a short moment. He was not slow in comprehending the cause of the unexpected phenomenon. The raft, no longer buoyed up, had sunk almost to the level of the surface; and the breeze now failed to impel it any faster than the casks themselves: so that both casks and *Catamaran* were making leeway at a like rate of speed, or rather with equal slowness.

Though the sailor-lad was dissatisfied on first perceiving this, after a moment's reflection, he saw that it was a favourable circumstance. Of course, it was not that the casks were making *more* way to leeward, but that the *Catamaran* was making *less*; and, therefore, if there was a chance of the swimmers coming up with the former, there was an equal probability of their overtaking the latter,—which would be better in every way. Indeed, the raft was now going at such a rate, that the slowest swimmer might easily overtake her, provided the distance between them was not too great.

It was this last thought that now occupied the mind of little William, and rendered him anxious. Had the swimmers fallen too far into the wake? Or would they still be able to swim on to the raft?

Where were they at that moment? He looked aft, towards the point from which he supposed himself to have been drifting. He was not sure of the direction; for the rude construction on which he stood had kept constantly whirling in the water,—now the stem, now the quarters, anon the bows, or beam-ends turned towards the breeze. He looked, but saw nothing. Only the sea-kit that by this time had got several hundred fathoms to windward, cask Number 1 a little nearer, and Number 2 still nearer. These, however, strung out in a line, enabled him to conjecture the direction in which the swimmers, if still above water, should be found.

Indeed, it was something more definite than a conjecture. Rather was it a certainty. He knew that the raft could not have made way otherwise than *down the wind*; and that those who belonged to it could not be elsewhere than to windward.

Guided, therefore, by the breeze, he gazed in this direction,—sweeping with his eye an arc of the horizon sufficiently large to allow for any deviation which the swimmers might have made from the true track.

He gazed in vain. The kit, the casks, a gull or two, soaring on snowy wings, were all the objects that broke the monotony of the blue water to windward.

He glided across the low-lying planks of the raft, and up to the empty cask still attached, which offered the highest point for observation. He balanced himself on its top, and once more scanned the sea to windward.

Nothing in sight, save kit, casks, and gulls lazily plying their long scimitar-shaped wings with easy unconcern, as if the limitless ocean was,—what in reality it was,—their habitat and home.

Suffering the torture of disappointment,—each moment increasing in agony,—little William leaped down from the cask; and, rushing amidships, commenced mounting the mast.

In a few seconds he had swarmed to its top: and, there clinging, once more directed his glance over the water. He gazed long without discovering any trace of his missing companions,—so long that his sinews were tried to the utmost; and the muscles both of his arms and limbs becoming relaxed, he was compelled to let go, and slide down despairingly upon the planks forming the deck of the *Catamaran*.

He stayed below only long enough to recover strength; and then a second time went swarming up the stick. If kit and casks should serve no better purpose, they at least guided him as to the direction; and looking over both, he scanned the sea beyond.

The gulls guided him still better; for both—there was a brace of them—had now descended near to the surface of the sea; and, wheeling in short flights, seemed to occupy themselves with some object in the water below. Though they were at a great distance off, he could hear an occasional scream proceeding from their throats: as if the object attracting them excited either their curiosity or some passion of a more turbulent character.

Their evolutions,—constantly returning towards a centre,—guided the eye of the observer until it rested on an object just visible above the sheen of the water. The colour of this object rendered it the more easy of being distinguished amidst the blue water that surrounded it; for it was blacker than anything which the sea produces,—unless it were the bone of the giant *Mysticetus*. Its shape, too—almost a perfect sphere—had something to do in its identification: for William was able to identify it, and by a process of negative reasoning. It was not the black albatross, the frigate-bird, nor the booby. Though of like colour, there was no bird of such form as that. There was neither beast nor fish belonging to the sea that could show such a shape above its surface. That sable globe, rounded like a sea-hedgehog, or a Turk's-head clew, and black as a tarred tackle-block, could be nothing else than the woolly pate of Snowball, the sea-cook!

A little beyond were two other objects of dark colour and founded shape; but neither so dark nor so round as that already identified. They must be the heads of the English sailor and Lilly Lalee. They appeared to be equally objects of attraction to the gulls, that alternately flew from one to the other, or kept hovering above them,—and continuously uttering their shrill, wild screams,—now more distinctly heard by little William, clinging high up on the mast of the *Catamaran*.

Chapter Forty Two
Once more aboard

The sailor-lad did not remain longer on the top of the mast than just to satisfy himself that what he saw were his companions, still afloat and alive. They were not at such a distance neither as to render it altogether impossible for them to recover their lost way; and, stimulated by this hope, little William determined upon continuing his efforts to assist them.

Gliding back upon the planks of the raft, he laid hold of the detached oar; and once more plying it as a paddle, he endeavoured to propel the *Catamaran* up the wind.

It is true he made but slight progress in this direction but he had the satisfaction of knowing that the craft held her ground, and something more; as he could tell from the fact of the casks last set loose by him, falling a little to leeward. This showed that he must himself be making way to the windward.

The sea-chest and the cask first loosed from its lashings, had been launched long before any of the others,—for it was only after an interval of reflection that he had set free the rest,—and the former were now far to windward. When looking from the masthead he had noted that the position of the swimmers was not so far beyond the kit; and it was scarce possible at that time, that they could have failed to discover it. Without staying to consider whether they had done so or not, William had come down from his perch; and now that he had reapplied himself to the oar, and saw that he was gaining ground in the right direction, he did not like to desist. Every fathom he made to windward was a fathom nearer to the saving of the lives of his companions,—a stroke less for the swimmers to make,—to whom, wearied as they must now be, the saving of even a single stroke might be an object.

With this thought urging him to perseverance, the sailor-lad stuck to his oar, wielding it with all the strength in his arms, and only thinking of the one purpose,—to make way against the wind. Fortunately the breeze, already gentle, seemed each moment to grow gentler, —as if unwilling to oppose his efforts in the cause of humanity; and little William perceived, to his great gratification, that the casks already passed by the *Catamaran* were falling far into her wake. This proved that he must be gaining upon the others.

All at once a glad sight came suddenly under his eyes. Earnestly occupied with the oar, he had permitted more than a minute to elapse without casting a glance ahead. When at length he renewed his lookout to windward, he was surprised to see, not only the cask and the sea-chest still nearer but on the top of the latter, a something that was not there before. Something that lay along the lid, with arms stretched downwards, and hands clutching its projecting edges. He also perceived two dark rounded objects in the water, —one near each end of the chest, —one rounder and blacker than the other, but both easily distinguishable as the heads of human beings.

The singular tableau was at once understood. Lilly Lalee was on the top of the sea-kit; Snowball and Ben Brace were flanking it, one at each end. The chest was supporting all three. Hurrah! they were saved!

Little William, at that moment, felt certain they would be saved; though that joyful certainty had not yet been communicated to them. Standing erect upon an elevated part of the raft, the boy had the advantage of them, and could note every movement they were making, without being seen by them.

He did not spend much time in merely looking at them. He knew that that would be of no avail; and after giving utterance to one or two joyous ejaculations, he returned to the oar, if possible plying it with greater energy than ever, from the renewed encouragement which he now derived from the confidence of success.

When he turned again and stood upright, looking to windward, the tableau had changed. Lilly Lalee was still lying along the lid of the chest, but only one head was seen in the water! It was that of the sailor, as the white face and the long flowing hair told him.

Where was the cranium of the sea-cook? Where was the skull of Snowball? Gone with his body to the bottom?

These interrogatories flashed across the brain of the lad, causing him a feeling of alarm. It was of short continuance, however. In the next moment they were answered, and to his satisfaction. The Coromantee was seen astride of the cask, more conspicuous than ever: only, being now in a slightly different direction, he had not been seen at the first glance.

Without shouting, or making any other idle demonstration, the intelligent youth once more applied himself to the oars, and vigorously propelled the raft to windward.

He did not again desist, until a voice falling upon his ear and, pronouncing his name, caused him to look once more in the direction of the swimmers.

Then, instead of seeing the Coromantee astride of the cask, he perceived the round black physiognomy of that individual above the surface of the water, and scarce a cable's length from the *Catamaran*!

A double line of frothy ripple proceeding from each of his large spread ears, and running rapidly into his wake, indicated the direction in which he was swimming,—towards the raft,—while his eyeballs showing fearfully, and white as the froth itself,—the spluttering and blowing that proceeded from his thick lips, and the agitation of the sea around him,—all told that he was doing his very best to come up with the *Catamaran*.

"Golly!" he gasped out, on perceiving himself within safe distance of being heard. "Row dis way, lilly Willy! Row like de debbil, good lad! I'se most done up,—dat I be. In de space ob anoder cable length dis chile he muss a gub up!"

And ending his speech with a loud "Whugh," partly to clear the water from his throat, and partly to express the satisfaction he felt at the near prospect of deliverance, he continued to strike on towards the raft.

In a few seconds more the long-protracted struggle was brought to a termination. Snowball succeeded in reaching the raft, and, assisted by the sailor-lad, clambered aboard.

Only staying to catch a little breath, the negro laid hold of the second oar; and the *Catamaran*, under the double stroke, was soon brought *en rapport* with the sea-chest; when the remainder of the crew were restored to her decks, and delivered from a death that but a short time before had framed so certain as to be inevitable.

Chapter Forty Three
Refitting the Raft

On once more setting foot on the deck of the *Catamaran* the strong sailor was so thoroughly exhausted that he was unable to stand erect, and after scrambling aboard, and staggering a pace or two, he lay down along the planks. Lilly Lalee was taken care of by little William; who, half-leading, half-lifting her in his arms, tenderly placed her upon some pieces of canvas near the foot of the mast.

For this service, so fondly yet delicately performed, the boy felt himself amply rewarded by the glance of gratitude that shone in the eyes of the child,—even without the thanks faintly murmured by her on perceiving she was safe.

Snowball, equally exhausted, dropped into a recumbent position. All three remained silent for a considerable length of time, and without stirring either hand or foot,—as though to speak or move in their state of extreme weariness was impossible.

Little William, however, did not resign himself to inaction. As soon as he had disposed of Lalee, he made direct to that corner of the *Catamaran* where a small barrel or keg, half submerged under the water, was attached to one of the timbers of the craft. It was the keg containing the precious "Canary."

Carefully extracting the bung,—which, in the lashing of the keg, had been purposely kept upwards,—he inserted a dipper,—that is to say, a small tin vessel, or drinking "taut,"—which had turned up among the stores of the sea-kit, and which, having been already used for the same purpose, was provided with a piece of cord attached around its rim, like the vessel in use among the gaugers or wine-merchants for drawing their wine from the wood. This was hoisted out again, filled with the sweet fluid which the keg contained; and which was at once administered,—first to Lilly Lalee, then to William's own especial protector, Ben Brace; and lastly, after a fresh draw from the keg, to the real owner of the wine,—the Coromantee. The spirit of the grape, grown upon the declivities of Teneriffe, acted like magic on all three; and in a few minutes both sailor and sea-cook were sufficiently restored to think about taking certain prudent measures, that had now become necessary, and that would require a fresh exertion of their strength.

These measures were the recovery of the empty casks which William had detached from the *Catamaran*; and for the want of which that improvised craft not only lay much lower in the water than when they had left her, but was altogether a less seaworthy structure.

The sailor's chest,—for which its owner now felt increased affection,— was the first thing secured; and next the cask upon which Snowball had bestraddled himself to get a better view. Both were near, and easily reached by a little rowing.

The other three casks had drifted to a considerable distance to leeward, and were still continuing their course; but as all three were in sight, the crew of the *Catamaran* anticipated no great difficulty in overtaking them.

Nor did any occur. A pair of oars handled by the sailor and sea-cook, with the sailor-boy standing up to direct the course in which they should pull, soon brought the raft down upon the straying hogsheads; and they were picked up one after the other, the severed ropes respliced, and all of them set back in their old positions,—so that but for the wet garments clinging around the bodies of those who had been overboard, and perhaps the pale and wearied expression upon their countenances, no one could have told that anything had gone wrong on board the *Catamaran*.

As to their wet clothes, none of them cared much for that; and if there had been any discomfort in it, it was not likely to continue long under the hot sun then shining down upon them. So rapidly was this part of the damage becoming repaired that all three,—but more especially Snowball— were now surrounded by a cloud of evaporation that would soon dry every stitch of clothing they had on.

The negro,—partly from the natural heat proceeding from his own body, and partly from the strong sunbeams,—was smoking like a fresh kindled pit of charcoal: so that, through the strata of steam that encompassed his head and shoulders, it would have been impossible to tell whether he was black or white. In the midst of this Juno-like *nimbus* however, the negro continued to talk and act, helping the sailor and little William, until not only were the water-casks restored to their proper places, but the sail was hauled up to the mast, and the *Catamaran* once more scudding before the breeze, as if not the slightest accident had occurred either to craft or crew.

Care was taken, however, this time to make fast the halliard rope with a proper "belay"; and although Snowball might have deserved a caution to be more vigilant for the future, it was not deemed necessary to administer it, as it was thought the peril out of which they had so miraculously escaped would prove to him a sufficient reminder.

There was but one misfortune arising out of the adventure that might have caused the crew of the *Catamaran* any serious regret. This was the loss of a large portion of their stock of provisions,—consisting of the dried fish,—partly those that had been half cured by Snowball previous to the union of the two rafts, and partly the flitches of shark-meat, that had been taken from the lesser raft, and added to Snowball's store.

These, with the object of having them thoroughly dried, had been exposed to the sun, on the tops of the water-casks which little William had let loose. In the hurry and excitement of the moment, it was not likely the lad should give a thought to the flitches of fish. Nor did he; and while freeing the water-casks from their fastenings, and pushing them off from the raft, the pieces were all permitted to slide off into the water, and either swim or go to the bottom, as their specific gravity might dictate. The consequence was, that, when everything else was recovered, these were lost,—having actually gone to the bottom, or floated out of sight; or, what was more probable than either, having been picked up by the numerous predatory birds hovering in the heavens above, or the equally voracious fish quartering the depths of the ocean underneath.

It was not without some chagrin that Snowball contemplated his reduced stores,—a chagrin in which his companions could equally participate. At the time, however, they felt the misfortune less bitterly than they might otherwise have done,—their spirits being buoyed up by the miraculous escape they had just made, as well as by a hope that the larder so spent might be replenished, and by a process similar to that by which it had been originally stocked.

Chapter Forty Four
The Albacores

The hope of replenishing their larder was likely to be realised easily, and ere long. Scarce had their sail caught the breeze, when they perceived alongside the *Catamaran* a shoal of the most beautiful fish that are to be found in any part of the boundless ocean. There were several hundreds in the shoal; like mackerel, all nearly of one size, and swimming, moreover in the same direction,—just as a school of mackerel are seen to do.

They were much larger, however, than the common mackerel,—each being about four feet in length, with a stout, though well-proportioned body, having that peculiar elegance of shape which belongs to all the mackerel tribe.

Their colour was sufficient of itself to entitle them to the appellation of beautiful creatures. It was a bright turquoise blue or azure, showing, in certain lights, a tinge of gold. This was the colour of their backs; while underneath they were of a silvery white, gleaming with a lively iridescence. A row of spurious fins above the tail, and another underneath, were of a bright yellow; while their large round eyes exhibited an iris of silver.

Their pectoral fins were very long and sickle-shaped; while the dorsal one, also well developed, presented a structural peculiarity in having a deep groove running longitudinally down the spine of the back, into which the fin,—when at rest and depressed,—exactly fitted: becoming so completely sheathed and concealed, as to give to the fish the appearance of being without this apparatus altogether!

If we except their lovely hues, their greater size, and a few other less notable circumstances, the fishes in question might have been taken for mackerel; and it would have been no great mistake to so describe them: since they were in reality of this genus. They were of a different species, however,—the most beautiful species of the mackerel tribe.

"Albacore!" cried Ben Brace, as soon as he saw them shooting alongside the raft. "Albacore be they. Now, Snowy, out wi' your hooks an' lines. In this fresh breeze they be a'most sure to bite; and we'll be able, I hope, to make up for the loss o' the others. Hush all o' ye! Ne'er a word; ne'er a movement to scare 'em off. Softly, Snowy! Softly, ye ole sea-cook."

"No fear, Massa Brace,—no fear o' dem leabin dis ole *Cat'maran*, so long's de be a-gwine on dat fashion. Looker dar! Fuss to one side, den de todder,—back and for'rad as ef de cudn't be content nowha."

While Snowball was speaking, and before he had commenced, the albacores had entered upon a peculiar movement. On first joining company with the *Catamaran*, they swam for a time alongside,—the starboard side,— keeping pace with the raft, and evidently making no exertion to go ahead of her, as they might easily have done. On the contrary, they scarce moved their fins; but floated slowly along at the exact rate of speed at which the craft was sailing, and not one bit faster. As they swam parallel to the raft, and also parallel to each other, one might have fancied them all joined together by some invisible link, that kept them from changing their relative positions both to the *Catamaran* and to one another!

All at once, however, and quick as the change of a kaleidoscope, this parallelism was terminated,—not as regarded each other, but with respect to the course of the *Catamaran* By a single flutter of their tails, the whole *school* was seen simultaneously turning head towards the craft; and then, like a flash of lightning, they passed underneath.

For a moment they were out of sight; but in the next they appeared on the starboard beam, swimming parallel as before, both to the course of the *Catamaran* and to each other. The manoeuvre was executed with such precision and uniformity, as could not be imitated among men,—even under the tuition of the ablest drill-sergeant that ever existed. They swerved from right to left, as if each and all were actuated by the same impulse, and at the same instant of time. At the same instant their tails made a movement in the water,—at precisely the same point of time they turned together,— showing a list of its silvery abdomen, and with like simultaneous action did they dive under the keel of the *Catamaran*.

It was this peculiar manoeuvre on the part of the fish,—won after repeated by their shooting back to the starboard, and again returning to larboard,—that had elicited from Snowball the assertion, so confidently put forward, that there was no fear of their leaving the *Catamaran* so long as they were going in that fashion.

Of those upon the raft, Ben Brace alone comprehended Snowball's meaning. To little William it was a matter of some surprise when the ex-sea-cook spoke so confidently, and acted, moreover, as if he had no fear of frightening the shy-looking creatures that were swimming alongside.

"Why, Snowy?" asked the lad,—"why is there no fear of their being scared off?"

"Kase, lilly Willy, I hab de idea dar be something else not far off, dat dem albacore am more feerd on dan we. I no see dat someting yet. We sure see de *long snout*, by 'm by."

"The long snout!—what do you mean by that, Snowy?"

"Wha do a mean?—de long-nose a mean. Tole ye so! dar he be yonner,— right on de la'bord quarter. Dis nigger knew he no far off. Da's why de beauties hab come roun de raff; an dat I hope keep um hyar till we hab cotch a few ob dem!"

"A shark!" cried the boy-sailor, catching a glance of some large fish at some distance out in the water on the larboard bow,—the direction in which Snowball had pointed.

"Shark! nuffin ob de kind," rejoined the negro; "diff'rent sort ob fish altogedder. If him wa shark, de albacore no stay hyar. Dey go up to him, and dart all 'bout im,—jess like de lilly birds when dey see big hawk or de vulture. No shark he,—dat ere skulkin' fella. He am massa long-nose,—de real enemy ob de albacore. No fear ob dem leabin' us, while he anywhar in sight."

Saying this the Coromantee proceeded to single out his hooks; and, assisted by Ben Brace, commenced baiting them with an unconcern that testified a full confidence in the truth of his assertion.

Chapter Forty Five
The Sword-Fish

Little William,—whose curiosity had become excited at the appearance of the strange fish,—stood looking over the larboard quarter, in hopes of getting a better view of it.

As yet, he had only obtained a slight glimpse of it: for the larboard quarter lay towards the south-west, and the sun, just then sinking down upon the sea, hindered him from having a fair opportunity to scan the surface in that particular direction.

Shading his eyes with the palm of his hand, he gazed for some time, but saw nothing,—either upon the surface or under it. Snowball, notwithstanding that he seemed wholly occupied with the hooks and lines, took notice of the reconnoissance of the sailor-lad.

"No use you look dat way, lilly Willy," said he. "Doan you see dat de abbacores are now on de larbord side. Wheneber dey am on de larbord, you look for long-nose on de starbord. Truss dem take care dey no get on de same side wit' dat ere fella."

"There, Will'm!" interposed Ben. "Look out that way! there he be,—right astern,—don't ye see?"

"I see, I see!" cried William. "O, look, Lalee! What in odd fish it is! I never saw one like it before."

This was true; for although the young sailor had already traversed many a long league of the Atlantic Ocean, he had not yet seen a fish of the same kind; and he might traverse hundreds of long leagues of any of the oceans without seeing the like again.

It was, in truth, one of the most singular denizens of the great deep that had thus come under the observation of the *Catamaran's* crew,—so peculiar in its appearance that, without the intervention of Ben Brace, who at that moment called out in name, the boy could have pronounced it for himself.

It was a fish of some eight or ten feet in length; with a long bony snout, projecting horizontally forward, at least one third of the length of its body. This snout was nothing more than a prolongation of the upper jaw,— perfectly straight, of osseous structure, and tapering towards the end like the blade of a rapier.

Otherwise the fish was not ill-formed; nor did it present that hideous aspect characteristic of the more predatory creatures that inhabit the ocean. For all that, there was a certain shyness combined with great swiftness in its motion,—a skulking in its attitudes: as Snowball's speech had already declared,—a truculent, trap-like expression in its quick watchful eyes, that told of an animal whose whole existence was passed in the pursuit of prey.

It was not to be wondered at that William should have mistaken the creature for a shark: for, in addition to the fact of the sun being in his eyes, there were points of similarity between the fish in question, and certain species of sharks, requiring a good view and an experienced observer to tell the difference. William perceived a large crescent shaped fin rising several inches above the surface of the water,—a tail lunated like that of the shark,—a hungry eye, and prowling attitude: the very characteristics of the dreaded tyrant of the deep.

There was one thing in which the creature in question differed materially from all the individuals of the *squalus* tribe. Instead of swimming slowly, it appeared to be one of the swiftest of fishes: for at each instant as the albacores changed their position from one side of the raft to the other, the long-snouted creature was seen to shoot to the same side with a velocity that almost baffled the sight to keep pace with it.

In fact, the eye could scarcely have traced its course, had it not been aided by two circumstances altogether strange and peculiar. The first was that the strange fish, while darting from point to point, caused a rushing sound in the water; like that produced by heavy rain falling upon the leaves of a forest. The second peculiarity was, that while thus progressing its hues became completely changed. Instead of the dull brown,—its colour when at rest,—its body presented a striated appearance,—a brindling of bright and dark blue,—sometimes heightened to a uniform azure!

It was not these peculiarities that had guided little William to the identification of the species; but the long, tapering snout, straight as a rapier, that projected in front of its body. This was a token not to be mistaken,—

never to be forgotten by one who had seen it before. And the young sailor had before seen such a one; not at sea, nor under the sea, but in a collection of "natural curiosities," that had by chance been carried through his native town; and whose inspection, perhaps, had much to do with that impulse that first caused him to "run away to sea." Under a glass-case he had examined that piece of osseous structure, described by the showman as the sword of the *sword-fish*. Under the waves of the tropical Atlantic,—but little less translucent than the glass,—he had no difficulty in identifying the formidable weapon!

Chapter Forty Six
The Swordsman of the Sea

While William was gazing upon the strange fish, it was seen all at once to make a rush in the direction of the raft. They could hear a "swishing" sound, as its huge body passed through the water, at the same time that its great scimitar-shaped dorsal fin, projecting above the surface, rapidly traced a rippling line through the whole of its course.

The dash was evidently directed against the shoal of albacore swimming alongside the *Catamaran*.

But these creatures were constantly on the alert. Although exhibiting every symptom of fright, they did not seem for an instant to lose their presence of mind; and as the sword-fish was seen rushing towards them, all turned as if by a common impulse, and, quick as lightning, passed to the other side of the raft.

The sword-fish, seeing himself foiled, checked the velocity of his charge with a suddenness that displayed his great natatory powers; and, instead of pursuing the albacores under the *Catamaran*, he continued to follow after the craft, in a sort of skulking, cowardly fashion, — as if he designed to use stratagem rather than strength in the capture of his prey.

It soon became evident to little William that the albacores had sought the companionship of the *Catamaran* less from the idea of obtaining any droppings there might be from her decks, than as a protection against their formidable pursuer, — the sword-fish. Indeed, this is most probably the reason why not only the albacores and their kindred the bonitos, but several other kinds of shoal-fish, attach themselves to ships, whales, and other large objects, that they may encounter floating or sailing upon the open ocean.

The mode in which the sword-fish makes his attack, — by rushing irresistibly upon his prey, and impaling it on his long, slender beak, — is full of risk to himself; for should his "sword" come in contact with the sides of a ship, or any substance of sufficient strength to withstand his impetuous "thrust," the chances are that the weapon either gets broken off altogether, or so embedded that the owner of it falls a victim to his rash voracity.

Under the excitement of fear, and occupied in watching the movements of their enemy, Snowball knew there was no chance of the albacores paying any attention to the hooks he had baited for them. Instead, therefore, of throwing them over the side, he permitted them to lie upon the planks, and waited until the sword-fish should either take his departure or fall far enough into the wake of the *Catamaran* to permit, on the part of the creatures swimming alongside, a temporary forgetfulness of his presence.

"It am no use trowin' dem de hook," said he, addressing himself to the sailor, "no use jess yet, so long de sharp snout am dar. We mus' wait till he go out ob dar sight an out ob dar hearin too."

"I suppose we must," rejoined Ben; "that be a pity too. They'd bite greedy enough, if the ugly thing warn't there. That I know, for I've seed 'em many's the time."

This was not the only bit of information concerning the albacore and their enemy communicated by the sailor to his companions on the raft, but more especially to his *protégé*, who, feeling a strange interest in those creatures, had asked several questions concerning them. During the interval, while they were waiting for some change in the tactics of the pursuer,—hoping that he might get ahead and abandon the pursuit,—Ben imparted to his audience several chapters of his experience,—in which either albacore or sword-fish, and sometimes both, had figured as the principal actors. Among others, he related an anecdote of a ship in which he had sailed having been pierced by the beak of a sword-fish.

At the time the incident occurred there was no one on board who had any suspicion of its nature. The crew were below at their dinner; when one of the sailors who chanced to be on deck heard a loud splashing in the water. On looking over the ship's side, and seeing a large body just sinking below the surface, the sailor supposed it to be some one of the crew who had gone over, and instantly raised the cry of "A man overboard!"

The crew were paraded; when it was ascertained that no one was missing. Though the sailors were at a loss to account for the singular appearance, the alarm soon subsided; and nothing more was thought of the matter. Shortly after, one of the men,—Ben Brace himself, it was,—chanced to ascend the rigging; and while aloft he perceived a rugged mass projecting from the side of the ship, just below the water line. On a boat being lowered and the thing examined, it proved to be the *rostrum* of a sword-fish, broken off from the animal's head. It was the body of the animal,—no doubt, killed by the concussion,—which the sailor had seen sinking in the water.

The "sword" had pierced completely through the copper sheathing and solid timbers of the larboard bow of the ship; and on the sailors going below, they found eight or ten inches of its top projecting into the inside, embedded among some coals contained in the hold!

Singular as the sailor's story might appear, it was not in the least an exaggeration. Snowball knew it was not: for the ex-sea-cook could have told of like experiences; and William was also satisfied of its truth, from having read the account of a similar incident, and heard that the evidences of it,—that is, a piece of the solid wood of the ship's timbers, with the sword imbedded in it,—were to be seen at any time in the British Museum.

Just as Ben had finished his curious relation, a movement upon the part of the pursuer told an intention of changing his tactics,—not as if he was about to retreat, but rather to assume a bolder attitude of offence. The sight of such a fine shoal of fat albacores,—so near and yet so long keeping clear of his attack, appeared to have tantalised him to a point beyond endurance; and, being extra hungry, perhaps he was determined to dine upon them, *coute qui coute*.

With this intent he drew nearer to the *Catamaran* swooping from quarter to quarter, then along the sides, and once or twice darting ahead, so as to create in the shoal a degree of excitement that might force them into irregularity of action.

This very effect he at length succeeded in producing; for the pretty creatures became more frightened than ever; and instead of swimming, as hitherto, in concert, and parallel to each other as they had been doing, they got huddled into a crowd, and commenced darting, pell-mell, in every direction.

In the midst of their confusion a large band became separated,—not only from the others, but from the *Catamaran*,—and fell several fathoms' length into the wake of the craft.

Upon these the hungry eyes of the prowling monster were now fixed; but only for a moment: for in the next he was charging down among them with a velocity that caused the water to spray upwards against his dorsal fin, while the rushing sound made by his body could be heard afar off over the ocean, "Look, Will'm!" cried Ben, anxious that his *protégé* should not miss seeing the curious spectacle. "Look, lad! yonder's a sight worth seein'. Shiver my timbers, if he han't got a brace o' 'em on his toastin' fork!"

While Ben was speaking, the sword-fish had charged into the middle of the frightened flock. There was a momentary plashing,—as several of the albacores leaped up out of the water and fell back again,—there was a surging and bubbling over a few yards of surface, which hindered a clearer view of what was passing; and then outside reappeared the sword-fish, with his long weapon projected above the water, and a brace of the beautiful albacores impaled upon its point!

The wretched creatures were struggling to free themselves from their painful position; but their struggles were not for long. They were terminated almost on the instant,—by the sword-fish giving a quick jerk of his head, and tossing, first one and then the other of his victims high into the air!

As they came down again, it was to fall, not upon the water, but into the throat of the voracious tyrant; who, although toothless and without any means of masticating, made shorter work of it by introducing them *untoothed*, and at a single gulp, into his capacious maw!

Chapter Forty Seven
Angling for Albacore

After a while the crew of the *Catamaran* watched the manoeuvres of the sword-fish with a degree of interest that almost caused them to forget their own forlorn situation. Little William and Lilly Lalee were especially delighted with the singular spectacle; and long after the sailor and Snowball had turned their attention to other and more necessary matters, the two stood side by side gazing out upon the ocean in the direction in which the sea-swordsman had been seen.

We say *had been* seen: for, after swallowing the brace of albacores, the voracious monster had suddenly disappeared, either by diving deep down into the sea, or shooting off to some distant point.

Little William and Lalee looked everywhere,—first astern, where the swordsman had made the display of his skill; then on both sides; and, finally, ahead. They looked in these different directions,—because, from what they had already seen of its natative powers, they knew that the great fish could pass in a few seconds through a hundred fathoms of water, and therefore was as likely to be on one side as the other.

On no side, however, could the fish be seen; and, although both the sailor-lad and Lalee would have been pleased to witness a little more of that same sword exercise, they were at length forced to the conclusion that the performance was over and the performer gone away,—perhaps, to exhibit his prowess in some other quarter of the aquatic world.

"Berry like,—berry like he gone way," said Snowball, in reply to the interrogatory of little William. "A good ting if dat am de fack; fo' den we hab chance to hook up some o' dese hya abbacore. See dem now! Doan' you see how berry different dey are behavin'. Dey no longer 'feerd. Dat am sign dat de long snout hab turn him nose in some oder direcshun. He gone fo' sartin."

Sure enough the *behaviour* of the albacores was very much altered, as Snowball had affirmed. Instead of flashing about from one side of the raft to the other, and exhibiting manifest symptoms of alarm, they now swam placidly alongside, at a regular rate of speed, just keeping up with the *Catamaran*.

They looked, moreover, as if they would now take the bait, which during the presence of the sword-fish they had obstinately refused to touch, though frequently flung, both by Snowball and the sailor, right under their snouts.

Both were again preparing to repeat their angling operations; and in a few seconds' time each had his hook ready, with a piece of shark-meat temptingly attached to it, the bait being rendered still more attractive from having a little shred of scarlet flannel looped around the shank of the hook, while several fathoms of stout sennit-cord served as trolling-lines.

Plash into the water went the two baited hooks, both at once; and, almost before the ripples caused by the plunge had ceased to circle upon the surface, a still louder plashing could be heard, and a much rougher ripple seen, — in short, a large space of the surface agitated into foam, where a brace of albacores were fluking and struggling on the respective hooks of Snowball and the sailor.

Right rapidly were they hauled aboard, and their struggles brought to a termination by a smart tap on the head administered to each in succession, by a handspike, which had suddenly found its way into the grasp of the sailor.

No time was thrown away in contemplating the captives, or triumphing over their capture. Little William and Lalee alone examined the two beautiful creatures thus brought within their reach; while Snowball and the sailor, rapidly readjusting the baits upon their hooks, that had been slightly disarranged by the teeth of the *tunnies*, — for the albacore is a species of tunny fish, — once more flung them forth.

This time the baits were not so greedily "grabbed" at. As if the "school" had become suspicious, they all for a considerable time fought shy of it; but, as it was trolled so temptingly under their very snouts, first one and then another began to make approach, — now nearer and nearer, one or two taking a nibble at it, and then dropping it again, and suddenly shying off, — as if they had discovered something unpleasant either in its taste or touch.

This delicate nibbling continued for several minutes when, at length, an albacore more courageous than its companions, or perhaps with an emptier stomach than the rest, at sight of the tempting morsel suddenly took leave of his discretion; and, darting forward, seized the bait upon Ben's hook, swallowing bait, hook, and several inches of the sennit-cord, at a single gulp!

There was no danger of its being able to detach itself from that hook. The barb was already fast in its entrails before Ben gave the jerk to secure it. Another jerk brought the fish out of its native element, landing it amidships on board the *Catamaran*, where, like its two predecessors, it was instantly knocked on the head.

Snowball continued to "troll" his line in the most approved fashion; and was soon again joined by his brother "piscator," who, after settling the scores with the second fish he had caught, had adjusted a fresh bait, and once more flung his line into the water.

For some reason or other, the albacores became suddenly shy,—not as if alarmed at the action of the anglers, but rather from having their attention attracted to some other object invisible to the eyes of those on the *Catamaran*. The fish were so near the raft, that every movement made by them could be easily observed,—even to the glancing of their silvery irides,—and those who observed them could see that they were looking aloft.

Up went the eyes of the *Catamarans*, both anglers and idlers turning their glances towards the sky. There was nothing to be seen there,—at least, nothing to account for the shyness of the fish, or the upward cast of their eyeballs. So thought three of the party,—little William, Lalee, and the sailor,—who beheld only the blue, cloudless canopy of the heavens.

Snowball, however, whose single experience of ocean-life was greater than the sum total of the other three twice told, did not, like the rest, desist all at once from his scrutiny of the sky, but remained gazing with upturned look for period of several minutes.

At the termination of that time, an exclamatory phrase, escaping from his lips, proclaimed the discovery of some object that, to his mind, accounted for the odd behaviour of the albacores.

"De frigate-bird!" was the phrase that came mutteringly from between Snowball's teeth. "Ya, ya,—dar am two ob dem,—de cock an' hen, I s'pose. Dat 'counts for de scariness of dese hya fish. Dat's what am doin' it."

"O, a frigate-bird!" said Ben Brace, recognising in Snowball's synonyme one of the most noted wanderers of the ocean,—the *Pelicanus aquila* of the naturalists, but which, from its swift flight and graceful form, is better known to mariners under the appellation given to it by Snowball.

"Where away?" interrogated the sailor. "I don't see bird o' any sort. Where away, Snowy?"

"Up yonner,—nearly straight ober head,—close by dat lilly 'peck ob cloud. Dar dey be, one on de one side, odder on fodder,—de ole cock an' de ole hen, I'se be boun'!"

"Your daylights be uncommon clear, nigger. I don't see ne'er a bird— Ah, now I do!—two of 'em, as you say. Ye're right, Snowy. Them be frigates to a sartainty. It's easy to tell the cut o' thar wings from any other bird as flops over the sea. Beside, there be no other I knows on as goes up to that height. Considerin' that thar wings be spread nigh a dozen feet, if not all o' that, and that they don't look bigger than barn-swallows, I reckon they must be mor'n a mile overhead o' us. Don't you think so, Snowy?"

"Mile, Massa Brace! Ya, dey am two mile 'bove us at de berry lees. Dey doan' 'peer to move an inch from dat same spot. Dar be no doubt dat boaf o' 'em am sound 'sleep."

"Asleep!" echoed little William, in a tone that betokened a large measure of astonishment. "You don't say, Snowball, that a bird can go to sleep upon the wing?"

"Whoo! lilly Willy, dat all you know 'bout de birds in dis hya part ob do worl'? Sleep on de wing! Sartin dey go 'sleep on de wing, an' some time wif de wing fold close to dar body, an' de head tuck under 'im,—don't dey, Mass' Brace?"

"I ain't sartin as to that," doubtingly answered the ex-man-o'-war's-man. "I've heerd so: but it *do* seem sort o' unnat'ral."

"Whoo!" rejoined Snowball, with a slightly derisive inclination of the head; "why for no seem nat'ral? De frigate herself she sleep on de water widout sails set,—not eben a stitch ob her canvas. Well, den: why no dem frigate-birds in de air? What de water am to de ship de air am to de birds. What hinder 'em to take dar nap up yonner, 'ceptin' when dar's a gale ob wind? Ob coos dat u'd interrup' dar repose."

"Well, nigger," rejoined the sailor, in a tone that betokened no very zealous partisanship for either side of the theory, "you may be right, or you may be wrong. I ar'n't goin' to gi'e you the lie, one way or t' other. All I know is, that I've seed frigates a-standing in the air, as them be now, making way neyther to windart or leuart; f'r all that I didn't believe they was asleep. I kud see thar forked tails openin' and closin' jist like the blades o' a pair o' shears; and that inclined me to think they war wide awake all the time. If they was asleep, how kud they a-kep waggin' thar tails? Though a bird's tail be but feathers, still it must ha' some feelin' in it."

"Law, Massa Ben!" retorted the negro, in a still more patronising tone, as if pitying the poverty of the sailor's syllogism, "you no tink it possible that one move in dar sleep? You nebber move you big toe, or you foot, or some time de whole ob you leg? Beside," continued the logician, passing to a fresh point of his argument, "how you s'pose de frigate-bird do 'idout sleep? You know berry well he not got de power to swim,—him feet only half web. He no more sit on de water dan a guinea-fowl, or a ole hen ob de dunghill. As for him go 'sleep on de sea, it no more possyble dan for you or me, Massa Ben."

"Well, Snowy," slowly responded the sailor, rather pushed for a reply, "I'm willin' to acknowledge all that. It look like the truth, an' it don't,—both at the same time. I can't understan' how a bird can go to sleep up in the air, no more'n I could hang my old tarpaulin' hat on the corner o' a cloud. Same time I acknowledge that I'm puzzled to make out how them thar frigates can take thar rest. The only explanation I can think o' is, that every night they fly back to the shore, an' turns in thar."

"Whoogh! Massa Brace, you knows better dan dat. I'se heerd say dat de frigate-bird nebber am seed more'n a hunder league from de shore. Dam! Dis nigga hab seed dat same ole cock five time dat distance from land,—in de middle ob de wide Atlantic, whar we sees 'um now. Wish it was true he nebber 'tray more dan hunder knots from de land; we might hab some chance reach it den. Hunder league! Golly! more'n twice dat length we am from land; and dere 's dem long-wing birds hov'rin' 'bove our heads, an sleepin' as tranquil as ebber dis nigga did in de caboose ob de ole *Pandora*."

Ben made no reply. Whether the reasoning of the Coromantee was correct or only sophistical, the facts were the same. Two forms were in the sky, outlined against the back ground of cerulean blue. Though distant, and apparently motionless, they were easily distinguishable as living things,— as birds,—and of a kind so peculiar, that the eye of the rude African, and even that of the almost equally rude Saxon, could distinguish the species.

Chapter Forty Eight
The Frigate-Bird

The frigate-bird (*Pelicanus aquila*), which had thus become the subject of conversation on board the *Catamaran*, is in many respects very different from other ocean-birds. Although generally classed with the pelicans, it bears but a very slight resemblance to any species of these misshapen, unwieldy, goose-like creatures.

It differs from most other birds frequenting the sea in the fact of its feet being but slightly webbed, and its claws being *talons*, like those of hawks or eagles.

Otherwise, also, does it resemble these last birds,—so much that the sailors, noting the resemblance, indifferently call it "sea-hawk," "man-of-war hawk," and "man-of-war eagle." The last appellation, however, is sometimes given to the great wandering albatross (*Diomedea exulans*).

The male frigate-bird is jet black all over the body; having a red bill, very long, vertically flattened, and with the mandibles abruptly hooked downwards at the point. The female differs in colour: being sooty black above, and having a large white disc on the abdomen.

The legs are short in proportion to the bulk of the bird; the toes, as already stated, being furnished with talons,—the middle one scaly, and notched underneath; while the legs are feathered to the feet, showing another point of affinity with predatory birds of the land. Still another may be pointed out: in the innermost toe or *pollex*, being turned outwards, as if intended for perching,—which the frigate-bird actually does when it visits the shore, often making its nest upon trees, and roosting among the branches.

In fact, this creature may be regarded as a sort of connecting link between the birds of prey who make their home on the dry land, and the web-footed birds that equally lead a predatory life upon the sea. Perhaps it continues the chain begun by the ospreys and sea-eagles, who take most of their food out of the water, but do not stray far from the shore in search of it.

The frigate-bird, a true sea-hawk,—sea-eagle, it may be called, since its bold, noble qualities entitle it to the name,—makes its excursions so far from the shore that it is not unfrequently seen in the very middle of the Atlantic. Now, this is the most curious circumstance in its history, and one that has hitherto perplexed ornithologists. Since its feet are not provided with the "web," it cannot swim a stroke; nor has it ever been seen to alight on the water for the purpose of taking rest. It is not likely that it can settle on the wave,—the conformation of its feet and body making this an impossibility.

How, then, does it find rest for its tired wings? This is the question to which an answer is not easily given.

There is a belief, as Ben alleged, that it returns every night to roost upon the land; but when it is considered that to reach its roost would often require a flight of a thousand miles,—to say nothing of the return journey to its fishing-ground,—the statement at once loses all *vrai-semblance*, Many sailors say that it goes to sleep suspended aloft in the air, and so high up as to be sometimes invisible. This was the belief of Snowball.

Now, this belief, or conjecture, or whatever you may—term it, on the part of Jack tar, though sneered at as impossible, and even scoffed at as ridiculous, may, after all, not be so very far beyond the truth. Jack has told some rare tales in his time,—"yarns" that appear to be "spun" out of his fancy, quite as much as this one,—which, after having run the gauntlet of philosophic ridicule on the part of closet naturalists, have in the long run turned out to be true! Has not his story of the "King of the Cannibal Islands,"—Hokee-pokee-winkee-wum, with his fifty wives as black as "sut," and all his belongings, just as Jack described them,—actually "turned up" in reality, in the person of Thakombau and a long line of similar monsters inhabiting the Fiji Islands?

Why, then, may not his statements, about the frigate-bird going to sleep upon the wing be a correct conjecture, or observation, instead of a "sailor's yarn,"—as sage and conceited, but often mistaken, professors of "physical science" would have us regard it?

Such professors as are at this moment, in almost every newspaper in the country,—scientific journals among the number,—abusing and ridiculing the poor farmer for destroying the birds that destroy his grain; and telling him, if he were to let the birds alone, they would eat the insects that commit far greater devastation on his precious *cerealia*! Conceited theorists! it has never occurred to them, that the victims of the farmer's fowling-piece— *the birds that eat corn—would not touch an insect if they were starving!* The farmer does not make war on the insect-eating birds. Rarely, or never, does he expend powder and shot on the swallow, the wagtail, the tomtit, the starling, the thrush, the blackbird, the wren, the robin, or any of the grub and fly-feeders. His "game" are the buntings and *Fringillidae*,—the larks, linnets, finches, barley-birds, yellowhammers, and house sparrows, that form the great flocks afflicting him both in seed-time and harvest; and none of which (excepting, perhaps, the last-mentioned gentry, who are at times slightly inclined towards a wormy diet) would touch an insect, even with the tips of their bills. Ha! ye scribblers of closet conceits! you have been sneering at "Chaw-bacon" long enough. He may turn and scoff at you; for, in very truth, the boot (of ignorance) is upon the other leg!

Let us make sure then, lest Jack's theory regarding the lumbers of the sea-hawk be not mythical in the mirror of our own incredulity.

That the bird can take rest in the air is perfectly certain. It may be seen—as the crew of the *Catamaran* saw it—suspended on outspread wing, without any perceptible motion except in its tail; the long, forked feathers of which could be observed opening and closing at intervals; according to the sailor's simile, like the blades of a pair of scissors. But this motion might be merely muscular, and compatible with a state of slumber or unconscious repose. At all events, the bird has been seen to keep its place in the air for many minutes at a time, with no other motion observable than that of the long and gracefully-forking feathers of its tail.

A fish sleeps suspended in the water without any apparent effort. Why not certain birds in the air, whose body is many times lighter than that of a fish, and whose skeleton is constructed with air vessels to buoy them up into the azure fields of the sky? The sea-hawk may seldom require what is ordinarily termed rest. Its smooth, graceful flight upon wings, which, though slender, are of immense length,—often often feet spread,—shows that it is, perhaps, as much at ease in the air as if perched upon the bough of a tree; and it is certain that its claws never clasp branch, nor do its feet find rest on any other object, for weeks and months together.

It is true that while fishing near the shore it usually retires to roost at night; but afar over the ocean it keeps all night upon the wing. It does not, like many other ocean-birds,—as the booby, one of its own genus,—seek rest upon the spars of ships, though it often hovers above the mastheads of sailing vessels, as if taking delight in this situation, and not unfrequently seizes in its beak, and tearing away the pieces of coloured cloth fixed upon the vane.

A curious anecdote is told of a frigate-bird taken while thus occupied,—its captor being a man who had swarmed up to the masthead and seized it in his hand. As this individual chanced to be a landsman, serving temporarily on board the ship, and being remarkably tall and slender, the crew of the vessel would never have it otherwise, than that the bird, accustomed only to the figure of a sailor, had mistaken its captor for a spare spar, and thus fallen a victim to its want of discernment!

Strictly speaking, the frigate-bird does not *fish*, like other predatory birds of the ocean. As it cannot either dive or swim, of course it cannot take fish out of the water. How, then, does it exist? Where finds it the food necessary to sustain existence? In a word, it captures its prey in the air; and this commonly consists in the various species of flying-fish, and also the *loligo*, or "flying squids." When these are forced out of their own proper element to seek safety in the air, the frigate-bird, ready to pounce down from aloft, clutches them before they can get back into the equally unsafe element out of which they have sprung.

Besides the flying-fish, it preys upon those that have the habit of leaping above the surface, and also others that have been already captured by boobies, terns, gulls, and tropic birds, all of which can both swim and dive.

These the frigate-bird remorselessly robs of their legitimate prize,— first compelling them to relinquish it in the air, and then adroitly seizing it before it gets back to the water.

The storm is the season of plenty to this singular bird of prey; as then it can capture many kinds of fish upon the surface of the waves. It is during those times when the sea is tranquil or perfectly calm, that it resorts to the other method,—of forcing the fishing-birds to yield up their prey, often even to disgorge, after having swallowed it!

Its wondrous powers of flight not only enable it to seize with certainty the morsel thus rejected, but so confident is it of its ability in the performance of this feat, that, if a fish chance to be awkwardly caught in its beak, it will fearlessly fling it into the air, and, darting after, grasp it again and again, until it gets the mouthful in a convenient position for being gulped down its own greedy throat.

Chapter Forty Nine
Between two Tyrants

The two birds which had attracted the attention of the *Catamaran's* crew were seen suddenly to abandon their fixed poise in the air, and commence wheeling in circles, or rather in spiral lines that gradually descended towards the surface of the sea.

In a short while they were so low that the scarlet pouch under the throat of the male was easily recognisable, swollen out like a goitre; while the elegant conformation of the birds, with their long, scimitar-shaped wings, and slender forked tails, was sharply defined against the blue background of the sky.

The albacores no longer took any notice of the baited hooks; but, instead, commenced darting through the water in various directions, until they had got scattered about over the sea.

Was it fear of the predatory birds hovering above that was producing this change in their tactics?

It could not be that. They did not appear to be acting under any alarm; but rather as if prowling in search of something not yet visible either to them or to those who were watching them from the deck of the *Catamaran*.

Ben Brace and Snowball knew the fish were not frightened by the presence of the birds; but William, whose experience of sea-life was more limited,—although the albacores did not look alarmed,—thought, doubtingly, that they were so.

"Surely," said he, appealing to his older companions, "such big fish needn't be scared of them?"

As he put the interrogatory, he pointed upward to the two birds, now within a hundred fathoms of the surface. "Surely they can't kill an albacore? If they did, they could never swallow it, I should think?"

"'T ain't the albacore they be after," replied Ben Brace, "nor be the albacore afeerd o' them,—not a bit. There be another sort o' fishes not far away, though we can't see 'em. No more do these sky-blue chaps as be swimming around us. They be now lookin' for 'em,—mighty sharp, as ye see; an' they'll be sartin to scare 'em up in three shakes o' a shark's tail."

"What other sort of fish?" inquired William.

"Flyin'-fish, lad; same's you an' I made our first meal on, when we wur wellnigh starvin'. There's a school not far off. The frigates has spied 'em from aloft, an' that's what's brought them hoverin' over. They've seed the albacores too; and as they know that these preys on the flyin'-fish, they've come down to be nearer thar game. Unless the albacores get thar eyes on the winged fish, and run down among 'em, there'll be no chance for the frigates. They can do nothin' till t' other jumps 'em out o' the water. The sky-blues don't seem to see 'em yet; but I dare say it'll not be long afore they do, judgin' by their manoeuvres. Thar! Didn't I tell thee, lad? See yonder! They be off after something."

As the sailor spoke, several of the albacores were seen suddenly heading in a direction parallel to the course of the *Catamaran* and passing rapidly through the transparent water.

In an instant after, several white objects were seen springing up before them, which, after glancing for a moment in the air, plunged back again into the water.

Not any of the *Catamaran's* crew were ignorant of the character of these objects. The silvery sheen of translucent wings, as they glittered under the bright sunbeams, proclaimed the creatures to be a "flock" of flying-fish, of which the albacores—of all their many enemies the most dangerous—were now in pursuit.

There may have been several of the flying-fish that did not rise into the air, but fell a prey to their pursuers under the water; and of those that did succeed in springing above the surface there were two that never came down again,—at least not in the shape of flying-fish.

The sea-hawks, wheeling above both pursuers and pursued, had been watching their opportunity; and as the pretty creatures made their appearance above water, both the birds swooped straight down among the prinkling cohort, each selecting a victim. Both made a successful swoop; for they were observed to turn and fly with a slant upwards, each with a flying-fish in its beak.

One of them, the male bird, didn't appear to be satisfied with the hold he had taken; for, with a sudden jerk of his head, he let go again, pitched the prey several feet upward, and again as it came down took a fresh "grip" upon it.

No doubt this was to his satisfaction, for almost in the same instant that the flying-fish returned within the mandibles of his beak it disappeared, wings and all, down that dark passage, where, no doubt, many another of its kind had preceded it.

It was evident that neither of the birds considered one flying-fish sufficient for a meal; for as soon as they had swallowed those already taken, they again placed themselves in position for shooting down upon a second victim.

And now the crew of the *Catamaran* had the fortune to witness one of those singular incidents that may sometimes be seen upon the ocean,—a little drama of Nature, in which three of her creatures,—all three differing in kind,—formed the *dramatis persona*.

The cock frigate-bird, on turning to look for a fresh victim, espied one, or that which was likely to become one, almost directly beneath him.

It was a single flying-fish, which by some chance,—perhaps from not being either so fast a swimmer or so swift upon the wing as its fellows,— had lagged behind the "school."

It was no longer playing laggard, and for a very good reason: since an albacore, nearly full three feet in length, was swimming after it and doing his very best to overtake it. Both were exerting every bit of muscular strength that lay in their fins,—the former to make its escape, the latter to prevent this consummation.

It was evident, however, to those on board the *Catamaran*, that the pursuer was gaining upon the pursued; and this at length became also evident to the flying-fish. The tiny creature, as it cut through the clear water, could be seen quivering with fear; and the spectators looked to see it shoot upward into the air, and thus disappoint the greedy tyrant at its tail.

No doubt this would have been the very course of conduct for the flying-fish to have pursued; and no doubt it was on the eve of adopting it, when, all at once, the long, shadowy wings and outstretched neck of the frigate-bird were seen outlined above.

The sight was sufficient to keep the fish under water a while longer, but only a very little while. Above were that ugly red pouch and craning neck; below, those hideous jaws, ready to open and engulf it.

There seemed no chance of escape. It was only a question of choice as to the mode of death: whether it would prefer to become food for a fish, or be devoured by a bird.

As, in itself, it partook a little of the nature of, or, at all events, of the habits of both, there was not much to choose between them; but whether it did not desire to deliver itself over to the enemy most like to itself, or whether it was that the latter was now so near as to be almost certain of seizing it, it declared its preference for the bird by making a sudden spring which carried it clear out of the water, and into the air.

The sea-hawk hovering above in eager expectation lost no time in making the attempt to secure it; but whether he was too sure of his prize, or from some other unexplained reason, certain it is that he gave a practical illustration of the old and well-known adage about the cup and the lip, by failing to clutch the prey.

He was seen darting towards it with open beak,—his talons cruelly extended for its capture; but, notwithstanding all his activity, the white object that shot glittering past him, and dropped into the sea far beyond, proclaimed to the Catamarans that the *Exocetus* had escaped.

Chapter Fifty
Snowball making a Somersault

And now all eyes were turned towards the sea-hawk, and became fixed upon him with glances that expressed surprise; for, instead of again soaring upward, and renewing his pursuit either of the creature that he had so clumsily permitted to escape him, or some other of its kind, the bird was seen to stay down upon the surface of the sea,—his wings spread to their full extent, and flapping the water with such violence as to raise the spray in a thick cloud over and around him!

He was heard, too, giving utterance to loud and repeated screams,—not in the tone of a conqueror; but as if he was in danger of being vanquished, or had already become the victim of some ocean tyrant stronger than himself!

For some seconds this inexplicable movement,—a struggle it seemed,—continued; not in one place, but over a space of many square yards of surface,—which appeared to be also agitated by the exertions of some creature underneath; the bird all the while repeating its cries, and beating the water into froth, like a huge pelican at play!

The crew of the *Catamaran,* utterly unable to account for this strange conduct on the part of the old cock, stood upon the deck of their craft, looking on with feelings of intense astonishment.

Even Snowball, who thought himself *au fait* to every incident of ocean-life, was surprised and puzzled equally with the rest.

"What be the matter wi' the creetur, Snowy?" inquired Ben, thinking Snowball could explain its odd behaviour. "The frigate 'pears to ha' got on its beam-end; shiver my timbers if 't ain't goin' to founder!"

"Shibber ma timber, too," rejoined Snowball, rudely pirating the sailor's favourite shibboleth; "shibber 'um, if dis nigga know what am de matter. Golly! someting got de ole hawk by de legs,—dat seem sartin. Maybe 'um be shark, maybe 'um be long-nose—de—"

Snowball was going to say "sword-fish," had he been permitted to finish his speech. But he was not; for while in the act of its delivery, with the whites of his eyes rolling in conjectural wonder, something from below struck the plank, upon which he was standing, and with such a shock that the piece of timber was started from its fastenings, and impelled suddenly upwards,—not only knocking the ex-sea-cook out of his perpendicular position, but pitching him, as from a catapult, clear across the *Catamaran*, and into the sea on the opposite side!

This was not all. The plank from which Snowball had been projected instantly fell back into its place,—in consequence of its being one of the heaviest pieces of timber in the raft,—but instead of remaining there, it was again seen to shoot upward, then fall back upon the water, as if dragged down by a powerful but invisible hand,—the hand of some sea-god or demon,—perhaps of Neptune himself!

Not only the plank, but the whole raft moved under this inexplicable impulsion,—which had communicated to it a rocking motion, not from side to side, but upwards and downwards! So quick and violent was this mysterious oscillation, that it was with difficulty the three individuals who still occupied the decks of the craft could keep either their balance or their feet.

Along with the motion of the raft there was a corresponding commotion in the water,—accompanied by a loud splashing noise that seemed to proceed from under the timbers, on which, like so many acrobats, they were endeavouring to balance themselves; and in a few seconds after they had felt the great shock, the sea all around exhibited a surface of high waves crested with foam!

Snowball, who had risen to the surface after the somersault that had plunged him deep down into the sea, perceiving that the raft still continued to heave upward and downward, made no attempt to get on board; but swimming alongside, sputtered forth his terrified ejaculations. Even the brave man-o'-war's-man, who had faced death in a thousand shapes, was, at that moment, the victim of fear.

How could it be otherwise? He could think of nothing in nature capable of causing that mysterious commotion and who, without trembling, could withstand the assaults of the supernatural?

"Shiver my timbers!" cried Ben, himself shivering as he spoke the words, "what in old Nick's name has got under us? Be it a whale that's bumpin' its back against the rail? Or—"

Before he could pronounce the second interrogatory, a loud crash sounded in the ears of all,—as if the plank heaving so mysteriously had been suddenly torn in twain!

This sound, whatever had caused it, seemed to proclaim the climax of the commotion: for immediately after the *Catamaran* began to compose herself, the waves caused by her continued rocking gradually grew less, until at length, once more "righted," she lay in her customary position upon the tranquil surface of the sea.

Chapter Fifty One
A Thrust through and through

As soon as the *Catamaran* had fairly recovered her equilibrium, Snowball condescended to climb aboard. The ludicrous appearance of the negro, as he stood dripping upon the deck, might have excited laughter; but neither Ben Brace, nor his acolyte, nor the little Lalee, were in a mood for mirth. On the contrary, the curious incident that had just occurred was yet unexplained; and the awe with which it had inspired them still continued to hold all three in a sort of speechless control. Snowball himself was the first to break silence.

"Good Gorramity!" he exclaimed, his teeth chattering like castanets, as the words passed between them. "Wha's all de rumpus 'bout? Wha you tink, Massa Ben? Wha make dat dratted fuss under de raff? De water be plash bout so I've see nuffin, 'cepting a big black heap o' someting. Golly! I b'lieve it war de *jumbe*,—de debbil!"

The terrified looks of the speaker, while giving utterance to these words,—especially when pronouncing the dreaded name of the *jumbe*—told that he was serious in what he said; and that he actually believed the devil to have been the agent who had been causing the mysterious commotion!

The English sailor, though not entirely free from a certain tinge of superstition, did not share Snowball's belief. Though unable, by any experience he had ever gone through, to account for the odd incident, still he could not ascribe it to supernatural agency. The blow which started the plank on which Snowball had been standing had communicated a shock to the whole structure. It might have been given by some huge fish, or other monster of the deep; and though unaccountable and unexpected, might, nevertheless, be quite natural. It was the shaking which the *Catamaran* kept up afterwards,—almost to the spilling of the whole crew into the water,— that most perplexed the old man-o'-war's-man. He could not imagine why a fish, or any other creature, having butted its head once against the "keel" of the craft, would not instantly desist from such an idle encounter, and make off as fast as fins could carry it.

Ben's first impression was, that a whale had by chance risen under the raft; as he had known them to do against the sides of ships. But then the persistence of the creature, whatever it was, in its odd attack, argued something more than accident. On the other hand, if the attack was designed, and had been made by a whale, of whatever species, the sailor knew that it would not have left off after merely shaking the raft. A whale, with a single flirt of his tail, would have sent the whole structure flying into the air, sunk it down into the deep, or scattered it in fifty fragments over the surface of the water.

One of these things a whale would undoubtedly have done. So believed Ben Brace; and therefore the creature that had come so near capsizing them could not be a whale. What was it, then? A shark? No. It could not be a shark. Though there are two or three species of these monsters, quite as large as good-sized whales, the sailor never knew of their assaulting anything after that fashion.

As they stood speculating on the cause of their curious adventure, a shout from Snowball announced that the ex-cook had at length discovered the explanation.

Snowball's first thought, after having partially recovered from his fright, was to examine the plank from which, like an acrobat from his spring-board, he had made that involuntary somersault.

There, just by the spot on which he had been standing, appeared an object that explained everything: a sharp, bony, proboscis-like implement, standing up a full foot's length out of the timber, slightly obliqued from the perpendicular, and as firmly imbedded in the wood as if it had been driven in by the blows of a blacksmith's hammer!

That it had penetrated the plank from underneath could be easily seen, by the ragged edge, and split pieces around the orifice where it came out.

But the negro did not stay to draw deductions of this nature. On catching sight of the object, —which he knew had not been there before, —his terror at once came to an end; and a long cachinnation, intended for a peal of laughter, announced that "Snowball was himself again."

"Golly!" he exclaimed. "Look dar, Massa Brace. Look at de ting dat hab gub us sich a frightnin. Whuch! Who'd a beliebed dat de long-nose had got so much 'trength in im ugly body? Whuch!"

"A sword-fish!" cried Ben. The rostrum of one of these singular creatures was the sharp bone protruding above the plank. "You're right, Snowy, it be a sword-fish, and nothing else."

"Only de snout o' one," jocularly rejoined the negro. "De karkiss ob de anymal an't dar any more. Dat was de black body I seed under de raff; but he an't dar now. He hab broke off him long perbossus; and no doubt dat hab killed him. He gone dead, and to de bottom, boaf at de same time."

"Yes," assented the sailor. "It must have broke off while he was struggling to get clear, I heerd the crash o't, like the partin' o' a spar; and just after, the raft stopped shakin', an' began to settle down again. Lor ha mercy on us! what a thrust he have made! That plank be five inches thick, at the very least, an' you see he's stuck his snout through it more'n a foot! Lor 'a mercy on us! What wonderful queery creeturs the ocean do contain!"

And with this philosophic reflection, from the lips of the man-o'-war's-man, ended the adventure.

Chapter Fifty Two
An awkward Grip

To the two oldest of the *Catamaran's* crew the curious circumstances of the sword-fish thrusting his rostrum through the raft, and snapping it asunder, needed no explanation. Both knew that it was not with an intention of attacking the *Catamaran* that the "stab" had been given; nor was the act a voluntary one, in any way.

Not likely, indeed; since it had proved fatal to the swordsman himself. No one doubted his having gone dead to the bottom of the sea: for the bony "blade" was found to have been broken close to the "hilt," and it was not possible the owner could exist without this important weapon. Even supposing that the fearful "fracture" had not killed him outright, the loss of his long rapier, the only tool by which he could obtain his living, would be sure to shorten his lease of life, and the final moment could not be long delayed.

But neither sailor nor ex-sea-cook had any doubt of the fish having committed suicide, no more than that the act was involuntary.

The explanation given by Ben Brace to his *protégé* was simple, as it was also rational. The sword-fish had been charging into a shoal of albacores. Partly blinded by the velocity of its impetuous rush, and partly by its instinct of extreme voracity,—perhaps amounting to a passion, it had seen nothing of the raft until its long weapon struck the plank, piercing the latter through and through. Unable to withdraw its rostrum from the fibrous wood, the fish had instantly inaugurated that series of struggles, and continued them, until the crash came, caused, no doubt, by the upheaved raft lurching suddenly down in a direction transverse to its snout.

Only a part of this explanatory information was extended to little William: for only a part was required. From some previous talk that had occurred on the same subject, he was already acquainted with a few of the facts relating to this foolish fencing on the part of the sword-fish.

Nor was there at that moment any explanation either offered or asked; for, as soon as the *Catamaran* had settled into her proper position, and Snowball had got aboard, the eyes of her whole crew,—those of the Coromantee among the rest,—became once more directed to that which had occupied their attention previous to receiving the shock,—the strange behaviour of the frigate-bird.

This creature was still down on the surface of the water, darting from point to point, fluttering and flopping, and throwing up the little clouds of spray, that, surrounding it like a nimbus, seemed to follow it wherever it went!

Though Ben Brace and Snowball had been able to explain the action of the fish, they were both at fault about the behaviour of the bird. In all their sea experience neither had ever witnessed the like conduct before,—either on the part of a frigate-bird, or any other bird of the ocean.

For a long time they stood watching the creature, and exchanging conjectures as to the cause of its singular action. It was clear this was not voluntary; for its movements partook of the nature of a struggle. Besides, its screams,—to which it gave an almost continuous utterance,—betokened either terror or pain, or both.

But why did it keep to the surface of the sea, when it was well-known to be a bird that could rise almost vertically into the air, and to the highest point that winged creatures might ascend?

This was the query to which neither sailor nor sea-cook could give a reply, either with positive truth or probable conjecture.

For full ten minutes it remained unanswered; that is, ten minutes after the sword-fish adventure had ended, and twenty from the time the frigate-bird had been seen to swoop at the flying-fish. Then, however, the problem received its solution; and the play of the *Pelicanus aquila* was at length explained.

It was no play on the part of the unfortunate bird, but a case of involuntary and fearful captivity.

The bird had begun to show symptoms of exhaustion, and as its strength became enfeebled, its wings flopped more gently against the water, the spray no longer rose around it, and the sea underneath was less agitated.

The spectators could now see that it was not alone. Beneath, and apparently clutching it by the leg, was a fish whose shape, size, and sheen of azure hue proclaimed it an albacore,—no doubt, the one that simultaneously with the bird itself had been balked in the pursuit of the flying-fish.

So far the detention of the frigate-bird upon the surface of the sea was explained; but not sufficiently. There was still cause for conjecture. The albacore seemed equally tired of the connection,—equally exhausted; and as it swam slowly about,—no longer darting swiftly from point to point, as at the beginning of the strife,—the spectators could now see that the foot of the sea-hawk, instead of being held between the jaws of the fish,—as at first they had supposed it to be,—appeared to be resting on the back of its head, as if the bird had perched there, and was balancing itself on one leg!

Mystery of mysteries! What could it all mean?

The struggles of both bird and fish seemed coming to a termination: as they were now only continued intermittently. After each interval, the wings of the former and the fins of the latter moved with feebler stroke; until at length both wings and fins lay motionless,—the former on, the latter *in*, the water.

But that the bird's wings were extended, it would, no doubt, have sunk under the surface; and the fish was still making feeble endeavours to draw it down; but the spread pinions, extending over nearly ten feet of surface, frustrated the design.

It so chanced that the curious spectacle had occurred directly ahead of the *Catamaran*, and the craft, making way down the wind, kept gradually approaching the scene of the strife.

Every moment the respective positions of the two parties revealed themselves more clearly; but it was not until the raft swept within reach, and the exhausted adversaries were both taken up, that the connection between them became thoroughly understood.

Then it was discovered that the contest which had occurred between them was on both sides an involuntary affair,—had not been sought by either; but was the result of sheer accident.

How could it be otherwise: since the albacore is too strong for the beak of the frigate-bird,—too big for even *its* capacious throat to swallow; while, on the other hand, the frigate-bird never ventures to intrude itself on the cruising-ground of this powerful fish?

The accident which had conducted to this encounter, leading to a fatal entanglement, had been caused by a creature which is the common prey of both,—the little flying-fish, that for once had escaped from his enemies of both elements,—the air and the water.

In dashing down upon the flying-fish, the curving talons of the bird, missing the object for which they had been braced, entered the eye of the albacore. Partly because they fitted exactly into the socket, and partly becoming imbedded among the fibrous sutures of the skull, they remained fixed; so that neither bird nor fish—equally desirous of undoing the irksome yoke—was able to put an end to the partnership!

Snowball gave them a divorce, as effectual as could have been obtained in the court, ever to be noted as that of Sir Cresswell Cresswell.

The process was brief,—the execution following quick upon the judgment; though the sentences pronounced upon the criminals were not exactly the same.

The fish was knocked on the head; while a different, though equally expeditious, mode of punishment was executed upon the bird. Its head was twisted from its body!

Thus, somewhat after the fashion of Kilkenny cats, perished two tyrants of the sea. Let us hope that the tyrants of the land may all receive an analogous compensation for their crimes!

Chapter Fifty Three
Gloomy Prospects

The reappearance of the sword-fish,—if it was the same that had already paid them a visit,—or more likely the discovery and pursuit of the "school" of flying-fish,—had caused the albacores to decamp from the neighbourhood of the *Catamaran*; so that with the exception of that taken from the talons of the frigate-bird, not one was any longer to be seen.

Once recovered from the excitement, caused by the singular accident that happened to the *Catamaran*,—as well as the other incident almost as singular,—her crew made an inspection of their craft, to see if any damage had accrued from the shock.

Fortunately there was none. The piercing of the plank, in which the bony rostrum remained firmly imbedded, was of no consequence whatever; and, although several feet of the "sword,"—the whole of the blade, in fact, excepting that which protruded above,—could be perceived jutting out underneath, they made no attempt to "extract" it: since it could not greatly interfere with the sailing qualities of the *Catamaran*.

The plank itself had been started slightly out of place aid one or two other timbers loosened. But in such able hands as those of Snowball and the sailor, these trifling damages were soon made good again.

The two baited hooks were once more dropped into the water, but the sun went down over the ocean without either of them receiving a nibble. No albacore,—no fish whatever,—no bird,—no living creature of any kind,—was in sight at the setting of that sun; which, slowly descending, as it were, into the silent depths of the ocean, left them in the purple gleam of the twilight.

Notwithstanding the interesting events which had transpired,— enough to secure them against a single moment of *ennui*,—they were far from being cheerful in that twilight hour. The stirring incidents of the day had kept them from thinking of their real situation; but when all was once more tranquil,—even to the ocean around them,—their thoughts naturally reverted to their very narrow chances of ultimately escaping from that wide, wild waste, stretching, as it seemed, to the ends of the world!

With wistful glances they had watched the sun sinking over the sea. The point where the golden luminary disappeared from their sight was due westward,—the direction in which they desired to go. Could they have only been at that moment where his glorious orb was shining down from the vertex, they would have been upon dry land; and, O what a thrilling thought is that of firm stable earth, to the wretched castaway clinging upon his frail raft in the middle of the endless ocean!

They were discouraged by the dead calm that reigned around them; for every breath of the breeze had died away before sunset. The surface of the sea was tranquil even to glassiness; and as the twilight deepened, it began to mirror the millions of twinkling stars gradually thickening in the sky.

There was something awful in the solemn stillness that reigned around them; and with something like awe did it inspire them.

It was not unbroken by sounds; but these were of a character to sadden rather than cheer them, for they were sounds to be heard only in the wilderness of the great deep,—such as the half-screaming laugh of the sea-mew, and the wild whistle of the boatswain-bird.

Another cause of discouragement to our castaways,—one which had that day arisen,—was the loss of their valuable dried fish.

It is true that only a portion of their stock had been spilled into the engulfing ocean; but even this was a cause of regret; since it might not be so easy to make up the quantity lost.

While angling among the albacores, with the prospect of making a successful troll, they had thought less of it. Now that these fish had forsaken them,—leaving only three in their possession,—and they were in doubt whether they might ever come across another "school,"—more acutely did they feel the misfortune.

Their spirits sank still lower, as the descending twilight darkened around them; and for an hour or more not a cheerful word was heard or spoken by that sad quartette composing the crew of the *Catamaran*.

Chapter Fifty Four
Thanksgiving

Despondency cannot endure forever. Kind Nature has not ordained that it should be so. It may have its periods, longer or shorter as the case may be; but always to be succeeded by intervals, if not of absolute cheerfulness, at least of emotions less painful to endure.

About an hour after the going down of the sun, the spirits of those on board the *Catamaran* became partially freed from the weight that for some time had been pressing upon them.

Of coarse this change was attributable to some cause; and as it was a physical one, there could be no difficulty in tracing it.

It was simply the springing up of a breeze,—a fine breeze blowing steadily, and to the west,—the very direction in which it was desirous they should make way.

And they *did* make way; the *Catamaran*, in spite of the terrible "stab" she had received, scudding through the water, as if to show that the assault of the sword-fish had in no way disabled her.

Motion has always a soothing effect upon anyone suffering from despondent spirits; more especially when the movement is being made in the right direction. A boat stationary in the water, or drifting the wrong way against the stroke of the rower,—a railway carriage at a stand, or gliding back to the platform, contrary to the direction in which the traveller intends to go,—such experiences always produce a feeling of irksome uneasiness. When either begins to progress in its proper course,—no matter how slowly,—the unpleasant feeling instantly passes away; for we know that we are going "onward!"

"Onward!" a word to cheer the drooping spirit,—a glorious word for the despondent.

It was not that anyone on board the *Catamaran* had the slightest idea that that breeze would waft them to land; or even last long enough to bear them many leagues over the ocean. It was the thought that they were making progress in the right course,—going *onward*,—simply that thought that cheered them.

It roused them from their despondency sufficiently to beget thoughts of supper; and Snowball was seen starting up with some alacrity, and scrambling towards his *stores*.

His "locker" lay amidships; and as he had not far to go, nor any great variety of comestibles to choose from, he soon returned to the stern,—near which the others were seated,—carrying in his outstretched claws half a dozen of the "pickled" biscuits, and some morsels of cured fish.

It was a coarse and meagre meal; at which even a pauper would have pouted his lips; but to those for whom it was intended it had relish enough to make it not only acceptable, but welcome.

A greater delicacy was before their eyes, lying on the deck of the *Catamaran*. That was the albacore,—a fish whose *flesh* is equal in excellence to that of any taken out of the ocean. But the flesh of the albacore was *raw*; while that of Snowball's stock, if not cooked, was at least cured; and this, in the opinion of the Catamarans, rendered it more palatable.

With a little "Canary" to wash it down, it was not to be despised,—at least, under the circumstances in which they were who supped upon it; but the wine was sparingly distributed, and drunk with a large admixture of water.

The bump of economy stood high upon the skull of the Coromantee. Perhaps to this might be attributed the fact of his being still in existence: since but for the industry he had exhibited in collecting his stores, and his careful hoarding of them, he might, with his *protégé*, have long before succumbed to starvation.

While eating their frugal supper, Snowball expressed regret at not having a fire,—upon which he might have cooked a cut from the albacore. The *chef-de-caboose* was not ignorant of the excellence of the fish.

He really felt regret,—less on his own account, than in consideration of his *protégé*, Lilly Lalee; whose palate he would fain have indulged with something more delicate than sun-dried fish and salty biscuit.

But as fire was out of the question, he was compelled to forego the pleasure of cooking Lalee's supper; and could only gain gratification by giving to the girl more than her share of the sweet Canary.

Small as was the quantity distributed to each, it had the effect of still further cheering them; and, after supper, they sat for some time indulging in lighter converse than that to which they had lately accustomed themselves.

"Somethin'" said the sailor, "seem to tell me—jest as if I heerd it in a whisper—that we'll yet reach land, or come in sight o' a ship. I doan' know what puts it in my head; unless it be because we've been so many times near going down below, an' still we're above water yet, an' I hope likely to keep so."

"Ya—ya! Massa Ben. We float yet,—we keep so long 's we kin,—dat fo' sartin. We nebba say die,—long 's de *Catamaran* hold togedda."

"I war 'stonished," continued the sailor, without heeding the odd interpolation of the sea-cook, "wonderful 'stonished when that flyin'-fish chucked itself aboard our bit o' plankin', an' it no bigger than the combin' o' a hatchway. What kud 'a conducted it thear,—to that spot above all others o' the broad ocean? What but the hand o' that angel as sits up aloft? No, Snowy! ye may talk as ye like 'bout your Duppys and Jumbes, and that other creetur ye call your Fetush; but I tell ye, nigger, thear be somethin' up above us as is above all them,—an' that's the God o' the Christyun. He be thear; and He sent the flyin'-fish into our wee bit o' raft, and He sent the shower as saved me and little Will'm from dyin' o' thust; and He it war that made you an' me drift to'rds each other,—so as that we might work thegither to get out o' this here scrape, as our own foolishness and wickedness ha' got us into."

"Dat am de troof, Massa Brace, dat las' remark,—only not altogedder! 'T want altogedder our own fault dat brought us on board de slabe-ship *Pandora*,—neider you not maseff. It mite a been our foolishness, dat I do admit; but de wickedness war more de fault ob oder men, dat am wickeder dan eider you or dis unfortunate Coromantee nigga."

"Never mind, Snowy," responded the sailor, "I know there be still some good in ye; and maybe there be good in all o' us, to be favoured and protected as we've been in the midst o' so many dangers. I think after what's happened this day,—especially our escaping from that sharks an' the long swim as we had to make after'ards,—we ought to be uncommon thankful, and say somethin' to show it, too."

"Say something! say what, Massa Brace?"

"I mean a prayer."

"Prayer! wha's dat?"

"Surely, Snowy, you know what a prayer be?"

"Nebba heerd ob de ting,—nebba in all ma life!"

"Well, it be to say somethin' to Him as keeps watch up aloft,—either by way o' askin' for somethin' you want to get, or thankin' Him for what you ha' got arready. The first be called a prayer,—the t'other be a thanksgivin'. Thear ain't much difference, as I could ever see; tho' I've heerd the ship's chaplain go through 'em both,—ay, scores o' times; but the one as we want now be the thanksgivin'; an' I know little Will'm here can go through it like a breeze. Did you ever hear Will'm pray, Snowy?"

"Nebba! I tell ye, Massa Brace, a nebba heer anybody pray in de fashun you 'peak 'bout. Ob coas, I hab heer de nigga talk to da Fetish, de which I, tho' I be a nigga maseff, nebba belieb'd in. Dis child no belieb in anyting he no see, an' he see many ting he no belieb in."

To this frank confession of faith on the part of the Coromantee Ben made no rejoinder that might signify either assent or opposition. His reply was rather a continuation of the train of thought that had led to his last interrogative.

"Ah, Snowy, if you heerd the lad! He do pray beautiful! Most equal to the parson, as we had aboard the frigate; an' he warn't slow at it, eyther. Do 'ee think, Will'm," continued the sailor, turning to the lad with an inquiring look, "do 'ee think ye can remember that prayer as is in the Church Sarvice, and which I've heerd the frigate chaplain go through,—specially after a storm,—as speaks about deliverin' us from all dangers by sea and by land? You've heerd it at home in the church. D'ye think ye could gie it as?"

"O," answered William, "you mean the 'Thanksgiving for Deliverance from our Enemies.' Certainly I remember it. How could I forget what I've heard so many Sundays in church, besides often on week-days at home? O yes, Ben, I can repeat it, if you wish!"

"I do, lad. Gie it us, then. It may do good. At all events, we *owe* it, for what's been done to us. So take a reef out o' your tongue, lad, an' fire away!"

Notwithstanding the *bizarrerie* of manner in which the request was made, the boy-sailor hesitated not to comply with it; and turning himself round upon his knees,—a movement imitated by all the others,—he repeated that *thanksgiving* of the Church Service, which, though well-known, is fortunately only heard upon very unfrequent occasions.

The thanksgiving appeared an appropriate finale to the toils and dangers of the day; and after it was offered up, Snowball, William, and Lalee lay down to rest,—leaving Ben Brace to attend to the steering-oar, and otherwise perform the duties of the dog-watch.

Chapter Fifty Five
Snowball sees Land

The man-o'-war's-man kept watch during the long hours of the night. True to his trust, he attended to the steering-oar: and as the breeze continued to blow steadily in the same direction, the raft, under the double propulsion of the wind and the "line current," made considerable way to the westward.

A sort of filmy fog had arisen over the ocean, which hid the stars from sight. This might have rendered it impossible for the steersman to keep his course; but, under the belief that there was no change occurring in the direction of the wind, Ben guided himself by that, and very properly, as it afterwards proved.

Just before daybreak, he was relieved by Snowball; who entered upon his watch, at the same time taking his turn at the steering-oar.

Ben had not aroused the negro for this purpose; and he would have generously remained at his post until morning, had Snowball desired to prolong his slumbers.

The act of arousing himself was not altogether voluntary on the part of the negro; though neither was it the doing of his comrade. It was in consequence of a physical feeling—a cold shivering caused by the damp sea-fog—that Snowball had been disturbed from his sleep; and which, on his awaking, kept him for some minutes oscillating in a sort of ague, his ivories "dingling" against each other with a continuous rattle that resembled the clattering of some loose bolt in a piece of machinery out of repair.

It was some time before Snowball could recover his exact equilibrium; for, of all sorts of climate, that least endurable to the Coromantee negro is a cold one.

After repeated flopping his arms over his broad chest, and striking crosswise, until the tips of his fingers almost met upon the spinal column of his back, Snowball succeeded in resuscitating the circulation; and then, perceiving it was full time to take his turn at the helm, he proposed relieving the sailor.

This proposal was agreed to; Ben, before putting himself in a position for repose, giving Snowball the necessary directions as to the course in which the *Catamaran* was to be kept.

In five minutes after, the sailor was asleep; and the sea-cook was the only one of the Catamarans who was conscious that the craft that carried them was only a frail structure drifting in mid-ocean hundreds of miles from land.

Little William was, perhaps, dreaming of his English, and Lilly Lalee of her African, home; while the sailor, in all probability, was fancying himself safely "stowed" in the forecastle of a British frigate, with all sail rightly set, and a couple of hundred jolly Jacks like himself stretched out in their "bunks" or swinging in their hammocks around him.

During the first hour of his watch, Snowball did not embarrass his brain with any other idea than simply to follow the instructions of the sailor, and keep the *Catamaran* before the wind.

There had been something said about keeping a look-out, in the hope of espying a sail; but in the dense fog that surrounded them there would be no chance of seeing the biggest ship,—even should one be passing at an ordinary cable's length from the *Catamaran*.

Snowball, therefore, did not trouble himself to scan the sea on either side of their course; but for all that he kept the look-out enjoined on him by the sailor,—that is, he *kept it with his ears!*

Though a ship might not be seen, the voices of her crew or other sounds occurring aboard might be heard; for in this way the presence of a vessel is often proclaimed in a very dark night or when the sea is obscured by a fog.

Oftener, however, at such times, two ships will approach and recede from one another, without either having been conscious of the proximity of the other,—meeting in mid-ocean and gliding silently past, like two giant spectres,—each bent on its own noiseless errand.

Daybreak arrived without the black pilot having heard any sound, beyond that of the breeze rustling against the sail of the *Catamaran* or the hollow "sough" of the water as it surged against the empty casks lashed along their sides.

As the day broke, however, and the upper edge of the sun's disk became visible above the horizon,—the fog under the influence of his rays growing gradually but sensibly thinner,—a sight became disclosed to the eyes of Snowball that caused the blood to course with lightning quickness through his veins; while his heart, beating delightfully within his capacious chest, bounded far above the region of his diaphragm.

At the same instant he sprang to his feet, dropped the steering-oar, as if it had been a bar of red-hot iron; and, striding forward to the starboard bow of the *Catamaran* stood gazing outward upon the ocean!

What could have caused this sudden commotion in both the mind and body of the Coromantee? What spectacle could have thus startled him?

It was the sight of *land*!

Chapter Fifty Six
Is it Land?

A sight so unexpected, and yet so welcome, should have elicited from him a vociferous announcement of the fact.

It did not. On the contrary, he kept silent while stepping forward on the deck, and for some time after, while he stood gazing over the bow.

It was the very unexpectedness of seeing land—combined with the *desirability* of such a sight—that hindered him from proclaiming it to his companions; and it was some time before he became convinced that his senses were not deceiving him.

Though endowed with only a very limited knowledge of nautical geography, the negro knew a good deal about the lower latitudes of the Atlantic. More than once had he made that dreaded middle passage,—once in fetters, and often afterwards assisting to carry others across in the same unfeeling fashion. He knew of no land anywhere near where they were now supposed to be; had never seen or heard of any,—neither island, rock, nor reef. He knew of the Isle of Ascension, and the lone islet of Saint Paul's. But neither of these could be near the track on which the *Catamaran* was holding her course. It could not be either.

And yet what was it he saw? for, sure as eyes were eyes, there was an island outlined upon the retina, so plainly perceptible, that his senses could *not be deceiving him*!

It was after this conviction became fully established in his mind, that he at length broke silence; and in a voice that woke his slumbering companions with a simultaneous start.

"Land 'o!" vociferated Snowball.

"Land ho!" echoed Ben Brace, springing to his feet, and rubbing the sleep out of his eyes, "Land, you say, Snowy? Impossible! You must be mistaken, nigger."

"Land?" interrogated little William. "Whereaway, Snowball?"

"Land?" cried the Portuguese girl, comprehending that word of joyful signification, though spoken in a language not her own.

"Whar away?" inquired the sailor, as he scrambled over the planks of the raft, to get on the forward side of the sail, which hindered his field of view.

"Hya!" replied Snowball. "Hya, Massa Brace, jess to la'bord, ober de la'bord bow."

"It do look like land," assented the sailor, directing his glance upon something of a strange appearance, low down upon the surface of the sea, and still but dimly discernible through the fog. "Shiver my timbers if it don't! An island it be,—not a very big 'un, but for all that, it seem a island."

"My gollies! dar am people on it! D'you see um, Massa Brace? movin' 'bout all ober it I see 'um plain as de sun in de hebbens! Scores o' people a'gwine about back'ard an' forrads. See yonner!"

"Plain as the sun in the heavens," was not a very appropriate simile for Snowball to make use of at that moment; for the orb of day was still darkly obscured by the fog; and for the same reason, the outlines of the island,—or whatever they were taking for one,—could be traced only very indistinctly.

Certain it is, however, that Snowball, who had been gazing longer at the supposed land, and had got his eyes more accustomed to the view, did see some scores of figures moving about over it; and Ben Brace, with little William as well, now that their attention was called to them, could perceive the same forms.

"Bless my stars!" exclaimed the sailor, on making out that the figures were in motion, "thear be men on 't sure enough,—an' weemen, I should say,—seein' as there's some o' 'em in whitish clothes. Who and what can they be? Shiver my timbers if I can believe it, tho' I see it right afore my eyes! I never heerd o' a island in this part of the Atlantic, an' I don't believe thear be one, 'ceptin' it's sprung up within the last year or two. What do you think, Snowy? Be it a Flyin' Dutchman, or a rock, as if just showin' his snout above water, or a reg'lar-built island?"

"Dat 'ere am no Flyin' Dutchman,—leas'wise a hope um no' be. No, Massa Brace, dis nigga wa right in de fuss speckelashun. 'Tarn a island,—a bit ob do real terrer firmer, as you soon see when we puts de *Cat'maran* 'bout an' gits a leetle nearer to de place."

This hypothetic suggestion on the part of the Coromantee was also intended as a counsel; and, acting upon it, the sailor scrambled back over the raft, and seizing hold of the steering-oar, turned the *Catamaran's* head straight in the direction of the newly-discovered land.

The island,—if such it should prove to be,—was of no very great extent. It appeared to run along the horizon a distance of something like a hundred yards; but estimates formed in this fashion are often deceptive,—more especially when a fog interferes, such as at that moment hung over it.

The land appeared to be elevated several feet above the level of the sea,—at one end having a bold bluff-like termination, at the other shelving off in a gentle slope towards the water.

It was principally upon the more elevated portion that the figures were seen,—here standing in groups of three or four, and there moving about in twos, or singly.

They appeared to be of different sizes, and differently dressed: for, even through the film, it could be seen that their garments were of various cuts and colours. Some were stalwart fellows, beside whom were others that in comparison were mere pygmies. These Snowball said were the "pickaninnies,"—the children of the taller ones.

They were in different attitudes too. Some standing erect, apparently carrying long lance-like weapons over their shoulders; others similarly armed, in stooping positions; while not a few appeared to be actively engaged, handling huge pickaxes, with which they repeatedly struck downwards, as if excavating the soil!

It is true that their manoeuvres were seen only indistinctly: and it was not possible for the Catamarans to come to any certain understanding, as to what sort of work was going on upon the island.

It was still very doubtful whether what they saw was in reality an island, or that the figures upon it were those of human beings. Snowball believed them to be so, and emphatically asserted his belief; but Ben was slightly incredulous and undecided, notwithstanding that he had several times "shivered his timbers" in confirmation of the fact.

It was not the possibility of the existence of an island that the sailor disputed. That was possible and probable enough. At the time of which we speak, new islands were constantly turning up in the ocean, where no land was supposed to exist; and even at the present hour, when one might suppose that every inch of the sea has been sailed over, the discovery of rocks, shoals, and even unknown islands, is far from unfrequent.

It was not the island, therefore, that now puzzled the ex-man-o'-war's-man, but the number of people appearing upon it.

Had there been only a score, or a score and a half, he could have explained the circumstance of its being inhabited; though the explanation would not have been productive of pleasure either to himself or his companions. In that case he would have believed the moving forms to be the shipwrecked crew of the *Pandora* who on this ocean islet had found a temporary resting-place; while the pickaxes, which were being freely employed, would have indicated the sinking of wells in search after fresh water.

The number of people on the island, however, with other circumstances observed, at once contradicted the idea that it could be the crew of the shipwrecked slaver; and the certainty that it was *not* these ruffians whom they saw emboldened the Catamarans in their approach.

In spite of appearances, still was the sailor disposed to doubt the existence of an island; or, at least, that the forms moving to and fro over its surface were those of human beings.

Nor could he be cured of his incredulity until the *Catamaran*, approaching still nearer to the shore of the doubtful islet, enabled him to see and distinguish beyond the possibility of doubt a flag floating from the top of its staff, which rose tall and tapering from the very highest point of land which the place afforded!

The flag was of crimson cloth, — apparently a piece of bunting. It floated freely upon the breeze; which the filmy mist, though half disclosing, could not altogether conceal. The deep red colour was too scarce upon the ocean to be mistaken for the livery of any of its denizens. It could not be the tail-feathers of the tropic bird so prized by the chiefs of Polynesia; nor yet the scarlet pouch of the sea-hawk.

It could be nothing else than a "bit o' buntin'."

So, at length, believed Ben Brace, and his belief, expressed in his own peculiar *patois*, produced conviction in the minds of all, that the object extending along a hundred fathoms of the horizon, "must be eyther a rock, a reef, or a island; and the creeturs movin' over it must be men, weemen, an' childer!"

Chapter Fifty Seven
The King of the Cannibal Islands

The emphatic declaration of the sailor,—that the dark disc before them must be an island, and that the upright forms upon it were those of human beings,—dispelled all doubts upon the subject; and produced a feeling of wild excitement in the minds of all three of his companions.

So strong was this feeling, that they could no longer control themselves; but gave vent to their emotions in a simultaneous shout of joy.

Acting prudently, they would have restrained that mirthful exhibition, for although, for reasons already stated, the people appearing upon the island could not be the wicked castaways who had composed the crew of the Pandora, still might they be a tribe of savages equally wicked and murderous.

Who could tell that it was not a community of *Cannibals*. No one aboard the *Catamaran*.

It may seem singular that such a thought should have entered the mind of any of the individuals who occupied the raft. But it did occur to some of them; and to one of the four in particular. This was Ben Brace himself.

The sailor's experience, so far from destroying the credences of boyhood,—which included the existence of whole tribes of cannibals,—had only strengthened his belief in such anthropophagi.

More than strengthened it: for it had been confirmed in every particular.

He had been to the Fiji islands, where he had seen their king, Thakombau,—a true descendant of the lineage of "Hokey-Pokey-Winkey-Wum,"—with other dignitaries of this man-eating nation. He had seen their huge caldron for cooking the flesh of men,—their pots and pans for stewing it,—their dishes upon which it was served up,—the knives with which they were accustomed to carve it,—their larders stocked with human flesh, and redolent of human blood! Nay, more; the English sailor had been an eye-witness of one of their grand festivals; where the bodies of men and women, cooked in various styles,—stewed, roasted, and boiled,—had been served out and partaken of by hundreds of Thakombau's courtiers; the sailor's own captain,—the captain of a British frigate,—ay, the commodore of a British squadron,—with cannon sufficient to have blown the island of Viti Vau out of the water,—sitting alongside, apparently a tranquil and contented spectator of the horrid ceremonial!

It is difficult to account for the behaviour of this Englishman, the Hon. — by name. The only explanation of his conduct one can arrive at is, to believe that his weak mind was fast confined by the trammels of that absurd, but often too convenient, theory of international non-interference,—the most dangerous kind of red-tape that ever tethered the squeamish conscience of an official imbecile.

How different was the action of Wilkes,—that Yankee commander we are so fond of finding fault with! He, too, paid a visit to the cannibal island of Viti Vau; and while there, taught both its king and its people a lesson by the fire of his forty-pounders that, if not altogether effective in extinguishing this national but unnatural custom, has terrified them in its practice to this very day.

Non-interference, indeed! International delicacy in the treatment of a tribe of cruel savages! A nation of man-eaters,—forsooth, a nation! Why not apply the laws of nationality to every band of brigands who chances to have conquered an independent existence? Bah! The world is full of frivolous pretences,—drunk with the poison-cup of political hypocrisy.

It was not Ben Brace who thus reasoned, but his biographer. Ben's reflections were of a strictly practical character His belief in cannibalism was complete; and as the craft to which he had so involuntarily attached himself drifted on towards the mysterious islet, he was not without some misgivings as to the character of the people who might inhabit it.

For this reason he would have approached its shores with greater caution; and he was in the act of enforcing this upon his companions, when his intention was entirely frustrated by the joyous *huzza* uttered by Snowball; echoed by little William; and chorussed by the childish, feminine voice of Lilly Lalee.

The sailor's caution would have come too late,—even had it been necessary to the safety of the *Catamaran's* crew. Fortunately it was not: for that imprudent shout produced an effect which at once changed the current of the thoughts, not only of Ben Brace, but of those who had given utterance to it.

Their united voices, pealing across the tranquil bosom of the deep, caused a sudden change in the appearance of the island; or rather among the people who inhabited it. If human beings, they must be of a strange race,— very strange indeed,—to have been furnished with wings! How otherwise could they have forsaken their footing on *terra firma*,—if the island was such,—and soared upward into the air, which one and all of them did, on hearing that shout from the *Catamaran?*

There was not much speculation on this point on the part of the *Catamaran's* crew. Whatever doubts may have been engendered as to the nature of the island, there could be no longer any about the character of its inhabitants.

"Dey am birds!" suggested the Coromantee; "nuffin more and nuffin less dan birds!"

"You're right, Snowy," assented the sailor. "They be birds; and all the better they be so. Yes; they're birds, for sartin. I can tell the cut o' some o' their jibs. I see frigates, an' a man-o'-war's-man, an' boobies among 'em; and I reckon Old Mother Carey has a brood o' her chickens there. They be all sizes, as ye see."

It was no more a matter of conjecture, as to what kind of creatures inhabited the island. The forms that had been mystifying the crew of the *Catamaran*, though of the biped class, were no longer to be regarded as human beings, or even creatures of the earth. They had declared themselves denizens of the air; and, startled by the shouts that had reached them,—to them, no doubt, sounds strange, and never before heard,—they had sought security in an element into which there was no fear of being followed by their enemies, either of the earth or the water.

Chapter Fifty Eight
Very like a Whale

Though the birds by their flight had dissolved one half of the speculative theory which the crew of the *Catamaran* had constructed, the other half still held good. The island was still there, before their eyes; though completely divested of its inhabitants,—whose sudden eviction had cost only a single shout!

The flag was still waving over it; though, to all appearance, there was not a creature on shore that might feel pride in saluting that solitary standard!

There could be no one; else why should the birds have tarried so long undisturbed, to be scared at last by the mere sound of human voices?

Since there was nobody on the island, there was no need to observe further caution in approaching it,—except so far as regarded the conduct of their craft; and in the belief that they were about to set foot upon the shores of a desert isle, the sailor and Snowball, with little William assisting them, now went to work with the oars and hastened their approach to the land.

Partly impelled by the breeze, and partly by the strength of the rowers, the *Catamaran* moved, briskly through the water; and, before many minutes had elapsed, the craft was within a few hundred fathoms of the mysterious island, and still gliding nearer to it. This proximity,—along with the fact that the morning mist had meanwhile been gradually becoming dispelled by the rays of the rising sun,—enabled her crew to obtain a clearer view of the object before them; and Ben Brace, suspending his exertions at the oar, once more slewed himself round to have a fresh look at the supposed *land*.

"Land!" he exclaimed, as soon as his eyes again rested upon it. "A island, indeed! Shiver my timbers if 't be a island after all! That be no land,—ne'er a bit o't. It look like a rock, too; but there be something else it look liker; an' that be a *whale*. 'Tis wery like a whale!"

"Berry,—berry like a whale!" echoed Snowball, not too well satisfied at discovering the resemblance.

"It *be* a whale!" pronounced the sailor, in a tone of emphatic confidence,—"a whale, an' nothin' else. Ay," he continued speaking, as if some new light had broken upon him, "I see it all now. It be one o' the great *spermaceti* whales. I wonder I didn't think o't afore. It's been killed by some whaling-vessel; and the flag you see on its back's neyther more nor less than one o' their *whifts*. They've stuck it there, so as they might be able to find the sparmacety when they come back. Marcy heaven! I hope they *will* come back."

As Ben finished this explanatory harangue, he started into an erect attitude, and placed himself on the highest part of the *Catamaran's* deck,— his eyes no longer bent upon the whale, but, with greedy glances, sweeping the sea around it.

The object of this renewed reconnoissance may be understood from the words to which he had given utterance,—the hope expressed at the termination of his speech. The whale must have been killed, as he had said. He was looking for the *whaler*.

For full ten minutes he continued his optical search over the sea,—until not a fathom of the surface had escaped his scrutiny.

At first his glances had expressed almost a confident hope; and, observing them, the others became excited to a high degree of joy.

Gradually, however, the old shadow returned over the sailor's countenance, and was instantly transferred to the faces of his companions.

The sea,—as far as his eye could command a view of it,—showed neither sail, nor any other object. Its shining surface was absolutely without a speck.

With a disappointed air, the captain of the *Catamaran* descended from his post of observation; and once more turned his attention to the dead *cachalot* from which they were now separated by less than a hundred fathoms,—a distance that was constantly decreasing, as the raft, under sail, continued to drift nearer.

The body of the whale did not appear anything like as large as when first seen. The mist was no longer producing its magnifying effect upon the vision of our adventurers; but although the carcass of the *cachalot* could no more have been mistaken for an island, still was it an object of enormous dimensions; and might easily have passed for a great black rock standing several fathoms above the surface of the sea. It was over twenty yards in length; and, seen sideways from the raft, of course appeared much longer.

In five minutes after, they were close up to the dead whale; and, the sail being lowered, the raft was brought to. Ben threw a rope around one of the pectoral fins; and, after making it fast, the *Catamaran* lay moored alongside the *cachalot*, like some diminutive tender attached to a huge ship of war! There were several reasons why Ben Brace should mount up to the summit of that mountain of whalebone and blubber; and, as soon as the raft had been safely secured, he essayed the ascent.

It was not such a trifling feat,—this climbing upon the carcass of the dead whale. Nor was it to be done without danger. The slippery epidermis of the huge leviathan,—lubricated as it was with that unctuous fluid which the skin of the sperm-whale is known to secrete,—rendered footing upon it extremely insecure.

It might be fancied no great matter for a swimmer like Ben Braco to slide off: since a fall of a few feet into the water could not cause him any great bodily hurt. But when the individual forming this fancy has been told that there was something like a score of sharks prowling around the carcass, he will obtain a more definite idea of the danger to which such a fall would have submitted the adventurous seaman.

Ben Brace was the last man to be cowed by a trifling danger, or even one of magnitude; and partly by Snowball's assistance, and using the pectoral flipper to which the raft was attached as a stirrup, he succeeded in mounting upon the back of the defunct monster of the deep.

As soon as he had steadied himself in his new position, a piece of rope was thrown up to him,—by which Snowball was himself hoisted to the shoulders of the *cachalot*; and then the two seamen proceeded towards the tail,—or, as the sailor pronounced it, the "starn" of this peculiar craft.

A little aft of "midships" a pyramidal lump of fatty substance projected several feet above the line of the vertebras. It was the spurious or rudimentary dorsal fin, with which the sperm-whale is provided.

On arriving at this protuberance,—which chanced to be the highest point on the carcass where the flag was elevated on its slender shaft,— both came to a halt; and there stood together, gazing around them over the glittering surface of the sunlit sea.

Chapter Fifty Nine
Aboard the Body of a Whale

The object of their united reconnoissance was the same which, but a few moments before, had occupied the attention of the sailor. They were standing on the dead body of a whale that had been killed by harpoons. Where were the people who had harpooned it?

After scanning the horizon with the same careful scrutiny as before, the sailor once more turned his attention to the huge leviathan, on whose back they were borne.

Several objects not before seen now attracted the attention of himself and companion. The tall flag, known among whalers by the name of "whiff," was not the only evidence of the manner in which the *cachalot* had met its death. Two large harpoons were seen sticking out of its side, their iron arrows buried up to the socket in its blubber; while from the thick wooden shanks, protruding beyond the skin, were lines extending into the water, at the ends of which were large blocks of wood floating like buoys upon the surface of the sea.

Ben identified the latter as the "drogues," that form part of the equipment of a regular whale-ship. He knew them well, and their use. Before becoming a man-o'-war's-man, he had handled the harpoon; and was perfectly *au fait* to all connected with the calling of a whaler.

"Yes," resumed he, on recognising the implements of his *ci-devant* profession, "it ha' been jest as I said. A whaler 'a been over this ground, and killed the spermacety. Maybe I'm wrong about that," he added, after reflecting a short while. "I may be wrong about the ship being over this very ground. I don't like the look o' them drogues."

"De drogue?" inquired the Coromantee. "Dem block o' wood dat am driffin' about? Wha' for you no like dem, Massa Brace?"

"But for their bein' thear I could say for sartin a ship had been here."

"Must a' been!" asserted Snowball. "If no', how you count for de presence ob de flag and de hapoons?"

"Ah!" answered the sailor, with something like a sigh; "they kud a' got thear, without the men as throwed 'em bein' anywhere near this. You know nothin' o' whalin', Snowy."

This speech put Snowball in a quandary.

"You see, nigger," continued the sailor, "the presence o' them drogues indercates that the whale warn't dead when the boats left her." (The *ci-devant* whaler followed the fashion of his former associates, in speaking of the whale, among whom the epicene gender of the animal is always feminine.) "She must a' been still alive," continued he, "and the drogues were put thear to hinder her from makin' much way through the water. In coorse there must a' been a school o' the spermacetys; and the crew o' the whaler didn't want to lose time with this 'un, which they had wounded. For that reason they have struck her with this pair o' drogued harpoons; and stuck this whift into her back. On fust seein' that, I war inclined to think different. You see the whift be stickin' a'most straight up, an' how could that a' been done by them in the boats? If the whale hadn't a' been dead, nobody would a' dared to a clombed on to her an' fix the flag that way."

"You are right dar," interrupted Snowball.

"No," rejoined the sailor, "I ain't. I thought I war; but I war wrong, as you be now, Snowy. You see the flag-spear ain't straight into the back o' the anymal. It's to one side, though it now stand nearly on top; because the body o' the whale be canted over a bit. A first-rate '*heads-man*' o' a whale-boat could easily a' throwed it that way from the bottom o' his boat, and that's the way it ha' been done."

"Spose 'im hab been jest dat way," assented Snowball. "But wha' matter 'bout dat? De whale have been kill all de same."

"What matter? Everything do it matter."

"'Splain, Massa Brace!"

"Don't ye see, nigger, that if the spermacety had been dispatched while the boats were about it, it would prove that the whale-ship must a' been here while they were a killin' the creature; an' that would go far to prove that she couldn't be a great ways off now."

"So dat wud, —so im wud, fo' sa'tin sure."

"Well, Snowy, as the case stands, thear be no sartinty where the whaler be at this time. The anymal, after being drogued, may a' sweemed many a mile from the place where she war first harpooned. I've knowed 'em to go a score o' knots afore they pulled up; an' this bein' a' old bull,—one o' the biggest spermacetys I ever see,—she must a sweemed to the full o' that distance afore givin' in. If that's been so, thear ain't much chance o' eyther her or we bein' overhauled by the whaler."

As the sailor ceased speaking he once more directed his glance over the ocean; which, after another minute and careful scrutiny of the horizon, fell back upon the body of the whale, with the same expression of disappointment that before had been observable.

Chapter Sixty
A curious Cuisine

During all that day, the sailor and the ex-cook of the *Pandora* kept watch from the *summit* of the dead *cachalot*.

It was not altogether for this purpose they remained there, —since the mast of the *Catamaran* would have given them an observatory of equal and even greater elevation.

There were several reasons why they did not cast off from the carcass, and continue their westward course: the most important being the hope that the destroyers of the whale might return to take possession of the valuable prize which they had left behind them.

There was, moreover, an undefined feeling of security in lying alongside the leviathan, —almost as great as they might have felt if anchored near the beach of an actual island, —and this had some influence in protracting their stay.

But there was yet another motive which would of itself have caused them to remain at their present moorings for a considerable period of time.

During the intervals of their protracted vigil, they had not been inattentive to the objects immediately around them: and the carcass of the whale had come in for a share of their consideration. A consultation had been held upon it, which had resulted in a determination not to leave the leviathan until they had rendered its remains, or at least a portion of them, useful for some future end.

The old whaleman knew that under that dark epidermis over which, for two days, they had been recklessly treading, there were many valuable substances that might be made available to their use and comfort, on board the *Catamaran*.

First, there was the "blubber," which, if boiled or "tried," would, from the body of an old bull like that, yield at the very least, a hundred barrels of oil.

This they cared nothing about: since they had neither the pots to boil, the casks to hold, nor the craft to carry it,—even if rendered into oil for the market.

But Ben knew that within the skull of the *cachalot* there was a deposit of pure sperm, that needed no preparation, which would be found of service to them in a way they had already thought of.

This sperm could be reached by simply removing the "junk" which forms the exterior portion of a *cachalot's* huge snout, and sinking a shaft into the skull. Here would, or should, be found a cavity filled with a delicate cellular tissue, containing ten or a dozen large barrels full of the purest spermaceti.

They did not stand in need of anything like this quantity. A couple of casks would suffice for their need; and these they desired to obtain for that want which had suggested itself to both Snowball and the sailor. They had been long suffering from the absence of fuel,—not wherewith to warm themselves,—but as a means of enabling them to cook their food. They need suffer no longer. With the spermaceti to be extracted from the "case" of the *cachalot*, they could lay in a stock that would last them for many a day. They had their six casks,—five of them still empty. By using a couple of them to contain the oil, the raft would still be sufficiently buoyant to carry all hands, and not a bit less worthy of the sea.

Both of these brave men had observed the repugnance with which Lilly Lalee partook of their raw repasts. Nothing but hunger enabled her to eat what they could set before her. It had touched the feelings of both; and rendered them desirous of providing her with some kind of food more congenial to the delicate palate of the child.

Long before they had any intention of abandoning the dead body of the whale,—in fact shortly after taking possession of it,—Ben Brace, assisted by Snowball and little William,—the latter having also mounted upon the monster's back,—cut open the great cavity of the "case" with the axe; and then inserting a large tin pot,—which had turned up in the sailor's sea-kit,—drew it put again full of liquid spermaceti.

This was carried down to the deck of the *Catamaran* when the process of making a fire was instantly proceeded with.

By means of some untwisted strands of tarry rope, ingeniously inserted into the oil, the pot was converted into a sort of open lamp,—which only required to be kindled into a flame.

But Ben Brace had not been smoking a pipe for a period of nearly thirty years, without being provided with the means of lighting it. In the same depository from which the tin pot had been obtained was found the proper implements for striking a light, — flint, steel, and tinder, — and, as the latter, within the water-tight compartment of the man-o'-war's-man's chest, having been preserved perfectly dry, there was no difficulty in setting fire to the oil.

It was soon seen burning up over the rim of the pot with a bright clear flame; and a large flake of the dried fish being held over the blaze, in a very short space of time became done to a turn.

This furnished all of them with a meal much more palatable than any they had eaten since they had been forced to flee from the decks of the burning *Pandora*.

Chapter Sixty One
An Assembly of Sharks

As the spermaceti in the pot still continued to blaze up,—the wick not yet having burnt out,—it occurred to Snowball to continue his culinary operations, and broil a sufficient quantity of the dead fish to serve for supper. The ex-cook, unlike most others of his calling, did not like to see his fuel idly wasted: and therefore, in obedience to the thought that had suggested itself, he brought forth another flake of shark-flesh, and submitted to the flames, as before.

While observing him in the performance of this provident task, a capital idea also occurred to Ben Brace. Since it was possible thus to cook their supper in advance, why not also their breakfast for the following morning, then dinner for the day, their supper of to-morrow night,—in short, all the raw provisions which they had on their hands? By doing this, not only would a fire be no longer necessary, but the fish so cooked,—or even thoroughly dried in the blaze and smoke,—would be likely to keep better. In fact, fish thus preserved,—as is often done with herrings, ling, codfish, mackerel, and haddock,—will remain good for months without suffering the slightest taint of decomposition. It was an excellent idea; and, Ben having communicated it to the others, it was at once determined that it should be carried out.

There was no fear of their running short in the staple article of fuel. Ben assured them that the "case" of a *cachalot* of the largest size,—such as the one beside them,—often contained five hundred gallons of the liquid spermaceti! Besides, there was the enormous quantity of junk and blubber,—whole mountains of it,—both of which could be rendered into oil by a process which the whalers term "trying." Other inflammable substances, too, are found in the carcass of the sperm-whale: so that, in the article of fuel, the crew of the *Catamaran* had been unexpectedly furnished with a stock by which they might keep up a blazing fire for the whole of a twelvemonth.

It was no longer any scarcity of fuel that could hinder them from cooking on a large scale, but a scantiness of the provisions to be cooked; and they were now greatly troubled at the thought of their larder having got so low.

While Ben Brace and Snowball stood pondering upon this, and mutually murmuring their regrets, a thought suddenly came into the mind of the sailor which was calculated to give comfort to all.

"As for the provisions in our locker," said he, "we can easily 'plenish them, such as they be. Look there, nigger. There be enough raw meat to keep ye a' cookin' till your wool grows white."

The sailor, as he said this, simply nodded toward the sea.

It needed no further pointing out to understand what he meant by the phrase "raw meat." Scores of sharks,—both of the blue and white species,— attended by their pilots and suckers, were swimming around the carcass of the *cachalot*. The sea seemed alive with them. Scarce a square rod, within a circle of several hundred fathoms' circumference, that did not exhibit their stiff, wicked-looking dorsal fins cutting sharply above the surface.

Of course the presence of the dead whale accounted for this unusual concourse of the tyrants of the deep. Not that they had any intention of directing their attack upon it: for, from the peculiar conformation of his mouth, the shark is incapable of feeding upon the carcass of a large whale. But having, no doubt, accompanied the chase at the time the *cachalot* had been harpooned, they were now staying by a dead body, from an instinct that told them its destroyers would return, and supply them with its flesh in convenient morsels,—while occupied in *flensing* it.

"Ugh!" exclaimed the sailor; "they look hungry enough to bite at any bait we may throw out to them. We won't have much trouble in catchin' as many o' 'em as we want."

"A doan b'lieve, Massa Brace, we hab got nebba such a ting as a shark-hook 'board de *Cat'maran*."

"Don't make yourself uneasy 'bout that," rejoined the sailor, in a confident tone. "Shark-hook be blowed! I see somethin' up yonder worth a score o' shark-hooks. The brutes be as tame as turtles turned on their backs. They're always so about a dead spermacety. Wi' one o' them ere tools as be stickin' in the side o' the old bull, if I don't pull a few o' them out o' water, I never handled a harpoon, that's all. Ye may stop your cookin' Snowy, an' go help me. When we've got a few sharks catched an' cut up, then you can go at it again on a more 'stensive scale. Come along, my hearty!"

As Ben terminated his speech, he strode across the deck of the raft, and commenced clambering up on the carcass.

Snowball, who perceived the wisdom of his old comrade's design, let go the flake of fish he had been holding in the blaze; and, parting from the pot, once more followed the sailor up the steep side of the *cachalot*.

Chapter Sixty Two
A dangerous Equilibrium

Ben had taken along with him the axe; and, proceeding towards one of the harpoons,—still buried in the body of the whale,—he commenced cutting it out.

In a few moments a deep cavity was hewn out around the shank of the harpoon; which was further deepened, until the barbed blade was wellnigh laid bare. Snowball, impatiently seizing the stout wooden shaft, gave it a herculean pluck, that completely detached the arrow from the soft blubber in which it had been imbedded.

Unfortunately for Snowball, he had not well calculated the strength required for clearing that harpoon. Having already made several fruitless attempts to extract it, he did not expect it to draw out so easily; and, in consequence of his making an over-effort, his balance became deranged; his feet, ill-planted upon the slippery skin, flew simultaneously from beneath him; and he came down upon the side of the leviathan with a loud "slap,"—similar to what might have been heard had he fallen upon half-thawed ice.

Unpleasant as this mishap may have been, it was not the worst that might have befallen him on that occasion. Nor was it the fall itself that caused him to "sing out" at the top of his voice, and in accents betokening a terrible alarm.

What produced this manifestation was a peril of far more fearful kind, which at the moment menaced him.

The spot where the harpoon had been sticking was in the side of the *cachalot*, and, as the carcass lay, a broad space around the weapon presented an inclined plane, sloping abruptly towards the water. Lubricated as it was with the secreted oil of the animal, it was smooth as glass. Upon this slope Snowball had been standing; and upon it had he fallen.

But the impetus of the fall not only hindered him from lying where he had gone down, but also from being able to get up again; and, instead of doing either one or the other, he commenced sliding down the slippery surface of the leviathan's body, where it shelved towards the water.

Good heavens! what was to become of him? A score of sharks were just below,—waiting for him with hungry jaws, and eyes glancing greedily upward. Seeing the two men mounted upon the carcass of the whale, and one wielding an axe, they had gathered upon that side,—in the belief that the *flensing* was about to begin!

It was a slight circumstance that saved the sea-cook from being eaten up,—not only raw, but alive. Simply the circumstance of his having held on to the harpoon. Had he dropped that weapon on falling, it would never have been grasped by him again. Fortunately, he had the presence of mind to hold on to it; or perhaps the tenacity was merely mechanical. Whatever may have been the reason, he *did* hold on. Fortunately, also, he was gliding down on the side *opposite* to that on which floated the "drogue."

These two circumstances saved him.

When about half-way to the water,—and still sliding rapidly downwards,—his progress was suddenly arrested, or rather impeded,—for he was not altogether brought to a stop,—by a circumstance as unexpected as it was fortunate. That was the tightening of the line attached to the handle of the harpoon. He had slidden to the end of his tether,—the other end of which was fast to the drogue drifting about in the sea, as already said, on the opposite side of the carcass.

Heavy as was the piece of wood,—and offering, as it did, a considerable amount of resistance in being dragged through the water,—it would not have been sufficient to sustain the huge body of the Coromantee. It only checked the rapidity of his descent; and in the end he would have gone down into the sea,—and shortly after into the stomachs of, perhaps, half a score of sharks,—but for the opportune interference of the ex-man-o'-war's-man; who, just in the nick of time,—at the very moment when Snowball's toes were within six inches of the water's edge, caught hold of the cord and arrested his farther descent.

But although the sailor had been able to accomplish this much, and was also able to keep Snowball from slipping farther down, he soon discovered that he was unable to pull him up again. It was just as much as his strength was equal to,—even when supplemented by the weight of the drogue,—to keep the sea-cook in the place where he had succeeded in checking him.

There hung Snowball in suspense,—holding on to the slippery skin of the *cachalot*, literally "with tooth and toe-nail."

Snowball saw that his position was perilous,—more than that: it was frightful. He could hear noises beneath him,—the rushing of the sharks through the water. He glanced apprehensively below. He could see their black triangular fins, and note the lurid gleaming of their eyeballs, as they rolled in their sunken sockets. It was a sight to terrify the stoutest heart; and that of Snowball did not escape being terrified.

"Hole on, Massa Brace!" he instinctively shouted. "Hole on, for de lub o' God! Doan't leab me slip an inch, or dese dam brute sure cotch hold ob me! Fo' de lub o' de great Gorramity, hole on!"

Ben needed not the stimulus of this pathetic appeal. He was holding on to the utmost of his strength. He could not have added another pound to the pull. He dared not even renew either his attitude, or the grip he had upon the rope. The slightest movement he might make would endanger the life of his black-skinned comrade.

A slackening of the cord, even to the extent of twelve inches, would have been fatal to the feet of Snowball—already within six of the surface of the water and the snouts of the sharks!

Perhaps never in all his checkered career had the life of the negro been suspended in such dangerous balance. The slightest circumstance would have disturbed the equilibrium,—an ounce would have turned the scale,— and delivered him into the jaws of death.

It is scarcely necessary to conjecture what would ultimately have been the end of this perilous adventure, had the sailor and sea-cook been permitted to terminate it between themselves. The strength of the former was each instant decreasing; while the weight of the latter,—now more feebly clinging to the slippery epidermis of the whale,—was in like proportion becoming greater.

With nothing to intervene, the result might be easily guessed. In figurative parlance Snowball must have "gone overboard."

But his time was not yet come; and his comrade knew this, when a pair of hands,—small, but strong ones,—were seen grasping the cord, alongside of his own. They were the hands of Little Will'm!

At the earliest moment, after Snowball had slipped and fallen, the lad had perceived his peril; and "swarming" up by the flipper of the whale, had hurried to the assistance of Ben, laying hold of the rope,—not one second too soon.

It was soon enough, however, to save the suspended Coromantee; whose body, now yielding to the united strength of the two, was drawn up the slippery slope,—slowly, but surely,—until it rested upon the broad horizontal space around the summit of that mountain of bones and blubber.

Chapter Sixty Three
A Harpoon well handled

It was some time before either his breath or the tranquillity of his spirits was restored to the Coromantee.

The sailor was equally suffering from the loss of the former; and both remained for a good many minutes without taking any further steps towards the accomplishment of the design which had brought them on the back of the whale.

As soon, however, as Snowball could find wind enough for a few words, they were uttered in a tone of gratitude,—first to Ben, who had hindered him from sinking down into something worse than a watery grave; and then to little William, who had aided in raising him up from it.

Ben less regarded the old comrade whom he had rescued than the young one who had been instrumental in aiding him.

He stood gazing upon the youth with eyes that expressed a lively satisfaction.

The promptitude and prowess which his *protégé* had exhibited in the affair was to him a source of the greatest gratification.

Many a boy old as he,—ay, older, thought Ben Brace,—instead of having the sense shown by the lad in promptly running to the rescue, would have remained upon the raft in mute surprise; or, at the best, have evinced his sympathy by a series of unserviceable shouts, or a continued and idle screaming.

Ben did not wish to spoil his *protégé* by any spoken formula of praise, and therefore he said nothing: though, from his glances directed towards little William, it was easy to see that the bosom of the brave tar was swelling with a fond pride in the youth, for whom he had long felt an affection almost equalling that of a father.

After indulging a short while in the mutual congratulations that naturally follow such a crisis of danger, all three proceeded to the execution of the duty so unexpectedly interrupted.

William had succeeded Snowball in that simple culinary operation which the latter, commanded by his captain, had so suddenly relinquished.

The lad now returned to the raft, partly to complete the process of broiling the fish; but perhaps with a greater desire to tranquillise the fears of Lilly Lalee,—who, ignorant of the exact upshot of what had transpired, was yet in a state of unpleasant agitation.

Ben only waited for the return of his breath; and as soon as that was fairly restored to him, he once more set about the design that had caused him for the second time to climb upon the back of the *cachalot*.

Taking the harpoon from the hands of the Coromantee,—who still kept clutching it, as if there was danger in letting it go,—the sailor proceeded to draw up the drogue. Assisted by Snowball, he soon raised it out of the water, and hoisted it to the horizontal platform, on which they had placed themselves.

He did not want the block of wood just then,—only the line tied to it; and this having been detached, the drogue was left lying upon the carcass.

Armed with the harpoon, the *ci-devant* whaleman now took a survey,— not of the land, but of the sea around him.

There was an assemblage of sharks close in to the body of the whale,— at the spot where they had so lately threatened Snowball.

Some of them had since scattered away, with a full consciousness of their disappointment; but the greater number had stayed, as if unsatisfied, or expecting that the banquet that had been so near their noses might be brought back to them.

Ben's purpose was to harpoon some half-dozen of these ill-featured denizens of the deep, and with their flesh replenish the stores of the *Catamaran*; for repulsive as the brutes may appear to the eye, and repugnant to the thoughts, they nevertheless,—that is, certain species of them, and certain parts of these species,—afford excellent food: such as an epicure,—to say nothing of a man half-famished,—may eat with sufficient relish.

There could have been no difficulty in destroying any of the sharks so late threatening to swallow Snowball, had the harpooner been able to get within striking distance of them. But the slippery skin of the whale deterred the sailor from trusting himself on that dangerous incline; and he determined, therefore, to try elsewhere.

In the direction of the *cachalot's* tail the descent was gradual. Scarcely perceptible was its declination towards the water, upon which lay the two great flukes, slightly sunk below the surface, and extending on each side to a breadth of many yards.

There were several sharks playing around the tail of the *cachalot*. They might come within the pitch of a harpoon. If not, the old whaleman knew how to attract them within easy reach of that formidable weapon.

Directing Snowball to bring after him some of the pieces of blubber,— which, in cutting out the harpoon, had been detached from the carcass,— Ben proceeded towards the tail. Here and there as he advanced, with the sharp edge of the harpoon blade; he cut out a number of holes in the spongy skin, in order to give both himself and his follower a more sure footing on the slimy surface.

At the point where he intended to take his stand,—close in by the "crutch" of the *cachalot's* tail-fin,—he made three excavations with more care. At length, satisfied with his preparations, he stood, with pointed harpoon, waiting for we of the sharks to come within striking distance. They "fought shy" at first; but the old whaleman knew a way of overcoming their shyness. It only required that "chunk" of blubber, held in the hands of Snowball, to be thrown into the water, and simultaneous with the plunge a score of sharks would be seen rushing, open-mouthed, to seize upon it.

This in effect was precisely what transpired.

The blubber was dropped into the sea, close as possible to the carcass of the whale,—the sharks came charging towards it,—nearly twenty of them. The same number, however, did not go back as they had come; for one of them, impaled by the harpoon of Ben Brace, was dragged out of his native element, and hauled up the well-greased incline towards the highest point on the carcass of the *cachalot*.

There, notwithstanding his struggles and the desperate as well as dangerous fluking of his posterior fins, he was soon despatched by the axe, wielded with all the might and dexterity which the Coromantee could command.

Another shark was "hooked," and then despatched in a similar fashion; and then another and another, until Ben Brace believed that enough shark-flesh had been obtained to furnish the *Catamaran* with stores for the most prolonged voyage.

At all events, they would now have food—such as it was—to last as long as the water with which the hand of Providence alone seemed to have provided them.

Chapter Sixty Four
The thick Waters

The most palatable portions of the sharks' flesh having been stripped from the bones and cut into thin slices, were now to be submitted to a drying, or rather broiling process. This was to be accomplished by a fire of spermaceti.

As already stated, there was no scarcity on the score of this fuel. The "case" of the *cachalot* contained enough to have roasted all the sharks within a circle of ten mile around it; and, to all appearance, there were hundreds of them inside that circumference. Indeed, that part of the ocean where the dead whale had been found, though far from any land, is at all times most prolific in animal life. Sometimes the sea for miles around a ship will be seen swarming with fish of various kinds, while the air is filled with birds. In the water may be seen large "schools" of whales, "basking"—as the whalers term it—at intervals, "spouting" forth their vaporous breath, or moving slowly onward,—some of them, every now and then, exhibiting their uncouth gambols. Shoals of porpoises, albacores, bonitos, and other gregarious fishes will appear in the same place,—each kind in pursuit of its favourite prey, while sharks, threshers, and sword-fish, accompanied by their "pilots" and "suckers," though in lesser numbers, here also abound,— from the very abundance of the species on which these sea-monsters subsist "Flocks" of flying-fish sparkle in the sun with troops of bonitos gliding watchful below, while above them the sky will sometimes be literally clouded with predatory birds,—gulls, boobies, gannets, tropic and frigate-birds, albatrosses, and a score of other kinds but little known, and as yet undescribed by the naturalist.

It may be asked why so many creatures of different kinds congregate in this part of the ocean? Upon what do they subsist? what food can they find so far from land?

A ready reply to these questions may be given, by saying, that they subsist upon each other; and this would be, to some extent, true. But then there must be a base forming the food for all, and produced by some process of nature. What process can be going on in the midst of the ocean to furnish the subsistence of such myriads of large and voracious creatures? In the waters of the great deep, apparently so pure and clear, one would think that no growth,—either animal or vegetable, could spring up,—that nothing could come out of nothing. For all this, in that pure, clear water, there is a continual process of production,—not only from the soil at the bottom of the sea, but the salt-water itself contains the germs of material substances, that sustain life, or become, themselves, living things, by what appears, to our ignorant eyes, spontaneous production.

There is no spontaneity in the matter. It is simply the principle of creation, and acting under laws and by ways that, however ill-understood by us, have existed from the beginning of the world.

It is true that the whole extent of the great oceans are not thus thickly peopled. Vast tracts may be traversed, where both fish and birds of all kinds are extremely scarce; and a ship may sail for days without seeing an individual of either kind. A hundred miles may be passed over, and the eye may not be gratified by the sight of a living thing,—either in the water or the air. These tracts may truly be termed the deserts of the sea; like those of the land, apparently uninhabited and uninhabitable.

It may be asked, Why this difference, since the sea seems all alike? The cause lies not in a difference of depth: for the tracts that teem with life are variable in this respect,—sometimes only a few fathoms in profundity, and sometime unfathomable.

The true explanation must be sought for elsewhere. It will be found not in *depth*, but in *direction*,—in the direction of the currents.

Every one knows that the great oceans are intersected here and there by currents,—often hundreds of miles in breadth, but sometimes narrowing to a width of as many "knots." These oceanic streams are regular, though not regularly defined. They are not caused by mere temporary storms, but by winds having a constant and regular direction; as the "trades" in the Atlantic and Pacific, the "monsoons" in the Indian Ocean, the "pamperos" of South America, and the "northers" of the Mexican Gulf.

There is another cause for these currents, perhaps of more powerful influence than the winds, yet less taken into account. It is the *spinning* of the earth on its axis. Undoubtedly are the "trades" indebted to this for their direction towards the west,—the simple centrifugal tendency of the atmosphere. Otherwise, would these winds blow due northward and southward, coming into collision on the line of the equator.

But it is not my purpose to attempt a dissertation either on winds or oceanic streams. I am not learned enough for this, though enough to know that great misconception prevails on this subject, as well as upon that of the *tides*; and that meteorologists have not given due credit to the revolving motion of our planet, which is in truth the principal producer of these phenomena.

Why I have introduced the subject at all is, not because our little book is peculiarly a book of the ocean, but, because that ocean currents have much to do with "Ocean Waifs," and that these last afford the true explanation of the phenomenon first-mentioned,—the fact that some parts of the ocean teem with animal life, while others are as dead as a desert. The currents account for it, thus:—where two of them meet,—as is often the case,—vast quantities of material substances, both vegetable and animal, are drifted together; where they are held, to a certain extent, stationary; or circling around in great *ocean eddies*. The wrack of sea-weed,—waifs from the distant shores,—birds that have fallen lifeless into the ocean, or drop their excrement to float on its surface,—fish that have died of disease, violence, or naturally,—for the finny tribes are not exempt from the natural laws of decay and death,—all these organisms, drifted by the currents, meet upon the neutral "ground,"—there to float about, and furnish food to myriads of living creatures,—many species of which are, to all appearance, scarce organised more highly than the decomposed matters that appear first to give them life, and afterwards sustain their existence.

In such tracts of the ocean are found the lower marine animals, in incalculable numbers; the floating shell-fish, as *Janthina, Hyalaea* and *Cleodora*; the sea-lizards, as *Velellae, Porpitae,* and their kindred; the squids, and other molluscs; with myriads of *medusa*.

These are the oceanic regions known to the sailors as "thick waters," the favourite resort of the whale and its concomitant creatures, whose food they furnish; the shark, and its attendants; the dolphins, porpoises, sword-fish and flying-fish; with other denizens of the water; and a like variety of dwellers in the air, hovering above the surface, either as the enemies of those below, or aids to assist them in composing the inscrutable "chain of destruction."

Chapter Sixty Five
A Whale on Fire!

Perhaps we have *drifted* too far adown the currents of the ocean. From our digression let us return to out special "Waifs." We left them making preparations to roast the shark-flesh,—not in single steaks, but in a wholesale fashion,—as if they had intended to prepare a "fish dinner" for the full crew of a frigate.

As already stated, fuel they had in sufficiency; or, at all events, the best of oil, that would serve as such. The spermaceti could not be readily kindled, nor its blaze kept up, without wicks. But neither was there any difficulty about this. There was a quantity of old rope trash on the raft, which had been fished up among the wreck of the *Pandora*, and kept in case of an emergency. It needed only to restore this to its original state of tarry fibre, when they would be provided with wick enough to keep the lamp long burning. It was the lamp itself, or rather the cooking furnace, that caused them uneasiness. They had none. The tiny tin vessel that had already served for a single meal would never do for the grand *roti* they now designed making. With it, along with time and patience, they might have accomplished the task; but time to them was too precious to be so wasted; and as to patience,—circumstanced as they were, it could scarcely be expected.

They stood in great need of a cooking-stove. There was nothing on board the *Catamaran* that could be used as a substitute. Indeed, to have kindled such a fire as they wanted on the raft,—without a proper material for their hearth,—would have seriously endangered the existence of the craft; and might have terminated in a conflagration.

It was a dilemma that had not suggested itself sooner—that is, until the shark-steaks had been made ready for roasting. Then it presented itself to their contemplation in full force, and apparently without any loophole to escape from it.

What was to be done for a cooking-stove?

Snowball sighed as he thought of his caboose, with all its paraphernalia of pots and pans,—especially his great copper, in which he had been accustomed to boil mountains of meat and oceans of pea-soup.

But Snowball was not the individual to give way to vain regrets,—at least, not for long. Despite that absence of that superior intellect,—which flippant gossips of so-called a "Social Science" delight in denying to his race, themselves often less gifted than he,—Snowball was endowed with rare ingenuity,—especially in matters relating to the *cuisine,* and in less than ten minutes after the question of a cooking-stove had been started, the Coromantee conceived the idea of one that might have vied with any of the various "patents" so loudly extolled by the ironmongers, and yet not so effective when submitted to the test. At all events, Snowball's plan was suited to the circumstances in which its contriver was placed; and perhaps it was the only one which the circumstances would have allowed.

Unlike other inventors, the Coromantee proclaimed the plan of his invention as soon as he had conceived it.

"Wha' for?" he asked, as the idea shaped itself in his skull,—"wha' for we trouble 'bout a pot fo' burn de oil?"

"What for, Snowy!" echoed the sailor, turning upon his interrogator an expectant look.

"Why we no make de fire up hya?"

The conversation was carried on upon the back of the whale,—where the sharks had been butchered and cut up.

"Up here!" again echoed the sailor, still showing surprise. "What matter whether it be up here or down theear, so long's we've got no vessel,—neyther pot nor pan?"

"Doan care a dam fo' neyder," responded the ex-cook. "I'se soon show ye, Mass' Brace, how we find vessel, big 'nuff to hold all de oil in de karkiss ob de ole cashlot, as you call him."

"Explain, nigger, explain!"

"Sartin I do. Gib me dat axe. I soon 'splain de whole sarkumstance."

Ben passed the axe, which he had been holding, into the hands of the Coromantee.

The latter, as he had promised, soon made his meaning clear, by setting to work upon the carcass of the *cachalot,* and with less than a dozen blows of the sharp-edged tool hollowing out a large cavity in the blubber.

"Now, Mass' Brace," cried he, when he had finished, triumphantly balancing the axe above his shoulder, "wha' you call dat? Dar's a lamp hold all de oil we want set blaze. You d'sire me 'crow' de hole any wida or deepa,

I soon make 'im deep's a draw-well an' wide as de track ob a waggon. Wha' say, Mass' Brace?"

"Hurraw for you, Snowy! It be just the thing. I dar say it's deep enough, and wide as we'll want it. You ha got good brains, nigger,—not'ithstanding what them lubbers as they call filosaphurs say. I'm a white, an' niver thought o' it. This'll do for the furness we want. Nothin' more needed than to pour the sparmacety into it, chuck a bit o' oakum on the top, an' set all ablaze. Let's do it, and cook the wittles at once."

The cavity, which Snowball had "crowed" in the carcass of the whale was soon filled with oil taken from the case. In this was inserted with due care a quantity of the fibre, obtained by "picking" the old ropes into oakum.

A crane was next erected over the cavity,—a handspike forming one support and an oar the other. The crane itself consisted of the long iron arrow and socket of one of the harpoons found in the carcass of the *cachalot*.

Upon this was suspended, as upon a spit, so many slices of shark-meat as could be accommodated with room, and when all was arranged, a "taper" was handed up from below, and the wick set on fire.

The tarry strands caught like tinder; and soon after a fierce bright blaze was seen rising several feet above the back of the *cachalot*,—causing the shark-steaks to frizzle and fry, and promising in a very short space of time to "do them to a turn."

Any one who could have witnessed the spectacle from distance, and not understanding its nature, might have fancied that the *whale was on fire*!

Chapter Sixty Six
The big Raft

While the strange phenomenon of a blazing fire upon the back of a whale was being exhibited to the eyes of ocean-birds and ocean-fishes,—all doubtless wondering what it meant,—another and very different spectacle was occurring scarce twenty miles from the spot,—of course also upon the surface of the ocean.

If in the former there was something that might be called comic, there was nothing of this in the latter. On the contrary, it was a true tragedy,—a drama of death.

The stage upon which it was being enacted was a platform of planks and spars, rudely united together,—in short, a raft. The *dramatis persona* were men,—all men; although it might have required some stretch of imagination,—aided by a little acquaintanceship with the circumstances that had placed them upon that raft,—to have been certain that they were human beings. A stranger to them, looking upon them in reality,—or upon a picture, giving a faithful representation of them,—might have doubted their humanity, and mistaken them for *fiends*. No one could have been blamed for such a misconception.

If human beings in shape, and so in reality, they were fiends in aspect, and not far from it in mental conformation. Even in appearance they were more like skeletons than men. One actually was a skeleton,—not a living skeleton, but a corpse, clean-stripped of its flesh. The ensanguined bones, with some fragments of the cartilage still adhering to them, showed that the despoliation had been recent. The skeleton was not perfect. Some of the bones were absent. A few were lying near on the timbers of the raft, and a few others might have been seen in places where it was horrible to behold them!

The raft was an oblong platform of some twenty feet in length by about fifteen in width. It was constructed out of pieces of broken masts and spars of a ship, upon which was supported an irregular sheeting of planks, the fragments of bulwarks, hatches, cabin-doors that had been wrested from their hinges, lids of tea-chests, coops, and a few other articles,—such as form the paraphernalia of movables on board a ship. There was a large hogshead with two or three small barrels upon the raft; and around its edge were lashed several empty casks, serving as buoys to keep it above water. A single spar stood up out of its centre, or "midships," to which was rigged—in a very slovenly manner—a large lateen sail,—either the spanker or spritsail of a ship, or the mizzen topsail of a bark.

Around the "step" of the mast a variety of other objects might have been seen: such as oars, handspikes, pieces of loose boards, some tangled coils of rope, an axe or two, half a dozen tin pots and "tots,"—such as are used by sailors,—a quantity of shark-bones clean picked, with two or three other bones, like those already alluded to, and whose size and form told them to be the *tibia* of a human skeleton.

Between twenty and thirty men were moving amid this miscellaneous collection,—not all moving: for they were in every conceivable attitude, of repose as of action. Some were seated, some lying stretched, some standing, some staggering,—as if reeling under the influence of intoxication, or too feeble to support their bodies in an erect attitude. It was not any rocking on the part of the raft that was producing these eccentric movements. The sea was perfectly quiescent, and the rude embarkation rested upon it like a log.

The cause might have been discovered near the bottom of the mast, where stood a barrel or cask of medium size, from which proceeded an exhalation, telling its contents to be rum.

The staggering skeletons were *drunk*!

It was not that noisy intoxication that tells of recent indulgence, but rather of the nervous wreck which succeeds it; and the words heard, instead of being the loud banterings of inebriated men, were more like the ravings and gibbering of maniacs. No wonder: since they who uttered them *were* mad,—mad with *mania potu*! If they were ever to recover, it would be the last time they were likely to be afflicted by the same disease,—at least on board that embarkation. Not from any virtuous resolve on their parts, but simply from the fact that the cause of their insanity no longer existed.

The rum-cask was as dry inside as out. There was no longer a drop of the infernal liquor on the raft; no more spirit of any kind to produce fresh drunkenness or renewed *delirium tremens*!

The madmen were not heeded by the others; but allowed to totter about, and give speech to their incoherent mumblings!—sometimes diversified by yells, or peals of mania laughter,—always thickly interlarded with oaths and other blasphemous utterances.

It was only when disturbing the repose of some one less *exalted* than themselves, or when two of them chanced to come into collision, that a scene would ensue,—in some instances extending to almost every individual on the raft, and ending by one or other of the delirious disputants getting "chucked" into the sea, and having a swim before recovering foothold on the frail embarkation. This the ducked individual would be certain to do. Drunk as he might have been, and maudlin as he might be, his instincts were never so benumbed as to render him regardless of self-preservation. Even from out his haggard eyes still gleamed enough of intelligence to tell that those dark triangular objects, moving in scores around the raft, and cutting the water, so swift and sheer, were the dorsal fins of the dreaded sharks. Each one was a sight that, to a sailor's eye, even when "blind drunk," brings habitual dread.

The *douche*, and the fright attending it, would usually restore his reason to the delirious individual,—or, at all events, would have the effect of restoring tranquillity upon the raft,—soon after to be disturbed by some scene of like, or perhaps more terrible, activity.

The reader, unacquainted with the history of this raft and the people upon it, may require some information concerning them. A few words must suffice for both.

As already stated, at the beginning of our narrative, a raft was constructed out of such timbers as could be detached from the slave-bark *Pandora*,—after that vessel had caught fire, and previous to her blowing up. Upon this embarkation the slaver's crew had escaped, leaving her *cargo* to perish,—some by the explosion, some by drowning, and not a few by the teeth of sharks. The *Pandora's* captain, along with five others,—including the mates and carpenter,—had stolen away with the gig. As this was the only boat found available in the fearful crisis of the conflagration, the remainder of the crew had betaken themselves to the large raft, hurriedly constructed for the occasion.

As already related, Snowball and the Portuguese girl were the only individuals on board the *Pandora* who had remained by the wreck, or rather among its *débris*. There the Coromantee, by great courage and cunning, had succeeded not only in keeping himself and his *protégé* afloat, but in establishing a chance for sustaining existence, calculated to last for some days. It is known also that Ben Brace with *his protégé*, having been informed by the captain's parting speech that there was a barrel of gunpowder aboard the burning bark, apprehensive of the explosion, had silently constructed a little raft of his own; which, after being launched from under the bows of the slaver, he had brought *en rapport* with the "big raft," and thereto attached it. This "tender," still carrying the English sailor and the boy, had been afterwards cut loose from its larger companion in the dead hour of night, and permitted to fall far into the wake. The reason of this defection was simply to save little William from being eaten up by the ex-crew of the *Pandora*, then reduced to a famished condition,—if we may use the phrase, screwed up to the standard of anthropophagy.

Since the hour in which the two rafts became separated from each other, the reader is acquainted, in all its minute details, with the history of the lesser: how it joined issue with the embarkation that carried the ex-cook and his *protégé*; how the union with the latter produced a cross between the two,—afterwards yclept the *Catamaran*; with all the particulars of the *Catamaran's* voyage, up to the time when she became moored alongside the carcass of the *cachalot*; and for several days after.

During this time, the "big raft" carrying the crew of tin burnt bark,— being out of sight, may also have escaped from the reader's mind. Both it and its occupants were still in existence. Not all of them, it is true, but the greater number; and among these, the most prominent in strength of body, energy of mind; and wickedness of disposition.

It is scarce necessary to say, that the raft now introduced as lying upon the ocean some twenty miles from the dead *cachalot* was that which some days before had parted from the *Pandora*, or that the fiendish forms that occupied it were the remnant of the *Pandora's* crew.

These were not all there: nearly a score of them were absent. The absence of the captain, with five others who had accompanied him in his gig, has been explained. The ex-cook, the English sailor and sailor-boy, with the cabin passenger, Lilly Lalee, have also been accounted for; but there were several others aboard the big raft, on its first starting "to sea," that were no longer to be seen amidst the crowd still occupying this ungainly embarkation. Half a dozen,—perhaps more,—seemed to be missing. Their absence might have appeared mysterious, to anyone who had not been kept "posted" up in the particulars of the ill-directed cruise through which the raft had been passing; though the skeleton above described, and the dissevered *tibia* scattered around, might have given a clew to their disappearance,—at least, to anyone initiated into the shifts and extremities of starvation.

To those of less experience,—or less quick comprehension,—it may be necessary to repeat the conversation which was being carried on upon the raft,—at the moment when it is thus reintroduced to the notice of the reader. A correct report of this will satisfactorily explain why its original crew had been reduced, from over thirty, to the number of six-and-twenty, exclusive of the skeleton!

Chapter Sixty Seven
A Crew of Cannibals

"*Allons!*" cried a black-bearded man, in whose emaciated frame it was not easy to recognise the once corpulent bully of the slave-ship,—the Frenchman, Le Gros. "*Allons! messieurs!* It's time to try fortune again. *Sacré!* we must eat, or die!"

The question may be asked, What were these men to eat? There appeared to be no food upon the raft. There *was* none,—not a morsel of any kind that might properly be called meat for man. Nor had there been, ever since the second day after the departure of the raft from the side of the burning bark. A small box of sea-biscuits, that, when distributed, gave only two to each man, was all that had been saved in their hurried retreat from the decks of the *Pandora*. These had disappeared in a day. They had brought away water in greater abundance, and caught some since in their shirts, and on the spread sail,—nearly after the same fashion and in the same rain-storm that had afforded the well-timed supply to Ben Brace and his *protégé*.

But the stock derived from both sources was on the eve of being exhausted. Only a small ration or two to each man remained in the cask; but thirsty as most of them might be, they were suffering still more from the kindred appetite of hunger.

What did Le Gros mean when he said they must eat? What food was there on the raft, to enable them to avoid the terrible alternative appended to his proposal,—"eat, or die"! What *had* kept them from dying: since it was now many days, almost weeks, since they had swallowed the last morsel of biscuit so sparingly distributed amongst them?

The answer to all these interrogatories is one and the some. It is too fearful to be pronounced,—awful even to think of!

The clean-stripped skeleton lying upon the raft, and which was clearly that of a human being; the bones scattered about,—some of them, as already observed, held in hand, and in such fashion as to show the horrid use that was being made of them,—left no doubt as to the nature of the food upon which the hungering wretches had been subsisting.

This, and the flesh of a small shark, which they had succeeded in luring alongside, and killing with the blow of a handspike, had been their only provision since parting with the *Pandora*. There were sharks enough around them now. A score, at the very least, might have been quartering the sea, within sight of the raft; but these monsters, strange to say, were so shy, that not one of them would approach near enough to allow them an opportunity of capturing it! Every attempt to take them had proved unsuccessful. Such of the crew as kept sober had been trying for days. Some were even at that moment engaged with hook and line, angling for the ferocious fish,—their hooks floating far out in the water, baited with *human flesh*.

It was only the mechanical continuation of a scheme that had long since proved to be of no avail,—a sort of despairing struggle against improbability. The sharks had taken the alarm; perhaps from observing the fate of that one of their number that had gone too near the odd embarkation; or, perhaps, warned by some mysterious instinct, that, sooner or later, they would make a grand banquet on those who were so eager to feast upon them.

In any case, no sharks had been taken, or were likely to be taken; and once more the eyes of the famishing castaways were wolfishly turned upon one another, while their thoughts reverted to that horrible alternative that was to save them from starvation.

Le Gros—on board the raft, as upon the deck of the slave-ship—still held a sort of fatal ascendency over his comrades; and with Ben Brace no longer to oppose his despotic propensities, he had established over his fellow-skeletons a species of arbitrary rule.

His conduct had all along been guided by no more regard for fair-play than was just necessary to keep his subordinates from breaking out into open mutiny; and among these the weaker ones fared even worse than their fellows, bad as that was.

A few of the stronger,—who formed a sort of bodyguard to the bully, and were ready to stand up for him in case of extremity,—shared his ascendency over the rest; and to these were distributed larger rations of water, along with the more choice morsels of their horrid food.

This partiality had more than once led to scenes, that promised to end in bloodshed; and but for this occasional show of resistance, Le Gros and his party might have established a tyranny that would have given them full power over the *lives* of their feebler companions.

Things were fast tending in this direction,—merging, as it were, into absolute monarchy,—a monarchy of "cannibals," of which Le Gros himself would be "king." It had not yet, however, quite come to that,—at least when it became a question of life and death. When the necessity arose of finding a fresh victim for their horrible but necessary sacrifice, there was still enough republicanism left among the wretches to influence the decision in a just and equitable manner, and cause the selection to be made by lot. When it comes to crises like these,—to questions of life and death,—men must yield up their opposition to the *ballot*, and acknowledge its equity.

Le Gros and his cruel bodyguard would have opposed it had they been strong enough,—as do equally cruel politicians who are strong enough,—but the bully still doubted the strength of his party. A proposal so atrocious had beep made, in the case of little William, at the very outset, and had met with but slight opposition. Had it not been for the brave English sailor, the lad would certainly have fallen a sacrifice to the horrid appetites of these horrid men. With one of themselves, however, the case was different. Each had a few adherents, who would not have submitted to such an arbitrary cruelty; and Le Gros was influenced by the fear of a general "skrimmage," in which more than one life,—among the rest perhaps his own,—might be forfeited. The time for such a high-handed measure had not yet arrived; and when it came to the question of "Who dies next?" it was still found necessary to resort to the *ballot*.

That question was once more propounded,—now for the third time,— Le Gros himself acting as the spokesman. No one said anything in reply, or made any sign of being opposed to an answer being given. On the contrary, all appeared to yield, if not a cheerful, at least a tacit assent to what they all knew to be meant for a proposal,—knowing also its fearful nature and consequences.

They also comprehended whence the answer was to come. Twice before had they consulted that dread oracle, whose response was certain death to one of their number. Twice before had they recognised and submitted to its decree. No preliminaries needed to be discussed. These had been long ago arranged. There was nothing more to do than cast the lots.

On the moment after Le Gros had put the question, a movement was visible among the men to whom it was addressed. One might have expected it to startle them; but it did not appear to do this,—at least, to any great extent. Some only showed those signs of fear distinguishable by blanched cheeks and white lips; but there were some too delirious to understand the full import of what was to follow; and the majority of the crew had become too callow with suffering to care much even for life!

Most that could, however,—for there were some too feeble to stand erect,—rose to their feet, and gathered around the challenger, exhibiting both in their words and attitudes, an earnestness that told them not altogether indifferent to death.

By a sort of tacit agreement among them, Le Gros acted as master of the ceremonies,—the dispenser of that dread lottery of life and death, in which he himself was to take a share. Two or three of his fellows stood on each side of him, acting as aids or *croupiers*.

Solemn and momentous as was the question to be decided, the mode of decision was simple in the extreme. Le Gros held in his hand a canvas bag, of oblong bolster shape,—such as sailors use to carry their spare suit of "Sunday go-ashores." In the bottom of this bag,—already carefully counted into it,—were twenty-six buttons: the exact number of those who were to take part in the drawing. They were the common black buttons of horn,—each pierced with four holes,—such as may be seen upon the jacket of the merchant sailor. They had been cut from their own garments for the purpose in which they were now, a third time, to be employed, and all chosen so exactly alike, that even the eye would have found it difficult to distinguish one from the other. One, however, offered an exception to this statement. While all its fellows were jet black, it exhibited a reddish hue,—a dark crimson,—as if it had been defiled with blood. And so it had been; stained on purpose,—that for which it was to be employed,—to be the exponent of the *prize*, in that lottery of blood, of which its colour was an appropriate emblem.

The difference between it and the others was not perceptible to the touch. The fingers of a man born blind could not have distinguished it among the rest,—much less the callous and tar-bedaubed "claws" of a sailor.

The red button was cast into the bag along with the others. *"He who should draw it forth must die."*

As we have said, there was no settling about preliminaries, no talking about choice as to the time of drawing. These matters had been discussed before, both openly and by secret mental calculations. All had arrived at the conclusion that the chances were even, and that it could make no difference in the event as to whose fate was first decided. The red button might be the last in the bag, or it might be the first drawn out of it.

Under this impression, no one hesitated to inaugurate the dread ceremony of the drawing; and as soon as Le Gros held out the bag,—just open enough to admit a hand,—a man stepped up, and, with an air of reckless indifference, plunged his arm into the opening!

Chapter Sixty Eight
The Lottery of Life and Death

One by one the buttons were drawn forth from the bag, —each man, as he drew his, exhibiting it in his open palm, to satisfy the others as to its colour, and then placing it in a common receptacle, —against the contingency of its being required again for another like lottery!

Solemn as was the character of the ceremony, it was not conducted either in solemnity or silence. Many of the wretches even jested while it was in progress; and a stranger to the dread conditions under which the drawing was being made might have supposed it a raffle for some trifling prize!

The faces of a few, however, would have contradicted this supposition. A few there were who approached the oracle with cowed and craven looks; and their trembling fingers, as they inserted them into the bag, proclaimed an apprehension stronger than could have arisen from any mere courting of chance in an ordinary casting of lots.

Those men who were noisiest and most gleeful *after* they had drawn were the ones who before it had shown the strongest signs of fear, and who trembled most while performing the operation.

Some of them could not conceal even their demoniac joy at having drawn blank, but danced about over the raft as if they had suddenly succeeded to some splendid fortune.

The difference between this singular lottery and most others, was that the blanks were the prizes, —the prize itself being the true blank, —the ending of existence.

Le Gros continued to hold the bag, and with an air of nonchalance; though anyone closely observing his countenance could tell that it was assumed. As had been already proved, the French bully was at heart a coward. Under the influence of angry passion, or excited by a desire for revenge, he could show fight, and even fling himself into positions of danger; but in a contest such as that in which he was now engaged a cool strife, in which Fortune was his only antagonist, and in which he could derive no advantage from any unfair subterfuge, his artificial courage had entirely forsaken him.

So long as the lottery was in its earlier stages, and only a few buttons had been taken out of the bag, he preserved his assumed air of indifference. There were still many chances of life against that one of death,—nearly twenty to one. As the drawing proceeded, however, and one after another exhibited his black button, a change could be observed passing over the features of the Frenchman. His apparent *sangfroid* began to forsake him; while his glances betokened a feverish excitement, fast hastening towards apprehension.

As each fresh hand came up out of the dark receptacle bearing the evidence of its owner's fate, Le Gros was seen to cast hurried and anxious glances towards the tiny circle of horn, held between the thumb and forefinger, and each time that he saw the colour to be black his countenance appeared to darken at the sight.

When the twentieth button had been brought forth, and still the red one remained in the bag, the master of the ceremonies became fearfully excited. He could no longer conceal his apprehension. His chances of life were diminished to a point that might well inspire him with fear. It was now but six to one,—for there were only six more tickets to be disposed of.

At this crisis, Le Gros interrupted the drawing to reflect. Would he be in a better position, if some one else held the bag? Perhaps that might change the run of luck hitherto against him; and which he had been cursing with all his might ever since the number had been going through the teens. He had tried every way he could think of to tempt the red ticket out of the bag. He had shaken the buttons time after time,—in hopes of bringing it to the top, or in some position that might insure its being taken up. But all to no purpose. It would obstinately stay to the last.

What difference could it make were he to hand the bag over to some other holder, and try his luck for the twenty-first chance? "Not any!" was the mental reply he received to this mental inquiry. Better for him to hold on as he had been doing. It was hardly possible—at least highly improbable— that the red button should be the last. There had been twenty-five chances to one against its being so. It is true twenty black buttons had been drawn out before it,—in a most unexpected manner,—still it was as likely to come next as any of the remaining six.

It would be of no use changing the process,—so concluded he, in his own mind,—and, with an air of affected recklessness, the Frenchman signified to those around him that he was ready to continue the drawing.

Another man drew forth Number 21. Like those preceding it, the button, was black!

Number 22 was fished out of the bag,—black also!

23 and 24 were of the like hue!

But two buttons now remained,—two men only whose fate was undecided. One of them was Le Gros himself,—the other, an Irish sailor, who was, perhaps, the least wicked among that wicked crew. One or other of them must become food for their cannibal comrades!

It would scarce be true to say that the interest increased as the dread lottery progressed towards its ending. Its peculiar conditions had secured an interest from the first as intense as it was possible for it to be. It only became changed in character,—less selfish, if we may use the phrase,—as each individual escaped from the dangerous contingency involved in the operation. As the drawing approached its termination, the anxiety about the result, though less painful to the majority of the men, was far more so to the few whose fate still hung suspended in the scale; and this feeling became more intensified in the breasts of the still smaller number, who saw their chances of safety becoming constantly diminished. When, at length, only two buttons remained in the bag, and only two men to draw them out, the interest, though changed in character, was nevertheless sufficiently exciting to fix the attention of every individual on the raft.

There were circumstances, apart from the mere drawing, that influenced this attention. Fate itself seemed to be taking a part in the dread drama; or, if not, a very singular contingency had occurred.

Between the two men, thus left to decide its decree, there existed a rivalry,—or, rather, might it be called a positive antipathy,—deadly as any *vendetta* ever enacted on Corsican soil.

It had not sprung up on the raft. It was of older date—old as the earliest days of the *Pandora's* voyage, on whose decks it had originated.

Its first seeds had been sown in that quarrel between Le Gros and Ben Brace,—in which the Frenchman had been so ignominiously defeated. The Irish sailor,—partly from some slight feeling of co-nationality, and partly from a natural instinct of fair-play,—had taken sides with the British tar;

and, as a consequence, had invoked the hostility of the Frenchman. This feeling he had reciprocated to its full extent; and from that time forward Larry O'Gorman—such was the Irishman's name—became the true *bête noir* of Le Gros, to be insulted by the latter on every occasion that might offer. Even Ben Brace was no longer regarded with as much dislike. For him the Frenchman had been taught, if not friendship, at least, a certain respect, springing from fear; and, instead of continuing his jealous rivalry towards the English sailor, Le Gros had resigned himself to occupy a secondary place on the slaver, and transferred his spite to the representative of the Emerald Isle.

More than once, slight collisions had occurred between them,—in which the Frenchman, gifted with greater cunning, had managed to come off victorious. But there had never arisen any serious matter to test the strength of the two men to that desperate strife, of which death might be the ending. They had generally fought shy of each other; the Frenchman from a latent fear of his adversary,—founded, perhaps, on some suspicion of powers not yet exhibited by him, and which might be developed in a deadly struggle,—the Irishman from a habitude, not very common among his countrymen, of being little addicted to quarrelling. He was, on the contrary, a man of peaceful disposition, and of few words,—also a rare circumstance, considering that his name was Larry O'Gorman.

There were some good traits in the Irishman's character. Perhaps we have given the best. In comparison with the Frenchman, he might be described as an angel; and, compared with the other wretches on the raft, he was, perhaps, the *least bad*: for the word *best* could not, with propriety, be applied to anyone of that motley crew.

Personally, the two men were unlike as could well be. While the Frenchman was black and bearded, the Irishman was red and almost beardless. In size, however, they approximated nearer to each other,—both being men of large stature. Both had been stout,—almost corpulent.

Neither could be so described as they assisted at that solemn ceremonial that was to devote one or other of them to a doom—in which their *condition* was a circumstance of significant interest to those who were to survive them.

Both were shrunken in shape, with their garments hanging loosely around their bodies, their eyes sunk in deep cavities, their cheek-bones prominently protruding, their breasts flat and fleshless, the ribs easily discernible,—in short, they appeared more like a pair of skeletons, covered with shrivelled skin, than breathing, living men. Either was but ill-adapted for the purpose to which dire necessity was about to devote one or other of them.

Of the two, Le Gros appeared the less attenuated. This may have arisen from the fact of his greater ascendency over the crew of the raft,—by means of which he had been enabled to appropriate to himself a larger share of the food sparsely distributed amongst them. His ample covering of hair may have had something to do with this appearance,—concealing as it did the unevenness of the surface upon which it grew, and imparting a plumper aspect to his face and features.

If there was a superiority in the quantity of flesh still clinging to his bones, its quality might be questioned,—at all events, in regard to the use that might soon be made of it. In point of tenderness, his muscular integuments could scarcely compare with those of the Irishman, whose bright skin promised—

These are horrid thoughts. They should not be her repeated, were it not to show in its true light the terrible extremes, both of thought and action, to which men may be reduced by starvation. Horrid as they may appear, they were entertained at that crisis by the castaway crew of the *Pandora*!

Chapter Sixty Nine
A Challenge declined

When it came to the last drawing,—for there needed to be only one more,—there was a pause in the proceedings, such as usually precedes an expected climax.

It was accompanied by silence; so profound that, but for the noise made by the waves as they dashed against the hollow hogsheads, a pin might have been heard if dropped upon the planking of the raft. In the sound of the sea there was something lugubrious: a fit accompaniment of the unhallowed scene that was being enacted by those within hearing of it. One might have fancied that spirits in fearful pain were confined within the empty casks, and that the sounds that seemed to issue out of them were groans elicited by their agony.

The two men, one of whom was doomed to die, stood face to face; the others forming a sort of circle around them. All eyes were bent upon them, while theirs were fixed only upon each other. The reciprocated glance was one of dire hostility and hate,—combined with a hope on the part of each to see the other dead, and then to survive him.

Both were inspired by a belief—in the presence of such an unexpected contingency it was not unreasonable—that Fate had singled them out from their fellows to stand in that strange antagonism. They were, in fact, convinced of it.

Under the influence of this conviction, it might be supposed that neither would offer any further opposition to Fate's decree, but would yield to what might appear their "manifest destiny."

As it was, however, fatalism was not the faith of either. Though neither of them could lay claim to the character of a Christian, they were equally unbelievers in this particular article of the creed of Mahomet; and both were imbued with a stronger belief in strength or stratagem than in chance.

On the first-mentioned the Irishman appeared most to rely, as was evidenced by the proposal he made upon the occasion.

"I dar yez," said he, "to thry which is the best man. To dhraw them buttons is an even chance between us; an' maybe the best man is him that'll have to die. By Saint Pathrick! that isn't fair, nohow. The best man should be allowed to live. Phwat do *yez* say, comrades?"

The proposal, though unexpected by all, found partisans who entertained it. It put a new face upon the affair. It was one that was not more than reasonable.

The crew, no longer interested in the matter,—at least, so far as their own personal safety was concerned,—could now contemplate the result with calmness; and the instinct of justice was not dead within the hearts of all of them. In the challenge of the Irishman there appeared nothing unfair. A number of them were inclined to entertain it, and declared themselves of that view.

The partisans of Le Gros were the more numerous; and these remained silent,—waiting until the latter should make reply to the proposal of his antagonist.

After the slight luck he had already experienced in the lottery,—combined with several partial defeats erst inflicted upon the man who thus challenged him,—it might have been expected that Le Gros would have gladly accepted the challenge.

He did not. On the contrary, he showed such an inclination to trust to *chance* that a close observer of his looks and actions might have seen cause to suspect that he had also some reliance upon *stratagem*.

No one, however, had been thus closely observing him. No one—except the individual immediately concerned—had noticed that quick grasp of hands between him and one of his partisans; or, if they had, it was only to interpret it as a salute of sympathy, extended towards a comrade in a situation of danger.

In that salute, however, there passed between the two men something of significance; which, if exhibited to the eyes of the spectators, would have explained the indifference to death that from that moment characterised the demeanour of Le Gros.

After that furtive movement, he no longer showed any hesitancy as to his course of action; but at once declared his willingness, as well as his determination, to abide by the decision of the drawing.

"*Sacré!*" cried he, in answer to the challenge of the Irishman; "you don't suppose, *Monsieur Irlandais,* that I should fear the result as you propose it? *Parbleu!* nobody will believe that. But I'm a believer in Fortune,—notwithstanding the scurvy tricks she has often served me—even now that she is frowning upon me black as ever. Neither of us appears to be in favour with her, and that will make our chances equal. So then, I say, let us try her again. *Sacré!* it will be the last time she can frown on one of us,—that's certain."

As O'Gorman had no right to alter the original programme of the lottery, of course the dissenting voices to its continuance were in the minority; and the general clamour tailed upon fate to decide which of the two men was to become food for their famishing companions.

Le Gros still held the bag containing the two buttons. One of them should be black, the other red. It became a subject of dispute, which was to make the draw. It was not a question of who should draw first, since one button taken out would be sufficient. If the red one came out, the drawer must die; if the black, then the other must become the victim.

Some proposed that a third party should hold the bag, and that there should be a toss up for the first chance. Le Gros showed a disposition to oppose this plan. He said that, as he had been intrusted with the superintendence so far, he should continue it to the end. They all saw,—so urged he,—that he had not benefited by the office imposed upon him; but the contrary. It had brought nothing but ill-luck to him; and, as everybody knew, when a run of ill-luck once sets in, there was no knowing where it might terminate. He did not care much, one way or the other: since there could be no advantage in his holding the bag; but as he had done so all through,—as he believed to his disadvantage,—he was willing to hold on, even if it was death that was to be his award.

The speech of Le Gros had the desired effect. The majority declared themselves in favour of his continuing to hold the bag; and it was decided that the Irishman should make choice of the *penultimate* button.

The latter offered no opposition to this arrangement. There appeared no valid grounds for objecting to it. It was a simple toss of heads and tails,—"Heads I win, and tails you lose"; or, to make use of a formula more appropriate to the occasion, "Heads I live, and tails you die." With some such process of reasoning current through the brain of Larry O'Gorman, he stepped boldly up to the bag; plunged his fist into its obscure interior; and drew forth—*the black button!*

Chapter Seventy
An unexpected Termination

The red button remained in the bag. It was a singular circumstance that it should be the last; but such strange circumstances will sometimes occur. It belonged to Le Gros. The lottery was over; the Frenchman had forfeited life.

It seemed idle for him to draw the button out; and yet, to the astonishment of the spectators, he proceeded to do so.

"*Sacré!*" he exclaimed, "the luck's been against me. *Eh bien!*" he added, with a *sangfroid* that caused some surprise, "I suppose I must make a die of it. Let me see the accursed thing that's going to condemn me!"

As he said this, he held up the bag in his left hand,—at the same time plunging his right into its dark interior. For some seconds he appeared, to grope about, as if he had some difficulty in finding the button. While fumbling in this fashion he let go the mouth of the wallet, which he had been holding in his left hand,—adroitly transferring his hold to its bottom. This was done apparently for the purpose of getting the button into a corner,—in order that he might lay hold of it with his fingers.

For some moments the bag rested upon his left forearm, while he continued his hunt after the little piece of horn. He appeared successful at length; and drew forth his right hand, with the fingers closed over the palm, as if containing something,—of course the dread symbol of death. Stirred by a kind of curiosity, his comrades pressed mechanically around, and stood watching his movements.

For an instant he kept his fist closed, holding it on high to that all might see it: and then, slowly extending his fingers, he exhibited his spread palm before their eyes. It held the button that he had drawn forth from the bag; but, to the astonishment of all, it was a *black* one, and not the *red* token that had been expected!

There were but two men who did not partake of this surprise. One was Le Gros himself,—though, to all appearance, he was the most astonished individual of the party,—the other was the man who, some minutes before, might have been observed standing by his side, and stealthily transferring something from his own fingers to those of the Frenchman.

This unexpected termination of the lottery led to a scene of terrific excitement. Several seized hold of the bag,—jerking it out of the hand of him who had hitherto been holding it. It was at once turned inside out; when the red button fell upon the planking of the raft.

Most of the men were furious, and loudly declared that they had been cheated,—some offering conjectures as to how the cheat had been accomplished. The confederate of Le Gros—backed by the ruffian himself— suggested that there might have been no deception about the matter, but only a mistake made in the number of buttons originally thrown into the bag. "Like enough,—damned like enough!"—urged Le Gros's sharping partner; "there's been a button too many put into the bag,—twenty-seven instead of twenty-six. That's how it's come about. Well, as we all helped at the counting of 'em, therefore it's nobody's fault in particular. We'll have to draw again, and the next time we can be more careful."

As no one appeared able to contradict this hypothesis, it passed off, with a number, as the correct one. Most of the men, however, felt sure that a trick had been played; and the trick itself could be easily conjectured. Some one of the drawers had procured a button similar to those inside the bag; and holding this button, had simply inserted his hand, and drawn it out again.

Out of twenty-six draws it would have been impossible to fix upon the individual who had been guilty of the cheat, though there were not a few who permitted their suspicions to fall on Le Gros himself. There had been observed something peculiar in his mode of manipulation. He had inserted his hand into the wallet with the fist closed; and had drawn it out in similar fashion. This, with one or two other circumstances, looked suspicious enough; but it was remembered that some others had done the same; and as there was not enough of evidence to bring home the infamous act to its perpetrator, no one appeared either able or willing to risk making the accusation.

Yes, there *was* one who had not yet declared himself; nor did he do so until some time had elapsed after the final and disappointing draw made by the master of the ceremonies. This man was Larry O'Gorman.

While the rest of the crew had been listening to the arguments of the Frenchman's confederate,—and one by one signifying their acquiescence,—

the Irishman stood apart, apparently busied in some profound mental calculation.

When at length all seemed to have consented to a second casting of lots, he roused himself from his reverie; and, stepping hastily into their midst, cried out in a determined manner, "No—

"No, yez don't," continued he, "no more drawin', my jewels, till we've had a betther undherstandin' ov this little matther. That there's been chatin' yez are all agreed; only yez can't identify the chate. Maybe I can say somethin' to point out the dirty spalpeen as hasn't the courage nor the dacency to take his chance along wid the rest ov us."

This unexpected interpolation at once drew the eyes of all parties upon the speaker; for all were alike interested in the revelation which O'Gorman was threatening to make.

Whoever had played foul,—if it could only be proved against him,— would be regarded as the man who ought to have drawn the red button; and would be treated as if he had done so. This was tacitly understood; even before the suggestion of such a course had passed the lips of anyone. Those who were innocent were of course desirous of discovering the "black sheep,"—in order to escape the danger of a second drawing,—and, as these comprehended almost the entire crew, it was natural that an attentive ear should be given to the statement which the Irishman proposed to lay before them.

All stood gazing upon him with expectant eyes. In those of Le Gros and his confederate there was a different expression. The look of the Frenchman was more especially remarkable. His jaws had fallen; his lips were white and bloodless; his eyes glared fiend-like out of their sunken sockets; while the whole cast of his features was that of a man threatened with some fearful and infamous fate, which he feels himself unable to avert.

Chapter Seventy One
Le Gros upon Trial

As O'Gorman gave utterance to the last words of his preparatory speech, he fixed his eyes steadfastly upon the Frenchman. His look confirmed every one in the belief that the allusion had been to the latter.

Le Gros at first quailed before the Irishman's glance; but, perceiving the necessity of putting a bold front on the matter, he made an endeavour to reciprocate it.

"*Sacré bleu!*" he exclaimed. "*Monsieur Irlandais* why do you look at me? you don't mean to insinuate that I've acted unfairly?"

"The divil a bit," replied the Irishman. "If it's insinivation yez be talkin' about, the divil a bit ov that do I mane. Larry O'Gorman isn't agoin' to bate about the bush wan way or the tother, Misther Laygrow. He tells ye to yer teeth that it was yer beautiful self putt the exthra button into the bag,—yez did it, Misther Laygrow, and nobody else."

"Liar!" vociferated the Frenchman, with a menacing gesture. "Liar!"

"Kape cool, Frenchy. It isn't Larry the Galwayman that's goin' to be scared at yer blusther. I repate,—it was you yourself that putt that button into the bag."

"How do you know that, O'Gorman?" "Can you prove it?"

"What proof have you?" were questions that were asked simultaneously by several voices,—among which that of the Frenchman's confederate was conspicuous.

"Phwy, phwat more proof do yez want, than phwat's alriddy before yez? When I had me hand in the wallet, there wasn't only the two buttons,—the divil a more. I feeled thim both while I was gropin' about to make choice betwixt them; an if there had been a third, I wud a feeled that too. I can swear by the holy cross of Saint Pathrick there wasn't wan more than the two."

"That's no proof there wasn't three," urged the friend of Le Gros. "The third might have been in a wrinkle of the bag, without your feeling it!"

"The divil a wrinkle it was in, except the wrinkles in the palm of that spalpeen's fist! That's where it was; and I can tell yez all who putt it there. It was this very chap who is so pit-a-pat at explainin' it. Yez needn't deny it, Bill Bowler. I saw somethin' passin' betwixt yerself and Frenchy,—jest before it come his turn to dhraw. I saw yer flippers touchin' van another, an' somethin' slippin' in betwane them. I couldn't tell phwat it was, but, by Jaysus! I thought it quare for all that. I know now phwhat it was,—it was the button."

The Irishman's arguments merited attention; and received it. The circumstances looked at the least suspicious against Le Gros. To the majority they were conclusive of his guilt.

The accusation was supported by other evidence. The man who had preceded O'Gorman in the drawing positively avowed that he could feel only three buttons in the bag; while the one before him, with equal confidence, asserted that when *he* drew, there were but four. Both declared that they could not be mistaken as to the numbers. They had separately "fingered" each button in the hope of being able to detect that which was bloodstained, and so avoid bringing it forth.

"Ach!" ejaculated the Irishman, becoming impatient for the conviction of his guilty antagonist; "phwat's the use ov talkin'. Frenchy's the wan that did it. That gropin' an fumblin' about the bottom of the wallet was all pretince. He had the button in his shut fist all the time, an' by Jaysus! he's entitled to the prize, the same as if he had dhrawn it. It's him that's got to die!"

"*Canaille!* liar!" shouted Le Gros; "if I have, you—"

And as the words issued from his lips he sprang forward, knife in hand, with the evident design of taking the life of his accuser.

"Kape cool!" cried the latter, springing out of reach of his assailant; and with his own blade bared, placing himself on the defensive. "Kape cool, ye frog-atin' son av a gun, or ye'll make mate for us sooner than ye expected, ay, before yez have time to put up a *pater* for yer ugly sowl, that stans most disperately in nade ov it.

"Now," continued the Irishman, after he had fairly placed himself in an attitude of defence; "come an whiniver yer loike. Larry O'Gorman is riddy for ye, an' another av the same at yer dhirty back. *Hoch,—faugh-a-ballah,— hiloo,—whallabaloo!*"

Chapter Seventy Two
A Duel to the Death

The strange ceremonial upon the raft,—hitherto carried on with some show of solemnity,—had reached an unexpected crisis.

A second appeal to the goddess of Fortune was no longer thought of. The deadly antagonism of the two chief castaways—Le Gros and O'Gorman— promised a result likely to supply the larder of that cannibal crew, without the necessity of their having recourse to her decrees.

One or other,—perhaps both,—of these men must soon cease to live; for the determined attitude of each told, beyond mistaking, that his bared blade would not be again sheathed, except in the flesh of his adversary.

There was no attempt at intervention. Not one of their comrades interposed to keep them apart. There was friendly feeling,—or, to use a more appropriate phrase, partisanship,—on the side of each; but it was of that character which usually exists among the brutal backers of two "champions of the ring."

Under other circumstances, each party might have regretted the defeat of the champion they had adopted; but upon that raft, the death of one or other of the combatants was not only desirable; but, rather than it should not occur, either side would have most gladly assented to see its especial favourite the victim.

Every man of that ruffian crew had a selfish interest in the result of the threatened conflict; and this far outweighed any feeling of partisanship with which he might have been inspired. A few may have felt friendlier than others towards their respective champions; but to the majority it mattered little which of the two men should die; and there were even some who, in the secret chambers of their hearts, would have reflected gleefully to behold both become victims of their reciprocal hostility. Such a result would cause a still further postponement of that unpopular lottery,—in which they had been too often compelled to take shares.

There was no very great difference in the number of the "friends" on either side. The partisans of the Frenchman would have far outnumbered those of his Irish adversary, but ten minutes before. But the behaviour of

Le Gros in the lottery had lost him many adherents. That he had played the trick imputed to him was by most believed; and as the result of his unmanly subterfuge was of personal interest to all, there were many, hitherto indifferent, now inspired with hostility towards him.

Apart from personal considerations,—even amongst that conglomeration of outcasts,—there were some in whom the instinct of "fair-play" was not altogether dead; and the foul play of the Frenchman had freshly aroused this instinct within them.

As soon as the combatants had shown a fixed determination to engage in deadly strife, the crowd upon the raft became separated, as if by mechanical action, into two groups,—one forming in the rear of Le Gros, the other taking stand behind the Irishman.

As already stated, there was no great inequality between them in point of numbers; and as each occupied an end of the raft, the balance was preserved, and the stage upon which the death drama was about to be enacted—set horizontally—offered no advantage to either.

Knives were to be their weapons. There were others on the raft. There were axes, cutlasses, and harpoons; but the use of these was prohibited to either of the intended combatants: as nothing could be fairer than the sailor's knife,—with which each was provided,—and no weapon in close combat could be used with more certain or deadlier effect.

Each armed with his own knife, released from its lanyard fastenings in order to be freely handled,—each with his foot planted in front of him, to guard against the onset of his adversary,—each with an arm upraised, at the end of which appeared six inches of sharp, glittering steel,—each with muscles braced to their toughest tension, and eyes glaring forth the fires of a mutual hatred,—a hostility to end only in death,—such became the attitude of the antagonists.

Behind each stood their respective partisans, in a sort of semicircle, of which the champion was in the centre,—all eagerly intent on watching the movements of the two men, one of whom—perhaps both—was about to be hurried into eternity.

It was a setting sun that was to afford light for this fearful conflict. Already was the golden orb declining low upon the western horizon. His disc was of a lurid red,—a colour appropriate to the spectacle it was to illumine. No wonder that both combatants instinctively turned their eyes towards the west, and gazed upon the god of day. Both were under the belief they might never more look upon that luminary!

Chapter Seventy Three
Hate against Hate

The combatants did not close on the instant. The sharp blades shining in their hands rendered them shy of a too near approach, and for some time they kept apart. They did not, however, remain motionless or inactive. On the contrary, both were on the alert, —moving in short curves from one side to the other, and all the while keeping *vis-à-vis*.

At irregular intervals one of them would make a feint to attack; or by feigning a retreat endeavour to get the other off guard; but, after several such passes and counter-passes had been delivered between them, still not a scratch had been given, —not a drop of blood drawn.

The spectators looked on with a curious interest. Some showed not the slightest emotion, —as if they cared not who should be the victor, or which the victim. To most it mattered but little if both should fall; and there were even some upon the raft who, for certain secret reasons, would have preferred such a termination to the sanguinary struggle.

A few there were slightly affected with feelings of partisanship. These doubtless felt a deeper interest in the result, at least they were more demonstrative of it; and by words of exhortation and cries of encouragement endeavoured to give support to their respective champions.

There were spectators of a different kind, that appeared to take as much interest in the fearful affair as any of those already described. These were the sharks! Looking at them, as they swam around the raft, —their eyes glaring upon those who occupied it, —one could not have helped thinking that they comprehended what was going on, —that they were conscious of a deed of violence about to be enacted, —and were waiting for some contingency that might turn up in their favour!

Whatever the crisis was to be, neither the spectators *in* the sea, nor those *upon* it, would have long to wait for the crisis. Two men, mutually enraged, standing in front of each other, armed with naked knives; each desperately desirous of killing the other, —with no one to keep them apart, but a score of spectators to encourage them in their intent of reciprocal destruction,—were not likely to be long in coming to the end of the affair. It was not a question of swords, where skilful fencing may protract a combat to an indefinite period of time; nor of pistols, where unskilful shooting may equally retard the result. The combatants knew that, on closing within arms' length, one or other must receive a wound that might in a moment prove mortal.

It was this thought that—for some minutes after their squaring up to each other—had influenced them to keep at a wary distance.

The cries of their companions began to assume an altered tone. Mingled with shouts of exhortation could be heard taunts and jeers,—several voices proclaiming that the "two bullies were afraid of each other."

"Go in, Le Gros! give him the knife!" cried the partisans of the Frenchman.

"Come, Larry! lay on to him!" shouted the backers of his antagonist.

"Bear a hand, both of you! go it like men!" vociferated the voice of some one, who did not seem particularly affected to the side of either.

These off-hand counsels, spoken in a varied vocabulary of tongues, seemed to produce the desired effect. As the last of them pealed over the heads of the spectators, the combatants rushed towards each other,—as they closed inflicting a mutual stab. But the blade of each was met by the left arm of his antagonist, thrown out to ward off the strokes and they separated again without either having received further injury than a flesh wound, that in no way disabled them. It appeared, however, to produce an irritation, which rendered both of them less careful of consequences: for in an instant after they closed again,—the spectators accompanying their collision with shouts of encouragement.

All were now looking for a quick termination to the affair; but in this they were disappointed. After several random thrusts had been given on both sides, the combatants again became separated without either having received any serious injury. The wild rage which blinded both, rendering their blows uncertain,—combined with the weakness of their bodies from long starvation,—may account for their thus separating for the second time, without either having received a mortal wound.

Equally innocuous proved the third encounter,—though differing in character from either of those that preceded it. As they came together, each grasped the right arm of his antagonist,—that which wielded the weapon,—in his left hand; and firmly holding one another by the wrists, they continued the strife. In this way it was no longer a contest of skill, but of strength. Nor was it at all dangerous, as long as the "grip" held good; since neither could use his knife. Either could have let go with his left hand at any moment; but by so doing he would release the *armed* hand of his antagonist, and thus place himself in imminent peril.

Both were conscious of the danger; and, instead of separating, they continued to preserve the reciprocal "clutch" that had been established between them.

For some minutes they struggled in this strange fashion,—the intention of each being to throw the other upon the raft. That done, he who should be uppermost would obtain a decided advantage.

They twisted, and turned, and wriggled their bodies about; but both still managed to keep upon their feet.

The contest was not carried on in any particular spot, but all over the raft; up against the mast, around the empty casks, among the osseous relics of humanity,—the strewed bones rattling against their feet as they trod over them. The spectators made way as they came nearer, nimbly leaping from side to side; while the stage upon which this fearful drama was being enacted,—despite the ballast of its water-logged beams, and the buoyancy of its empty casks,—was kept in a continual commotion.

It soon became evident that Le Gros was likely to get the worst of it, in this trial of strength. The muscular power of the Frenchman was inferior to that of his island antagonist; and had it been a mere contest of toughness, the former would have been defeated.

In craft, however, Le Gros was the Irishman's superior: and at this crisis stratagem came to his aid.

In turning about, the Frenchman had got his head close to the sleeve of O'Gorman's jacket,—that one which encircled his right wrist, and touched the hand holding the dangerous knife. Suddenly craning his neck to its fullest stretch, he seized the sleeve between his teeth, and held it with all the strength of his powerful jaws. Quick as thought, his left hand glided towards his own right; his knife was transferred to it; and the next moment gleamed beneath, threatening to penetrate the bosom of his antagonist.

O'Gorman's fate appeared to be sealed. With both arms pinioned, what chance had he to avoid the blow? The spectators, silent and breathless, looked for it as a certain thing. There was scarce time for them to utter an exclamation, before they were again subjected to surprise at seeing the Irishman escape from his perilous position.

Fortunate it was for him, that the cloth of his pea-jacket was not of the best quality. It had never been, even when new; and now, after long-continued and ill-usage, it *was* almost rotten. For this reason, by a desperate wrench, he was enabled to release his arm from the dental grip which his antagonist had taken upon it,—leaving only a rag between the Frenchman's teeth.

The circumstances had suddenly changed! the advantage being now on the side of the Irishman. Not only was his right arm free again; but with the other he still retained his hold upon that of his antagonist. Le Gros could only use his weapon with the left arm; which placed him at a disadvantage.

The shouts that had gone up to hail the Frenchman's success—so late appearing certain—had become suddenly hushed; and once more the contest proceeded in silence.

It lasted but a few seconds longer; and then was it terminated in a manner unexpected by all.

Beyond doubt, O'Gorman would have been the victor, had it ended as every one was anticipating it would,—in the death of one or other of the combatants. As it chanced, however, neither succumbed in that sanguinary strife. Both were preserved for a fate equally fearful: one, indeed, for a death ten times more terrible.

As I have said, the circumstances had turned in favour of the Irishman. He knew it; and was not slow to avail himself of the advantage.

Still retaining his grasp of Le Gros's right wrist, he plied his own dexter arm with a vigour that promised soon to settle the affair; while the left arm of the Frenchman could offer only a feeble resistance, either by thrusting or parrying.

Their knife-blades came frequently in collision; and for a few passes neither appeared to give or receive a wound. This innocuous sparring, however, was of short continuance and ended by the Irishman making a dexterous stroke, by which his blade was planted in the hand of his antagonist,—transfixing the very fingers which were grasping the knife!

The weapon fell from his relaxed clutch; and passing through the interstices of the timber, sank to the bottom of the sea! A scream of despair escaped from the lips of the Frenchman, as he saw the blade of his antagonist about to be thrust into his body!

The thrust was threatened, but not made. Before it could be given, a hand interfered to prevent it. One of the spectators had seized the uplifted arm of the Irishman, —at the same time vociferating, in a stentorian voice—

"Don't kill him! we won't need to eat him! Look yonder! We're saved! we're saved!"

Chapter Seventy Four
A Light!

The man who had so unexpectedly interrupted the deadly duello, while giving utterance to his strange speech, kept one of his arms extended towards the ocean, —as if pointing to something he had descried above the horizon.

The eyes of all were suddenly turned in the direction thus indicated. The magic words, "We are saved!" had an immediate effect, —not only upon the spectators of the tragedy thus intruded upon, but upon its actors. Even rancour became appeased by the sweet sound; and that of the Irishman, as with most of his countrymen, being born "as the flint bears fire," subsided on the instant.

He permitted his upraised arm to be held in restraint; it became relaxed, as did also his grasp on the wrist of his antagonist; while the latter, finding himself free, was allowed to retire from the contest.

O'Gorman, among the rest, had faced round; and stood looking in the direction where somebody had seen something that promised salvation of all.

"What is it?" inquired several voices in the same breath, — "the land?"

No: it could not be that. There was not one of them such a nautical ignoramus as to believe himself within sigh of land.

"A sail? —a ship?"

That was more likely: though, at the first glance, neither tail nor ship appeared upon the horizon, "What is it?" was the interrogatory reiterated by a dozen voices.

"A light! Don't you see it?" asked the lynx-eyed individual, whose interference in the combat had caused this sudden departure from the programme. "Look!" he continued; "just where the sun's gone down yonder. It's only a speck; but I can see it plain enough. It must be the light from a ship's binnacle!"

"*Carrajo!*" exclaimed a Spaniard; "it's only a spark the sun's left behind him. It's the *ignis fatuus* you've seen, *amigo!*"

"Bah!" added another; "supposing it is a binnacle-lamp, as you say, what would be the use, except to tantalise us. If it be in the binnacle, in course the ship as carries it must be stern towards us. What chance would there be of our overhaulin' her?"

"*Par Dieu!* there be von light!" cried a sharp-eyed little Frenchman. "Pe Gar! I him see. Ver true, vraiment! An—pe dam!—zat same est no lamp in ze binnacle!"

"I see it too!" cried another.

"And I!" added a third.

"*Io tambien!*" (I also) echoed a fourth, whose tongue proclaimed him of Spanish nativity.

"*Ich sehe!*" drawled out a native of the German Confederacy; and then followed a volley of voices,—each saying something to confirm the belief that a light was really gleaming over the ocean.

This was a fact that nobody—not even the first objectors—any longer doubted.

It is true that the light seen appeared only a mere sparkle, feebly glimmering against the sky, and might have been mistaken for a star. But it was just in that part of the heavens where a star could not at that time have been seen,—on the western horizon, still slightly reddened by the rays of the declining sun.

The men who speculated upon its appearance,—rude as they were in a moral sense,—were not so intellectually stupid as to mistake for a star that speck of yellowish hue, struggling to reveal itself against the almost kindred colour of the occidental sky.

"It isn't a star,—that's certain," confidently declared one of their number; "and if it be a light aboard ship, it's no binnacle-lamp, I say. Bah! who'd call that a binnacle glim, or a lamp of any kind? If't be a ship's light at all, it's the glare o' the galley-fire,—where the cook's makin' coffee for all hands."

The superb picture of comfort thus called forth was too much for the temper of the starving men, to whom the idea was addressed; and a wild cry of exultation responded to the speech.

A galley; a galley-fire; a cook; coffee for all hands; lobscouse; plum-duff; sea-pies; even the much-despised pea-soup and salt junk, had been long looked upon as things belonging to another world,—pleasures of the past, never more to be indulged in!

Now that the gleam of a galley-fire—as they believed the light to be—rose up before their eyes, the spirits of all became suddenly electrified by the wildest imaginings; and the contest so lately carried on,—as well as the combatants engaged in it,—was instantaneously forgotten; while the thoughts, and eager glances, of every individual on the raft were now directed towards that all-absorbing speck,—still gleaming but obscurely against the reddish background of the sun-stained horizon.

As they continued to gaze, the tiny spark seemed to increase, not only in size, but intensity; and, before many minutes had elapsed, it proclaimed itself no longer a mere spark, but a blaze of light, with its own luminous halo around it. The gradual chastening of colour in the western sky, along with the increased darkness of the atmosphere around it, would account for this change in the appearance of the light. So reasoned the spectators,—now more than ever convinced that what they saw was the glare of a galley-fire.

Chapter Seventy Five
Towards the Beacon!

As soon as they were satisfied that the bright spark upon the horizon was a burning light, every individual on the raft became inspired with the same impulse, — to make for the spot where the object appeared. Whether in the galley or not, — and whether the glow of a fire or the gleam of a lamp, — it must be on board a ship. There was no land in that part of the ocean; and a light could not be burning upon the water, without something in the shape of a ship to carry it.

That it was a ship, no one for a moment doubted. So sure were they, that several of the men, on the moment of making it out, had vociferated, at the top of their voices, "Ship ahoy!"

The voices of none of them were particularly strong just then. They were weak, in proportion to their attenuated frames; but had they been ten times as strong as they were, they could not have been heard at such a distance as that light was separated from the raft.

It was not less than twenty miles from them. In the excited state of their senses, — arising from thirst, starvation, and all the wild emotions which the discovery itself had roused within them, — they had formed a delusive idea of the distance; many of them fancying that the light was quite near!

There were some among them who reasoned more rationally. These, instead of wasting their strength in idle shouting, employed their time in impressing upon the others the necessity of making some exertion to approach the light.

Some thought that much exertion would not be required; as the light appeared to be approaching them. And, in truth, it did appear so; but the wiser ones knew that this might be only an optical illusion, — caused by the sea and sky each moment assuming a more sombre hue.

These last—both with voice and by their example—urged their companions to use every effort towards coming up with what they were sure must be a ship.

"Let us meet her," they said, "if she's standing this way; if not, we must do all we can to overtake her."

It needed no persuasion to put the most slothful of the crew upon their mettle. A new hope of life,—an unexpected prospect of being rescued from what most of them had been contemplating as almost certain death,—inspired all to the utmost effort; and with an alacrity they had never before exhibited in their raft navigation,—and a unanimity of late unknown to them,—they went to work to propel their clumsy craft across the ocean.

Some sprang to the oars, while others assisted at the sail. For days the latter had received no attention; but had been permitted to hang loosely from the mast,—flopping about in whatever way the breeze chanced to blow it. They had entertained no idea of what course they ought to steer in; or if they did think of a direction, they had not sufficient decision to follow it. For days they had been drifting about over the surface of the sea, at the discretion of the currents.

Now the sail was reset, with all the trimness that circumstances would admit of. The sheets were drawn home and made fast; and the mast was stayed *taut*, so as to hinder it from slanting.

As the object upon which they were directing their course was not exactly to leeward, it was necessary to manage the sail with the wind slightly abeam; and for this purpose two men were appointed to the rudder,—which consisted of a broad plank, poised on its edge and hitched to the stern timbers of the raft. By means of this rude rudder, they were enabled to keep the raft "head on" towards the light.

The rowers were seated along both sides. Nearly every individual of the crew, who was not occupied at the sail or steering-board, was employed in propelling. A few only were provided with oars; others wielded handspikes, capstan-bars, or pieces of split plank,—in short, anything that would assist in the "pulling," if only to the value of a pound.

It was,—or, at all events, they thought it was,—a life and death struggle. They were sure that a ship was near them. By reaching her they would be saved; by failing to do so they would be doomed. Another day without food would bring death, at least to one of them; another day without water would bring worse than death to almost every man of them.

Their unanimous action, assisted by the broad sail, caused the craft, cumbersome as it was, to make considerable way through the water,—

though by far too slow to satisfy their wishes. At times they kept silent; at times their voices could be heard mingled with the plunging of the oars; and too often only in profane speech.

They cursed the craft upon which they were carried,—its clumsiness,— the slowness with which they were making way towards the ship,—the ship itself, for not making way towards them: for, as they continued on, those who formerly believed that the light was approaching them, no longer held to that faith. On the contrary, after rowing nearly an hour, all were too ready to agree in the belief that the ship was wearing away.

Not an instant passed, without the eyes of some one being directed towards the light. The rowers, whose backs were turned upon it, kept occasionally twisting their necks around, and looking over their shoulders,— only to resume their proper attitudes with countenances that expressed disappointment.

There were not wanting voices to speak discouragement. Some declared that the light was growing less; that the ship was in full sail, going away from them; and that there would not be the slightest chance of their coming up with her.

These were men who began to feel fatigued at the oar.

There were even some who professed to doubt the existence of a ship, or a ship's light. What they saw was only a bright spot upon the ocean,— some luminous object—perhaps the carcass of some phosphorous fish, or "squid," floating upon the surface. They had many of them seen such things; and the conjecture was not offered to incredulous ears.

These surmises produced discontent,—which in time would have exhibited itself in the gradual dropping of the oars, but for a circumstance which brought this climax about, in a more sudden and simultaneous manner,—the *extinction of the light.*

It went out while the eyes of several were fixed upon it; not by any gradual disappearance,—as a waning star might have passed out of sight,— but with a quick "fluff;"—so one of the spectators described it,—likening its extinction to "a tub of salt-water thrown over the galley-fire."

On the instant of its disappearance, the oars were abandoned,—as also the rudder. It would have been idle to attempt steering any longer. There was neither moon nor stars in the sky. The light was the only thing that had been guiding them; and that gone, they had not the slightest clue as to their course. The breeze was buffeting about in every direction; but, even had it been blowing steadily, every one of them knew how uncertain it would be to trust to its guidance,—especially with such a sail, and such a steering apparatus.

Already half convinced that they had been following an *ignis fatuus*,—and half resolved to give over the pursuit,—it needed only what had occurred to cause a complete abandonment of their nocturnal navigation.

Once more giving way to despair,—expressed in wild wicked words,—they left the sail to itself, and the winds to waft them to whatever spot of the ocean fate had designed for the closing scene of their wretched existence.

Chapter Seventy Six
A double Darkness

The night was a dark one; by a Spanish figure of speech, comparable to a "pot of pitch." It was scarce further obscured by a thick fog that shortly after came silently over the surface of the ocean, enveloping the great raft along with its ruffian crew.

Through such an atmosphere nothing could be seen,—not even the light, had it continued to burn.

Before the coming on of the fog, they had kept a look-out for the light,— one or other remaining always on the watch. They had done so, with a sort of despairing hope that it might reappear; but, as the surrounding atmosphere became impregnated with the filmy vapour, this dreary vigilance was gradually relaxed, and at length abandoned altogether.

So thick fell the fog during the mid-hours of the night, that nothing could be seen at the distance of over six feet from the eye. Even they who occupied the raft could only distinguish those who were close by their side; and each appeared to the others as if shrouded under a screen of grey gauze.

The darkness did not hinder them from conversing. As nearly all hope of succour from a supposed ship had been extinguished, along with that fanciful light, it was but natural that their thoughts should lapse into some other channel; and equally so, that they should turn back to that from which they had been so unexpectedly diverted.

Hunger,—keen, craving hunger,—easily transported them to the spectacle which the sheen of that false torch had brought to an unsatisfactory termination; and their minds now dwelt on what would have been the different condition of affairs, had they not yielded to the delusion.

Not only had their thoughts reference to this theme, but their speeches; and in the solemn hour of midnight,—in the midst of that gloomy vapour, darkly overshadowing the great deep,—they might have been heard again discussing the awful question, "Who dies next?"

To arrive at a decision was not so difficult as before. The majority of the men had made up their minds as to the course that should be pursued. It was no longer a question of casting lots. That had been done already; and the two who had not yet drawn clear—and between whom the thing still remained undecided—were undoubtedly the individuals to determine the matter.

Indeed, there was no debate. All were unanimous that either Le Gros or O'Gorman should furnish food for their famishing companions,—in other words, that the combat, so unexpectedly postponed, should be again resumed.

There was nothing unfair in this,—except to the Irish man. He had certainly secured his triumph, when interrupted. If another half-second had been allowed him, his antagonist would have lain lifeless at his feet.

Under the judgment of just umpires this circumstance would have weighed in his favour; and, perhaps, exempted him from any further risk; but, tried by the shipwrecked crew of a slaver,—more than a moiety of whom leaned towards his antagonist,—the sentence was different; and the majority of the judges proclaimed that the combat between him and Le Gros should be renewed, and continued to the death.

The renewal of it was not to take place on the moment. Night and darkness both forbade this; but the morning's earliest light was to witness the resumption of that terrible strife.

Thus resolved, the ex-crew of the *Pandora* laid themselves down to sleep,—not quite so calmly as they might have done in the forecastle of the slaver; for thirst, hunger, and fears for a hopeless future,—without saying anything of a hard couch,—were not the companions with which to approach the shrine of Somnus. As a counterpoise, they felt lassitude both of mind and body, approaching to prostration.

Some of them slept. Some of them could have slept within the portals of Pluto, with the dog Cerberus yelping in their ears!

A few there were who seemed either unable to take rest or indifferent to it. All night long some one or other—sometimes two at a time—might be seen staggering about the raft, or crawling over its planks, as if unconscious of what they were doing. It seemed a wonder that some of them—semisomnambulists in a double sense—did not fall overboard into the water. But they did not. Notwithstanding the eccentricity of their movements, they all succeeded in maintaining their position on the raft. To tumble over the edge would have been tantamount to toppling into the jaws of an expectant shark, and getting "scrunched" between no less than six rows of sharp teeth. Perhaps it was an instinct—or some presentiment of this peril—that enabled these wakeful wanderers to preserve their equilibrium.

Chapter Seventy Seven
A whispered Conspiracy

Although most of the men had surrendered themselves to such slumber as they might obtain, the silence was neither profound nor continuous. At times no sounds were heard save the whisperings of the breeze, as it brushed against the spread canvas, or a slight "swashing" in the water as it was broken by the rough timbers of the craft.

These sounds were intermingled with the loud breathing of some of the sleepers,—an occasional snore,—and now and then a muttered speech the involuntary utterance of someone dreaming a dreadful dream.

At intervals other noises would arise, when one or more of the waking castaways chanced to come together, to hold a short conversation; or when one of them, scarce conscious of what he did, stumbled over the limbs of a prostrate comrade,—perhaps awaking him from a pleasant repose to the consciousness of the painful circumstances under which he had been enjoying it.

Such occurrences usually led to angry altercations,—in which threats and ribald language would for some minutes freely find vent from the lips both of the disturbed and the disturber; and then both would growlingly subside into silence.

At that hour, when the night was at its darkest, and the fog at its thickest, two men might have been seen,—though only by an eye very close to where they were,—in a sitting posture at the bottom of the mast. They were crouching rather than seated; for they were upon their knees, with their bodies bent forward, and one or both of their hands resting upon the planks.

The attitude was plainly not one of repose; and anyone near enough to have observed the two men, or to have heard the whispered conversation that was being carried on between them, would have come to the conclusion that sleep was far from their thoughts.

In that deep darkness, however, no one noticed them; and although several of their companions were lying but a few feet from the bottom of the mast, these were either asleep or too distant to hear the whisperings that passed between the two men kneeling in juxtaposition.

They continued to talk in very low whispers,—each in turn putting his lips close to the ear of the other; and while doing so the subject of their conversation might have been guessed at by their glances, or at least the individual about whom they conversed.

This was a man who was lying stretched along the timbers, not far from the bottom of the mast, and apparently asleep. In fact he must have been asleep, as was testified by the stentorian snores that occasionally escaped from his wide-spread nostrils.

This noisy slumberer was the Irishman, O'Gorman,—one of the parties to that suspended fight, to be resumed by day break in the morning. Whatever evil deeds this man may have done during his life,—and he had performed not a few, for we have styled him only the least guilty of that guilty crew,— he was certainly no coward. Thus to sleep, with such a prospect on awaking, at least proved him recklessly indifferent to death.

The two men by the mast,—whose eyes were evidently upon him,—had no very clear view of him where he lay. Through the white mist they could see only something like the shape of a human being recumbent along the planks; and of that only the legs and lower half of the body. Even had it been daylight they could not, from their position, have seen his head and shoulders; for both would have been concealed by the empty rum-cask, already mentioned, which stood upon its end exactly by the spot where O'Gorman had rested his head.

The Irishman, above all others, had taken a delight in the contents of that cask,—so long as a drop was left; and now that it was all gone, perhaps the smell of the alcohol had influenced him in choosing his place of repose.

Whether or not, he was now sleeping on a spot which was to prove the last resting-place of his life. Cruel destiny had decreed that from that slumber he was never more to awaken!

This destiny was now being shaped out for him; and by the two individuals who were regarding him from the bottom of the mast.

"He's sound asleep," whispered one of them to the other. "You hear that snore? *Parbleu!* only a hog could counterfeit that."

"Sound as a top!" asserted the other.

"*C'est bon!*" whispered the first speaker, with a significant shrug of the shoulders. "If we manage matters smartly, he need never wake again. What say you, comrade?"

"I agree to anything you may propose," assented the other. "What is it?"

"There need be no noise about it. A single blow will be sufficient,—if given in the right place. With the blade of a knife through his heart, he'll not make three kicks. He'll never know it till he's in the next world. *Peste!* I could almost envy him such an easy way of getting out of this!"

"You think it might be done without making a noise?"

"Easy as falling overboard. One could hold something over his mouth, to keep his tongue quiet; while the other—You know what I mean?"

The horrid act to be performed by the other was left unspoken,—even in those confidential whisperings.

"But," replied the confederate, objectingly, "suppose the thing done,—how about matters in the morning? They'd know who did it. Leastwise, their suspicions would fall upon us,—upon you to a certainty, after what's happened. You haven't thought of that?"

"Haven't I? But I have, *mon ami!*"

"Well; and what?"

"First place. They're not in the mind to be particular,—none of them,—so long as they get something to eat. Secondly; if they should kick up a row, our party is the strongest; and I don't care what comes of it. We may as well all die at once, as die by bits."

"That's true enough."

"But there's no fear of any trouble from the others. I've got an idea that'll prevent that. To save appearances, he can commit suicide."

"What do you mean?"

"Bah! *camarade!* how dull you are. The fog has got into your skull. Don't you know the *Irlandais* has got a knife, and a sharp one. *Peste!* I know it. Well,—perhaps it can be stolen from him. If so, it can also be found sticking in the wound that will deprive him of life. Now do you comprehend me?"

"I do,—I do!"

"First, to steal the knife. Go you: I daren't: it would look suspicious for me to be seen near him,—that is, if he should wake up. You may stray over that way, as if you were after nothing particular. It'll do no harm to try."

"I'll see if I can hook it then," responded the other. "What if I try now?"

"The sooner the better. With the knife in our possession, we'll know better how to act. Get it, if you can."

The last speaker remained in his place. The other, rising into an erect attitude, stepped apart from his fellow-conspirator, and moved away from the mast,—going apparently without any design. This, however, led him towards the empty rum-cask,—alongside of which the Irishman lay asleep, utterly unconscious of his approach.

Chapter Seventy Eight
A foul Deed done in a Fog

It is scarce necessary to tell who were the two men who had been thus plotting in whispers. The first speaker was, of course, the Frenchman, Le Gros,—the other being the confederate who had assisted him in the performance of his unfair trick in the lot-casting.

Their demoniac design is already known from their conversation,—nothing more nor less than to murder O'Gorman in his sleep!

The former had two motives prompting him to this horrid crime,—either sufficiently strong to sway such a nature as his to its execution. He had all along felt hostility to the Irishman,—which the events of that day had rendered both deep and deadly. He was wicked enough to have killed his antagonist for that alone. But there was the other motive, more powerful and far more rational to influence him to the act. As above stated, it had been finally arranged that the suspended fight was to be finished by the earliest light of the morning. Le Gros knew that the next scene in that drama of death was to be the last; and, judging from his experience of the one already played, he felt keenly apprehensive as to the result. He had been fully aware, before the curtain fell upon the first act, that his life could then have been taken; and, conscious of a certain inferiority to his antagonist, he now felt cowed, and dreaded the final encounter.

To avoid it, he was willing to do anything, however mean or wicked,—ready to commit even the crime of murder!

He knew that if he should succeed in destroying his adversary,—so long as the act was not witnessed by their associates,—so long as there should be only circumstantial evidence against him,—he would not have much to fear from such judges as they. It was simply a question as to whether the deed could be done silently and in the darkness; and that question was soon to receive an answer.

The trick of killing the unfortunate man with his own knife,—and making it appear that he had committed self-destruction,—would have been too shallow to have been successful under any other circumstances;

but Le Gros felt confident that there would be no very strict investigation; and that the inquest likely to be held on the murdered man would be a very informal affair.

In any case, the risk to him would be less than that he might expect on the consummation of the combat,—the *finale* of which would in all probability, be the losing of his life.

He was no longer undecided about doing the foul deed. He had quite determined upon it; and the attempt now being made by his confederate to steal the knife was the first stop towards its perpetration.

The theft was too successfully accomplished. The wretch on getting up to the rum-cask, was seen to sit down silently by its side; and, after a few moments passed in this position he again rose erect, and moved back towards the mast. Dark as was the night, Le Gros could perceive something glittering in the hand of his accomplice, which he knew must be the coveted weapon.

It was so. The sleeper had been surreptitiously disarmed.

For a moment the two men might have been seen standing in juxtaposition; and while thus together the knife was furtively transferred from the hand of the accomplice into that of the true assassin.

Then both, assuming a careless attitude, for a while remained near the mast, apparently engaged in some ordinary conversation. An occasional shifting of their position, however, took place,—though so slight that, even under a good light, it would scarce have been observed. A series of these movements, made at short intervals, ended in bringing the conspirators close up to the empty hogshead; and then one of them sat down by it. The other, going round it, after a short lapse of time, imitated the example of his companion by seating himself on the opposite side.

Thus far there was nothing in the behaviour of the two men to have attracted the attention of their associates on the raft,—even had the latter been awake. Even so, the obscurity that surrounded their movements would have hindered them from being very clearly comprehended.

There was no eye watching the assassins, as they sat down by the side of their sleeping victim; none fixed upon them as both simultaneously leant over him with outstretched arms,—one holding what appeared a piece of blanket over his face, as if to stifle his breath,—the other striking down upon his breast with a glittering blade, as if stabbing him to the heart.

The double action occupied scarce a second of time. In the darkness, no one appeared to perceive it, except they were its perpetrators. No one seemed to hear that choking, gurgling cry that accompanied it; or if they did, it was only to shape a half conjecture, that some one of their companions was indulging in a troubled dream!

The assassins, horror-stricken at what they had done, skulked tremblingly back to their former position by the mast.

Their victim, stretched on his back, remained motionless upon the spot where they had visited him; and anyone standing over him, as he lay, might have supposed that he was still slumbering!

Alas! it was the slumber of death!

Chapter Seventy Nine
Dousing the Glim

We left the crew of the *Catamaran* in full occupation,—"smoking" shark-flesh on the back of a *cachalot* whale.

To make sure of a sufficient stock,—enough to last them with light rations for a voyage, if need be, to the other side of the Atlantic,—they had continued at the work all day long, and several hours into the night. They had kept the fire ablaze by pouring fresh spermaceti into the furnace of flesh which they had constructed, or rather excavated, in the back of the leviathan; and so far as that kind of fuel was concerned, they might have gone on roasting shark-steaks for a twelvemonth. But they had proved that the spermaceti would not burn to any purpose without a wick; and as their spare ropes were too precious to be all picked into oakum, they saw the necessity of economising their stock of the latter article. But for this deficiency, they might have permitted the furnace-lamp to burn on during the whole night, or until it should go out by the exhaustion of the wick.

As they were not yet quite satisfied with the supply of broiled shark-meat, they had resolved to take a fresh spell at roasting on the morrow; and in order that the wick should not be idly wasted, they had "doused the glim" before retiring to rest.

They had extinguished the flame in a somewhat original fashion,—by pouring upon it a portion of the liquid spermaceti taken out of the case. The light, after giving a final flash, had gone out, leaving them in utter darkness.

But they had no difficulty in finding their way back to the deck, of their craft, where they designed passing the remainder of the night. During the preceding days they had so often made the passage from *Catamaran* to *cachalot*, and *vice versa*, that they could have gone either up or down blindfolded; and indeed they might as well have been blindfolded on this their last transit for the night, so dense was the darkness that had descended over the dead whale.

After groping their way over the slippery shoulders of the leviathan, and letting themselves down by the rope they had attached to his huge pectoral fin, they made their supper upon a portion of the hot roast they had brought along with them; and, washing it down with a little diluted "canary," they consigned themselves to rest.

Better satisfied with their prospects than they had been for some time past, they soon fell asleep; and silence reigned around the dark floating mass that included the forms of *cachalot* and *Catamaran*.

At that same moment a less tranquil scene was occurring scarce ten miles from the spot; for it is scarce necessary to say that the light seen by the ruffians on the great raft—and which they had fancifully mistaken for a ship's galley-fire,—was the furnace fed by spermaceti on the back of the whale.

The extinction of the flame had led to a scene which was reaching its maximum of noisy excitement at about the time that the crew of the *Catamaran* were munching their roast shark-meat and sipping their canary. This scene had continued long after every individual of the latter had sunk into a sweet oblivion of the dangers that surrounded them.

All four slept soundly throughout the remainder of the night. Strange to say, they felt a sort of security, moored alongside that monstrous mass, which they would not have experienced had their frail tiny craft been by itself alone upon the ocean. It was but a fancied security, it is true: still it had the effect of giving satisfaction to the spirit, and through this, producing an artificial incentive to sleep.

It was daylight before any of them awoke,—or it should have been daylight, by the hour: but there was a thick fog around them,—so thick and dark that the carcass of the *cachalot* was not visible from the deck of the *Catamaran*, although only a few feet of water lay between them.

Ben Brace was the first to bestir himself. Snowball had never been an early riser; and if permitted by his duties, or the neglect of them either, he would have kept his couch till midday. Ben, however, knew that there was work to be done, and no time to be wasted in idleness. The captain of the *Catamaran* had given up all hopes of the return of the whaler; and therefore the sooner they could complete their arrangements for cutting adrift from the carcass, and continuing their interrupted course towards the west, the better would be their chance of ultimately reaching land.

Snowball, *sans cérémonie*, was shaken out of his slumbers; and the process of restoring him to wakefulness also awoke little William and Lilly Lalee,—so that the whole crew were now up and ready for action.

A hasty *déjeuner à la matelot* served for the morning repast; after which Snowball and the sailor, accompanied by the boy, climbed once more upon the back of the *cachalot* to resume the operations which had been suspended for the night; while the girl, as usual, remained in charge of the *Catamaran*.

Chapter Eighty
Suspicious Sounds

The ex-cook, in the lead of those who ascended to the summit of the carcass, had some difficulty in finding his kitchen; but, after groping some time over the glutinous epidermis of the animal, he at length laid his claws upon the edge of the cavity.

The others joined him just as he had succeeded in inserting a bit of fresh wick; and soon after a strong flame was established, and a fresh spitful of shark-steaks hung frizzling over it.

Nothing more could be done than wait until the meat should be *done*. There was no "basting" required,—only an occasional turning of the steaks and a slight transposition of them on the harpoon spit,—so that each should have due exposure to the flame.

These little culinary operations needed only occasional attention on the part of the cook. Snowball, who preferred the sedentary *pose*, as soon as he saw his "range" in full operation, squatted down beside it. His companions remained standing.

Scarcely five minutes had passed, when the negro was seen to make a start as if some one had given him a kick in the shin. Simultaneously with that start the exclamation "Golly!" escaped from his lips.

"What be the matter, Snowy?" interrogated Brace.

"Hush! Hab ye no hear nuffin'?"

"No," answered the sailor,—little William chiming in with the negative.

"I hab den,—I hab hear someting."

"What?"

"Dat I doan know."

"It's the frizzlin' o' those shark-steaks; or, maybe, some sea-bird squeaking up in the air."

"No, neyder one nor todder. Hush! Massa Brace, I hab hear some soun' 'tirely diffrent,—somethin' like de voice ob human man. You obsarb silence. Maybe we hear im agen."

Snowball's companions, though inclined to incredulity, obeyed his injunction. They might have treated it with less regard, had they not known the Coromantee to be gifted with a sense of hearing that was wonderfully acute. His largely-developed ears would have proved this capacity; but they knew that he possessed it, from having witnessed many exhibitions of it previous to that time. For this reason they yielded to his double solicitation,—to remain silent and listen.

At this moment, to the surprise of Ben Brace and William, and not a little to the astonishment of the negro, a tiny voice reached them from below,— which they all easily recognised as that of Lilly Lalee.

"O Snowball," called out the girl, addressing herself to her especial protector, "I hear people speaking. It's out upon the water. Do you not hear them?"

"Hush! Lilly Lally," answered the negro, speaking down to his *protégé* in a sort of hoarse whisper; "hush, Lilly, pet; doan you 'peak above him Lilly Breff. Keep 'till, dat a good gal."

The child, restrained by this string of cautionary appeals, offered no further remark; and Snowball, making a sign for his companions to continue silent, once more resumed his listening attitude.

Ben Brace and the boy, convinced by this additional testimony that the Coromantee must have heard something more than the frizzling of the shark-flesh, without saying a word, imitated his example, and eagerly bent their ears to listen.

They had not long to wait before becoming convinced that Snowball *had* heard something besides the spirting of the shark-steaks. They heard something more themselves. They heard sounds that could not be mistaken for those of the sea. *They were the voices of Men!*

They were still at some distance,—though, perhaps, not so distant as they seemed. The thick fog, which, as every one knows, has the effect of deadening sound, was to be taken into account; and, making allowance for this, the voices heard might not be such a great way off.

Whatever was the distance, it was constantly becoming less. The listeners could tell this, ere they had stood many minutes listening. Whoever gave utterance to those sounds—words they were—must be moving onward,— coming towards the carcass of the *cachalot*.

How were they coming? They could not be walking upon the water: they must be aboard a ship?

This interrogatory occurred to those who stood upon the whale. Could they have answered it in the affirmative, their own voices would soon have been uplifted in a joyous huzza; while the hail "Ship ahoy!" would have been sent through the sombre shadows of the mist, in the hope of its receiving an answer.

Why was the hail not heard? Why did the crew of the *Catamaran* stand listening to those voices without making challenge, and with looks that betokened apprehension rather than relief?

Six words that escaped from the lips of Ben Brace will explain the silence of himself and his companions, as well at the dissatisfied air that had impressed itself upon their faces. The six words were:—

"Dangnation! it be the big raft!"

Chapter Eighty One
Unpleasant Conjectures

"Dangnation! it be the big raft."

Such was the singular speech that fell from the lips of the sailor, and with an accent that proclaimed it ominous. And why ominous? Why should the presence of that embarkation—known to them as the "big raft"—cause apprehension to the crew of the *Catamaran*?

So far as Ben Brace and little William were concerned, the question has been already answered. It may be remembered with what feelings of alarm they first listened to the voices of Snowball and Lilly Lalee,—heard in a similar manner during the darkness of the night,—and with what suspicious caution they had made their approach to the Coromantee in the middle of his casks. It may be remembered for what reason they were thus suspicious, for it was then given,—a dread on the part of William—and a great one, too—of being devoured by that cannibal crew; and on the part of his generous protector a fear of becoming a victim to their revenge.

The same motive for their fears still existed; and their apprehension of being approached by the raft was as unabated as ever.

Snowball's dread of the *Pandora's* people might not have been so acute, but for a certain circumstance that came before his mind. He had been made aware,—by sundry ill-usage he had received from the slaver's captain and mate, just previous to the climax of the catastrophe,—that he was himself regarded as the author of it. He knew he had been; and he supposed that the thing must have become known to the rest of the crew. He had not encountered them afterwards; and well had it been for him,—for certainly they would have wreaked their vengeance upon him without stint Snowball had sense enough to be aware of this; and therefore his aversion to any further intercourse with the castaways of the lost ship was quite as strong as that of either Ben Brace or the boy.

As for Lilly Lalee, her fears were due to a less definite cause, and only arose from observing the apprehension of her companions.

"De big raff," said Snowball, mechanically repeating the sailor's last words. "You b'lieve 'im be dat, Massa Brace?"

"Shiver my timbers if I know what to think, Snowy! If it be that—"

"Ef 'im be dat, wha' den?" inquired the Coromantee, seeing that Brace had stopped short in what he was going to say.

"Why, only that we're in an ugly mess. There's no reason to think they have picked up a stock o' provisions, since we parted wi' them. I don't know how they've stuck it out,—that is, supposin' it be them. They may have got shark-meat like ourselves; or they have lived upon—"

The sailor suddenly suspended his speech, glancing towards William, as if what he was about to say had better not reach the ears of the lad.

Snowball, however, understood him,—as was testified by a significant shake of the head.

"As for water," continued the sailor, "they had some left; but not enough to have lasted them to this time. They had rum,—oceans o' that,—but it 'ud only make things worse. True, they mout a caught some o' the rain in their shirts and tarpaulins, as we did; but they weren't the sort to be careful o' it wi' a rum-cask standin' by; an' I dar say, by this time, though they may have some'at to eat,—as you knows, Snowy,—they'll be dyin' for a drop o' drink. In that case—"

"In dat case, dey rob us ob de whole stock we hab save. Den we perish fo' sartin."

"Sure o' that, at least," continued the sailor. "But they wouldn't stop by robbin' us o' our precious water. They'd take everything; an' most likely our lives into the bargain. Let us hope it ain't them we've heard."

"Wha' you say, Master Brace? 'Pose 'um be de capten an' dem odders in de gig? Wha' you tink?"

"It mout," answered the sailor. "I warn't thinkin' o' them. It mout be; an' if so, we han't so much to fear as from t' other 'uns. They arn't so hard up, I should say; or even if they be, there arn't so many o' 'em to bully us. There were only five or six o' them. I should be good for any three o' that lot myself; an' I reckon you an' Will'm here could stan' a tussle wi' the others. Ah! I wish it war them. But it arn't likely: they had a good boat an' a compass in it; and if they've made any use o' their oars, they ought to be far from here long afore this. You've got the best ears, nigger: keep them well set, an' listen. You know the voices o' the ole *Pan's* crew. See if you can make 'em out."

During the above dialogue, which had been carried on in an undertone,—a whisper, in fact,—the mysterious voices had not been again distinguished. When first heard, they appeared to proceed from two or more men engaged in conversation; and, as we have said, were only very indistinct,—either from the speakers being at a distance or talking in a low tone of voice.

The Catamarans now listened, expecting to hear some words pronounced in a louder tone; and yet not wishing to hear them. Rather would they that those voices should never again sound in their ears.

For a time it seemed us if they were going to have this wish gratified. Full ten minutes elapsed, and no sound reached their ears, either of human or other voice.

This silence was at first satisfactory; but all at once a reflection came across the mind of Ben Brace, which gave a new turn to his thoughts and wishes.

What if the voices heard had come from a different sort of men? Why should they be those of the slaver's castaway crew,—either the ruffians on the raft or the captain's party in the gig? What, after all, if they had proceeded from the decks of the whaler?

The old whalesman had not thought of this before; and, now that he did think of it, it caused such a commotion in his mind, that he could hardly restrain himself from crying out "Ship ahoy!"

He was hindered, however, by a quick reflection that counselled him to caution. In case of its not being the whaler's men that had been heard it must be those of the slaver; and the hail would but too certainly be the precursor to his own destruction, as well as that of his companions.

In a whisper he communicated his thoughts to Snowball, who became equally affected by them,—equally inclined to cry "Ship ahoy!" and alike conscious of the danger of doing so.

A strife of thought was now carried on in the bosoms of both. It was lamentable to reflect, that they might be close to a ship,—within hailing distance of her,—which could at once have rescued them from all the perils that surrounded them; and that this ship might be silently gliding past, shrouded from their sight under that thick fog,—in another hour to be far off upon the ocean, never to come within hailing distance again!

A single word—a shout—might save them; and yet they dared not utter it; for the same shout might equally betray, and lead to their destruction.

They were strongly tempted to risk the ambiguous signal. For some seconds they stood wavering between silence and "Ship ahoy!" but caution counselled the former, and prudence at length triumphed.

This course was not adopted accidentally. A process of reasoning that passed through the mind of the old whalesman,—founded upon his former professional experiences,—conducted him to it.

If it be the whale-ship, reasoned he, she must have come back in search of the *cachalot*. Her crew must have known that they had killed it. The "drogues" and flag proved that belief on their part, and the ex-whalesman knew that it would be well worth their while to return in search of the whale. It was this very knowledge that had sustained his hopes, and delayed him so long by its carcass. A whale, which would have yielded nearly a hundred barrels of spermaceti, was a prize not to be picked up every day in the middle of the ocean; and he knew that such a treasure would not be abandoned without considerable search having first been made to recover it.

All this was in favour of the probability that the voices heard had proceeded from the whale-ship; and if so, it was farther probable that in the midst of that fog, while bent upon such an errand, the crew would not care to make way; but, on the contrary, would "lay to," and wait for the clearing of the atmosphere.

In that case the Catamarans might still expect to see the welcome ship when the fog should rise; and with this hope they came to the determination to keep silence.

The hour was still very early,—the sun scarce yet above the horizon. When that luminary should appear, his powerful rays would soon dissipate the darkness; and then, if not before, would they ascertain whether those voices had proceeded from the throats of monsters or of men.

Chapter Eighty Two
An informal Inquest

They did not have to stay for the scattering of the fog. Long before the sun had lifted that veil from off the face of the sea, the crew of the *Catamaran* had discovered the character of their neighbours. They were not friends, but dire enemies,—the very enemies they so much dreaded.

The discovery was not delayed. It was made soon after, and in the following manner:—

The three—Snowball, the sailor, and little William—had kept their place on the carcass of the *cachalot*, all three attentively listening,—the two last standing up, and the former in a reclining attitude, with his huge ear laid close to the skin of the whale,—as though he believed that to be a conductor of sound. There was no need for them to have been thus straining their ears: for when a sound reached them at length, it was that of a voice,—so harsh and loud, that a deaf man might almost have heard it.

"*Sacré!*" exclaimed the voice, apparently pronounced in an accent of surprise, "look here, comrades! Here's a dead man among us!"

Had it been the demon of the mist that gave utterance to these speeches, they could not have produced a more fearful effect upon those who heard them from the back of the *cachalot*. The accent, along with that profane shibboleth, might have proceeded from anyone who spoke the language of France; but the tone of the voice could not be mistaken. It had too often rung in their ears with a disagreeable emphasis. "Massa Le Grow, dat am," muttered the negro. "Anybody tell dat."

Snowball's companions made no reply. None was required. Other voices rose up out of the mist.

"A dead man!" shouted a second. "Sure enough. Who is it?"

"It's the Irishman!" proclaimed a third. "See! He's been killed! There's a knife sticking between his ribs! He's been murdered!"

"That's his own knife," suggested some one. "I know it; because it once belonged to me. If you look you'll find his name on the haft. He graved it there the very day he bought it from me."

There was an interval of silence, as if they had paused to confirm the suggestion of the last speaker.

"You're right," said one, resuming the informal inquest. "There's his name, sure enough,—*Larry O'Gorman*."

"He's killed himself!" suggested a voice not hitherto heard. "He's committed suicide!"

"I don't wonder at his doing so," said another, confirmingly. "He expected to have to die anyhow; and I suppose he thought the sooner it was off his mind the better it would be for him."

"How's that?" inquired a fresh speaker, who appeared to dissent from the opinions of those that had preceded him. "Why should he expect to die any more than the rest of us?"

"You forget, mate, that the fight was not finished between him and Monsieur Le Gros?"

"No, I don't forget it. Well?"

"Well, yourself!"

"It don't follow he was to be the next to die,—not as I can see. Look at this, comrades! There's been foul play here! The Irishman's been stabbed with his own knife. That's plain enough; but it is not so sure he did it himself, Why should he? I say again, there's been foul play?"

"And who do you accuse of foul play?"

"I don't accuse anyone. Let them bring the charge, as have seen something. Somebody must know how this came about. There's been a murder. Can anyone tell who did it?"

There was a pause of silence of more than a minute in duration. No one made answer. If anyone knew who was the murderer, they failed to proclaim it.

"Look here, mates!" put in one, whose sharp voice sounded like the cry of a hyena, "I'm hungry as a starved shark. Suppose we suspend this inquest, till we've had breakfast. After that we can settle who's done the deed,—if there's been anyone, except the man himself. What say ye all?"

The horrid proposal was not replied to by anyone. The loud shout that succeeded it sprang from a different cause; and the words that were afterwards uttered had no reference to the topic under consideration.

"A light! a light!" came the cry, vociferated by several voices.

"It's the light we saw last night. It's the galley-fire! There's a ship within a hundred yards of us!"

"Ship ahoy! ship ahoy!"

"Ship ahoy! what ship's that?"

"Why the devil don't you answer our hail?"

"To the oars, men! to the oars. *Sacré-dieu*! The lubbers must be asleep. Ship ahoy! ship ahoy!"

There was no mistaking the signification of these speeches. The sailor and Snowball exchanged glances of despair. Both had already looked behind them. There, blazing fiercely up, was the fire of spermaceti, with the shark-steaks browning in its flame. In the excitement of the moment they had forgotten all about it. Its light, gleaming through the fog, had betrayed their presence to those upon the raft; and the order issued to take to the oars, with the confused plashing that quickly followed, told the Catamarans that the big raft was about to bear down upon them!

Chapter Eighty Three
Slipping the Cable

"Dar coming on!" muttered Snowball. "Wha' we better do, Massa Brace? Ef we stay hya dey detroy us fo' sartin."

"Stay here!" exclaimed the sailor, who no longer spoke in whispers, since such would no longer avail. "Anything but that. Quick, Snowy,—quick, Will'm! Back down to the deck o' our craft. Let's make all speed, and cast off from the karkiss o' the whale. There be time enough yet; and then it'll be, who's got the heels. Don't be so bad skeeart, Snowy. The ole *Catamaran* be a trim craft. I built her myself, wi' your help, nigger; an' I've got faith in her speed. We'll outsail 'em yet."

"Dat we will, Massa Brace," assented Snowball, as, close following the sailor, he glided down the rope on to the deck of the *Catamaran*, where little William had already arrived.

It was the work of only a few minutes to cut the tiny cable by which the little embarkation had been attached to the fin of the *cachalot*, and push the craft clear of its moorings.

But, short as was the time, during its continuance the sun had produced a wonderful change in that oceanic panorama.

The floating fog, absorbed by his fervid rays, had almost disappeared from the deep, or at all events had become so dissipated that the different objects composing that strange tableau in the proximity of the dead *cachalot* could all be seen by a single *coup d'oeil*; and were also in sight of one another.

There was the huge carcass itself, looming like a great black rock above the surface of the sea. Just parting from its side was the little *Catamaran*, with its sail set, and its crew,—consisting of two men and a boy,—the little Portuguese girl appearing as a passenger,—the two men energetically bending to the oars while the boy held hold of the rudder.

Scarce a hundred yards astern was the larger embarkation,—supporting its score of dark forms,—some seated, and straining at the oars,—some steering,—others attending to the sail; and one or two standing by the head, shouting directions to the rest,—all apparently in wonder at the tableau thus suddenly disclosed, and uncertain what to make of it, or what course to pursue!

The occupants of the great raft were infinitely more astonished than those of the *Catamaran*. On the part of the latter there was no longer any astonishment. On recognising the voices taking part in that ceremonious inquest they had comprehended all. The surprise they had at first felt was now changed into terror.

The men on the raft were still under the influence of astonishment; and no wonder. The apparition that had so suddenly loomed up before their eyes,—at first obscurely seen through the fog, but gradually becoming more distinct,—was enough to cause any amount of surprise. Such a grouping of strange objects in such a situation! The huge carcass of a whale,—a fire upon its back, with bright flames blazing upward,—a crane over the fire with the curious flitches suspended from it,—a raft, in some respects resembling their own, supported by empty casks, and carrying a sail, with four human beings seen upon its deck,—all these formed a series of phenomena, or facts, that was enough to have excited the surprise of the most indifferent observers. Some of the men were even speechless with wonder, and so continued for a time, while others gave vent to their astonishment in loud shouts and excited gesticulations.

That first order issued by Le Gros—for it was his voice that had been heard giving it—had no other object than to cause a rapid movement towards the dark mass, or rather the beacon seen blazing upon its summit. The order had been instantly obeyed; for there was an instinctive apprehension on the part of all that, as before, the light might again vanish from their view.

As they drew nearer, however, and the fog continued to disperse, they obtained a fairer view. Their surprise was not much diminished, though their comprehension of the objects before them became rapidly clearer.

The retreat of the Catamarans—for the movements of the latter proclaimed this design—was of itself suggestive; and, perhaps, more than aught else, enabled those from whom they were retreating to comprehend the situation.

At first they could not even conjecture who they were that occupied the little raft. They saw four human beings upon it; but the mist was still thick enough to hinder them from having a clear view of either their forms, faces, or features. Through the filmy atmosphere to recognise them was impossible. Had there been but two, and had the embarkation that carried them been a mere platform of planks, they might have shaped a conjecture. They remembered that upon such a structure Ben Brace and the boy had given them the slip; and it might be them. But who were the two others? And whence came the six water-casks, the sail, and other paraphernalia seen upon the escaping craft?

They did not stay to waste time in conjectures. It was enough for them to perceive that the four individuals thus seen were trying to get out of their reach. This was *prima facie* proof that they had something worth carrying along with them; perhaps water!

Some one made use of the word. It was like proclaiming a reprieve to a wretch upon the scaffold about to be launched into eternity. It caused such excitement in the minds of the motley crew—all of them suffering from extreme thirst—that, without further hesitancy, they bent eagerly to their oars,—putting forth the utmost effort of their strength in chase of the *Catamaran*.

Chapter Eighty Four
Chapter Lxxxiv

The Chase.

Half pulling, half trusting to the sail, in a few seconds they were alongside the carcass of the *cachalot*. They saw what it was and divined how it came to be there; though still puzzled by the pyrotechnic display exhibited on its summit.

As they passed under the shadow of the huge mass some proposed that they should stay by it, — alleging that it would furnish food for all; but this proposal was rejected by the majority.

"*Pardieu!*" exclaimed the directing voice of Le Gros; "we have food a plenty. It's drink we want now. There's no water upon the whale; and there must be some in possession of these runaways, whoever they be. Let us first follow *them*! If we overhaul them, we can come back. If not, we can return all the same!"

This proposal appeared too reasonable to be rejected. A muttered assent of the majority decided its acceptance; and the raft, yielding to the renewed impulse of the rowers, swept past the carcass, — leaving both the black mass and the blazing beacon astern.

As if further to justify the course of action he had counselled, Le Gros continued —

"No fear about our finding the dead fish. This fog is clearing away. In half an hour there won't be a trace of it. We shall be able to make out the carcass if the whale twenty miles off, — especially with the smoke of that infernal fire to guide us. Pull like the devil! Be sure of it, there's water in one of those casks we see. Only think of it, — *water!*"

It scarce needed the repetition of this magic word to stimulate his thirsty companions. They were already pulling with all their strength.

For about ten minutes the chase continued, — both the pursued and the pursuer equally enveloped in vapour. They were less than two hundred yards apart, and virtually within view, — though not so near as to distinguish one another's features. Each crew could make out the forms of the other; but only to tell that they were human beings clad in some sort of costume.

In this respect the Catamarans had the advantage. They knew who were their pursuers; and all about them.

The latter were still in a state of ignorance as to who were the four individuals so zealously endeavouring to avoid an interview with them. They could perceive that only two of them were full-grown men, and that the other two were of smaller size; but this gave them no clew for the identification of the fugitives.

Of course it did not occur to any of them to think over the rest of the *Pandora's* people; and even if it had, there was no one who would have for a moment supposed that either the black cook, Snowball, or the little Portuguese pickaninny,—rarely seen upon the slaver's deck,—could be among the survivors.

Such a conjecture never occurred to any of the ruffians upon the great raft; and therefore they were continuing the chase still ignorant of the identity of those who seemed so desirous of escaping them.

It was only after the fog had floated entirely away,—or grown so thin as to appear but transparent film,—that the pursuers identified those they were pursuing.

Then did their doubts cease and their conjectures come to a termination.

Of the four forms distinguishable upon the deck of the escaping craft, there was one that could not be mistaken.

That huge, rounded bust covered with its sable epidermis—for the negro had stripped to his work,—surmounted by a spherical occiput,— could belong to no living creature but the ex-cook of the *Pandora*. It was Snowball to a certainty!

A general shout proclaimed the recognition; and for some moments the air was rent with the voices of his *ci-devant* comrades calling upon the Coromantee to "come to an anchor."

"Lie to, Snowball!" cried several of his old comrades. "Why have you cut your cable in that fashion? Hold on till we come up. We mean you no harm!"

Snowball did hold on; though not in the sense that his former associates desired. On the contrary, their request only stimulated him to fresh exertions, to avoid the renewal of an acquaintance which he knew would certainly end in his ruin.

The Coromantee was not to be cajoled. With Ben Brace by his side, muttering wholesome counsel, he lent a deaf ear to the proposal of the pursuers; and only answered it by pulling more energetically at his oar.

What had been only a request, now became a demand,—accompanied by threats and protestation. Snowball was menaced with the most dire vengeance; and told of terrible punishments that awaited him on his capture.

Their threats had no more influence than their solicitations; and they who had given utterance to them arriving after a time, at this conviction, ceased talking altogether.

Snowball's silent, though evidently determined, rejection of their demands had the effect of irritating those who had made them; and stimulated by their spite with more energy than ever did they bend themselves to the task of overtaking the fugitive craft.

Two hundred yards still lay between pursuer and pursued. Two hundred yards of clear, unobstructed ocean. Was that distance to become diminished, to the capture of the *Catamaran*; or was it to be increased, to her escape?

Chapter Eighty Five
Nearer and Nearer

Were the *Catamarans* to escape or be captured? Though not propounded as above, this was the question that occupied the minds of both crews,—the pursued and the pursuing.

Both were doing their very utmost,—the former to make their escape, the latter to prevent it; and very different were the motives by which the two parties were actuated. The occupants of the lesser raft believed themselves to be rowing and sailing for their lives; and they were not far astray in this belief; while those upon the larger embarkation were pulling after them with the most hostile intentions,—to rob them of everything they had got,— even their lives included.

So went they over the wide ocean: the pursued exerting themselves under the influence of fear; the pursuer, under that of a ferocious instinct.

In sailing qualities the *Catamaran* was decidedly superior to the larger raft; and had the wind been only a little fresher she would soon have increased the distance between herself and her pursuer.

Unfortunately it was a very gentle breeze that was blowing at the time; and therefore it was a contest of speed that would most likely have to be decided by the oars. In this respect the *Catamaran* laboured under a great disadvantage,—she could only command a single pair of oars; while, taking into account the various implements—capstan-bars and handspikes—possessed by her competitor, nearly a dozen oars might be reckoned upon. In fact, when her crew had got fairly settled down to the chase, quite this number of men could be seen acting as rowers.

Though their strokes were by no means either regular or efficient, still did they produce a rate of speed greater than that of the *Catamaran*; and the crew of the latter saw, to their dismay, that their pursuers were gaining upon them.

Not very rapidly, but sufficiently so to be perceived, and to inspire them with the dread belief, that in course of time they would be overtaken.

Under this belief, men of a despairing turn of mind would have ceased to exert themselves, and yielded to a fate that appeared almost certain to ensue.

But neither the English sailor nor the Coromantee sea-cook were individuals of the yielding kind. They were both made of sterner stuff,—and even when the chase was undoubtedly going *against* them, they were heard muttering to each other words of encouragement, and a mutual determination never to lay down their oars, so long as six feet of water separated them from their unpitying pursuers.

"No," ejaculated the sailor, "it 'ud be no use. They'd show us no more marcy than so many sharks. I know it by their ways. Don't lose a stroke, Snowy. We may tire 'em out yet."

"Nebba fear fo' me, Massa Brace!" replied the Coromantee. "A keep pullin' so long's de be a poun' o' trength in ma arms, or a bit o' breff in ma body. Nebba fear!"

It might appear as though the crew of the *Catamaran* were now contending against fate, and without hope. This, however, was not the case; for there was still something like a hope to cheer them on, and nerve them to continue their exertions. What was it?

The answer to this interrogatory would have been found by anyone who could have looked upon the sea,—at some distance astern of the chase.

There might have been observed an appearance upon the water, which betokened it different from that through which they were making their way.

It resembled a dark, shadowy line, extending athwart the horizon. It might not have attracted the notice of an ordinary observer, but to the eye of Ben Brace,—as he sat by his oar facing it,—that dark line had a peculiar signification.

He knew that it denoted rougher water, and a stiffer breeze than that blowing upon them; and from this, as well as the clouds fast gathering astern, he knew there was a wind coming from that quarter.

He had imparted his observation to Snowball, and it was this that continued to inspire them with a hope of ultimate escape. Both believed that, with a strong wind in their favour, they would have the advantage of the pursuer; and so, while still bending all their energies to the propulsion of the *Catamaran*, they kept their eyes almost continually fixed upon the sea astern,—even with a more anxious glance than that with which they regarded their pursuers.

"If we can keep out o' their way," muttered he to his fellow oarsman, "only twenty minutes longer! By that time yonder breeze 'll be down on us; and then we'll ha' some chance. There be no doubt but they're gainin' on us now. But the breeze be a gainin' on them,—equally, if not faster. O if we only had a puff o' yonder wind! It be blowin' fresh and strong. I can see it curlin' up the water not three knots astern o' the big raft. Pull for your life, Snowy. Shiver my timbers! they be a gainin' on us faster than ever!"

There was a despairing tone in these last words, that told how fearful appeared their situation to the captain of the *Catamaran*; and the sign of assent made by Snowball in reply,—an ominous shake of the head,— showed that the ex-cook shared the apprehensions of his comrade.

Chapter Eighty Six
Cut in Twain

For some seconds the sailor and Snowball remained silent,—both too busy with their oars, as well as their eyes, to find time for speech.

Their pursuers were noisy enough. They had kept quiet, so long as there appeared to be any uncertainty about the results of the chase; but as soon as they became assured that their clumsy craft was going faster than that of which they were in pursuit,—and they no longer felt doubt about overtaking the latter,—their fiendish voices once more filled the air; and commands for the Catamarans to come to,—with threats of revenge in case of non-compliance,—were hurled after the fugitives.

One man was conspicuous among the rest both for the position which he held upon the raft and the menacing words and gestures of which he made use. This man was Le Gros.

Standing prominently forward, near the head of the embarkation, with a long boat-hook in his hand, he appeared to direct the movements of the others,—urging them in every way to their utmost exertions. He was heard telling them that he saw both food and water in possession of the fugitives—a cask of the latter, as he stated, being lashed to the *Catamaran*.

It need scarce be said that the statement—whether true or fallacious,—acted as a stimulus to his comrades at the oar. The word "water" was music to their ears; and, on hearing it pronounced, one and all of them put forth their utmost strength.

The increased speed thus obtained for the larger craft war likely to bring about the crisis. She was now seen to gain upon the lesser more rapidly than ever; and, before another ten minutes had elapsed, she had forged so close to the stern timbers of the *Catamaran* that an active man might almost have leaped from one to the other.

The crew of the latter beheld the proximity with despair. They saw the black waves, with white curling crests, coming on behind. They saw the sky becoming overcast above their heads; but it appeared only to scowl upon them,—as if to make darker the dread doom that was now threatening so near.

"Shiver my timbers!" cried the sailor, alluding to that too tardy wind, "it will be too late to save us!"

"Too late!" echoed the voice of Le Gros from the big raft, his white teeth, as they shone through his black beard, imparting to him a ferocity of aspect that was hideous to behold. "Too late, you say, Monsieur Brace. For what, may I ask? Not too late for us to get a drink out of your water-cask. Ha! ha! ha!"

"You son of a sea-cook!" he continued, addressing himself to the negro; "why don't you hold your oars? *Sacré-Dieu*! what's the use, you ugly nigger? Don't you see we'll board you in six seconds more? Drop your oars, I say, and save time. If you don't, we'll skin you alive when we've got our flippers upon you."

"Nebba, Massa Grow!" defiantly retorted Snowball? "you nebba 'kin dis nigga 'live. He go die 'fore you do dat. He got him knife yet. By golly! me kill more than one ob you 'fore gib in. So hab a care, Massa Grow! You lay hand on ole Snowy, you cotch de tarnel goss."

To this threat of resistance the Frenchman did not vouchsafe reply: for the rafts were now so near to each other that his attention became engrossed by something that left no time for further speech.

He saw that the *Catamaran* was within reach of his boat-hook, and, leaning forwards with the long shaft extended, he struck its grappling-iron into her stern timber.

For a second or two there was a struggle, which would have ended in the two rafts being brought in contact with one another but for an adroit stroke given by the oar of the English sailor. This not only detached the boat-hook from its grip, but also from the grasp of Le Gros, and sent the implement shivering through the air.

At the same instant of time the Frenchman, losing his balance, was seen to stagger, and then sink suddenly downwards; not into a prostrate position, but perpendicularly,—as if his legs had penetrated between the timbers of the raft.

This was exactly what had occurred: for as soon as the spectators in both crafts could recover from their surprise, they saw only so much of

Monsieur Le Gros as lay between his armpits and the crown of his head,—his limbs and the lower half of his body being concealed between the planks that prevented him from sinking wholly into the water.

Perhaps it would have been better for him had he made a complete plunge of it. At all events, a bold "header" could not have had for him a more unfortunate ending. Scarce had he sunk between the timber when a wild shriek came forth from his throat,—accompanied by a pallor of countenance, and a contortion of his features, that proclaimed something more than a mere "start" received by suddenly sinking waist-deep into the sea.

One of his comrades,—the confederate ruffian already spoken of,—rushed forward to raise him out of the trap,—from which he was evidently unable to extricate himself.

The man caught hold of him by the arms, and was dragging him up; when, all at once, he was seen to let go, and start back with a cry of horror!

This singular conduct was explained on looking at the object from which he had made such a precipitate retreat. It was no longer Le Gros, nor even Le Gros's body; but only the upper half of it, cut off by the abdomen, as clean as if it had been severed by a pair of gigantic shears!

"A shark!" cried a voice, which only gave utterance to the thought that sprung up simultaneously in the minds of all,—both the occupants of the big raft, and the crew of the Catamaran.

Thus deplorably terminated the life of a sinful man; who certainly merited punishment, and, perhaps deserved no better fate.

Chapter Eighty Seven
An unlooked-for Deliverance

A spectacle so unexpected,—but, above all, of such a horrid nature,— could not fail to produce a powerful impression upon those who were witnesses to it. It even caused a change of proceedings on the part of the pursuers,—almost a suspension of the pursuit,—and on that of the pursued some relaxation in their efforts to escape. Both parties appeared for some seconds as if spellbound, and the oars on both rafts were for a while held "apeak."

This pause in the action was in favour of the *Catamaran*, whose sailing qualities were superior to those of her pursuer. Her crew, moreover, less caring for what had happened to Monsieur Le Gros, were the first to recover from their surprise; and before the comrades of the half-eaten Frenchman thought of continuing the chase, they had forced ahead several lengths of their craft from the dangerous contiguity so near being established between them.

The ruffian crew—now castaways—of the *Pandora* had been awed by the strange incident,—so much so as to believe, for a time, that something more than chance had interfered to bring it about. They were not all friends of the unfortunate man, who had succumbed to such a singular fate. The inquest that had been interrupted was still fresh in their minds, and many of them believed that the inquiry—had it proceeded to a just termination— would have resulted in proving the guilt of Le Gros, and proclaiming him the murderer of O'Gorman.

Under this belief, there were many aboard the big raft that would not have cared to continue the chase any further, had it merely been to avenge the death of their late leader. With them, as with the others, there was a different motive for doing so,—a far more powerful incentive,—and that was the thirst which tortured all, and the belief that the escaping craft carried the means to relieve it.

The moiety of their mutilated chief, lying along the planks of the raft, engaged their thoughts only for a very short while; and was altogether forgotten, when the cry of "Water!" once more rising in their midst, urged them to resume the pursuit.

Once more did they betake themselves to their oars,—once more did they exert their utmost strength,—but with far less effect than before. They were still stimulated by the torture of thirst; but they no longer acted with that unanimity which secures success. The head that had hitherto guided them with those imperious eyes—now glaring ghastly from the extremity of the severed trunk—was no longer of authority among them; and they acted in that undecided and irregular manner always certain to result in defeat.

Perhaps, had things continued as they were, they might have made up for the lost opportunity; and, in time, have overtaken the fugitives on the *Catamaran;* but during that excited interval a change had come over the surface of the sea, which influenced the fate both of pursuers and pursued.

The dark line, first narrowly observed by the crew of the *Catamaran* upon the distant verge of the horizon, was no longer a mere streak of shadowed water. It had developed during the continuance of the chase, and now covered both sea and sky,—the latter with black cumbrous clouds, the former with quick curling waves, that lashed the water-casks supporting both rafts, and proclaimed the approach, if not of a storm, at least a fresh breeze,—likely to change the character of the chase hitherto kept up between them.

And very quickly came that change to pass. By the time that the castaways on the great raft had once more headed their clumsy embarkation to the pursuit, they saw the more trim craft,—by her builders yclept the *Catamaran*—with her sails spread widely to the wind, gliding rapidly out of their reach, and "walking the water like a thing of life."

They no longer continued the pursuit. They might have done so, but for the waves that now, swelling up around the raft, admonished them of a danger hitherto unknown. With the spray rushing over them, and the sea, at each fresh assault, threatening to engulf their ill-governed craft, they found sufficient employment for their remaining strength, in clinging to the timbers of their rude embarkation.

Chapter Eighty Eight
A threatened Storm

Thus, once more, were the Catamarans delivered from a terrible danger,—almost literally "from the jaws of death"; and once more, too, by what appeared a providential interference.

Ben Brace actually believed it so. It would have been difficult for anyone to have thought otherwise; but the moral mind of the sailor had of late undergone some very serious transformations; and the perils through which they had been passing,—with their repeated deliverances, all apparently due to some unseen hand,—had imbued him with a belief that the Almighty must be everywhere,—even in the midst of the illimitable ocean.

It was this faith that had sustained him through the many trials through which they had gone; and that, in the very latest and last,—when the ruffians upon the raft were fast closing upon the *Catamaran*,—had led him to give encouraging counsels to Snowball to keep on. It had encouraged him, in fine, to strike the boat-hook from the grasp of Le Gros,—which act had ended by putting their implacable enemy *hors du combat*, and conducting to their final deliverance.

It was this belief that still hindered the brave mariner,—now that the sea began to surge around them, and the spray to dash over the deck of their frail craft,—hindered him from giving way to a new despair; and from supposing that they had been only delivered from one danger to be overwhelmed by another.

For some time did it seem as if this was to be their fate,—as if, literally, they were to be overwhelmed. The breeze which had so opportunely carried the *Catamaran* beyond the reach of the pursuing raft, soon freshened into a gale; and threatened to continue increasing to that still more dreaded condition of the ocean atmosphere,—a storm.

The rafts were no longer in sight of each other. Scarce five minutes had elapsed, after being grappled by Le Gros, when the breeze had caught hold of the *Catamaran*; and, from her superior sailing qualities, she had soon become separated from the more clumsy embarkation of the enemy.

In another hour, the *Catamaran*, under good steering, had swept several miles to westward; while the raft, no longer propelled by oars, and its rudder but ill-directed, had gone drifting about: as if they who occupied it were making only a despairing effort to keep it before the wind.

Despite the rising gale and the increasing roughness of the water, there were no despairing people upon the *Catamaran*. Supported by his faith in providential protection, Ben Brace acted as if there was no danger; and encouraged his companions to do the same.

Every precaution was adopted to provide against accidents. As soon as they saw that the pursuer was left behind,—and they were no longer in any peril from that quarter,—the sail was lowered upon the mast, as there was too great a breadth of it for the constantly freshening breeze. It was not taken in altogether, but only "shortened,"—reefed in a rude fashion,—so as to expose only half its surface to the wind; and this proved just sufficient to keep the *Catamaran* "trim" and steady upon her course.

It would not be correct to say that her captain and crew felt no fears for her safety. On the contrary, they experienced the apprehensions natural to such a situation; and for this reason did they take every precaution against the danger that threatened. The Coromantee might have given way to a feeling of fatalism,—peculiar to his country and class,—but there was no danger of Ben Brace doing so. Notwithstanding his faith about being protected by Providence, the sailor also believed, that self-action is required on the part of those who stand in need of such protection; and that nothing should be left undone to deserve it.

The situation was altogether new to them. It was the first thing in the shape of a storm, or even a gale, they had encountered since the construction of their curious craft. Ever since the burning of the *Pandora*, they had been highly favoured in this respect. They had been navigating their various embarkations through a "summer sea," in the midst of the tropical ocean,—where ofttimes whole weeks elapse without either winds or waves occurring to disturb its tranquillity,—a sea, in short, where the "calm" is more dreaded than the "storm." Up to this time they had not experienced any violent commotion of the atmosphere,—nothing stronger than what is termed a "fresh breeze," and in that the *Catamaran* had proved herself an accomplished sailer.

It was now to be seen how she would behave under a gale that might end in a storm,—perhaps a terrific tempest.

It would be untrue to say that her crew looked forward to the event without fear. They did not. As said, they suffered considerable apprehension; and would have felt it more keenly, but for the cheering influence of that faith with which her captain was sustained, and which he endeavoured to impart to his companions.

Leaning upon this, they looked with less dread upon the sky lowering above and the storm gathering around them.

As the day advanced the wind continued to freshen until about the hour of noon. It was then blowing a brisk gale. Fortunately for the crew of the *Catamaran*, it did not become a storm. Had it done so their frail craft must have been shivered, and her component parts once more scattered over the ocean.

It was just as much as her crew could accomplish to keep them together, in a sea only moderately rough, — compared with what it would have been in a storm. This they discovered during the afternoon of that day; and it was no great comfort to them to reflect that, in the event of a real storm being encountered, the *Catamaran* would undoubtedly go to pieces. They could only console themselves with the hope that such an event might not arise until they should reach land, or, which was perhaps more probable, be picked up by a ship.

The chances of terminating their perilous voyage in either way were so slight and distant, that they scarce gave thought to them. When they did, it was only to be reminded of the extreme hopelessness of their situation, and yield to despairing reflections. On that particular day they had no time to speculate upon such remote probabilities as the ultimate ending of their voyage. They found occupation enough, — both for their minds and bodies, — in insuring its continuance. Not only had they to watch every wave as it came rolling upon them, — and keep the *Catamaran* trimly set to receive it, — but they had to look to the timbers of the craft, and see that the lashings did not get loose.

Several times did the sea break quite over them; and but that Lilly Lalee and little William were fast tied to the foot of the mast, they would both have been washed off, and probably lost amidst the dark waste of waters.

It was just as much as the two strong men could do to keep aboard and even they had ropes knotted round their wrists and attached to the timbers of the raft, — in case of their getting carried overboard.

Once a huge billow swept over, submerging them several feet under the sea. At this crisis all four thought that their last hour had come, and for some seconds were under the belief that they were going to the bottom, and would never more look upon the light of day.

But for the peculiar construction of their raft this, in all likelihood, would have been the result; but those buoyant water-casks were not to be "drowned" in such a fashion and soon "bobbed" back to the surface, once more bringing the *Catamaran* and her crew above water.

It was fortunate for them that Ben Brace and Snowball had not trusted too much to fate while constructing their abnormal craft. The experienced sailor had foreseen the difficulties that on this day beset them; and, instead of making a mere temporary embarkation, to suit the conditions of the summer sea that then surrounded them, he had spared no pains to render it seaworthy as far as circumstances would allow. He and Snowball had used their united strength in drawing tight the cords with which the timbers were bound together,—as well as those that lashed them to the casks,—and their united skill in disposing the rude materials in a proper manner.

Even after "launching" the *Catamaran*,—every day, almost every hour, had they been doing something to improve her,—either by giving the craft greater strength and compactness, or in some other way rendering her more worthy both of the sea and her sailors.

By this providential industry they were now profiting: since by it, and it alone, were they enabled to "ride out" the gale.

Had they trusted to chance and given way to indolence,—all the more natural under the very hopelessness of their situation,—they would never have outlived that day. The *Catamaran* might not have gone to the bottom, but she would have gone to pieces; and it is not likely that any of her crew would have survived the catastrophe.

As it was, both raft and crew weathered the gale in safety. Before sunset the wind had fallen to a gentle zephyr; the tropical sea was gradually returning to its normal state of comparative calm; and the *Catamaran*, with her broad sail once more spread to the breeze, was scudding on,—guided in her course by the golden luminary slowly descending towards the western edge of a cloudless heaven.

Chapter Eighty Nine
A Startling Shriek

The night proved pleasanter than the day. The wind was no longer an enemy; and the breeze that succeeded was more advantageous than would have been a dead calm; since it steadied the craft amidst the rolling of the swell.

Before midnight the swell itself had subsided. It had never reached any great height, as the gale had been of short continuance; and for the same reason it had suddenly gone down again.

With the return of smooth water they were able to betake themselves to rest. They needed it, after such a series of fatigues and fears; and having swallowed a few morsels of their unpalatable food, and washed it down by a cup of diluted Canary, they all went to rest.

Neither the wet planking on which they were compelled to encouch themselves, nor the sea-soaked garments clinging round their bodies, hindered them from obtaining sleep.

In a colder clime their condition would have been sufficiently comfortless; but in the ocean atmosphere of the torrid zone the night hours are warm enough to render "wet sheets" not only endurable, but at times even pleasant.

I have said that all of them went to sleep. It was not their usual custom to do so. On other nights one was always upon the watch,—either the captain himself, the ex-cook, or the boy. Of course Lilly Lalee enjoyed immunity from this kind of duty: since she was not, properly speaking, one of the "crew," but only a "passenger."

Their customary night-watch had a twofold object: to hold the *Catamaran* to her course, and to keep a lookout over the sea,—the latter having reference to the chance if seeing a sail.

On this particular night their vigil,—had it been kept,—might have had a threefold purpose: for it is not to be forgotten that they were still not so very far from their late pursuers. They too must have been making way with the wind.

Neither had the Catamarans forgotten it; but even with this thought before their minds, they were unable to resist the fascinations of Morpheus; and leaving the craft to take her own course, the ships, if there were any, to sail silently by, and the big raft, if chance so directed it, to overtake them, they yielded themselves to unconscious slumber.

Simultaneously were they awakened, and by a sound that might have awakened the dead. It was a shriek that came pealing over the surface of the ocean,—as unearthly in its intonation as if only the ocean itself could have produced it! It was short, sharp, quick, and clear; and so loud as to startle even Snowball from his torpidity.

The Coromantee was the first to inquire into its character.

"Wha' de debbil am dat?" he asked, rubbing his ears to make sure that he was not labouring under a delusion.

"Shiver my timbers if I can tell!" rejoined the sailor, equally puzzled by what he had heard.

"Dat soun' berry like da voice o' some un go drown,—berry like. Wha' say you, Massa Brace?"

"It was a good bit like the voice of a man cut in two by a shark. That's what it minded me of."

"By golly! you speak de troof. It wa jess like that,—jess like the lass s'riek ob Massa Grow."

"And yet," continued the sailor, after a moment's reflection, "'t warn't like that neyther. 'T warn't human, nohow: leastwise, I niver heerd such come out o' a human throat."

"A don't blieb de big raff can be near. We hab been runnin' down de wind ebba since you knock off dat boat-hook. We got de start o' de *Pandoras*; an' dar's no mistake but we hab kep de distance. Dat s'riek no come from dem."

"Look yonder!" cried little William, interrupting the dialogue. "I see something."

"Whereaway? What like be it?" inquired the sailor.

"Yonder!" answered the lad, pointing over the starboard bow of the *Catamaran;* "about three cables' length out in the water. It's a black lump; it looks like a boat."

"A boat! Shiver my timbers if thee bean't right, lad. I see it now. It do look somethin' as you say. But what ul a boat be doin' here,—out in the middle o' the Atlantic?"

"Dat am a boat," interposed Snowball. "Fo' sartin it am."

"It must be," said the sailor, after more carefully scrutinising it. "It is! I see its shape better now. There's some un in it. I see only one; ah, he be standin' up in the middle o' it, like a mast. It be a man though; an' I dare say the same as gi'ed that shout, if he be a human; though, sartin, there warn't much human in it."

As if to confirm the sailor's last assertion, the shriek was repeated, precisely as it had been uttered before; though now, entering ears that were awake, it produced a somewhat different impression.

The voice was evidently that of a man. Even under the circumstances, it could be nothing else, but of a man who had taken leave of his senses. It was the wild cry of a maniac!

The crew of the *Catamaran* might have continued in doubt as to this had they been treated only to a repetition of the shriek; but this was followed by a series of speeches,—incoherent, it is true, but spoken in an intelligible tongue, and ending in a peal of laughter such as might be heard echoing along the corridors of a lunatic asylum!

One and all of them stood looking and listening.

It was a moonless night, and had been a dark one; but it was now close upon morning. Already had the aurora tinged the horizon with roseate hues. The grey light of dawn was beginning to scatter its soft rays over the surface of the ocean; and objects—had there been any—could be distinguished at a considerable distance.

Certainly there was an object,—a thing of boat-shape, with a human form standing near its middle. It was a boat, a man in it; and, from the exclamation and laughter to which they had listened, there could be no doubt about the man being mad.

Mad or sane, why should they shun him? There were two strong men on the raft, who need not fear to encounter a lunatic under any circumstances,—

even in the midst of the ocean. Nor did they fear it; for as soon as they became fully convinced that they saw a boat with a man in it, they "ported" the helm of the *Catamaran*, and stood directly towards it.

Less than ten minutes' sailing in the altered course brought them within fair view of the object that had caused them to deviate; and, after scrutinising it, less than ten seconds enabled them to satisfy their minds as to the strange craft and its yet stranger occupant.

They saw before them the "gig" of the slaver; and, standing "midships" in the boat, — just half-way between stem and stern, — they saw the captain of that ill-starred, ill-fated vessel!

Chapter Ninety
A Madman in mid-Ocean

In the minds of the *Catamaran's* crew there was no longer any cause for conjecture. The boat-shaped object on the water, and the human form standing up within it, were mysteries no more; nor was there any when that boat and that human being were identified.

If in the spectacle there was aught still to puzzle them, it was the seeing only one man in the boat instead of six.

There should have been six; since that was the number that the gig had originally carried away from the burning bark,—five others besides the one now seen,—and who, notwithstanding a great change in his appearance, was still recognisable as the slaver's captain.

Where were the missing men,—the mates, the carpenter and two common sailors, who had escaped along with him? Were they in the boat, lying down, and so concealed from the view of those upon the *Catamaran*? Or had they succumbed to some fearful fate, leaving only that solitary survivor?

The gig sat high in the water. Those upon the *Catamaran* could not see over its gunwale unless by approaching nearer, and this they hesitated to do.

Indeed, on identifying the boat and the individual standing in it, they had suddenly hauled down the sail and were lying to, using their oar to keep them from drifting any nearer.

They had done so from an instinctive apprehension. They knew that the men who had gone off in the gig were not a whit better than those upon the big raft; for the officers of the slaver, in point of ruffianism, were upon a par with their crew. With this knowledge, it was a question for consideration whether the Catamarans would be safe in approaching the boat. If the six were still in it, and out of food and water, like those on the large raft, they would undoubtedly despoil the *Catamaran*, just as the others had designed doing. From such as they no mercy need be expected; and as it was not likely any succour could be obtained from them, it would, perhaps, be better, in every way, to "give them a wide berth."

Such were the thoughts that passed hastily through the mind of Ben Brace, and were communicated to his companions.

Were the five missing men still aboard the boat?

They might be lying down along the bottom,—though it was not likely they could be asleep? That appeared almost impossible, considering the shouts and screams which the captain at intervals still continued to send forth.

"By de great gorramity!" muttered Snowball, "a doan't b'lieb one ob dem's leff 'board dat boat, 'ceptin de ole 'kipper himseff; an ob him dar am nuffin leff cep'n de body. Dat man's intlek am clar gone. He am ravin' mad!"

"You're right, Snowy," assented the sailor; "there be ne'er a one there but himself. At all events they ain't all there. I can tell by the way the gig sits up out o' the water. No boat o' her size, wi' six men aboard, could have her gunnel as high as that ere. No! If there be any besides the captain, there's only one or two. We needn't fear to go as nigh as we like. Let's put about, an' board the craft, anyhow. What say ye?"

"Haben't de leas' objecshun, Massa Brace, so long you link dar no fear. Dis chile ready take de chance. If dar be any odder cep'n de 'kipper, it no like dey am 'trong 'nuff to bully we nohow. De two ob us be equal match fo' any four ob dem,—say nuffin ob lilly Will'm."

"I feel a'most sartin," rejoined the sailor, still undecided, "there be only him. If that's the case, our best way is to close up, and take possession o' the boat. We may have some trouble wi' him if be's gone mad; an' from the way he be runnin' on, it do look like it. Never mind! I dare say we'll be able to manage him. Port about, an' let a see the thing through."

Snowball was at the steering-oar, and, thus commanded by her captain, he once more headed the *Catamaran* in the direction of the drifting boat,— while the sailor and William betook them to the oars.

Whether the occupant of the gig had yet perceived the raft was not certain. It is likely he had not, since the yells and incoherent speeches to which he had been giving utterance appeared to be addressed to no one, but were more like—what they believed them to be—the wild ravings of a lunatic.

It was still only the grey twilight of morning, with a slight fog upon the water; and although through this the Catamarans had recognised the gig and captain of the *Pandora* they had done so with certain souvenirs to guide them. Both the boat and its occupant had been seen only indistinctly: and it was possible that the latter had not seen them, and was still unsuspicious of their presence.

As they drew nearer, the light at each moment increasing in brightness, there was no longer any uncertainty as to their being seen; for, along with the yells uttered by the occupant of the gig, could be heard the significant speeches of, "Sail ho! Ship ahoy! What ship's that? Heave to, and be— Heave to, you infernal lubbers! if you don't I'll sink you!"

The manner in which these varied phrases were jumbled together, intermingled with screeching exclamations, as well as the excited and grotesque gestures that accompanied them, might have been ludicrous, but for the painful impression it produced.

There was no longer any doubt in the minds of those who witnessed his behaviour, that the ex-skipper of the *Pandora* was mad. None but a madman would have spoken, or acted, as he was doing.

In the state he was in, it would be dangerous to go near him. This was evident to the occupants of the raft; and when they had arrived within a half-cable's length of the boat, they suspended the stroke of the oars,—with the intention of entering upon a parley, and seeing how far their words might tranquillise him.

"Captain!" cried the sailor, hailing his former commander in a friendly tone of voice: "it's me! Don't you know me? It's Ben Brace, one o' the old *Pandora*. We've been on this bit o' raft ever since the burnin' o' the bark. Myself and Snowball—"

At this moment the sailor's epitomised narrative was interrupted by a fiendish yell, proceeding from the throat of the maniac. They were now near enough to have a clear view of his face, and could note the expression of his features. The play of these, and the wild rolling of his eyes, confirmed them in their belief as to his insanity. There could be no doubt about it; but if there had, what soon after succeeded was proof sufficient to satisfy them.

During the continuance of the discourse addressed to him by the sailor, he had kept silent, until the word "Snowball" fell upon his ears. Then all at once he became terribly excited,—as was testified by a terrible shriek, a twitching contortion of his features, and a glaring in his eyes that was awful to behold.

"Snowball!" screamed he; "Snowball, you say, do you? Snowball, the infernal dog! Show him to me! Ach! Blood and furies! it was he that fired my ship. Where is he? Let me at him! Let me lay my hands upon his black throat! I'll teach the sneaking nigger how to carry a candle that'll light him into the next world. Snowball! Where,—where is he?"

At this moment his rolling orbs became suddenly steadied; and all could see that his gaze was fixed upon the Coromantee with a sort of desperate identification.

Snowball might have quailed under that glance, had there been time for him to take heed of it. But there was not: for upon the instant it was given the madman uttered another wild screech, and, rising into the air, sprang several feet over the gunwale of the gig.

For a second or two he was lost to sight under the water. Then, rising to the surface, he was seen swimming with vigorous sweep towards the *Catamaran*.

Chapter Ninety One
The insane Swimmer

A dozen strokes would have carried him up to the craft; which they could not have hindered him from boarding, except by using some deadly violence. To avoid this, the oars were plied; and the raft rapidly pulled in a contrary direction.

For all this, so swiftly did the maniac make way through the water, that it was just as much as they could do to keep the *Catamaran* clear of his grasp; and it was only after Ben Brace and Snowball had got fairly bent to their oars, that they could insure themselves against being overtaken. Then became it a chase in which there was no great advantage in speed between the pursued and the pursuer; though what little there might have been was in favour of the former.

How long this singular chase might have continued, it is impossible to say. Perhaps until the lunatic had exhausted his insane strength, and sunk into the sea: since he appeared to have no idea of making an attempt to return to the boat. He never looked round to see how far he was leaving it behind him. On the contrary, he swam straight on, his eyes steadfastly fixed upon the one object that seemed to have possession of his soul,—the Coromantee! That it was of him only he was thinking could be told from his speech,—for even while in the water he continued to utter imprecations on the head of the negro,—his name being every moment mentioned in terms of menace.

The chase could not have lasted much longer,—even had it been permitted to terminate by the exhaustion of the insane swimmer. The supernatural strength of insanity could not forever sustain him; and in due time he would have sunk helplessly to the bottom of the sea.

But this was not the sort of death that Fate had designed for him. A still more violent ending of his life was in store for the unfortunate wretch. Though he himself knew it not, those aboard the *Catamaran* had now become aware of its approach.

Behind him,—scarce half a cable's length,—two creatures were seen moving through the water. Horrible-looking creatures they were: for they were hammer-headed sharks! Both were conspicuously seen: for they had risen to the surface, and were swimming with their dark dorsal fins protruded above, and set with all the triangular sharpness of staysails. Although they had not been observed before by those on the *Catamaran*, they appeared to have been swimming in the proximity of the gig,—on which, beyond doubt, they had been for some time attending.

They were now advancing side by side, in the same direction as the swimmer, and there could be no doubt as to their design. They were evidently in chase of *him*, with as much eagerness as he was in chase of the *Catamaran*.

The wretched man neither saw nor thought of them. Even had he seen them it is questionable whether he would have made any attempt to escape from them. They would, in all likelihood, have appeared a part of the fearful phantasmagoria already filling his brain.

In any case he could not have eluded those earnest and eager pursuers,— unless by the intervention of those upon the raft; and even had these wished to succour him, it would have required a most prompt and adroit interference. They *did* wish it, even became desirous to save him. Their hearts melted within them as they saw the unfortunate man, maniac though he was, in such a situation. Fear him as they might,—and deem him an enemy as they did,—still was he a human being,—one of their own kind,— and their natural instinct of hostility towards those ravenous monsters of the deep had now obliterated that which they might have felt for him about to become their prey.

Risking everything from the encounter which they might expect with a madman, they suspended their oars, and then commenced backing towards him. Even Snowball exerted himself to bring the *Catamaran* within saving distance of the wretch who, in his insane hatred, was threatening his own destruction.

Their good intentions, however, proved of no avail. The man was destined to destruction. Before they could get near enough to make any effective demonstration in his favour, the sharks had closed upon him. They who would have saved him saw it, and ceased their exertions to become spectators of the tragical catastrophe.

It was a brief affair. The monsters swam up, one on each side of their intended victim, till their uncouth bodies were parallel with his. He saw one of them first, and, with an instinct more true than his dethroned powers of reason, swerved out of the way to avoid it. The effort resulted in placing him within reach of the other, that, suddenly turning upon its side, grasped him between its extended jaws.

The shriek that followed appeared to proceed from only the half of his body; for the other half, completely dissevered, had been already carried off between the terrible teeth of the *zygaena*.

There was but one cry. There was not time for another, even had there been strength. Before it could have been uttered, the remaining moiety of the madman's body was seized by the second shark, and borne down into the voiceless abysm of the ocean!

Chapter Ninety Two
Boarding the Boat

Back to the boat! In the minds of the *Catamaran's* crew naturally did this resolve succeed to the spectacle they had just witnessed. There was nothing to stay them on that spot. The bloodstained water, which momentarily marked the scene of the tragedy, had no further interest for those who had been spectators to it; and once more heading their craft for the drifting gig, they made way towards it as fast as their oars and the sail, now reset, would carry them.

They no longer speculated as to the boat being occupied by a crew,— either sleeping or awake. In view of the events that had occurred, it was scarce possible that anyone, in either condition, could be aboard of her. She must have been abandoned, before that hour, by all but the solitary individual standing amidships, and pouring out his insane utterances to the ears of the ocean.

Where were the men that were missing? This was the question that occupied the crew of the *Catamaran*,—as they advanced towards the deserted gig—and to which they could give no satisfactory answer.

They could only shape conjectures,—none of which had much air of probability.

From what they knew or suspected to have occurred upon the large raft they could draw inferences of a revolting nature. It might be that the same course had been pursued among those in the gig; and yet it seemed scarce probable. It was known that the latter had gone off from the burning bark, if not sufficiently provided for a long voyage, at least with a stock of both food and water that should have sustained them for many days. Little William had been a witness of their departure, and could confirm these facts. Why then had their boat-voyage resulted so disastrously? It could not have arisen from want. It could not have been the gale.

In all probability, had the sea washed over them, the boat would either have been swamped or capsized. The captain alone could not have righted her. Besides, why should he be the only survivor of the six?

But there had not been storm enough for a disaster of this kind; and unless by some dire mismanagement, the men could not have fallen overboard.

Still puzzled to account for the strange condition of things, the crew of the *Catamaran* continued to pull towards the gig, and at length came up with it.

There they beheld a horrid spectacle, though it afforded no clue to what had occurred. In fact it left the affair as inexplicable as ever. What they saw gave them reason to believe that some terrible tragedy had transpired on board the boat; and that not the elements, but the hand of man, had caused the disappearance of the crew.

Along the bottom timbers lay stretched a human form. It was not only lifeless, but disfigured by many wounds,—anyone of which would have proved mortal. The face was gashed in the most frightful manner; and the skull crushed in several places, as if by repeated blows of a heavy hammer, while numerous wounds, that had been inflicted by some sharp-bladed weapon or implement, appeared over the breast and body.

This mutilated shape of humanity was lying half submerged in the bilge-water contained in the boat, and which looked more like blood. So deep was it in colour, and in such quantity, that it was difficult to believe it could have been stained by the blood of only that one body, to which in turn, as the red fluid went washing over it, had been imparted the same sanguinary hue.

The features of the hideous corpse could not be identified. The axe, knife, or whatever weapon it was, had defaced them beyond recognition; but for all this, both Ben Brace and Snowball recognised the mutilated remains. Something in the garments still clinging round the corpse was remembered, and by this they were enabled to identify it as that of one too well-known to them,—the first mate of the slaver.

Instead of elucidating the mystery, this knowledge only rendered it more inexplicable. It was evident the man had been murdered. The wounds proved that; for from the appearance of the extravasated blood they must have been given while he was still alive.

It was but natural to suppose that the deed had been done by his insane companion. The number and character of the wounds,—consisting of blows, cuts, and gashes, showed that they had been inflicted by some one out of his senses; for life must have been extinct before half of them could have been given.

So far the circumstances seemed clear enough. The maniac captain had murdered the mate. No motive could be guessed at; for no motive was needed to inspire a madman.

Beyond this all was shrouded in mystery. What was to explain the absence of the other four? What had become of them? The crew of the *Catamaran* could only frame conjectures, — all of a horrid nature. That of Snowball was the most rational that could be arrived at.

It suggested the probability that the first mate and captain had combined in the destruction of the others, — their motive being to get all the food and water themselves, and thus secure a better chance of prolonging their lives. They might have accomplished their atrocious design in various ways. There might have been a struggle in which these two men, — much stronger than their fellows, — had proved victorious; or there might not have been any contest at all. The foul crime could have been committed in the night, when their unsuspicious comrades were asleep; or even by the light of day, when the latter were under the spell of intoxication, — produced by the brandy that had furnished part of the stores of the gig.

All these were horrid imaginings; but neither Snowball nor the sailor could help giving way to them. Otherwise they could not account for the dreadful drama of which that bloodstained boat must have been the scene.

Supposing their conjectures to have been correct, no wonder that the sole survivor of such scenes should have been found a raving lunatic, — no wonder the man had gone mad!

Chapter Ninety Three
The Catamaran abandoned

For some time the crew of the *Catamaran* stood contemplating the gig and its lifeless occupant, with looks that betokened repugnance.

By reason of the many dread scenes they had already passed through, this feeling was the less intense, and gradually wore away. It was neither the time nor the place for any show of sentimentalism. Their own perilous situation was too strongly impressed on their minds to admit of unprofitable speculations; and instead of indulging in idle conjectures about the past, they directed their thoughts to the future.

The first consideration was, what was to be done with the gig?

They would take possession of her, of course. There could be no question about this.

It is true the *Catamaran* had done them good service. She had served to keep them afloat, and thus far saved their lives.

In calm weather they could have made themselves very comfortable on their improvised embarkation; and might have remained safe upon it, so long as their water and provisions lasted. But with such a slow-sailing craft the voyage might last longer than either; and then it could only result in certain death. They might not again have such good fortune in obtaining fish; and their stock of water once exhausted, it was too improbable to suppose they should ever be able to replenish it. There might not be another shower of rain for weeks; and even should it fall, it might be in such rough weather that they could not collect a single quart of it. Her slow-sailing was not the only objection to the *Catamaran*. Their experience in the gale of the preceding night had taught them, how little they could depend upon her in the event of a real storm. In very rough weather she would certainly be destroyed. Her timbers under the strain would come apart; or, even if they should stick together, and by the buoyancy of the empty casks continue to keep afloat, the sea would wash over them all the same and either drown or otherwise destroy them.

In such a long time as it must take before reaching land, they could not expect to have a continuance of fair weather.

With the gig,—a first-rate craft of its kind,—the case would be different.

Ben Brace well knew the boat, for he had often been one of its crew of rowers.

It was a fast boat,—even under oars,—and with a sail set to it, and a fair wind, they might calculate upon making eight or ten knots an hour. This would in no great time enable them to run down the "trades," and bring them to some port of the South American coast,—perhaps to Guiana, or Brazil.

These speculations occupied them only a few seconds of time. In fact they had passed through their minds long before they arrived alongside the gig; for they were but the natural considerations suggested by the presence of the boat.

They were now in possession of a seaworthy craft. It seemed as if Providence had thrown it in their way; and they had no idea of abandoning it. On the contrary, it was the raft which was to be deserted.

If they hesitated about transferring themselves and their chattels from the *Catamaran* to the gig, it was but for a moment; and that brief space of time was only spent in considering how they might best accomplish the transfer.

The boat had first to be got into a fit state for their reception; and as soon as they had recovered from the shock caused by that hideous spectacle, the sailor and Snowball set to work to remove the body out of sight, as well as every trace of the sanguinary strife that must have taken place.

The mutilated corpse was cast into the sea, and sank at once under the surface,—though perhaps never to reach the bottom, for those two ravenous monsters were still hovering around the spot, in greedy expectation of more food for their insatiable stomachs.

The red bilge-water was next baled out of the boat,—the inside timbers cleared of their ensanguined stains, and swilled with clean water from the sea; which was in its turn thrown out, until no trace remained of the frightful objects so lately seen.

A few things that had been found in the boat were permitted to remain: as they might prove of service to the crew coming into possession. Among these there was not a morsel of food, nor a drop of drinking water; but there was the ship's compass, still in good condition; and the sailor knew that this treasure was too precious to be parted with: as it would enable them to keep to their course under the most clouded skies.

As soon as the gig was ready to receive them, the "stores" of the *Catamaran* were transferred to it. The cask of water was carefully hoisted aboard the boat,—as also the smaller cask containing the precious "Canary." The dried fish packed inside the chest, the oars, and other implements were next carried over the "gangway" between the two crafts,—each article being stowed in a proper place within the gig.

There was plenty of room for everything: as the boat was a large one, capable of containing a dozen men; and of course ample for the accommodation of the *Catamaran's* crew, with all their *impedimenta*.

The last transfer made was the mast and sail, which were "unshipped" from the *Catamaran* to be set up on the gig, and which were just of the right size to suit the latter craft.

There was nothing left upon the raft that could be of any use to them on their boat-voyage; and after the mast and sail had been removed, the *Catamaran* appeared completely dismantled.

As they undid the lashings,—which during the transfer had confined her to the gig,—a feeling of sadness pervaded the minds of her former crew. They had grown to feel for that embarkation,—frail and grotesque as it was,—a sort of attachment; such as one may have for a loved home. To them it had been a home in the midst of the wilderness of waters; and they could not part from it without a strong feeling of regret.

Perhaps it was partly for this reason they did not at once dip their oars into the water and row away from the raft; though they had another reason for lingering in its proximity.

The mast had to be "stepped" in the gig and the sail bent on to it; and, as it seemed better that these things should be done at once, they at once set about doing them.

During the time they were thus engaged, the boat drifted on with the breeze, making two or three knots to the hour. But this caused no separation between the two crafts; for the same breeze carried the dismantled raft— now lying light upon the water—at the like rate of speed; and when at length the mast stood amidships in the gig, and the sailyard was ready to be hauled up to it, there was scarce a cable's length between them.

The *Catamaran* was astern, but coming on at a fair rate of speed,—as if determined not to be left behind in that lone wilderness of waters!

Chapter Ninety Four
A "School" of Sperm-Whales

To all appearance the hour had arrived when they were to look their last on the embarkation that had safely carried them through so many dangers. In a few minutes their sail would be spread before a breeze, that would impel their boat at a rapid rate through the water; and in a short time they would see no more of the *Catamaran*, crawling slowly after them. A few miles astern, and she would be out of sight,—once and forever.

Such was their belief, as they proceeded to set the sail.

Little were they thinking of the destiny that was before them. Fate had not designed such a sudden separation; and well was it for them that the *Catamaran* had clung so closely upon their track, as still to offer them an asylum,—a harbour of refuge to which they might retreat,—for it was not long before they found themselves in need of it.

As stated, they were proceeding to set the sail. They had got their rigging all right,—the canvas bent upon the yard, the halliards rove, and everything except hauling up and sheeting home.

These last operations would have been but the work of six seconds, and yet they were never performed.

As the sailor and Snowball stood, halliards in hand, ready to hoist up, an exclamation came from little William, that caused both of them to suspend proceedings.

The boy stood gazing out upon the ocean,—his eyes fixed upon some object that had caused him to cry out. Lalee was by his side also, regarding the same object.

"What is it, Will'm?" eagerly inquired the sailor, hoping the lad might have made out a sail.

William had himself entertained this hope. A whitish disk over the horizon had come under his eye; which for a while looked like spread canvas, but soon disappeared,—as if it had suddenly dissolved into air.

William was ashamed of having uttered the exclamation,—as being guilty of causing a "false alarm." He was about to explain himself, when the white object once more rose up against the sky,—now observed by all.

"That's what I saw," said the alarmist, confessing himself mistaken.

"If ye took it for a sail, lad," rejoined the sailor, "you war mistaken. It be only the spoutin' o' a sparmacety."

"There's more than one," rejoined William, desirous of escaping from his dilemma. "See, yonder's half a dozen of them!"

"Theer ye be right, lad,—though not in sayin' there's half a dozen. More like there be half a hundred o' 'em. There's sure to be that number, whar you see six a-blowin' at the same time. There be a 'school' o' them, I be bound,—maybe a 'body.'"

"Golly!" cried Snowball, after regarding the whales for a moment, "dey am a-comin' dis way!"

"They be," muttered the old whalesman, in a tone that did not show much satisfaction at the discovery. "They're coming right down upon us. I don't like it a bit. They're on a 'passage,'—that I can see; an' it be dangerous to get in their way when they're goin' so,—especially aboard a craft sich as this un'."

Of course the setting of the sail was adjourned at this announcement; as it would have been, whether there had been danger or not. A school of whales, either upon their "passage" or when "gambolling," is a spectacle so rare, at the same time so exciting, as not to be looked upon without interest; and the voyager must be engrossed in some very serious occupation who can permit it to pass without giving it his attention.

Nothing can be more magnificent than the movements of these vast leviathans, as they cleave their track through the blue liquid element,— now sending aloft their plume-like spouts of white vapour,—now flinging their broad and fan-shaped flukes into the air; at times bounding with their whole bodies several feet above the surface, and dropping back into the water with a tremendous concussion, that causes the sea to swell into huge foam-crested columns, as if a storm was passing over it.

It was the thought of this that came into the mind of the ex-whalesman; and rendered him apprehensive,—as he saw the school of *cachalots* coming on towards the spot occupied by the frail embarkation. He knew that the swell caused by the "breaching" of a whale is sufficient to swamp even a large-sized boat; and if one of the "body" now bowling down towards them should chance to spring out of the water while passing near, it would be just as much as they could do to keep the gig from going upon her beam-ends.

There was not much time to speculate upon chances, or probabilities. When first seen, the whales could not have been more than a mile distant: and going on as they were, at the rate of ten knots an hour, only ten minutes elapsed before the foremost was close up to the spot occupied by the boat and the abandoned raft.

They were not proceeding in a regular formation; though here and there four or five might have been seen moving in a line, abreast with one another. The whole "herd" occupied a breadth extending about a mile across the sea; and in the very centre of this, as ill-luck would have it, lay the cockle-shell of a boat and the abandoned raft.

It was one of the biggest "schools" that Ben Brace had ever seen, consisting of nearly a hundred individuals,—full-grown females, followed by their "calves,"—and only one old bull, the patron and protector of the herd. There was no mistaking it for a "pod" of whales,—which would have been made up of young males just escaped from maternal protection, and attended by several older individuals of their own sex,—acting as trainers and instructors.

Just as the *ci-devant* whalesman had finished making this observation, the *cachalots* came past, causing the sea to undulate for miles around the spot,—as if a tempest had swept over, and was succeeded by its swell. One after another passed with a graceful gliding, that might have won the admiration of an observer viewing it from a position of safety. But to those who beheld it from the gig, there was an idea of danger in their majestic movement,—heightened by the surf-like sound of their respirations.

They had nearly all passed, and the crew of the gig were beginning to breathe freely; when they perceived the largest of the lot—the old bull— astern of the rest and coming right towards them. His head, with several fathoms of his back, protruded above the surface, which at intervals he "fluked" with his tail,—as if giving a signal to those preceding him, either to direct their onward course, or warn them of some threatened danger.

He had a vicious look about him,—notwithstanding his patriarchal appearance,—and the ex-whalesman uttered an exclamation of warning as he approached.

The utterance was merely mechanical, since nothing could be done to ward off the threatened encounter.

Nothing was done. There was no time to act, nor even to think. Almost on the same instant in which the warning cry was heard the whale was upon them. He who had uttered it, along with his companions, felt themselves suddenly projected into the air, as if they had been tossed from a catapult, and their next sensation was that of taking "a tremendous header" into the depths of the fathomless ocean!

All four soon came to the surface again; and the two who had best retained their senses,—the sailor and Snowball,—looked around for the gig. There was no gig in sight, nor boat of any kind! Only some floating fragments; among which could be distinguished a cask or two, with a scattering of loose boards, oars, handspikes, and articles of apparel. Among these were struggling two youthful forms,—recognisable as little William and Lilly Lalee.

A quick transformation took place in the tableau.

A cry arose, "Back to the *Catamaran!*" and in a score of seconds the boy-sailor was swimming alongside the A.B. for the raft; while the Coromantee, with Lilly Lalee hoisted upon his left shoulder, was cleaving the water in the same direction.

Another minute and all four were aboard the embarkation they had so lately abandoned,—once more saved from the perils of the deep!

Chapter Ninety Five
Worse off than ever

There was no mystery about the incident that had occurred. It had scarce created surprise; for the moment that the old whalesman felt the shock, he knew what had caused it, as well as if he had been a simple spectator.

The others, warned by him that danger might be expected in the passage of the whales—though then unapprised of its exact nature—were fully aware of it now. It had come and passed,—at least, after mounting once more upon the raft, they perceived that their lives were no longer in peril.

The occurrence needed no explanation. The detached timbers of the gig floating about on the water, and the shock they had experienced, told the tale with sufficient significance. They had been "fluked" by the bull-whale, whose fan-shaped tail-fins, striking the boat in an upward direction, had shattered it as easily as an eggshell, tossing the fragments, along with the contents, both animate and inanimate, several feet into the air.

Whether it were done out of spite or wanton playfulness, or for the gratification of a *whalish* whim, the act had cost the huge leviathan no greater effort than might have been used in brushing off a fly; and after its accomplishment the old bull went bowling on after its frolicsome school, gliding through the water apparently with as much unconcern as if nothing particular had transpired!

It might have been nothing to him,—neither the capsize nor its consequences; but it was everything to those he had so unceremoniously upset.

It was not until they had fairly established themselves on the raft, and their tranquillity had become a little restored, that they could reflect upon the peril through which they had passed, or realise the fulness of their misfortune.

They saw their stores scattered about over the waves,—their oars and implements drifting about; and, what was still worse, the great sea-chest of the sailor, which, in the hurry of the late transfer, had been packed full of shark-flesh, they could not see. Weighted as it was, it must have gone to the bottom, carrying its precious contents along with it.

The water-cask and the smaller one containing the Canary were still afloat, for both had been carefully bunged; but what mattered drink if there was no meat?—and not a morsel appeared to be left them.

For some minutes they remained idly gazing upon the wreck,—a spectacle of complete ruin. One might have supposed that their inaction proceeded from despair, which was holding them as if spellbound.

It was not this, however. They were not the sort to give way to despair. They only waited for an opportunity to act, which they could not do until the tremendous swell, caused by the passage of the whales, should to some extent subside.

Just then the sea was rolling "mountains high," and the raft on which they stood—or rather, crouched—was pitching about in such a manner, that it was as much as they could do to hold footing upon it.

Gradually the ocean around them resumed its wonted tranquillity; and, as they had spent the interval in reflection, they now proceeded to action.

They had formed no definite plans, further than to collect the scattered materials,—such of them as were still above water,—and, if possible, re-rig the craft which now carried them.

Fortunately the mast, which had been forced out of its "stepping" in the timbers of the gig and entirely detached from the broken boat, was seen drifting at no great distance off, with the yard and sail still adhering to it. As these were the most important articles of which the *Catamaran* had been stripped, there would be no great difficulty in restoring her to her original entirety.

Their first effort was to recover some of the oars. This was not accomplished without a considerable waste of time and a good deal of exertion. On the dismantled embarkation there was not a stick that could be used for rowing; and it was necessary to propel it with their outspread palms.

During the interval of necessary inaction, the floating fragments of the wreck had drifted to a considerable distance,—or rather had the raft, buoyed up by its empty casks, glided past them, and was now several cable-lengths to leeward.

They were compelled, therefore, to work up the wind and their progress was consequently slow,—so slow as to become vexatious.

Snowball would have leaped overboard, and recovered the oars by swimming: but the sailor would not listen to this proposal, pointing out to his sable companion the danger to be apprehended from the presence of the sharks. The negro made light of this, but his more prudent comrade restrained him; and they continued patiently to paddle the raft with their hands. At length a pair of oars were got hold of; and from that moment the work went briskly on.

The mast and sail were fished out of the sea and dragged aboard; the casks of water and wine were once more secured; and the stray implements were picked up one after another,—all except those of iron, including the axe, which had gone to the bottom of the Atlantic.

Their greatest loss had been the chest and its contents. This was irreparable; and in all probability the precursor of a still more serious misfortune,—the loss of their lives.

Chapter Ninety Six
The darkest Hour

Death in all its dark reality once more stared them in the face. They were entirely without food. Of all their stores, collected and cured with so much care and ingenuity, not a morsel remained. Besides what the chest contained there had been some loose flitches of the dried fish lying about upon the raft. These had been carried into the boat, and must have been capsized into the sea. While collecting the other *débris*, they had looked for them in hopes that some stray pieces might still be picked up; not one had been found. If they floated at all, they must have been grabbed by the sharks themselves, or some other ravenous creatures of the deep.

Had any such waifs come in their way, the castaways just at that crisis might not have cared to eat them with the bitterness they must have derived from their briny immersion; still they knew that in due time they would get over any daintiness of this kind; and, indeed, before many hours had elapsed, all four of them began to feel keenly the cravings of a hunger not likely to refuse the coarsest or most unpalatable food. Since that hurried retreat from their moorings by the carcass of the *cachalot* they had not eaten anything like a regular meal.

The series of terrible incidents, so rapidly succeeding one another, along with the almost continuous exertions they had been compelled to make, had kept their minds from dwelling upon the condition of their appetites. They had only snatched a morsel of food at intervals, and swallowed a mouthful of water.

Just at the time the last catastrophe occurred they had been intending to treat themselves to a more ceremonious meal, and were only waiting until the sail should be set, and the boat gliding along her course, to enter upon the eating of it.

This pleasant design had been frustrated by the flukes of the whale; which, though destroying many other things, had, unfortunately, not injured their appetites. These were keen enough when they first reoccupied their old places on the *Catamaran*; but as the day advanced, and they continued to exert themselves in collecting the fragments of the wreck, their hunger kept constantly increasing, until all four experienced that appetite as keenly as they had ever done since the commencement of their prolonged and perilous "cruise."

In this half-famished condition it was not likely they should have any great relish for work; and as soon as they had secured the various waifs, against the danger of being carried away, they set themselves to consider what chance they had to provide themselves with a fresh stock of food.

Of course their thoughts were directed towards the deep, or rather its finny denizens. There was nothing else above, beneath, or around them that could have been coupled with the idea of food.

Their former success in fishing might have given them confidence,— and would have done so but for an unfortunate change that had taken place in their circumstances.

Their hooks were among the articles now missing. The harpoons which they had handled with such deadly effect upon the carcass of the *cachalot* had been there left,—sticking up out of the back of the dead leviathan composing that improvised spit erected for roasting the shark-steaks. In short, every article of iron,—even to their own knives, which had been thrown loosely into the boat,—was now at the bottom of the sea.

There was not a moiety of metal left out of which they could manufacture a fish-hook; and if there had been it would not have mattered much, since they could not discover a scrap of meat sufficient to have baited it.

There seemed no chance whatever of fishing or obtaining fish in any fashion; and after turning the subject ever and over in their minds, they at length relinquished it in despair.

At this crisis their thoughts reverted to the *cachalot*,—not the live, leaping leviathan, whose hostile behaviour had so suddenly blighted their bright prospects; but the dead one, upon whose huge carcass they had so lately stood. There they might still find food,—more shark-meat. If not, there was the whale-beef, or blubber: coarse viands, it is true, but such as may sustain life. Of that there was enough to have replenished the larder of a whole ship's crew,—of a squadron!

It was just possible they could find their way back to it, for the wind, down which they had been running, was still in the same quarter; and the whole distance they had made during the night might in time be recovered.

At the best, it would have been a difficult undertaking and doubtful of success, even if there had been no other obstacle than the elements standing in their way.

But there was,—one more dreaded than either the opposition of the wind or the danger of straying from their course.

In all likelihood their pursuers had returned to the spot which they had forsaken; and might at that very moment be mooring their craft to the huge pectoral fin that had carried the cable of the *Catamaran*.

In view of this probability, the idea of returning to the dead whale was scarce entertained, or only to be abandoned on the instant.

Cheerless were the thoughts of the Catamarans as they sat pondering upon that important question,—how they were to find food,—cheerless as the clouds of night that were now rapidly descending over the surface of the sea, and shrouding them in sombre gloom.

Never before had they felt so dispirited, and yet never had they been so near being relieved from their misery. It was the darkest hour of their despondency, and the nearest to their deliverance; as the darkest hour of the night is that which precedes the day.

Chapter Ninety Seven
A cheering Cup

They made no attempt to move from the spot upon which the sun saw them at setting.

As yet they had not restored the mast with its sail; and they had no motive for toiling at the oar. All the little way they might make by rowing was not worth the exertion of making it; and indeed it had now become a question whether there was any use in attempting to continue their westward course. There was not the slightest chance of reaching land before starvation could overtake them; and they might as well starve where they were. Death in that shape would not be more endurable in one place than another; and it would make no difference under what meridian they should depend the last few minutes of their lives.

Into such a state of mind had these circumstances now reduced them,—a stupor of despair rather than the calmness of resignation.

After some time had been passed in this melancholy mood,—passed under darkness and in sombre silence,—a slight circumstance partially aroused them. It was the voice of the sailor, proposing "supper!" One hearing him might have supposed that he too had taken leave of his senses. Not so, nor did his companions so judge him. They knew what he meant by the word, and that the assumed tone of cheerfulness in which he pronounced it had been intended to cheer them. Ben's proposal was not without some significance; though to call it "supper" of which it was designed they should partake was making a somewhat figurative use of the phrase.

No matter; it meant something,—something to supply the place of a supper,—if not so substantial as they would have wished, at least something that would not only prolong their lives, but for a while lighten their oppressed spirits. It meant a cup of Canary.

They had not forgotten their possession of this. Had they done so, they might have yielded to even a deeper despair. A small quantity of the precious grape-juice was still within the cask, safe stowed in its old locker.

They had hitherto abstained from touching it, with the view of keeping it to the last moment that it could be conveniently hoarded. That moment seemed to Ben Brace to have arrived, when he proposed a cup of Canary for their supper.

Of course no objection was made to a proposition equally agreeable to all; and the stopper was taken from the cask.

The little measure of horn, which had been found floating among the *débris* of the wrecked gig, was carefully inserted upon its string, drawn out filled with the sweet wine, and then passed from lip to lip,—the pretty lips of the Lilly Lalee being the first to come in contact with it.

The "dipping" was several times repeated; and then the stopper was restored to its place, and without any further ceremony, the "supper" came to an end.

Whether from the invigorating effects of the wine, or whether from that natural reaction of spirits ever consequent on a "spell" of despondency, both the sailor and Snowball, after closing the cask, began to talk over plans for the future. Hope, however slight, had once more made entry into their souls.

The subject of their discourse was whether they should not forthwith re-step the mast and set the sail. The night was as dark as pitch, but that signified little. They could manipulate the "sticks," ropes, and canvas without light; and as to the lashings that would be required, there could be no difficulty in making them good, if the night had been ten times darker than it was. This was a trope used by Snowball on the occasion, regardless of its physical absurdity.

One argument which the sailor urged in favour of action was, that by moving onward they could do no harm. They might as well be in motion as at rest, since, with the sail as their motive power, it would require no exertion on their part. Of course this reasoning was purely negative, and might not have gone far towards convincing the Coromantee,—whose fatalist tendencies at times strongly inclined him to inaction. But his comrade backed it by another argument, of a more positive kind, to which Snowball more readily assented.

"By keepin' on'ard," said Ben, "we'll be more like to come in sight o' somethin',—if there be anythin' abroad. Besides, if we lay here like a log, we'll still be in danger o' them ruffians driftin' down on us. Ye know they be a win'ard, an' ha' got theer sail set,—that is, if they bean't gone back to the sparmacety, which I dar say they've done. In that case there moutn't be much fear o' 'em; but whether or no, it be best for us to make sure. I say let's set the sail."

"Berra well, Massa Brace," rejoined the Coromantee, whose opposition had been only slight. "Dar am troof in wha you hab 'ledged. Ef you say set de sail, I say de same. Dar am a lubbly breeze bowlum. 'Pose we 'tick up de mass dis berry instam ob time?"

"All right!" rejoined the sailor. "Bear a hand, my hearties, and let's go at it! The sooner we spread the canvas the better."

No further words passed, except some muttered phrases of direction or command proceeding from the captain of the *Catamaran* while engaged with his crew in stepping the mast. This done, the yard was hauled "apeak," the "sheets" drawn "taut" and "belayed," and the wet canvas, spread out once more, became filled with the breeze, and carried the craft with a singing sound through the water.

Chapter Ninety Eight
A phantom Ship or a Ship on Fire?

With the *Catamaran* once more under sail, and going on her due course, her crew might have seemed restored to the situation held by them previous to their encountering the dead *cachalot* Unfortunately for them, this was far from being the case.

A change for the worse had occurred in their circumstances. Then they were "victualled" — if not to full rations, at least with stores calculated to last them for some time. They were provided, moreover, with certain weapons and implements that might be the means of replenishing their stores in the event of their falling short.

Now it was altogether different. The *Catamaran* was as true and seaworthy as ever, her "rig" as of yore, and her sailing qualities not in the least impaired. But her "fitting out" was far inferior, especially in the "victualling department"; and this weighed heavily upon the minds of her crew.

Notwithstanding the depression of their spirits, which soon returned again, they could not resist an inclination for sleep. It is to be remembered that they had been deprived of this on the preceding night through the violence of the gale, and that they had got but very little on the night before that from being engaged in scorching their shark-meat.

Exhausted nature called loudly for repose; and so universally, that the complete crew yielded to the call, not even one of them remaining in charge of the helm.

It had been agreed upon that the craft should be left to choose its own track; or rather, that which the wind might select for it.

Guided by the breath of heaven, and by that alone, did the *Catamaran* continue her course.

How much way she made thus left alone to herself is not written down in her "log." The time alone is recorded; and we are told that it was the hour of midnight before any individual of her crew awoke from that slumber, to which "all hands" had surrendered after setting her sail.

The first of them who awoke was little William. The sailor-lad was not a heavy sleeper at any time, and on this night in particular his slumbers had been especially *unsound*. There was trouble on his mind before going to sleep, an uneasiness of no ordinary kind. It was not any fear for his own fate. He was a true English tar in miniature, and could not have been greatly distressed with any apprehensions of a purely selfish nature. Those that harassed him were caused by his consideration for another,—for Lilly Lalee.

For days he had been observing a change in the appearance of the child. He had noticed the gradual paling of her cheek, and rapid attenuation of her form,—the natural consequence of such a terrible exposure to one accustomed all her days to a delicate and luxurious mode of existence.

On that day in particular, after the fearful shock they had all sustained, the young Portuguese girl had appeared,—at least, in the eyes of little William,—more enfeebled than ever; and the boy-sailor had gone to sleep under a sad foreboding that she would be the first to succumb,—and that soon,—to the hardships they were called upon to encounter.

Little William loved Lilly Lalee with such love as a lad may feel for one of his own age,—a love perhaps the sweetest in life, if not the most lasting.

Inspired by this juvenile passion, and by the apprehensions he had for its object, the boy-sailor did not sleep very soundly.

Fortunate that it was so; else that brilliant flame that near the mid-hours of night glared athwart the deck of the *Catamaran* might not have awakened him; and had it not done so, neither he nor his three companions might ever again have looked upon human face except their own, and that only to see one another expire in the agonies of death.

There was a flame far lighting up the sombre surface of the ocean that shone upon the sleepy Catamarans. Gleaming in the half-closed eye of the sailor-lad, it awoke him.

Starting up, he beheld an apparition, which caused him surprise, not unmingled with alarm. It was a ship beyond doubt, — or the semblance of one, — but such as the sailor-lad had never before seen.

She appeared to be on fire. Vast clouds of smoke were rising up from her decks, and rolling away over her stern, illuminated by columns of bright flame that jetted up forward of her foremast, almost to the height of her lower shrouds. No man unaccustomed to such a sight could have looked upon that ship without supposing that she was on fire.

Little William should have been able to judge of what he saw. Unfortunately for himself, the spectacle of a ship on fire was not new to him. He had witnessed the burning of the bark which had borne him into the middle of the Atlantic, and left him where he now was, in a position of extremest peril.

But the memory of that conflagration did not assist him in determining the character of the spectacle now before his eyes. On the decks of the *Pandora* he had seen men endeavouring to escape from the flames, in every attitude of wild terror. On the ship now in sight he beheld the very reverse. He saw human beings standing in front of the column of fire, not only unconcerned at its proximity, but apparently feeding the flames!

It was a spectacle to startle the most experienced mariner, and call forth the keenest alarm, — a sight to suggest the double interrogatory, — "Is it a phantom ship, or a ship on fire?"

Chapter Ninety Nine
A Whaler "Trying-Out"

In making the observations above detailed, the boy-sailor had been occupied scarce ten seconds of time, — only while his eye took in the singular spectacle thus abruptly brought before it. He did not stay to seek out of his own thoughts an answer to the question that suggested itself; but giving way to the terrified surprise which the apparition had caused him, he raised a shout which instantly awoke his companions.

Each of the three, on the instant of their awaking, gave utterance to a quick cry, but their shouts, although heard simultaneously, were significant of very different emotions. The cry of the girl was simply a scream, expressive of the wildest terror. That of Snowball was a confused mingling of surprise and alarm; while to the astonishment of William, and the other as well, the utterance of the sailor was a shout of unrestrained joy, accompanied by the action of suddenly springing to his feet, — so suddenly that the *Catamaran* was in danger of being capsized by the abrupt violence of the movement.

He did not give them time to ask for an explanation, but on the moment of getting himself into an erect attitude he commenced a series of shouts and exclamations, all uttered in the very highest key of which his voice was capable.

And among these utterances, and conspicuously intoned, was the well-known hail, "Ship ahoy!" followed by other nautical phrases, denoting the recognition of a ship.

"Golly! it am a ship," interposed Snowball, "a ship on de fire!"

"No! no!" impatiently answered the ex-whalesman, "nothing o' the sort. It's a whaler 'tryin'-out' her oil. Don't you see the men yonder, standin' by the try-works, are throwin' in the 'scraps'? Lord o' mercy! if they should pass us without hearing our hail! Ship ahoy! whaler ahoy!" And the sailor once more put forth his cries with all the power that lay in his lungs.

To this was added the stentorian voice of the Coromantee, who, quickly catching the explanation given by the ex-whalesman, saw the necessity of making himself heard.

For some moments the deck of the *Catamaran* rang with the shouts, "Ship ahoy!"

"Whaler ahoy!" that might have been heard far over the ocean,—much farther than the distance at which the strange vessel appeared to be; but, to the consternation of those who gave utterance to those cries, no answer was returned.

They could now distinctly see the ship, and almost everything aboard of her; for the two columns of flame rising high in forward of her foremast, out of the huge double furnace of the "try-works," illuminated not only the decks of the vessel, but the surface of the sea for miles around her.

They could see rolling sternward immense volumes of thick smoke, gleaming yellow under the light of the blazing fires; and the figures of men looming like giants in the glare of the garish flames,—some standing in front of the furnace, others moving about, and actively engaged in some species of industry, that to the eye of any other than a whalesman might have appeared supernatural.

Notwithstanding the distinctness with which they saw all these things, and the evident proximity of the ship, those on the raft could not make themselves heard, shout as loudly as they would.

This might have appeared strange to the Catamarans, and led them to believe that it was, in reality, a phantom ship they were hailing, and the gigantic figures they saw were those of spectres instead of men.

But the experience of the ex-whalesman forbade any such belief. He knew the ship to be a whaler, the moving forms to be men,—her crew,—and he knew, moreover, the reason why these had not answered his hail. They had not heard it. The roaring of the great furnace fires either drowned or deadened *every* other sound; even the voices of the whalesmen themselves, as they stood close to each other.

Ben Brace remembered all this; and the thought that the ship might pass them, unheard and unheeded, filled his mind with dread apprehension.

But for a circumstance in their favour this might have been the lamentable result. Fortunately, however, there was a circumstance that led to a more happy termination of that chance encounter of the two strange crafts,—the *Catamaran* and the whale-ship.

The latter, engaged, as appearances indicated, in the process of "trying-out" the blubber of some whale lately harpooned, was "laying-to" against the wind; and, of course not making much way, nor caring to make it, through the water.

As she was coming up slowly, her head set almost "into the wind's eye," the Catamarans, well to windward, would have no difficulty in getting their craft close up to her.

The sailor was not slow in perceiving their advantageous position; and as soon as he became satisfied that the distance was too great for their hail to be heard, he sprang to the steering-oar, turned the helm "hard a port," and set his craft's head on towards the whaler, as if determined to run her down.

In a few seconds the raft was surging along within a cable's length of the whaler's bows, when the cry of "Ship ahoy!" was once more raised by both Snowball and the sailor. Though the hail was heard, the reply was not instantaneous; for the crew of the whale-ship, guided by the shouts of those on the raft, had looked forth upon the illumined water, and, seeing such a strange embarkation right under their bows, were for some moments silent through sheer surprise.

The ex-whalesman, however, soon made himself intelligible, and in ten minutes after the crew of the *Catamaran*, instead of shivering in wet clothes, with hungry stomachs to make them still more miserable, might have been seen standing in front of an immense fire, with an ample supply of wholesome food set before them, and surrounded by a score of rude but honest men, each trying to excel the other in contributing to their comfort.

Chapter One Hundred
The End of the "Yarn"

Ocean Waifs no longer, the crew of the *Catamaran* became embodied with that of the ship, and her little passenger found kindness and protection in the cabin of the whaler.

The *Catamaran* herself was not "cut loose" in the nautical sense of the term, and abandoned, but she was cut loose in a literal sense, and in pieces hoisted aboard the ship to be employed for various purposes,—her ropes, spars, and sail to be used at some time as they had been originally intended— her other timbers to go to the stock of the carpenter, and her casks to the cooper, to be eventually filled with the precious sperm-oil which the ship's crew were engaged in trying out.

The old whalesman was not long aboard before getting confirmed in his conjecture that the ship was the same whose boats had harpooned and "drogued" the *cachalot*, the carcass of which had been encountered by the *Catamaran*. It was one of a large "pod" of whales, of which the boats had been in pursuit, and these, along with the ship, having followed its companions to a great distance, and killed several of them in the chase, had lost all bearings of the one first struck.

It had been their intention to go in search of it, as soon as they should try out the others that had been captured; and the information now given by Ben Brace to the captain of the whaler would enable the latter the more easily to discover the lost prize, which he estimated at the value of seventy or eighty barrels of oil, and therefore well worth the trouble of going back for. On the day after the castaways had been taken aboard, the whale-ship, having extinguished the fires of her try-works, started in search of the drogued whale.

The ex-crew of the *Catamaran* had by this time given a full account of their adventures to the whalesmen; at the same time expressing their belief that the ruffians on the big raft would be found by the carcass they were in search of. The prospect of such an encounter could not fail to interest the crew of the whaler; and as they advanced in the direction in which they expected to find the drogued *cachalot*, all eyes were bent searchingly upon the sea.

So far as the dead whale was concerned, they were successful in their search. Just as the sun was going down, they came in sight of it; and before the twilight had passed they "hove to" along side of it. The vast flock of sea birds perched upon the floating mass, and that rose into the air as the ship approached them, proclaimed the absence of human beings. The great raft was not there, nor were there any indications that it had revisited the carcass. On the contrary, that curious structure, the crane, which the Catamarans had erected on the summit of the floating mass, was still standing just as they had left it; only that the flakes of shark's flesh were scorched to the hue and texture of a cinder, and the fire that had burnt them was no longer blazing beneath.

The fate of the slaver's castaway crew did not long remain a mystery. Three days after, when the carcass of the *cachalot* had been "flensed" and tried out, and the whaler had once more proceeded upon her cruise, she chanced upon a spot where the sea was strewn with a variety of objects, among which were two or three spars of a ship, and several empty water-casks. In these objects there was no difficulty in recognising the wreck of the *Pandora's* raft, which was drifting at no great distance from the place where they had been cutting up the *cachalot*.

The conclusion was easily arrived at. The gale, which had been successfully weathered by the carefully constructed *Catamaran*, had proved too violent for the larger embarkation, loosely lashed together, and negligently navigated as it was. As a consequence it had gone to pieces; while the wretches who had occupied it, not having the strength to cling either to cask or spar, had indubitably gone to the bottom. As little William afterwards related—

"So perished the slaver's crew. Not one of them,—either those in the gig or on the raft, ever again saw the shore. They perished upon the face of the wide ocean—miserably perished, without hand to help or eye to weep over them!"

In truth did it seem as if their destruction had been an act of the Omnipotent Himself, to avenge the sable-skinned victims of their atrocious cruelty!

Were it our province to write the after history of the Catamarans, we could promise ourselves a pleasant task, perhaps pleasanter than recording the cruise of that illustrious craft.

We have space only to epitomise. The day after setting foot upon the deck of the whale-ship, Snowball was appointed *chef de caboose*, in which distinguished office he continued for several years; and only resigned it to accept of a similar situation on board a fine bark, commanded by *Captain Benjamin Brace*, engaged in the African trade. But not *that African trade* carried on by such ships as the *Pandora*. No; the merchandise transported in Captain Brace's bark was not black men, but white ivory, yellow gold-dust, palm-oil, and ostrich-plumes; and it was said, that, after each "trip" to the African coast, the master, as well as owner, of this richly laden bark, was accustomed to make a trip to the Bank of England, and there deposit a considerable sum of money.

After many years spent thus professionally, and with continued success, the *ci-devant* whalesman, man-o'-war's-man, ex-captain of the *Catamaran*, and master of the African trader, retired from active life; and, anchored in a snug craft in the shape of a Hampstead Heath villa, is now enjoying his pipe, his glass of grog, and his *otium cum dignitate*.

As for "Little William," he in turn ceased to be known by this designation. It was no longer appropriate when he became the captain of a first-class clipper-ship in the East Indian trade,—standing upon his own quarter-deck full six feet in his shoes, and finely proportioned at that,—so well as to both face and figure, that he had no difficulty in getting "spliced" to a wife that dearly loved him.

She was a very beautiful woman, with a noble round eye, jet black waving hair, and a deep brunette complexion. Many of his acquaintances were under the impression that she had Oriental blood in her veins, and that he had brought her home from India on one of his return voyages from that country. Those more intimate with him could give a different account,—one received from himself; and which told them that his wife was a native of Africa, of Portuguese extraction, and that her name was *Lalee*.

They had heard, moreover, that his first acquaintance with her had commenced on board a slave bark; and that their friendship as children,—afterwards ripening into love,—had been cemented while both were castaways upon a raft—Ocean Waifs in the middle of the Atlantic.